Cambridge School Shakespeare

中文详注剑桥莎士比

暴风雨

THE TEMPEST

原版创始主编：[英] 瑞克斯·吉布森（Rex Gibson）
原版主编：[英] 瑞查德·安褚斯（Richard Andrews）
　　　　　[英] 维姬·维南德（Vicki Wienand）
原版编注：[英] 琳孜·布雷迪（Linzy Brady）
　　　　　[英] 戴维·詹慕斯（David James）
总主编：陈国华（北京外国语大学）
分册主编：程丽霞（大连理工大学）

北京语言大学出版社
CAMBRIDGE UNIVERSITY PRESS

社图号 20024

Cambridge School Shakespeare: The Tempest [Third edition] [978-1-107-61553-3] was first published by Cambridge University Press in 2014. All rights reserved.
This Simplified Chinese edition for the People's Republic of China is published by arrangement with the Press Syndicate of the University of Cambridge, Cambridge, United Kingdom.
© Cambridge University Press & Beijing Language and Culture University Press 2020.
This book is in copyright. No reproduction of any part may take place without the written permission of Cambridge University Press or Beijing Language and Culture University Press.
本书版权由剑桥大学出版社和北京语言大学出版社共同所有。本书任何部分之文字及图片，如未获得出版者书面同意，不得用任何方式抄袭、节录或翻印。
This edition is for sale in the People's Republic of China (excluding Hong Kong SAR, Macao SAR and Taiwan Province) only.
此版本仅限在中华人民共和国境内（不包括香港特别行政区、澳门特别行政区及台湾省）销售。

北京市版权局著作权合同登记图字：01-2020-2128 号

图书在版编目（CIP）数据

中文详注剑桥莎士比亚精选．暴风雨 / 陈国华总主编；程丽霞分册主编．-- 北京：北京语言大学出版社，2020.6
ISBN 978-7-5619-5635-9

Ⅰ. ①中⋯　Ⅱ. ①陈⋯　②程⋯　Ⅲ. ①多幕剧－剧本－英国－中世纪　Ⅳ. ① I561.33

中国版本图书馆 CIP 数据核字（2020）第 070716 号

中文详注剑桥莎士比亚精选：暴风雨
ZHONGWEN XIANG ZHU JIANQIAO SHASHIBIYA JINGXUAN: BAOFENGYU

项目策划：李　亮	**责任编辑**：孙冠群

封面设计：乔　剑
排版制作：北京创艺涵文化发展有限公司
责任印制：武晓东

出版发行：北京语言大学出版社
社　　址：北京市海淀区学院路 15 号，100083
网　　址：www.blcup.com
电子信箱：service@blcup.com
电　　话：编辑部　8610-82301019/0178
　　　　　　发行部　8610-82303650/3591/3648
　　　　　　北语书店　8610-82303653
　　　　　　网购咨询　8610-82303908
印　　刷：北京中科印刷有限公司

版　　次：2020 年 6 月第 1 版　　**印　　次**：2020 年 6 月第 1 次印刷
开　　本：787 毫米 × 1092 毫米 1/16　**印　　张**：12.75
字　　数：327 千字
定　　价：65.00 元

PRINTED IN CHINA

序

由于观察角度不同，评判标准不同，关于哪个国家哪位诗人或小说家的成就最大，世人可能难以达成一致；可是说到剧作家，大家的共识是，莎士比亚不仅是英语国家有史以来最伟大的剧作家，也是全世界最伟大的剧作家，在知名度、影响力和传世作品的数量上，没有任何一位剧作家可以与之比肩。正是由于其公认的文学成就和人文精神，在过去400多年里，莎士比亚戏剧的演出在英语国家和许多非英语国家经久不衰，莎剧的阅读和鉴赏已成为这些国家英文教学的必选内容。

莎剧进入中国，已经有100多年历史，莎士比亚全集已经有了四个中文译本。不懂英文的人可以通过译本来欣赏莎士比亚剧作。然而文学作品的语言，尤其是诗歌的语言，具有相当程度的不可译性，而几乎所有莎剧的大部分台词都是素体诗（blank verse）。例如《哈慕雷》（*Hamlet*）里主人翁的名言"To be, or not to be, that is the question"，不论怎样译，都难以完全再现原文的深刻内涵和形式特点。要想真正欣赏莎士比亚的语言和戏剧艺术，还得阅读其英文原作。最早由剑桥大学出版社出版的这套莎剧精选，收录了最受读者和观众喜爱的14部剧目，涵盖莎剧的各个类别，以其独具匠心的设计和编排，成为所有英文原版莎剧中最适合英语学习者阅读、最适合戏剧爱好者排演的莎剧选集。

本选集的创始主编瑞克斯·吉布森（Rex Gibson）在本书引言（Introduction）里指出："不论做什么，都要记住，莎士比亚写下他的剧本是为了演出、观看和享受的。"秉承这一宗旨，这一新版莎剧选集有四个鲜明的区别性特点：

一、书的开本和页面的宽高比例特别适合学校的老师和学生以及剧团的导演和演员在排练莎剧时把书打开，拿在手里，随时参阅，而且左边页面上有许多有关排演活动的建议。

二、书中配有大量世界各国莎剧演出的彩色剧照，为莎剧爱好者和剧团排演莎剧提供了灵感。

三、书的正文部分打开后，右页是未经删减、原汁原味的剧本原文，左页是多种不同栏目，包括导演技巧（Stagecraft）、剧中语言（Language in the play）、人物分析（Characters）、主题分析（Themes）、写作练习（Write about it）、本幕回顾（Looking back at Act ...）、词语注释以及与剧情相关的各种思考题。

四、在剧本之后有各种针对全剧的专题论述，以《哈慕雷》为例，包括本剧回顾（Looking back at the play）、视角与主题（Perspectives and themes）、人物分析（Characters）、《哈慕雷》的语言（The language of *Hamlet*）、《哈慕雷》的演出（*Hamlet* in performance）、笔论莎士比亚（Writing about Shakespeare）、笔论《哈慕雷》（Writing about *Hamlet*），还有一份莎翁年表（William Shakespeare 1564–1616）。

左页上的栏目对于解读和排演莎剧特别有帮助，剧本后面的专题论述对于撰写有关莎士比亚的文章特别有帮助，而参加莎剧排演，背诵台词，撰写论文，又是提高英语水平的极好途径。

为了方便更多的中国读者阅读、欣赏、排演莎士比亚原作，北京语言大学出版社携手剑桥大学出版社，将这套莎剧精选引入中国。我有幸应邀担任这套书的中文版总主编，组织起一个团队，对原版进行一定程度的改编和汉化，以适应中国读者的需求。我们不仅将原版提供的关键注释基本译成了中文，而且针对中国英语学习者和莎剧爱好者阅读理解上的难点，主要做了以下四件事：

一、参考 The Oxford Dictionary of Original Shakespearean Pronunciation (David Crystal 2016), Oxford Dictionary of Pronunciation for Current English (Clive Upton 2003) 和 Shakespeare's Names: A Pronouncing Dictionary (Helge Kökeritz 1950)，给每个剧本前面人物表里的人名加上了国际音标。为了便于读者识别，我们将第一本发音词典里一般中国读者不认识的个别音标替换成了大家熟悉的近似音标。

二、为左页顶端的剧情简介添加中文译文。

三、左页中以及剧本后面论文部分里有一些具有挑战性的词和术语（如tableau），我们为其中的大部分添加了相应的中文释义。

四、适当增加了原版里没有的词语注释。

给剧中人物的名字加了国际音标之后，我们发现，现有莎剧中文译本里一些人名的中文译名与原文的读音差别较大且互不相同。根据定名不咎、译音循本、音义兼顾、音系对应的原则，我们给出了新译名。根据前两个原则，我们将剧本 Julius Caesar /ˈdʒuːlɪəsˈsiːzə(r)/ 译成《儒略·恺撒》，而没有采用《尤利/力乌斯·恺撒》《裘利/力斯·凯撒》《居里厄斯·恺撒》等现成译名中的任何一个，因为从公元前1世纪到公元16世纪西方使用的儒略历（Julian calendar）就是以这位 Julius Caesar（拉丁文读音是/ˈjuːlɪˌʊs ˈkaɛsar/）命名的。根据音义兼顾的原则，我们将剧本 Hamlet /ˈ(h)amlət/ 译成《哈慕雷》而不是《哈姆莱特》或《哈姆雷特》，因为"慕雷"比"姆莱"或"姆雷"更适合用来给男子起名，结尾的辅音/t/在实际说话中往往不发音。根据音系对应的原则，我们借鉴了曹禺的译法，将剧本 Romeo and Juliet 译成《柔密欧与茱丽叶》，没有将Romeo译成更常见的"罗密欧"，因为"柔/rou/"比"罗/luo/"更接近原名Romeo /ˈroːmɪoː/的读音；同时我们将Juliet /ˈdʒuːlɪət/译成"茱丽叶"而不是"朱丽叶"，因为这样做不容易让人误以为这个女孩姓"朱"。

这套经过改编并且带中文注释的《中文详注剑桥莎士比亚精选》不仅可以用作中国高中和大学的英文教材，而且适合中国所有具有较高英语能力的莎剧爱好者阅读和欣赏，将戏剧从书中提升到自己心中，将剧本从课堂搬演到戏台。

相信《中文详注剑桥莎士比亚精选》会带给中国广大英语爱好者一个惊喜。

陈国华

北京外国语大学
2020年5月于英国剑桥家中

Contents 目录

Introduction 引言	iv
Photo gallery 剧照精选	v

The Tempest 《暴风雨》

List of characters 人物表	1
Act 1 第 1 幕	3
Act 2 第 2 幕	45
Act 3 第 3 幕	79
Act 4 第 4 幕	105
Act 5 第 5 幕	125
Perspectives and themes 视角与主题	148
Characters 人物分析	156
The language of The Tempest 《暴风雨》的语言	164
The Tempest in performance 《暴风雨》的演出	170
Writing about Shakespeare 笔论莎士比亚	182
Writing about The Tempest 笔论《暴风雨》	184
William Shakespeare 1564–1616 莎翁年表	186
Acknowledgements 鸣谢	187

Cambridge School Shakespeare

Introduction 引言

This *The Tempest* is part of the **Cambridge School Shakespeare** series. Like every other play in the series, it has been specially prepared to help all students in schools and colleges.

The **Cambridge School Shakespeare** *The Tempest* aims to be different. It invites you to lift the words from the page and to bring the play to life in your classroom, hall or drama studio. Through enjoyable and focused activities, you will increase your understanding of the play. Actors have created their different interpretations of the play over the centuries. Similarly, you are invited to make up your own mind about *The Tempest*, rather than having someone else's interpretation handed down to you.

Cambridge School Shakespeare does not offer you a cut-down or simplified version of the play. This is Shakespeare's language, filled with imaginative possibilities. You will find on every left-hand page: a summary of the action, an explanation of unfamiliar words, and a choice of activities on Shakespeare's stagecraft, characters, themes and language.

Between each act and in the pages at the end of the play, you will find notes, illustrations and activities. These will help to encourage reflection after every act, and give you insights into the background and context of the play as a whole.

This edition will be of value to you whether you are studying for an examination, reading for pleasure or thinking of putting on the play to entertain others. You can work on the activities on your own or in groups. Many of the activities suggest a particular group size, but don't be afraid to make up larger or smaller groups to suit your own purposes. Please don't think you have to do every activity: choose those that will help you most.

Although you are invited to treat *The Tempest* as a play, you don't need special dramatic or theatrical skills to do the activities. By choosing your activities, and by exploring and experimenting, you can make your own interpretations of Shakespeare's language, characters and stories.

Whatever you do, remember that Shakespeare wrote his plays to be acted, watched and enjoyed.

Rex Gibson
Founding editor

This new edition contains more photographs, more diversity and more supporting material than previous editions, whilst remaining true to Rex's original vision. Specifically, it contains more activities and commentary on stagecraft and writing about Shakespeare, to reflect contemporary interest. The glossary has been enlarged too. Finally, this edition aims to reflect the best teaching and learning possible, and to represent not only Shakespeare through the ages, but also the relevance and excitement of Shakespeare today.

Richard Andrews and Vicki Wienand
Series editors

This edition of *The Tempest* uses the text of the play established by David Lindley in **The New Cambridge Shakespeare**. Please note that the line numbers in this edition differ in places from those of the Cambridge School Shakespeare first edition.

The play begins with a storm at sea raised by the spirit Ariel on the orders of his master, the sorcerer (术士) Prospero – the former duke of Milan.

▲ A ship carrying Alonso, the king of Naples, his son and courtiers (朝臣), is wrecked in the storm. In the confusion, they are separated and it is feared that the king has lost his only son.

▲ They are confused by their new surroundings on what seems to be a magic island. Two courtiers, one of them the king's brother, plan to murder him in order to take the crown on their return to Naples. What they do not know is that Prospero rules the island. Twelve years before, Prospero was overthrown as duke of Milan by his treacherous (奸诈的, 背叛的) brother Antonio and Alonso.

Prospero's magic art gives him control over the island and over Ariel, who has been freed from a life of torment and now serves Prospero by carrying out his commands.

Prospero lives on the island with his daughter Miranda (left). Another inhabitant is Caliban, the son of a witch, who was born on the island. Prospero keeps Caliban in slavery for attempting to assault Miranda, but Caliban accuses Prospero of stealing the island from him. He thinks of himself as the rightful owner.

▶ Prospero devises plans to confront Alonso and Antonio with the wrong they did to him. He also arranges for the king's son, Ferdinand (pictured), to make it safely to shore and to meet Miranda.

▼ Ferdinand and Miranda fall in love at first sight, but Prospero treats Ferdinand harshly. He secretly intends the two young people to marry, but first wants to test the sincerity of Ferdinand's love.

'You are three men of sin.' Ariel, in the form of a harpy (鸟身女妖), accuses Antonio, Alonso and Sebastian of their crimes against Prospero (centre, behind Ariel). The three are driven almost to madness by Ariel's enchantment (魔法) and their own guilt.

Prospero agrees to the marriage of Miranda and Ferdinand. To celebrate the betrothal (订婚), he arranges a spectacular entertainment.

Caliban (centre), Stephano and Trinculo plot to kill Prospero and make Stephano king of the island. But Ariel overhears and reports this to Prospero. The plotters suffer all kinds of humiliation when they are brought to Prospero.

Prospero finally has all his enemies in his power, but learning from Ariel (left) he decides that mercy is superior to revenge. He forgives all those who have done him wrong.

Naples and Milan are united by the marriage of Miranda and Ferdinand. Prospero sets Ariel free and bids farewell to the audience as he prepares to return home to Milan.

List of characters 人物表

The island 岛上

PROSPERO /ˈprɒspəroː/ (普饶斯普柔) the rightful Duke of Milan
MIRANDA /mɪˈrandə/ (蜜兰荙) Prospero's daughter
ARIEL /ˈeɪrɪəl/ (艾瑞尔) an airy spirit
CALIBAN /ˈkalɪban/ (凯力般) a savage and deformed slave
SPIRITS (精灵) in Prospero's service
IRIS /ˈəɪrɪs/ (爱蕊丝，朱娜的使者)
CERES /ˈsiːriːz/ (熹蕊丝，谷神)
JUNO /ˈdʒuːnoː/ (朱娜，众神之王朱庇特之妻) } characters in the masque
NYMPHS (仙女)
REAPERS (收割者)

The shipwrecked royal court 遭受海难的宫廷人员

ALONSO /əˈlɒnzoː/ (额朗佐) King of Naples
FERDINAND /ˈfɑː(r)dɪˌnænd/ (法迪南) Alonso's son
SEBASTIAN /səˈbastɪən/ (塞巴斯田) Alonso's brother
ANTONIO /anˈtoːnɪoː/ (安托纽) Prospero's brother, the usurping Duke of Milan
GONZALO /gənˈzɑːloː/ (艮扎娄) an honest old councillor
ADRIAN /ˈeɪdrɪən/ (艾颛)
FRANCISCO /franˈsɪskoː/ (伏冉希斯寇) } lords
STEPHANO /steˈfɑːnoː/ (斯迪法诺) a drunken butler
TRINCULO /ˈtrɪŋkjʊloː/ (淳丘娄) a jester

The ship's crew 船员

MASTER (船长) the captain
BOATSWAIN /ˈboːs(ə)n/ (水手长)
MARINERS (水手)

The play takes place on a ship and an island.

The Master commands the Boatswain to save the ship from running aground. The Boatswain gives instructions to the sailors but finds his work hampered by the courtiers. He orders them to go back to their cabins.

剧情简介：船长命令水手长避免让船搁浅。水手长向水手们发号施令，却遇上达官贵人干扰他的工作，于是命令他们回到自己船舱里去。

Stagecraft 导演技巧

Staging the storm (in large groups)

This opening scene is very dramatic: it takes place on a ship at sea during a terrible storm. How can the fury of the waves and wind be shown on stage? In some productions, the scene is played on a bare stage, without props (道具) or scenery – the illusion of a ship caught in a tempest is created only by lighting, sounds and the actors' movements. Other productions use an elaborate (精心制作的) set to create a realistic ship.

a Begin a Director's Journal, in which you write down ideas relating to the play in performance. Try to think like a director, focusing on bringing the words to life. Add to your journal as you read the play.

b Consider how you would perform this opening scene. In your group, hold a discussion using the prompts below, then act out the scene. There are six individual speaking parts, and you can have as many sailors as you want.

- Explore ways of performing the first stage direction: 'A tempestuous noise of thunder and lightning heard'.
- How can actors' movements suggest a ship caught in a storm?
- How might you convey the sense of fear and crisis? These are people who are desperately trying to save their lives: do they panic or are they well disciplined?
- What simple props might suggest a ship? One production had only a large ship's wheel at the back of the stage, and the sailors struggled to turn it to keep the ship on course. What would you use?

1 *tempestuous* 震耳欲聋
2 Boatswain 水手长
3 What cheer? 什么事？
4 Good 好伙计
5 mariners 水手们
6 Fall to't yarely 赶快全力以赴
7 Heigh 嗨
8 Cheerly 加油
9 Yare 赶快
10 Tend 注意听
11 Blow … enough! 风啊，你尽管吹吧，哪怕你吹断了气，只要这航道足够宽！
12 Play the men 拿出男人样来
13 keep below 待在（甲板）下面
14 mar 捣乱
15 Hence! 走开！
16 roarers 咆哮的海浪与狂风
17 whom (King Alonso)

Themes 主题分析

Challenging authority (in pairs)

Throughout the play, traditional authority is challenged. The Boatswain is the character with the lowest social status in this scene, but it is he who takes charge. He orders the king and the other aristocrats (贵族) off the deck.

- Do you think the Boatswain should defer to (遵从，听从) his social superiors, or is it important that he assumes control at this critical moment? Consider the possible consequences of the Boatswain's actions. Share your conclusions with other pairs.

The Tempest

Act 1 Scene 1
A ship at sea

A tempestuous[1] noise of thunder and lightning heard. Enter a
SHIPMASTER, *a* BOATSWAIN *and* MARINERS

MASTER Boatswain[2]!
BOATSWAIN Here, master. What cheer?[3]
MASTER Good[4]; speak to th'mariners[5]. Fall to't yarely[6], or we run ourselves aground. Bestir, bestir! *Exit*
BOATSWAIN Heigh[7], my hearts! Cheerly[8], cheerly, my hearts! Yare[9], yare! Take in the topsail. Tend[10] to th'master's whistle. [*To the storm*] Blow till thou burst thy wind, if room enough![11]

Enter ALONSO, SEBASTIAN, ANTONIO, FERDINAND,
GONZALO *and others*

ALONSO Good boatswain, have care. Where's the master? Play the men[12].
BOATSWAIN I pray now, keep below[13].
ANTONIO Where is the master, boatswain?
BOATSWAIN Do you not hear him? You mar[14] our labour – keep your cabins. You do assist the storm.
GONZALO Nay, good, be patient.
BOASTWAIN When the sea is. Hence![15] What cares these roarers[16] for the name of king? To cabin. Silence! Trouble us not.
GONZALO Good, yet remember whom[17] thou hast aboard.

The Boatswain reminds Gonzalo of humanity's weakness in the face of nature's violence. Gonzalo finds comfort in the Boatswain's face. The Boatswain again rebukes the courtiers, and is cursed in return.

🖋 **剧情简介**：水手长提醒贡扎娄在自然的狂暴面前人类的脆弱。贡扎娄从水手长的面相上看到了慰藉。水手长再次训斥那些达官贵人，却遭到他们的咒骂。

Themes 主题分析
Humans and nature (whole class)

In the script opposite, the Boatswain raises another theme that recurs throughout the play – the relationship between humans and nature: 'if you can command these elements to silence … use your authority' (lines 19–20).

- Hold a class debate. One side argues that nature is humanity's opponent and must be controlled. The other side argues that nature is humanity's friend and should be respected.

1 'he hath no drowning mark upon him' (in pairs)

Gonzalo seems to 'read' the Boatswain's face, deciding that he is not destined to die by drowning, but rather by hanging. Is Gonzalo trusting to fate, being cynical, or trying to find humour in a desperate situation?

a How would you advise the actor playing Gonzalo to deliver these words? Try out different readings.

b Write down the ideas that are explored in lines 18–29, considering in particular the themes of fate and chance.

2 'the rope of his destiny'

This play is rich in **imagery** (see 'The language of *The Tempest*', pp. 164–5). In lines 25–9, Gonzalo uses complex imagery of a hangman's noose (绳套, 套索) beginning to resemble an umbilical cord (脐带).

a Draw this image in a way that captures the richness of the language and the idea being expressed here.

b With others in your class, discuss what is lost and what is gained by turning these words into an image.

Characters 人物分析
What does the language tell us? (in fours)

Look at the language used by the Boatswain and Gonzalo in the script opposite. Compare it to that used by Sebastian and Antonio.

- Discuss what each character's choice of words reveals about them and then act out lines 32–41. What are the dominant emotions expressed here? Anger? Fear? Acceptance? Denial? Think about the humour as well as the terror of the scene.

---

1 None … myself 管他是谁，我只管好我自己
2 councillor 资政大臣
3 elements 风浪
4 work … present 让眼前的暴风雨平息
5 hand a rope 拉帆收缆
6 mischance 不幸
7 hap = happen
8 Methinks = I think
9 complexion 相貌
10 gallows 绞架
11 cable 三股绳拧成的船锚缆绳
12 for … advantage 我们的缆绳起不了多大作用
13 topmast 中桅
14 Bring … main-course 用主帆
15 office 船长的哨声
16 give o'er 放手
17 mind 故意，成心
18 bawling 骂骂咧咧的
19 blasphemous 亵渎神明的
20 whoreson 婊子养的
21 insolent 无礼
22 I'll … drowning 我担保他不会淹死
23 unstanched wench 饶舌或放荡的女人

BOATSWAIN None that I more love than myself[1]. You are a councillor[2]; if you can command these elements[3] to silence, and work a peace of the present[4], we will not hand a rope[5] more – use your authority. If you cannot, give thanks you have lived so long, and make yourself ready in your cabin for the mischance[6] of the hour, if it so hap[7]. [*To the Mariners*] Cheerly, good hearts. [*To the courtiers*] Out of our way, I say.

[*Exeunt Boatswain with Mariners, followed by Alonso, Sebastian, Antonio, Ferdinand*]

GONZALO I have great comfort from this fellow. Methinks[8] he hath no drowning mark upon him, his complexion[9] is perfect gallows[10]. Stand fast, good Fate, to his hanging; make the rope of his destiny our cable[11], for our own doth little advantage[12]. If he be not born to be hanged, our case is miserable.   *Exit*

Enter BOATSWAIN

BOATSWAIN Down with the topmast[13]! Yare, lower, lower! Bring her to try with main-course[14].

A cry within

Enter SEBASTIAN, ANTONIO *and* GONZALO

A plague upon this howling! They are louder than the weather, or our office[15]. [*To the lords*] Yet again? What do you here? Shall we give o'er[16] and drown? Have you a mind[17] to sink?

SEBASTIAN A pox o'your throat, you bawling[18], blasphemous[19], incharitable dog.

BOATSWAIN Work you then.

ANTONIO Hang, cur, hang, you whoreson[20], insolent[21] noisemaker, we are less afraid to be drowned than thou art.

GONZALO I'll warrant him from drowning[22], though the ship were no stronger than a nutshell, and as leaky as an unstanched wench[23].

The Boatswain orders action to save the ship, but disaster strikes. Antonio again curses the Boatswain. The crew abandon hope. Gonzalo accepts whatever is to come, but wishes for death on land.

剧情简介：水手长下令全力救船，但是大难还是临头。安托纽再次咒骂水手长。全体船员都丧失希望。艮扎娄只好认命，只是但愿自己能死在陆地上。

1 'All lost … all lost' (in small groups)

There is complete chaos on stage during the final part of this first scene. In what they believe are their final moments, all the characters behave in different ways. Some call on God's mercy in prayer. Others say farewell to each other. The Boatswain takes a drink (line 45).

- Each person takes a character from the script opposite. Prepare a **tableau** (亮相，舞台造型[演员全都静止不动]) (a 'freeze-frame', like a photograph) of these final moments. Think carefully about the expression on each character's face – what emotions do you want to portray? Practise your tableau, then show it to the rest of the class.
- Take it in turns to break out of your tableau and describe – in your own words – how your character feels at this moment.

Write about it 写作练习
The forces of fate

The fate of the sailors and their royal passengers seems to be decided. However, as we shall see, there are other forces at work that will decide whether they live or die.

- Read **Scene 1** again, then write three paragraphs explaining how much control you think the characters have over their lives at this point. What forces are shaping their actions? Think about what most affects what they are doing and saying. Remember to refer to the script in your writing.

1 Lay her a-hold （收起帆）停船
2 lay her off 往海里行驶，避开海岸（水手长改了命令）
3 must our mouths be cold 咱们喝点什么暖和暖和
4 merely 完全
5 wide-chopped 大嘴巴的
6 rascal 流氓，无赖
7 would 但愿
8 lie … tides 淹死后遭受十次海潮的冲刷（当时英国海盗在海滩上被绞死后，尸体须经三次海潮的冲刷才能收殓）
9 gape … him 把嘴张到最大来吞没他
10 a thousand furlongs 1000 弗隆（1弗隆约为200米）
11 long heath 石楠树
12 brown furze 荆豆花
13 The wills above be done 听天由命
14 fain 宁愿

THE TEMPEST ACT 1 SCENE 1
暴风雨

BOATSWAIN   Lay her a-hold[1], a-hold; set her two courses. Off to sea again; lay her off[2]!

Enter MARINERS, *wet*

MARINERS   All lost! To prayers, to prayers, all lost!
BOATSWAIN   What, must our mouths be cold[3]? 45
GONZALO   The king and prince at prayers! Let's assist them,
For our case is as theirs.
SEBASTIAN   I'm out of patience.
ANTONIO   We're merely[4] cheated of our lives by drunkards.
This wide-chopped[5] rascal[6] – would[7] thou mightst lie drowning
The washing of ten tides[8]!
GONZALO   He'll be hanged yet, 50
Though every drop of water swear against it,
And gape at wid'st to glut him[9].
                    [*Exeunt Boatswain and Mariners*]
A confused noise within
                    Mercy on us!
[VOICES OFF STAGE]   'We split, we split!' – 'Farewell, my wife and children!' –
'Farewell, brother!' – 'We split, we split, we split!'
ANTONIO   Let's all sink wi'th'king.
SEBASTIAN   Let's take leave of him. 55
                    [*Exeunt Sebastian and Antonio*]
GONZALO   Now would I give a thousand furlongs[10] of sea for an acre of barren ground – long heath[11], brown furze[12], anything. The wills above be done[13], but I would fain[14] die a dry death.   *Exit*

Miranda begs her father, Prospero, to calm the tempest. She feels the suffering of the shipwrecked people, and is full of pity for them. Prospero assures her that no harm has been done.

剧情简介：蜜兰达乞求父亲普饶斯普柔让暴风雨停下来，她对失事船上人的遭遇感同身受，充满怜悯。普饶斯普柔让她放心，没有任何人受到伤害。

1 Visualising Prospero (in pairs)

We learn from Miranda's first speech that her father, Prospero, has the power to create storms and control the seas.

a How do you visualise Prospero? With a partner, talk about how he might appear.

b Look at the ways in which different productions have presented Prospero in the photographs throughout this book. Which one is closest to your own imagining of this character? How would you present him differently? Sketch your own ideas for Prospero's 'look'.

Language in the play 剧中语言
Conjuring (施魔法召唤，变出) the storm (in fours)

Miranda's first speech (lines 1–13) is a vivid description of the storm as it is happening.

a Take it in turns to read the speech aloud, changing speaker at each punctuation mark. Emphasise the imagery she uses to describe the storm.

b Talk together about Miranda's 'storm' imagery. How does it create atmosphere for the audience? Make some notes and then share your thoughts with other groups.

c What does Miranda's language in the script opposite tell us about her character? Draw up a list of adjectives you would use to describe her.

2 'no harm done'? (in pairs)

a Look at the exchange between Prospero and Miranda in lines 13–21. Shakespeare uses **anaphora*** – the repetition of words in successive clauses (see p. 167) – in Prospero's words 'No harm'. It is as though he is trying to reassure his daughter that he is benevolent (仁慈). But what do you think are his motives? Discuss this in your pairs.

b What are your first impressions of Prospero and Miranda, and of their relationship? By yourself, write down your thoughts, then swap these notes with your partner. How are your impressions similar? How do they differ?

---

1 art 法术
2 roar 喧嚣
3 allay 使平息
4 welkin's cheek 老天爷的脸
5 The sky … out 天上像是要倾倒灼热融化的沥青，而大海却卷起巨浪冲上天际，要把天火浇灭
6 brave 宏伟，华丽
7 creature 人
8 ere 在……之前
9 fraughting souls 惊慌失措的人们
10 Be collected 镇定
11 amazement 惊骇
12 piteous 可怜，哀怨
13 woe 呜呼
14 meddle 干预

* anaphora 首语叠用，例如：The voice of the people is powerful, the voice of the people cannot be silenced, the voice of the people shakes the world.

Act 1 Scene 2
The island

Enter PROSPERO *and* MIRANDA

MIRANDA　If by your art[1], my dearest father, you have
　　　　　Put the wild waters in this roar[2], allay[3] them.
　　　　　The sky it seems would pour down stinking pitch,
　　　　　But that the sea, mounting to th'welkin's cheek[4],
　　　　　Dashes the fire out[5]. O, I have suffered　　　　　　5
　　　　　With those that I saw suffer! A brave[6] vessel,
　　　　　Who had no doubt some noble creature[7] in her,
　　　　　Dashed all to pieces. O, the cry did knock
　　　　　Against my very heart! Poor souls, they perished.
　　　　　Had I been any god of power, I would　　　　　　　10
　　　　　Have sunk the sea within the earth, or ere[8]
　　　　　It should the good ship so have swallowed, and
　　　　　The fraughting souls[9] within her.
PROSPERO　　　　　　　　　　　　　　Be collected[10];
　　　　　No more amazement[11]. Tell your piteous[12] heart
　　　　　There's no harm done.
MIRANDA　　　　　　　　　　O, woe[13] the day.
PROSPERO　　　　　　　　　　　　　　No harm.　　　　　　15
　　　　　I have done nothing but in care of thee –
　　　　　Of thee my dear one, thee my daughter – who
　　　　　Art ignorant of what thou art, nought knowing
　　　　　Of whence I am, nor that I am more better
　　　　　Than Prospero, master of a full poor cell,　　　　　20
　　　　　And thy no greater father.
MIRANDA　　　　　　　　　　　More to know
　　　　　Did never meddle[14] with my thoughts.

Prospero decides to tell Miranda her life story. He again assures her that no one was hurt in the shipwreck. He questions her about what she remembers, then reveals that he was once duke of Milan.

剧情简介：普饶斯普柔决定给蜜兰莐讲讲她的身世，并再次向她保证，失事的船上没有人受到伤害。他问蜜兰莐记得过去什么事，然后告诉蜜兰莐说自己曾经是米兰公爵。

1 Prospero's 'magic garment'

Prospero wears a 'magic garment', which gives him the supernatural powers that he calls his 'art'. In stage productions, this garment is often a cloak, richly decorated with magical symbols.

- Design your own version of Prospero's 'magic garment', using symbols to suggest particular powers.

Language in the play 剧中语言

'In the dark backward and abysm of time' (in pairs)

Line 50 is a good example of the rich imagery in *The Tempest*. Instead of saying 'long ago' or 'in the dim and distant past', Prospero says 'In the dark backward and abysm of time'.

- Try translating this line into modern English prose (散文；散体), then discuss your different versions. What has been lost from the original in your modern version?

2 'A prince of power'

Over the course of lines 53–88, we discover many things about Prospero and Miranda.

- After you have read this important exchange, write a short account (between one and three paragraphs) that explains their change of fortunes and their link with the passengers on the sunken ship.

Characters 人物分析

Prospero's story: a first impression (in pairs)

In lines 53–186, Prospero tells the story of how he and Miranda came to the island.

a Take parts and read the first part of this story (lines 53–88). Don't worry about words and phrases you may not understand. Just treat the read-through as a way of gaining a first impression of Prospero's overthrow and his journey to the island.

b Read through this part of the script again, taking turns in role as Prospero and as a voice coach, offering advice. What suggestions would you make about pitch, pace, pause and accompanying gestures to best portray Prospero's character and emotions?

---

1 pluck 脱
2 direful spectacle 惨状
3 wrack 海滩
4 very virtue of compassion 慈悲的本质
5 provision 先见之明
6 soul 人
7 perdition 丧失
8 Betid 发生
9 bootless inquisition 没有结果的探听
10 Stay 等着吧
11 ope = open
12 Out three years old 满三岁
13 Of … remembrance 对任何事情的印象，告诉我，你还记得什么
14 And … warrants 我回忆起来的更像一场梦，不是很清楚
15 tended 伺候
16 abysm = abyss （深渊）
17 aught ere 之前的任何事
18 thou mayst 你可能记得

PROSPERO   'Tis time
         I should inform thee farther. Lend thy hand
         And pluck[1] my magic garment from me – so –
                  [*Miranda assists Prospero; his cloak is laid aside*]
         Lie there my art. Wipe thou thine eyes; have comfort.   25
         The direful spectacle[2] of the wrack[3] which touched
         The very virtue of compassion[4] in thee,
         I have with such provision[5] in mine art
         So safely ordered, that there is no soul[6],
         No, not so much perdition[7] as an hair   30
         Betid[8] to any creature in the vessel
         Which thou heard'st cry, which thou saw'st sink. Sit down,
         For thou must now know farther.
                           [*Miranda sits*]
MIRANDA   You have often
         Begun to tell me what I am, but stopped
         And left me to a bootless inquisition[9],   35
         Concluding, 'Stay[10]: not yet.'
PROSPERO   The hour's now come;
         The very minute bids thee ope[11] thine ear,
         Obey, and be attentive. Canst thou remember
         A time before we came unto this cell?
         I do not think thou canst, for then thou wast not   40
         Out three years old[12].
MIRANDA   Certainly, sir, I can.
PROSPERO By what? By any other house, or person?
         Of any thing the image, tell me, that
         Hath kept with thy remembrance[13].
MIRANDA   'Tis far off;
         And rather like a dream, than an assurance   45
         That my remembrance warrants[14]. Had I not
         Four or five women once, that tended[15] me?
PROSPERO Thou hadst, and more, Miranda. But how is't
         That this lives in thy mind? What seest thou else
         In the dark backward and abysm[16] of time?   50
         If thou rememb'rest aught ere[17] thou cam'st here,
         How thou cam'st here thou mayst[18].
MIRANDA   But that I do not.
PROSPERO Twelve year since, Miranda, twelve year since,
         Thy father was the Duke of Milan and
         A prince of power –

Prospero again confirms that he was once the duke of Milan. As Prospero wanted to pursue his studies, he made his brother, Antonio, ruler of the state. The treacherous Antonio seized all power from Prospero.

剧情简介：普饶斯普柔再次证实自己原本是米兰公爵。当时他一心钻研法术，就让弟弟安托纽管理政务，然而奸诈的安托纽窃取了普饶斯普柔的所有权力。

Stagecraft 导演技巧

Prospero and Antonio: brothers and enemies (in fours)

Prospero describes how he was once the unchallenged ruler of Milan, the most important state in Italy: 'Through all the signories it was the first, / And Prospero the prime duke.' However, because of his overwhelming interest in acquiring magical skills, he entrusted the government of Milan to Antonio, his brother. This was a mistake – Antonio usurped (篡夺权力) him and took control of Milan.

a Split into two pairs. One pair takes the parts of Prospero and Miranda and reads lines 66–87 aloud. As they speak, the other pair mimes (演哑剧) the actions described. Afterwards, swap roles and repeat the activity. As you read, think about the range of emotions Prospero is feeling. (Consider how the language is disjointed, suggesting anger.)

b In the Director's Journal that you began on page 2, write down how you would want to depict the relationship between these characters during this scene.

Characters 人物分析

Miranda: disrespectful or distracted?

Miranda's language gives the impression that she is a dutiful daughter. However, she also appears to be rather distracted as Prospero recounts his story.

a Why do you think this is? What might she be thinking about? What tasks might she be doing around their home as Prospero tells his tale?

b Write notes to the actor playing Miranda, explaining how you think she should perform these lines.

1 'rapt in secret studies'

Consider Prospero's story from Antonio's perspective. He could argue that the duke had become too caught up in his magical studies, and that he was failing in his duties to the people of Milan.

- As you read Prospero's story, write down any ideas you have that might support Antonio's actions. Think about why Shakespeare may have wanted his audience to consider both sides of the situation.

---

1 piece of virtue 贞洁的典范
2 no worse issued 高贵的出身不亚于此
3 heaved thence 从那里被赶出去
4 blessedly holp hither 幸运地被带到了这里（holp = helped，hither = here）
5 o'th'teen 那些麻烦
6 is from my remembrance 我记不得了
7 perfidious 阴险，不忠，背信弃义
8 put … state 代理国事
9 signories 意大利城邦
10 prime 首席，地位最高
11 transported … studies 研究魔法走火入魔，神魂颠倒
12 heedfully 专心
13 Being once perfected 一旦达到炉火纯青的地步
14 grant suits 答应别人的请求
15 t'advance 提拔
16 trash 剪除
17 over-topping 僭越
18 created 委任
19 The creatures that were mine 原先效忠我的人
20 changed 'em … 'em 转变了他们 / 再造了他们
21 the key … office 职权和权术
22 verdure 生命力

MIRANDA   Sir, are not you my father?
PROSPERO   Thy mother was a piece of virtue[1], and
            She said thou wast my daughter; and thy father
            Was Duke of Milan; and his only heir,
            And princess, no worse issued[2].
MIRANDA   O the heavens!
            What foul play had we, that we came from thence?
            Or blessèd was't we did?
PROSPERO   Both, both, my girl.
            By foul play, as thou say'st, were we heaved thence[3],
            But blessedly holp hither[4].
MIRANDA   O, my heart bleeds
            To think o'th'teen[5] that I have turned you to,
            Which is from my remembrance[6]. Please you, farther.
PROSPERO   My brother and thy uncle, called Antonio –
            I pray thee mark me, that a brother should
            Be so perfidious[7] – he, whom next thyself
            Of all the world I loved, and to him put
            The manage of my state[8], as at that time
            Through all the signories[9] it was the first,
            And Prospero the prime[10] duke, being so reputed
            In dignity, and for the liberal arts
            Without a parallel; those being all my study,
            The government I cast upon my brother,
            And to my state grew stranger, being transported
            And rapt in secret studies[11]. Thy false uncle –
            Dost thou attend me? –
MIRANDA   Sir, most heedfully[12].
PROSPERO   Being once pèrfected[13] how to grant suits[14],
            How to deny them; who t'advance[15], and who
            To trash[16] for over-topping[17]; new created[18]
            The creatures that were mine[19], I say, or changed 'em,
            Or else new formed 'em[20]; having both the key
            Of officer, and office[21], set all hearts i'th'state
            To what tune pleased his ear, that now he was
            The ivy which had hid my princely trunk,
            And sucked my verdure[22] out on't – thou attend'st not!
MIRANDA   O good sir, I do.

Prospero describes how his neglect of his duties aroused his brother's evil nature. Enjoying the benefits of playing the duke, Antonio aspired to the position himself, and plotted with Alonso, the king of Naples.

剧情简介：普饶斯普柔讲述自己对政务的疏忽如何勾起了安托纽的邪恶本性。安托纽尝到了扮演公爵的甜头，渴望自己登上大位，于是与那不勒斯国王额朗佐密谋。

Language in the play 剧中语言

Antonio's ambition grows (in small groups)

Prospero passionately recalls his brother's treachery (背叛行为). Lines 88–116 show his angry state of mind. Match statements **a** to **k** below with the appropriate lines from the script opposite.

a I neglected the business of government.
b I sought privacy in order to study.
c But what I studied was beyond the citizens' interest or understanding.
d My retirement was the cause of my brother's evil acts.
e My absolute trust in him was completely betrayed.
f He abused my wealth and overtaxed my people,
g He came to believe his own lies that he was the duke.
h Therefore his ambition grew.
i He wished to become the part he played – the duke.
j I was content with my books. He took this as a sign that I was unfit to govern.
k Eager for power, he agreed to make Milan, hitherto (迄今) independent, subordinate to (从属于) the king of Naples.

Stagecraft 导演技巧

Prospero's growing anger

Miranda's line 106 ('Your tale, sir, would cure deafness') reveals just how worked up (激动) Prospero is becoming.

- In your Director's Journal, write out how you would stage this part of the scene. Have fun exploring Miranda as a long-suffering daughter and Prospero as an increasingly angry father. Think about where you would place the characters on the stage as these lines are spoken.

1 'Good wombs have borne bad sons'

In line 120, Miranda suggests that nature is not the sole determiner of character, but that we are also affected by our surroundings.

- From what you have read so far, write down five points that support Miranda's view, and five points that contradict it. Use quotations from the script to back up your points.

1 closeness 与世隔绝
2 retired 离群索居
3 but … rate 我这样退出了政坛，高估了我的（魔法）研究对民众的价值
4 beget 催生
5 sans bound 没有限制
6 thus lorded 像公爵一样
7 revènue 财富
8 exact 获取
9 into truth 编造事实
10 of it = of the lie
11 To credit 让……可信
12 o'th'substitution 由于我让他代理政务
13 executing th'outward face of royalty 冠冕堂皇地行使王权
14 prerogative 特权
15 Absolute Milan 真正的米兰公爵
16 temporal royalties 世俗权力
17 confederates 与……结盟
18 So … sway 如此急切地想要得到权力
19 tribute 贡品，贡金
20 homage 效忠
21 coronet （王子、贵族等戴的）小冠冕
22 yet unbowed 从未低头的
23 ignoble stooping 卑贱的屈服
24 condition 结盟条件
25 event 后果
26 wombs 子宫

THE TEMPEST ACT 1 SCENE 2
暴风雨

PROSPERO   I pray thee mark me:
I, thus neglecting worldly ends, all dedicated
To closeness¹, and the bettering of my mind   90
With that which, but by being so retired²,
O'er-prized all popular rate³, in my false brother
Awaked an evil nature; and my trust,
Like a good parent, did beget⁴ of him
A falsehood, in its contrary as great   95
As my trust was – which had indeed no limit,
A confidence sans bound⁵. He being thus lorded⁶,
Not only with what my revènue⁷ yielded,
But what my power might else exact⁸ – like one
Who, having into truth⁹ by telling of it¹⁰,   100
Made such a sinner of his memory
To credit¹¹ his own lie – he did believe
He was indeed the duke, out o'th'substitution¹²
And executing th'outward face of royalty¹³
With all prerogative¹⁴. Hence his ambition growing –   105
Dost thou hear?
MIRANDA   Your tale, sir, would cure deafness.
PROSPERO To have no screen between this part he played,
And him he played it for, he needs will be
Absolute Milan¹⁵. Me, poor man, my library
Was dukedom large enough. Of temporal royalties¹⁶   110
He thinks me now incapable; confederates¹⁷ –
So dry he was for sway¹⁸ – wi'th'King of Naples
To give him annual tribute¹⁹, do him homage²⁰,
Subject his coronet²¹ to his crown, and bend
The dukedom yet unbowed²² – alas, poor Milan –   115
To most ignoble stooping²³.
MIRANDA   O the heavens!
PROSPERO Mark his condition²⁴, and th'event²⁵, then tell me
If this might be a brother.
MIRANDA   I should sin
To think but nobly of my grandmother –
Good wombs²⁶ have borne bad sons.

15

Alonso made a treaty with Antonio to overthrow Prospero. Antonio treacherously admitted Alonso's army into Milan. Prospero and Miranda were captured and cast adrift in a tiny, unseaworthy boat.

剧情简介：额朗佐和安托纽狼狈为奸，要推翻普饶斯普柔的统治。安托纽卖国求荣，放额朗佐的军队进入米兰。普饶斯普柔和蜜兰达被俘后，被送上一条经不住海上风浪的小破船，抛到海上，随波逐流。

Stagecraft 导演技巧

Overthrowing Prospero (in small groups)

Prospero continues to tell his story. His old enemy, Alonso, king of Naples, agreed a treaty ('condition') with Antonio. The agreement was that, in exchange for ('in lieu o'th'premises') making Milan subordinate to Naples and for protection money ('tribute'), Alonso would overthrow Prospero and make Antonio duke of Milan. Under cover of darkness, the treacherous Antonio opened the city gates to give Alonso's accomplices (同谋犯) ('ministers') the opportunity to capture Prospero and Miranda. The conspirators (同谋者) dared not kill Prospero because of his popularity. Instead, they abandoned him and his infant daughter in a tiny, unseaworthy boat ('A rotten carcass of a butt').

The script opposite is only part of Prospero's story, but it has great potential for drama. Try one or more of the following activities.

a **What if?** The influential Russian theatre director Stanislavski (斯坦尼斯拉夫斯基) felt that the question 'What if?' was one of the most powerful tools for understanding a script. How many 'What ifs' can you ask of the speeches in the script opposite? For example, what if Prospero is exaggerating? How would we know? What if Miranda is becoming increasingly bored by the story? How would this affect the way the actors perform the scene? Split into pairs, with one of you asking 'What if …?' and the other answering the question. Afterwards, compare your ideas with other pairs in your group.

b **Notes for the actors** Each member of the group takes a speech (or part of a speech) from Prospero's story and writes detailed notes on how the two actors should speak and move. Then put your combined advice into action and perform the whole thing using your various notes.

c **Speak the lines** Experiment with ways of relating Prospero's story. For example, you could read his speeches rapidly, with the words tumbling out (三言并作两语) passionately as the former duke angrily recalls what happened. Alternatively, you could read the lines very slowly and reflectively, as if the experience was like a dream from long ago. Which style has the most dramatic impact?

1 inveterate 长期
2 hearkens my brother's suit 听取我弟弟（安托纽）的请求
3 in lieu o'th'premises 作为安托纽进贡的回报
4 presently extirpate 立即驱逐（或灭掉）
5 mine 我的家人
6 levied 召集
7 Fated 命中注定
8 ministers 奉命做事或当差的人
9 Alack 啊呀
10 hint 场合
11 wrings 促使
12 impertinent 不相干
13 wench 女儿
14 durst not = dared not (不敢)
15 In few 长话短说
16 barque 小船
17 leagues 里格（航海计程单位，1里格约为3海里，5.56公里）
18 carcass 骨架
19 butt 大木箱/桶
20 rigged 给船配备船帆等物
21 tackle 绳索
22 hoist 把……推上浪尖

THE TEMPEST ACT 1 SCENE 2
暴风雨

PROSPERO   Now the condition.   120
This King of Naples, being an enemy
To me inveterate[1], hearkens my brother's suit[2],
Which was, that he, in lieu o'th'premises[3]
Of homage, and I know not how much tribute,
Should presently extirpate[4] me and mine[5]   125
Out of the dukedom, and confer fair Milan,
With all the honours, on my brother. Whereon,
A treacherous army levied[6], one midnight
Fated[7] to th'purpose did Antonio open
The gates of Milan, and i'th'dead of darkness   130
The ministers[8] for th'purpose hurried thence
Me, and thy crying self.

MIRANDA   Alack[9], for pity!
I, not remembering how I cried out then,
Will cry it o'er again; it is a hint[10]
That wrings[11] mine eyes to't.

PROSPERO   Hear a little further,   135
And then I'll bring thee to the present business
Which now's upon's; without the which, this story
Were most impertinent[12].

MIRANDA   Wherefore did they not
That hour destroy us?

PROSPERO   Well demanded, wench[13];
My tale provokes that question. Dear, they durst not[14],   140
So dear the love my people bore me; nor set
A mark so bloody on the business; but
With colours fairer painted their foul ends.
In few[15], they hurried us aboard a barque[16],
Bore us some leagues[17] to sea, where they prepared   145
A rotten carcass[18] of a butt[19], not rigged[20],
Nor tackle[21], sail, nor mast – the very rats
Instinctively have quit it. There they hoist[22] us
To cry to th'sea, that roared to us; to sigh
To th'winds, whose pity sighing back again   150
Did us but loving wrong.

MIRANDA   Alack, what trouble
Was I then to you!

Prospero says that he found comfort and strength in Miranda's smile, in divine providence and in Gonzalo's help. He believes that Fortune now favours him, as his enemies are within his reach. He causes Miranda to fall asleep.

剧情简介：普饶斯普柔说，是蜜兰莎的笑容、神的力量和艮扎娄的帮助给了他安慰和力量。他觉得命运女神现在眷顾他，让仇敌落入他的手掌。普饶斯普柔施法让女儿陷入沉睡。

1 'Knowing I loved my books'

Gonzalo made sure that books were placed in the boat that carried Prospero unwillingly to exile (流放).

a If you had to choose five possessions to take with you to a desert island, what would they be? They must be portable and either useful or of personal value (or both). If appropriate, bring them in to class and discuss why you have chosen them.

b Now think about Prospero. What does the fact that his most cherished objects are his books tell us about him and the society in which he lived? Share your ideas in groups or as a whole-class discussion.

Write about it 写作练习

Duke and princess … father and daughter … exiles

The relationship between Prospero and Miranda is a complex one, and it raises a number of key themes that run through the play, including family, duty, status and exile.

- Reflect on these and other ideas in relation to the relationship described in this scene. Write either a 100-word summary of the story told by Prospero or an analysis of the representation of the father-daughter relationship in the first 186 lines of this scene.

1	cherubin	守护天使
2	Infusèd with a fortitude	充满毅力
3	decked	铺洒，装点
4	undergoing stomach	坚持下去的勇气
5	providence divine	天意
6	design	计谋
7	linens	床上用品
8	stuffs	器物，材料
9	steaded much	帮了大忙
10	profit	益处
11	prescience	先见之明
12	zenith	命运的顶峰
13	auspicious	大吉大利
14	influence	星座的影响力
15	court	追求，使用
16	omit	忽略
17	droop	衰减
18	good dullness	时机正好的困意
19	give it way	随它吧

PROSPERO	[*Sitting*] O, a cherubin[1]	
	Thou wast that did preserve me. Thou didst smile,	
	Infusèd with a fortitude[2] from heaven,	
	When I have decked[3] the sea with drops full salt,	155
	Under my burden groaned; which raised in me	
	An undergoing stomach[4], to bear up	
	Against what should ensue.	
MIRANDA	How came we ashore?	
PROSPERO	By providence divine[5].	
	Some food we had, and some fresh water, that	160
	A noble Neapolitan, Gonzalo,	
	Out of his charity – who being then appointed	
	Master of this design[6] – did give us, with	
	Rich garments, linens[7], stuffs[8], and necessaries	
	Which since have steaded much[9]. So, of his gentleness,	165
	Knowing I loved my books, he furnished me	
	From mine own library, with volumes that	
	I prize above my dukedom.	
MIRANDA	Would I might	
	But ever see that man.	
PROSPERO	[*Standing*] Now I arise,	
	Sit still, and hear the last of our sea-sorrow.	170
	Here in this island we arrived, and here	
	Have I, thy schoolmaster, made thee more profit[10]	
	Than other princes can, that have more time	
	For vainer hours, and tutors not so careful.	
MIRANDA	Heavens thank you for't. And now I pray you, sir –	175
	For still 'tis beating in my mind – your reason	
	For raising this sea-storm?	
PROSPERO	Know thus forth:	
	By accident most strange, bountiful Fortune,	
	Now my dear lady, hath mine enemies	
	Brought to this shore; and by my prescience[11]	180
	I find my zenith[12] doth depend upon	
	A most auspicious[13] star, whose influence[14]	
	If now I court[15] not, but omit[16], my fortunes	
	Will ever after droop[17]. Here cease more questions.	
	Thou art inclined to sleep. 'Tis a good dullness[18],	185
	And give it way[19]; I know thou canst not choose.	

Prospero calls Ariel, who reports that he has carried out Prospero's commands in exact detail. Ariel's miraculous display of fire caused terror on the ship. Ferdinand was the first passenger to leap overboard.

剧情简介：普饶斯普柔召唤艾瑞尔，艾瑞尔报告说他已经把普饶斯普柔交代的事情不折不扣地办好了。他巧施魔法，展现火焰，在船上造成一片恐慌。在乘客当中法迪南第一个跳下船去。

Stagecraft 导演技巧
The casting of Ariel

Ariel can be played by either a man or a woman. What sort of Ariel would you want in your production? How would you cast the part?

a   In your Director's Journal, list the famous actors you think would be good for the part. Give brief reasons for each choice.

b   Think about the relationship you would want to establish early on between Prospero ('great master') and his servant ('brave spirit'). Share your thoughts with a partner. Are your ideas similar?

1 Act Ariel's story of the shipwreck

Lines 187–215 offer exciting opportunities for acting.

a   **Whole class** Everyone learns a very short section of Ariel's lines from the script opposite. One person plays Prospero, and stands in the centre of the room. In turn, each Ariel runs to join Prospero, speaking 'his' words and making appropriate gestures. The person who has the words 'more momentary / And sight-outrunning were not' has a challenging task: how can you outrun sight?

b   **In pairs** Choose a short section for one of you to read out while the other echoes (随声附和) it. Try different styles of echoing, such as whispering, questioning, and speaking emphatically, slowly and rapidly. Discuss which is the more effective and why you think that is.

c   **On your own** Read Ariel's lines aloud while walking around. Change direction abruptly at each punctuation mark, and add suitable gestures.

Themes 主题分析
The use (and abuse) of power (in fours)

Ferdinand's actions convey something of the atmosphere on board the ship. Ariel's description of the chaos can be portrayed in different ways. Some productions emphasise its mischievousness (恶作剧); others depict it as something more terrifying.

- Discuss whether you think Prospero is right to take revenge on Antonio and all his crew. Two of you defend Prospero and two criticise him. Share your ideas with other groups and agree on the top five points made for and against Prospero's actions.

---

1   grave sir   尊贵的大人
2   task   吩咐
3   all his quality   他的所有同类
4   to point   不折不扣
5   beak   船头
6   in the waist   在船腹
7   flamed amazement   燃起骇人的烈火
8   divide   用分身术
9   yards and bowsprit   帆桁（吊在桅杆上用来支撑和展开船帆的长柱）和船首斜桁（支撑前桅的长柱）
10 distinctly   分别
11 Jove   天神乔武（即Jupiter——朱庇特，万神之王）
12 precursors   先行者
13 momentary   急促
14 sight-outrunning   目不暇接
15 sulphurous   带硫黄味
16 Neptune   （罗马神话中的）海神尼普顿
17 besiege   围困
18 trident   三叉戟
19 coil   骚乱
20 fever of the mad   疯子的癫狂
21 tricks of desperation   绝望时的怪异举动
22 brine   卤水（指海水）
23 hair up-staring   毛发耸立
24 nigh shore   靠近岸边

THE TEMPEST ACT 1 SCENE 2
暴风雨

[*Miranda sleeps*]
Come away, servant, come; I'm ready now.
Approach, my Ariel. Come!

Enter ARIEL

ARIEL All hail, great master, grave sir[1], hail! I come
To answer thy best pleasure; be't to fly, 190
To swim, to dive into the fire, to ride
On the curled clouds. To thy strong bidding task[2]
Ariel, and all his quality[3].

PROSPERO Hast thou, spirit, performed to point[4] the tempest
That I bade thee?

ARIEL To every article. 195
I boarded the king's ship. Now on the beak[5],
Now in the waist[6], the deck, in every cabin,
I flamed amazement[7]. Sometime I'd divide[8]
And burn in many places; on the topmast,
The yards and bowsprit[9], would I flame distinctly[10], 200
Then meet and join. Jove's[11] lightning, the precursors[12]
O'th'dreadful thunder-claps, more momentary[13]
And sight-outrunning[14] were not; the fire and cracks
Of sulphurous[15] roaring the most mighty Neptune[16]
Seem to besiege[17], and make his bold waves tremble, 205
Yea, his dread trident[18] shake.

PROSPERO My brave spirit!
Who was so firm, so constant, that this coil[19]
Would not infect his reason?

ARIEL Not a soul
But felt a fever of the mad[20], and played
Some tricks of desperation[21]. All but mariners 210
Plunged in the foaming brine[22] and quit the vessel,
Then all a-fire with me; the king's son Ferdinand,
With hair up-staring[23] – then like reeds, not hair –
Was the first man that leaped; cried 'Hell is empty,
And all the devils are here.'

PROSPERO Why that's my spirit. 215
But was not this nigh shore[24]?

ARIEL Close by, my master.

PROSPERO But are they, Ariel, safe?

Ariel reports that the ship's passengers are safe on shore, the sailors are asleep on board, and the rest of the fleet is returning to Naples, mourning Alonso. Ariel, to Prospero's annoyance, demands his freedom.

剧情简介：艾瑞尔报告说，船上的乘客都已安全上岸，水手们在甲板上熟睡，其他船只正返回那不勒斯，悼念额朗佐。艾瑞尔请求普饶斯普柔放了自己，引起普饶斯普柔的反感。

Write about it 写作练习

Making sense of the storm (in pairs)

Ariel explains that the other boats in the fleet are returning safely home, but that they have witnessed the destruction of the king's ship.

- One of you steps into role as a sailor in the fleet heading home. Write to a member of your family describing the events that have taken place. You can write your letter in Shakespearean prose or in modern English.
- The other person takes on the role of a crew member who is now safe and 'dispersed ... 'bout the isle'. Write his diary entry. How would he make sense of what has happened (look carefully at lines 217–19)? You can write in modern or Shakespearean prose, but whichever style you choose, you should try to convey the information using rich and evocative (引起共鸣的) language.

1 Ariel: a resentful (充满愤恨的) servant?

In traditional tales, the spirits who serve magicians are often resentful and the magicians are never completely in control. Prospero and Ariel seem to be no exception. How does Ariel make his demand for freedom: resentfully, politely or in some other way? How does Prospero reply?

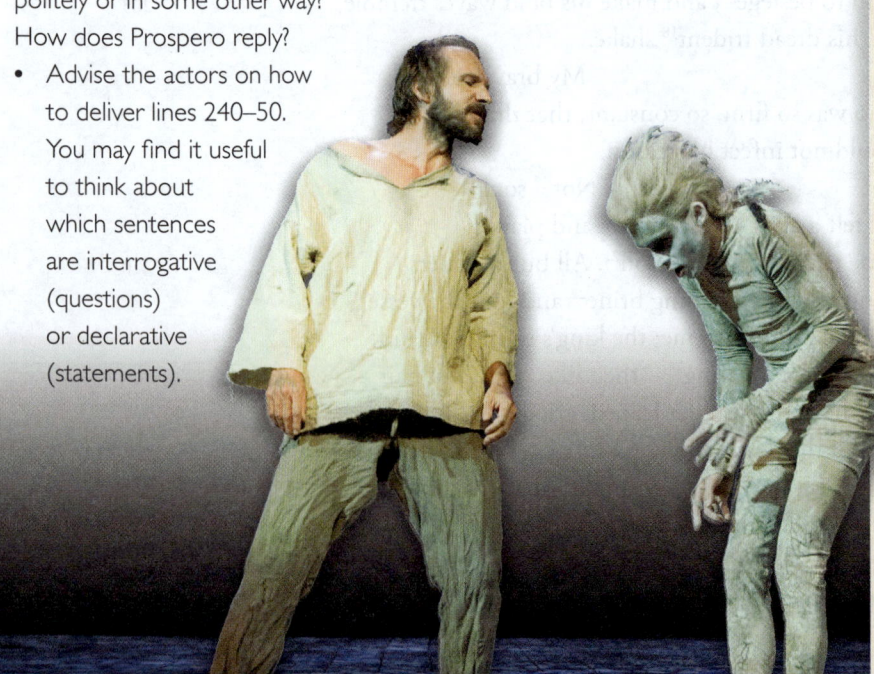

- Advise the actors on how to deliver lines 240–50. You may find it useful to think about which sentences are interrogative (questions) or declarative (statements).

1 Not a hair perished 没有一个人遇难
2 sustaining 漂浮
3 blemish 污渍
4 troops 群
5 dispersed 使分散
6 odd angle 偏僻的角落
7 His ... knot 手臂抱在一起，愁苦万分
8 deep nook 深邃的岬角
9 still-vexed 风暴仍然不断
10 Bermudas 百慕大群岛
11 under hatches 舱口下方
12 charm 魔咒，咒语
13 suffered labour 所经受的劳苦
14 float 海
15 perish 遇难
16 charge 任务，差事
17 mid-season 正午
18 two glasses （用沙漏计算的）两个钟点
19 'twixt six and now 在下午六点和现在（两点）之间（四个钟点）
20 most preciously 尽量珍惜时间
21 give me pains 差遣我做事
22 Moody 郁郁寡欢
23 Before the time be out 在说好的当差时限之前
24 prithee 求求您，拜托您
25 served ... grumblings 毫无怨言地听您差遣
26 bate me 放过我（免受役使）

ARIEL	Not a hair perished[1];

ARIEL On their sustaining[2] garments not a blemish[3],
But fresher than before. And as thou bad'st me,
In troops[4] I have dispersed[5] them 'bout the isle.   220
The king's son have I landed by himself,
Whom I left cooling of the air with sighs
In an odd angle[6] of the isle, and sitting,
His arms in this sad knot[7].

PROSPERO   Of the king's ship,
The mariners, say how thou hast disposed,   225
And all the rest o'th'fleet?

ARIEL   Safely in harbour
Is the king's ship, in the deep nook[8], where once
Thou call'dst me up at midnight to fetch dew
From the still-vexed[9] Bermudas[10], there she's hid;
The mariners all under hatches[11] stowed,   230
Who, with a charm[12] joined to their suffered labour[13],
I've left asleep. And for the rest o'th'fleet –
Which I dispersed – they all have met again,
And are upon the Mediterranean float[14]
Bound sadly home for Naples,   235
Supposing that they saw the king's ship wracked,
And his great person perish[15].

PROSPERO   Ariel, thy charge[16]
Exactly is performed; but there's more work.
What is the time o'th'day?

ARIEL   Past the mid-season[17].

PROSPERO At least two glasses[18]. The time 'twixt six and now[19]   240
Must by us both be spent most preciously[20].

ARIEL Is there more toil? Since thou dost give me pains[21],
Let me remember thee what thou hast promised,
Which is not yet performed me.

PROSPERO   How now? Moody[22]?
What is't thou canst demand?

ARIEL   My liberty.   245

PROSPERO Before the time be out[23]? No more.

ARIEL   I prithee[24],
Remember I have done thee worthy service,
Told thee no lies, made no mistakings, served
Without or grudge or grumblings[25]. Thou did promise
To bate me[26] a full year.

Prospero rebukes Ariel, accusing him of resentfulness. Prospero reminds Ariel of Sycorax who, enraged by Ariel's refusal to obey her, imprisoned him inside a tree, where he suffered agony for twelve years.

剧情简介：普饶斯普柔斥责艾瑞尔，说他不知感恩反而心怀怨恨。他提醒艾瑞尔，当初他因抗命而惹得巫婆悉柯拉克斯大发雷霆，被她禁锢在一棵树里，痛苦煎熬了12年。

1 What is your image of Ariel? (in pairs)

Ariel is Prospero's servant. His past errands (差事) have taken him to the ocean floor, to the freezing north wind, and to rivers running deep underground (lines 252–6).

- Look at the photographs of actors portraying Ariel on pages v, vii, x, 22, 26, 98, 103, 172 and 179. Which comes closest to your own image of an Ariel who could perform such amazing feats?

Language in the play 剧中语言
Ariel – from captivity to freedom

Lines 252–6 contrast with lines 274–80 in describing Ariel's experiences serving Prospero and enduring imprisonment by the witch Sycorax.

- Write a paragraph describing the visual imagery conjured by Prospero's language in these two passages. What does this imagery reveal about his character?

2 'The foul witch Sycorax' (in small groups)

No one really knows why Shakespeare decided to use the name Sycorax for the witch who tormented (折磨) Ariel. Perhaps the name comes from two Greek words: *sys* (sow) and *korax* (raven). Whatever Sycorax's name means, we know she 'with age and envy / Was grown into a hoop'. This physical deformity (畸形) was meant to indicate her moral deformity and evil nature.

- Compile a list of all references to witchcraft and evil as they relate to Sycorax in the script opposite.

Write about it 写作练习
Diary of a citizen of Algiers (阿尔及尔，今阿尔及利亚首都)

We are told that despite her 'mischiefs manifold' and 'sorceries terrible', Sycorax was not killed by the citizens of Algiers: 'For one thing she did / They would not take her life'. What was the amazing 'one thing' she did that so impressed (or frightened) the citizens that they spared her life?

- Imagine Sycorax's life story and write the diary of someone who observed her closely when she lived in Algiers, attracting the attention of the citizens through her 'mischiefs manifold'.

---

1 think'st it much　觉得了不起
2 tread the ooze　脚踩淤泥
3 do me business　替我办事
4 in the veins o'th'earth　在大地的裂缝沟渠中
5 malignant　恶毒
6 grown into a hoop　身体驼成了一个圈
7 mischiefs manifold　各式各样的灾祸
8 sorceries terrible　可怕的巫术
9 banished　流放
10 blue-eyed　眼窝青紫
11 hither　到此地
12 with child　有孕在身
13 delicate　柔弱纤巧
14 abhorred　心怀仇恨
15 grand hests　可怕的命令
16 potent ministers　强大的帮凶
17 unmitigable　难以平息
18 cloven　裂开的
19 rift　裂缝
20 vent　发出
21 as mill-wheels strike　像磨坊的水车轮打在水面上一样不间断
22 litter　产（崽）
23 whelp　小狗
24 hag-born　女巫生的

THE TEMPEST ACT 1 SCENE 2
暴风雨

PROSPERO   Dost thou forget   250
From what a torment I did free thee?
ARIEL   No.
PROSPERO   Thou dost! And think'st it much¹ to tread the ooze²
Of the salt deep,
To run upon the sharp wind of the north,
To do me business³ in the veins o'th'earth⁴   255
When it is baked with frost.
ARIEL   I do not, sir.
PROSPERO   Thou liest, malignant⁵ thing. Hast thou forgot
The foul witch Sycorax, who with age and envy
Was grown into a hoop⁶? Hast thou forgot her?
ARIEL   No, sir.
PROSPERO   Thou hast. Where was she born? Speak. Tell me.   260
ARIEL   Sir, in Algiers.
PROSPERO   O, was she so? I must
Once in a month recount what thou hast been,
Which thou forget'st. This damned witch Sycorax,
For mischiefs manifold⁷, and sorceries terrible⁸
To enter human hearing, from Algiers   265
Thou know'st was banished⁹. For one thing she did
They would not take her life. Is not this true?
ARIEL   Ay, sir.
PROSPERO   This blue-eyed¹⁰ hag was hither¹¹ brought with child¹²,
And here was left by th'sailors. Thou, my slave,   270
As thou report'st thyself, was then her servant;
And for thou wast a spirit too delicate¹³
To act her earthy and abhorred¹⁴ commands,
Refusing her grand hests¹⁵, she did confine thee,
By help of her more potent ministers¹⁶,   275
And in her most unmitigable¹⁷ rage,
Into a cloven¹⁸ pine, within which rift¹⁹
Imprisoned thou didst painfully remain
A dozen years; within which space she died,
And left thee there; where thou didst vent²⁰ thy groans   280
As fast as mill-wheels strike²¹. Then was this island –
Save for the son that she did litter²² here,
A freckled whelp²³, hag-born²⁴ – not honoured with
A human shape.
ARIEL   Yes, Caliban her son.

Prospero describes how he released Ariel, but threatens further punishment if Ariel continues to complain. He orders Ariel to disguise himself as an invisible sea-nymph, wakes Miranda and proposes to visit Caliban.

剧情简介：普饶斯普柔讲述他如何释放了艾瑞尔，但警告艾瑞尔，如果再抱怨，就进一步惩罚他。普饶斯普柔命令艾瑞尔化身为隐身的海上仙子，又唤醒蜜兰莶，提议二人去看看凯力般。

1 Imprisonment and release (in small groups)

Lines 286–93 vividly describe Ariel's torment as he was imprisoned in the 'cloven pine' (a split pine tree), and his subsequent release by Prospero.

a Read this section, then discuss how Prospero's violent imagery creates dramatic effect at this point in the play.

b In groups, create a tableau representing Ariel's imprisonment. Try to include the 'unmitigable rage' of Sycorax, the suffering of Ariel and the magic art of Prospero that set the spirit free.

2 Prospero and Ariel: master and servant (in pairs)

Read lines 290–305. Prospero reminds Ariel of his imprisonment on the island before his master's arrival. Reminded of how much he owes Prospero, Ariel promises not to be moody or keep demanding his liberty.

- Experiment with ways of reading these lines. What tone of voice should each character use? Does Ariel ask for pardon humbly and sincerely, or is he resentful? Is Prospero more like an indulgent (宽容的) teacher, an angry parent, a hard taskmaster (工头) or something else?

Stagecraft 导演技巧

Ariel's invisible shape

In lines 302–5, Prospero tells Ariel to make himself invisible to everyone except him.

- How would you ensure that the audience (and Prospero) can see Ariel, but no one else on stage knows he is there? Write your ideas in your Director's Journal.

1 penetrate the breasts 使人心生怜悯
2 made gape 打开
3 murmur'st （心怀不满地）嘟囔
4 rend 劈开
5 entrails 树干
6 correspondent 服从
7 gently 乖乖地
8 discharge thee 放了你（不再给你派差事）
9 diligence 认真
10 Heaviness 昏昏欲睡
11 Shake it off 打起精神，振作起来
12 Yields 屈从，被迫同意
13 villain 出身低贱的恶棍
14 cannot miss 不能没有
15 offices 差事
16 profit 对……有益
17 earth 泥块（与飘在空中的艾瑞尔形成鲜明对比）

PROSPERO	Dull thing, I say so: he, that Caliban	285
	Whom now I keep in service. Thou best know'st	
	What torment I did find thee in. Thy groans	
	Did make wolves howl, and penetrate the breasts[1]	
	Of ever-angry bears. It was a torment	
	To lay upon the damned, which Sycorax	290
	Could not again undo. It was mine art,	
	When I arrived and heard thee, that made gape[2]	
	The pine, and let thee out.	
ARIEL	I thank thee, master.	
PROSPERO	If thou more murmur'st[3], I will rend[4] an oak	
	And peg thee in his knotty entrails[5] till	295
	Thou hast howled away twelve winters.	
ARIEL	Pardon, master.	
	I will be correspondent[6] to command	
	And do my spiriting gently[7].	
PROSPERO	Do so;	
	And after two days I will discharge thee[8].	
ARIEL	That's my noble master! What shall I do?	300
	Say what? What shall I do?	
PROSPERO	Go make thyself	
	Like to a nymph o'th'sea. Be subject to	
	No sight but thine and mine, invisible	
	To every eye-ball else. Go take this shape	
	And hither come in't. Go! Hence with diligence[9].	305
	Exit [Ariel]	
	[*To Miranda*] Awake, dear heart, awake; thou hast slept well,	
	Awake.	
MIRANDA	The strangeness of your story put	
	Heaviness[10] in me.	
PROSPERO	Shake it off[11]. Come on,	
	We'll visit Caliban, my slave, who never	
	Yields[12] us kind answer.	
MIRANDA	'Tis a villain[13], sir,	310
	I do not love to look on.	
PROSPERO	But as 'tis	
	We cannot miss[14] him. He does make our fire,	
	Fetch in our wood, and serves in offices[15]	
	That profit[16] us. What ho! Slave! Caliban!	
	Thou earth[17], thou! Speak!	

Ariel is given secret orders by Prospero. Caliban curses Prospero and Miranda, and Prospero threatens painful punishments. Caliban recalls how Prospero had treated him kindly at first, but then enslaved him.

剧情简介：普饶斯普柔暗自给艾瑞尔交代了一些任务。凯力般诅咒普饶斯普柔和蜜兰达，普饶斯普柔则威胁要对他加以严惩。凯力般回忆普饶斯普柔一开始对他不错，后来却把他当成了奴隶。

Stagecraft 导演技巧

'Enter CALIBAN'

Prospero shouts for Caliban with insults (辱骂). He calls him his slave – a word he never uses to describe Ariel. Although Caliban answers him rudely from off stage, his entrance is delayed.

- How would you stage this entrance when it eventually occurs? What is going on both off stage and on stage while Prospero waits for Caliban? How does he look and act when he finally appears? Notice that 'Caliban' is almost an anagram* of 'cannibal' (食人怪) – does this affect how you imagine him to look and behave?
- Make notes in your Director's Journal, describing how you would stage this part of the scene in a modern performance.

1 'This island's mine' (in pairs)

Who has the right to own the island? Many people believe that Caliban's experience is typical of what happens to any race subjected to colonisation (see 'Perspectives and themes', pp. 154–5). When Prospero came to the island, he treated Caliban kindly, but then made him his slave.

- Explore the story that unfolds in lines 332–62 from the point of view of both Caliban and Prospero. Take parts as one of these two characters and argue for your own claim over the island. Use quotations from the play to support your case.

Language in the play 剧中语言

Punctuation

Think about how Caliban's language makes you feel as you read lines 331–45 while walking round the classroom. As you walk, change direction on each punctuation mark, using the following rules:

- At each full stop, make a full about-turn (180 degrees).
- At each comma, semi-colon and dash, make a half turn (90 degrees to your right or left).
- Think of a gesture to make at every exclamation mark (such as stamping your foot or clicking your fingers).

Which words or lines stood out for you during this activity? How did it change your understanding of Caliban's emotions and his feelings towards Prospero?

1 Fine apparition 装扮得很好
2 quaint 机灵
3 Hark 留神听着
4 got 被生养
5 dam 老娘
6 raven （女巫常用的）乌鸦
7 unwholesome fen 污秽的泥潭
8 south-west blow （易导致疾病的）西南风
9 blister 痛打
10 cramps 肌肉抽筋
11 Side-stiches 两肋刺痛
12 pen thy breath up 让你不敢呼吸
13 urchins 小妖
14 pinched / As thick as honeycomb 被掐捏出像蜂窝一样密密麻麻的印记
15 bigger … less 大亮（指太阳）……小亮（指月亮）
16 qualities 独特之处
17 brine-pits 卤水坑
18 subjects 臣民，子民
19 sty … rock 把我像猪一样圈在这岩石洞里

* anagram 字母异置词，例如把Elvis写成lives。

CALIBAN	(*Within*)	There's wood enough within.	315
PROSPERO	Come forth, I say; there's other business for thee.		
	Come, thou tortoise, when?		

Enter ARIEL *like a water-nymph*

Fine apparition[1]! My quaint[2] Ariel,
Hark[3] in thine ear.
             [*Whispers to Ariel*]

ARIEL	My lord, it shall be done.	*Exit*	
PROSPERO	Thou poisonous slave, got[4] by the devil himself		320
	Upon thy wicked dam[5], come forth.		

Enter CALIBAN

CALIBAN   As wicked dew as e'er my mother brushed
With raven's[6] feather from unwholesome fen[7]
Drop on you both! A south-west blow[8] on ye,
And blister[9] you all o'er!   325

PROSPERO   For this, be sure, tonight thou shalt have cramps[10],
Side-stitches[11] that shall pen thy breath up[12]; urchins[13]
Shall, for that vast of night that they may work,
All exercise on thee; thou shalt be pinched
As thick as honeycomb[14], each pinch more stinging   330
Than bees that made 'em.

CALIBAN   I must eat my dinner.
This island's mine by Sycorax my mother,
Which thou tak'st from me. When thou cam'st first
Thou strok'st me and made much of me; wouldst give me
Water with berries in't, and teach me how   335
To name the bigger light, and how the less[15],
That burn by day and night. And then I loved thee
And showed thee all the qualities[16] o'th'isle,
The fresh springs, brine-pits[17], barren place and fertile –
Cursèd be I that did so! All the charms   340
Of Sycorax – toads, beetles, bats – light on you!
For I am all the subjects[18] that you have,
Which first was mine own king; and here you sty me
In this hard rock[19], whiles you do keep from me
The rest o'th'island.

Prospero accuses Caliban of attempting to rape Miranda. Miranda tells Caliban that he deserves to be imprisoned because he is evil. Caliban curses her but, fearful of Prospero's threats, obeys the order to leave.

剧情简介：普饶斯普柔指控凯力般曾企图强奸蜜兰莶。蜜兰莶说凯力般生性邪恶，应该被囚禁。凯力般开始咒骂她，但由于畏惧普饶斯普柔，他还是服从命令离开了。

1 Who speaks the lines? (in small groups)

Some people think that lines 351–62 are too harsh to be spoken by Miranda. In some productions, therefore, the lines are given to Prospero instead.

- If you were directing a stage production, who would you want to speak the lines – Miranda or Prospero? Write notes to prepare for a director's meeting in which you will advise the actors playing these characters. Remember to refer to the script in detail as you explain your decision about who speaks the lines.

Write about it 写作练习

The official story? (by yourself)

What really happened when Prospero arrived on the island? Was Caliban an innocent, naturally good person whose genuine friendship towards Miranda was misinterpreted? Or was he a savage brute (畜生), tamed by Prospero, whose true nature came out when he tried to rape Miranda? Was Prospero a kind man who had no intention of seizing the island until Caliban's evil nature was revealed? Or was he deceitful and greedy, determined from the outset to exploit the island's natural resources and make Caliban his slave?

- Write an account of what you think happened, based on your knowledge of the characters in the play so far.

Characters 人物分析

'You taught me language' (in pairs)

Line 363 raises very important questions about language and race. Throughout history, conquerors and governments have tried to suppress the language of certain groups that they believed to be inferior. Caliban expresses the resentment of the enslaved:

> You taught me language, and my profit on't
> Is, I know how to curse. The red plague rid you
> For learning me your language!

- Search the script opposite (and elsewhere in this act) to find some of the curses Caliban uses. For each curse you find, write out what it means and try to find a modern equivalent.

---

1 stripes 鞭挞
2 lodged 安排……住在……
3 I … Calibans 否则我早让这个岛上住满凯力般的子孙
4 Abhorrèd 可恨，可怕
5 print 印记（引申义：教化，影响）
6 capable of all ill 有本事做各种恶事
7 gabble 嚎叫
8 brutish 粗野，野兽般
9 purposes 本意，想法
10 vile 邪恶
11 abide 容下，忍受
12 more than a prison 比监禁更严厉的惩罚（指处死，这里蜜兰莶指对强奸罪的惩罚）
13 curse （像巫婆一样）诅咒
14 red plague 红瘟疫（又称天花或丹毒）
15 rid 摧毁
16 learning 教诲
17 Hag-seed 巫婆之子
18 answer other business 做其他差事
19 malice 坏东西
20 rack 折磨
21 old cramps 抽筋这一老办法
22 din 惨叫
23 Setebos 南美洲的神明（凯力般和他母亲崇拜的神）
24 vassal 奴才

PROSPERO   Thou most lying slave,
            Whom stripes[1] may move, not kindness! I have used thee,
            Filth as thou art, with humane care, and lodged[2] thee
            In mine own cell, till thou didst seek to violate
            The honour of my child.

CALIBAN   O ho, O ho! Would't had been done.
            Thou didst prevent me – I had peopled else
            This isle with Calibans[3].

MIRANDA   Abhorrèd[4] slave,
            Which any print[5] of goodness wilt not take,
            Being capable of all ill[6]! I pitied thee,
            Took pains to make thee speak, taught thee each hour
            One thing or other. When thou didst not, savage,
            Know thine own meaning, but wouldst gabble[7] like
            A thing most brutish[8], I endowed thy purposes[9]
            With words that made them known. But thy vile[10] race –
            Though thou didst learn – had that in't which good natures
            Could not abide[11] to be with; therefore wast thou
            Deservedly confined into this rock,
            Who hadst deserved more than a prison[12].

CALIBAN   You taught me language, and my profit on't
            Is, I know how to curse[13]. The red plague[14] rid[15] you
            For learning[16] me your language!

PROSPERO   Hag-seed[17], hence!
            Fetch us in fuel; and be quick, thou'rt best,
            To answer other business[18]. Shrug'st thou, malice[19]?
            If thou neglect'st, or dost unwillingly
            What I command, I'll rack[20] thee with old cramps[21],
            Fill all thy bones with aches, make thee roar,
            That beasts shall tremble at thy din[22].

CALIBAN   No, pray thee.
            [*Aside*] I must obey; his art is of such power,
            It would control my dam's god Setebos[23],
            And make a vassal[24] of him.

PROSPERO   So, slave, hence.
                                        Exit Caliban

345

350

355

360

365

370

Ariel's first song is an invitation to dance upon the sands. Ferdinand is amazed by the music that has calmed both the storm and his grief. Ariel's second song describes a wonderful transformation after death.

剧情简介：艾瑞尔唱了第一首歌，邀请人到沙滩上跳舞。法迪南很惊讶，因为乐曲既平息了暴风雨又安抚了他的悲痛。艾瑞尔又唱了一首歌，描述人死后的奇妙转变。

1 Ariel's songs (in small groups)

Ariel's first song is about the calming of the tempest. It is an invitation to dance by the seashore where the waves kiss, becoming silent and calm. Ariel's second song tells how Alonso, the king, is magically transformed, having undergone 'a sea-change / Into something rich and strange'.

- Write a paragraph describing the kind of music you would choose to evoke the mood of these songs. Would it be harmonious and reassuring or eerie (令人毛骨悚然) and slightly frightening?

Language in the play 剧中语言

The power of music (by yourself)

The language in the script opposite has several musical qualities: rhyme, rhythm (节奏) and sound echoes all contribute to the musicality (乐感) of this scene.

a Find examples of the following language features in the script opposite: **alliteration***; **rhyming couplets** (押韵二行连句；对偶句); **onomatopoeia** (拟声); **personification** (拟人)(see pp. 166–7 for more information on these).

b Choose one of Ariel's songs or Ferdinand's speech, and read it aloud two or three times. Then write a paragraph describing the effect of this language on an audience.

2 First sight of Ferdinand

Ferdinand says that the music has calmed his feeling of grief for his father, whom he believes drowned during the storm.

- Read Ariel's description of Ferdinand earlier in this scene (lines 221–4). Write down a few words to describe his appearance. Is he bedraggled (全身湿透) or neatly dressed? Amazed or terrified? Then write a paragraph predicting what might happen to Ferdinand on the island.

Themes 主题分析

Transformation (in pairs)

a Memorise the first six lines of Ariel's second song (lines 396–401) and identify all the transformations Alonso has undergone.

b What do you think Ariel means by a 'sea-change', and what emotions are evoked as you read these lines?

---

1 *playing* 弹奏（边弹边唱，弹的很可能是类似琵琶的鲁特琴[lute]）
2 Curtsied 行屈膝礼
3 whist 平息
4 Foot it featly 轻盈起舞吧
5 sprites 精灵
6 burden bear 合唱
7 *dispersedly* 分散地
8 *burden* 衬歌，帮腔
9 strain 曲调
10 strutting Chanticleer 大摇大摆的雄鸡强啼克烈（Chanticleer是伊索寓言中一只自吹自擂的大公鸡的名字）
11 waits upon 唱给……听
12 Allaying 安抚
13 passion 悲痛
14 air 曲调
15 fathom 英寻（深度计量单位，一英寻约等于1.83米）
16 Full fathom five 足足五英寻（约9米）深
17 fade 腐烂
18 knell 丧钟

* alliteration 头韵，指诗句里两个或多个词的第一个辅音相同，如sing a song of sixpence，类似中文的双声。

The Tempest Act 1 Scene 2
暴风雨

Enter FERDINAND, *and* ARIEL *invisible, playing*[1] *and singing*

SONG

ARIEL
Come unto these yellow sands, 375
And then take hands.
Curtsied[2] when you have, and kissed,
The wild waves whist[3].
Foot it featly[4] here and there,
And sweet sprites[5] the burden bear[6]. 380
    Hark, hark
      The watch-dogs bark
        Bow wow, bow wow.
[*Spirits dispersedly*[7] *echo the burden*[8] *'Bow wow'*]
    Hark, hark! I hear
      The strain[9] of strutting Chanticleer[10], 385
        Cry cock-a-diddle-dow.
[*Spirits dispersedly echo the burden 'cock-a-diddle-dow'*]

FERDINAND
Where should this music be? I'th'air, or th'earth?
It sounds no more; and sure it waits upon[11]
Some god o'th'island. Sitting on a bank,
Weeping again the king my father's wrack, 390
This music crept by me upon the waters,
Allaying[12] both their fury and my passion[13]
With its sweet air[14]. Thence I have followed it –
Or it hath drawn me rather; but 'tis gone.
No, it begins again. 395

SONG

ARIEL
Full fathom[15] five[16] thy father lies,
Of his bones are coral made;
Those are pearls that were his eyes;
Nothing of him that doth fade[17],
But doth suffer a sea-change 400
Into something rich and strange.
Sea-nymphs hourly ring his knell[18].
Hark, now I hear them, ding dong bell.
[*Spirits dispersedly echo the burden 'ding dong bell'*]

Miranda wonders at Ferdinand, imagining him to be a spirit. Prospero assures her that Ferdinand is human. Ferdinand thinks that Miranda is a goddess, and is surprised to hear her speak his language.

剧情简介：蜜兰苂看到法迪南很惊奇，以为他是精灵，普饶斯普柔向女儿保证法迪南是人。法迪南以为蜜兰苂是女神，听到她跟自己说同样的语言，大为吃惊。

Language in the play 剧中语言

A fairy-tale world? (in small groups)

Prospero's line 407 is a formal and elaborate way of saying 'open your eyes'. Prospero uses another elaborate image in lines 413–14.

- Take turns in role as Prospero, and describe why you are using such formal and solemn language. What effect are you hoping it will have on Miranda? How do you want her to respond to what she sees? Remember, Miranda is still in a dream-like state and is being invited to look at something new and strange.

1 'It goes on, I see'

Prospero's plan is working. Write an extended **aside** (旁白) (see p. 168) for Prospero, to allow the audience to find out more about his desire to make Miranda and Ferdinand notice each other. Add at least four more lines to his aside in lines 418–19.

Stagecraft 导演技巧

How do you speak to a stranger? (in pairs)

With a partner, discuss how you think Ferdinand should speak and behave towards Miranda when he first sees her. Do you think the actor should be reminded that Ferdinand is a European prince who thinks that he is meeting a foreigner who doesn't speak his language? Or do you think this should be portrayed as a delicate moment, full of dream-like wonder?

◀ Write notes to the actors playing Ferdinand and Miranda, describing how you want them to behave during their first meeting.

1 ditty 歌曲
2 remember （让人）怀念
3 mortal 凡人
4 owes = owns
5 The fringèd … eye 带流苏的帘子（即眼皮）
6 advance 抬起
7 yond 在那边；那边的
8 brave form 英俊的外表
9 gallant 仪表堂堂的小伙儿
10 but 若不是
11 canker 溃疡，腐败
12 these airs 这些歌声
13 Vouchsafe 请恩准
14 remain 居住
15 bear me 行事
16 prime 最重要
17 maid 少女
18 best 最高贵（法迪南以为自己现在是那不勒斯国王了）

| FERDINAND | The ditty¹ does remember² my drowned father. |
| | This is no mortal³ business, nor no sound | 405
	That the earth owes⁴. I hear it now above me.
PROSPERO	[*To Miranda*] The fringèd curtains of thine eye⁵ advance⁶,
	And say what thou seest yond⁷.
MIRANDA	What is't? A spirit?
	Lord, how it looks about! Believe me, sir,
	It carries a brave form⁸. But 'tis a spirit.	410
PROSPERO	No, wench, it eats, and sleeps, and hath such senses
	As we have, such. This gallant⁹ which thou seest
	Was in the wrack; and but¹⁰ he's something stained
	With grief – that's beauty's canker¹¹ – thou might'st call him
	A goodly person. He hath lost his fellows,	415
	And strays about to find 'em.
MIRANDA	I might call him
	A thing divine, for nothing natural
	I ever saw so noble.
PROSPERO	[*Aside*] It goes on, I see,
	As my soul prompts it. [*To Ariel*] Spirit, fine spirit, I'll free thee
	Within two days for this.
FERDINAND	[*Seeing Miranda*] Most sure the goddess	420
	On whom these airs¹² attend. Vouchsafe¹³ my prayer
	May know if you remain¹⁴ upon this island,
	And that you will some good instruction give
	How I may bear me¹⁵ here. My prime¹⁶ request,
	Which I do last pronounce, is – O you wonder –	425
	If you be maid¹⁷, or no?
MIRANDA	No wonder, sir,
	But certainly a maid.
FERDINAND	My language? Heavens!
	I am the best¹⁸ of them that speak this speech,
	Were I but where 'tis spoken.

Ferdinand, believing his father dead, says he is king of Naples. Miranda and Ferdinand have fallen in love. To test their love, Prospero accuses Ferdinand of usurpation. Miranda defends Ferdinand.

剧情简介：法迪南以为父亲已死，便对蜜兰莐说自己是那不勒斯国王。蜜兰莐和法迪南坠入爱河。为了考验他们的爱情，普饶斯普柔指控法迪南篡夺王位，蜜兰莐为其辩护。

1 Getting a word in – and not listening (in threes)

Ferdinand has fallen head over heels in love with Miranda, and he has eyes and ears for her alone. He is so entranced (着迷) that Prospero finds it difficult to gain his attention.

a Read the script opposite and identify all the times Prospero asks Ferdinand for a 'word'. Notice how by line 451 Prospero seems to be getting exasperated (恼火) :'I charge thee / That thou attend me!'

b Create a tableau of these three characters as represented in the script opposite. Then create a second tableau that shows how Prospero is really feeling about the developing relationship between the young lovers.

1 How the best? 你怎么会是最高贵的?
2 single thing 孤身一人
3 Myself am Naples 我本人就是那不勒斯国王
4 ne'er since at ebb 一直流泪
5 faith 说真的
6 his brave son 他那优秀的儿子（这里暗示米兰公爵安托纽有一个儿子，但剧中此人并未出现）
7 twain 两个人
8 braver 更优秀
9 control 质疑
10 changed eyes 眉目传情
11 ungently 不客气
12 I sighed for 我爱慕
13 your affection not gone forth 你的芳心还没有归属
14 uneasy 不顺利
15 light = easy
16 light = cheap
17 usurp 篡夺
18 ow'st not 不拥有
19 dwell in 居住在

Stagecraft 导演技巧

Staging the asides

There are three asides in the script opposite: two are spoken by Prospero and one by Miranda. Remember that an aside allows the character speaking to take the audience into his or her confidence, and gives the audience a greater understanding of what is happening than the other characters on stage.

- How would you ensure that the audience hears these asides, without the other characters on stage knowing what is going on? Sketch a diagram to show how you would position the actors. Use arrows and annotations to indicate their movement at this point in the play.

Themes 主题分析

Does beauty equal goodness? (in pairs)

Is someone morally good because they are good-looking? Miranda thinks so. In lines 456–8, she says that Ferdinand's handsome face reflects his good character and that good drives out evil from beautiful people ('Good things will strive to dwell with't').

a Talk together about whether you believe a person's character shows in their face and general appearance.

b In role as Miranda, explain more fully what you mean in lines 456–8. Then script a response to her from Prospero, who probably has a different opinion and possesses a greater understanding of human nature than Miranda does.

PROSPERO   How the best[1]?
         What wert thou if the King of Naples heard thee?   430

FERDINAND   A single thing[2], as I am now, that wonders
         To hear thee speak of Naples. He does hear me,
         And that he does, I weep. Myself am Naples[3],
         Who, with mine eyes, ne'er since at ebb[4], beheld
         The king my father wracked.

MIRANDA   Alack, for mercy!   435

FERDINAND   Yes, faith[5], and all his lords, the Duke of Milan
         And his brave son[6] being twain[7].

PROSPERO   [Aside]   The Duke of Milan
         And his more braver[8] daughter could control[9] thee
         If now 'twere fit to do't. At the first sight
         They have changed eyes[10]. [To Ariel] Delicate Ariel,   440
         I'll set thee free for this! [To Ferdinand] A word, good sir;
         I fear you have done yourself some wrong; a word.

MIRANDA   [Aside] Why speaks my father so ungently[11]? This
         Is the third man that e'er I saw; the first
         That e'er I sighed for[12]. Pity move my father   445
         To be inclined my way.

FERDINAND   O, if a virgin,
         And your affection not gone forth[13], I'll make you
         The Queen of Naples.

PROSPERO   Soft, sir, one word more.
         [Aside] They are both in either's powers; but this swift business
         I must uneasy[14] make, lest too light[15] winning   450
         Make the prize light[16]. [To Ferdinand] One word more. I
             charge thee
         That thou attend me! Thou dost here usurp[17]
         The name thou ow'st not[18], and hast put thyself
         Upon this island as a spy, to win it
         From me, the lord on't.

FERDINAND   No, as I am a man.   455

MIRANDA   There's nothing ill can dwell in[19] such a temple.
         If the ill spirit have so fair a house,
         Good things will strive to dwell with't.

Prospero threatens harsh punishment on Ferdinand, who draws his sword. Prospero 'freezes' Ferdinand with a spell, and forces him to drop the sword. Prospero scolds Miranda for supporting Ferdinand.

剧情简介：普饶斯普柔威胁要严惩法迪南。法迪南拔剑，普饶斯普柔用咒语定住了法迪南，令他扔掉剑，并谴责女儿一心向着法迪南。

1 'My foot my tutor?' – is Prospero angry? (in pairs)

Prospero's rebuke to Miranda is a vivid way of saying 'Shall something inferior presume to teach me?' Does Prospero speak impatiently and angrily, or with amused irony (讽刺), or in some other tone? Is Miranda emotional and hysterical (情绪异常激动), or calming and appeasing (姑息，安抚)?

- Read through lines 465–82 and experiment with different tones and emphases for this exchange between father and daughter.

Write about it 写作练习

What is Ferdinand thinking?

We have seen Ferdinand shipwrecked, washed up on the island, weeping for his father (whom he believes to be dead), and overwhelmed by the beauty of Ariel's music. He then meets Miranda and falls in love with her, after which Prospero calls Ferdinand a spy and, at line 464, charms him from moving before imprisoning him.

- Write a diary entry for Ferdinand, in which he records these extraordinary events, how he feels about them, and his hopes and fears for the future.

▼ Find a line or stage direction from the script opposite that serves as a suitable caption for this picture (Ferdinand is on the right).

1 manacle 给……上镣铐
2 fresh-brook mussels 淡水溪里的贻贝（不可食用）
3 husks / Wherein the acorn cradled 曾经包裹橡果的干壳
4 entertainment 待遇
5 *draws* 拔剑
6 *charmed* 被施魔咒
7 too rash a trial 太严厉的考验
8 gentle 身份高贵
9 My foot my tutor? 脚丫子管起脑袋来了？
10 mak'st a show 装装样子
11 Come from thy ward 别再做出防守的架势了
12 stick 手杖
13 Beseech 恳求，哀求
14 surety 担保（人）
15 chide 责骂
16 advocate 辩护人
17 impostor 骗子
18 To = compared to
19 goodlier 更英俊

PROSPERO	[*To Ferdinand*] Follow me.
	[*To Miranda*] Speak not you for him: he's a traitor.
	[*To Ferdinand*] Come!
	I'll manacle[1] thy neck and feet together; 460
	Sea water shalt thou drink; thy food shall be
	The fresh-brook mussels[2], withered roots, and husks
	Wherein the acorn cradled[3]. Follow.
FERDINAND	No!
	I will resist such entertainment[4], till
	Mine enemy has more power.
	He draws[5], and is charmed[6] from moving
MIRANDA	O dear father, 465
	Make not too rash a trial[7] of him, for
	He's gentle[8], and not fearful.
PROSPERO	[*To Miranda*] What, I say,
	My foot my tutor[9]? [*To Ferdinand*] Put thy sword up, traitor,
	Who mak'st a show[10], but dar'st not strike, thy conscience
	Is so possessed with guilt. Come from thy ward[11], 470
	For I can here disarm thee with this stick[12],
	And make thy weapon drop.
MIRANDA	[*Kneeling*] Beseech[13] you, father!
PROSPERO	Hence! Hang not on my garments.
MIRANDA	Sir, have pity;
	I'll be his surety[14].
PROSPERO	Silence! One word more
	Shall make me chide[15] thee, if not hate thee. What, 475
	An advocate[16] for an impostor[17]? Hush!
	Thou think'st there is no more such shapes as he,
	Having seen but him and Caliban. Foolish wench,
	To[18] th'most of men this is a Caliban,
	And they to him are angels.
MIRANDA	My affections 480
	Are then most humble. I have no ambition
	To see a goodlier[19] man.

Ferdinand says that, in spite of all his troubles, he will be content if he is allowed to see Miranda once a day from his prison. Prospero promises Ariel freedom in return for his services.

剧情简介：法迪南说尽管饱受苦难，但只要每天能从牢房看一眼蜜兰达，他就心满意足。普饶斯普柔答应艾瑞尔这次任务完成后会还他自由。

1 The romance tradition (in pairs)

The episode in this scene involving Ferdinand echoes two major elements of the romance and fairy-tale traditions that probably influenced Shakespeare as he wrote *The Tempest* (see p. 148).

- the harsh father who submits (使服从) the young lover to trials and ordeals (严酷的考验) in order to test his love
- the power of love to overcome all suffering.

Find examples or quotations from the end of Act 1 Scene 2 that show both the trials of love and the power of love to overcome difficulties.

Stagecraft 导演技巧

Setting the scene

a Step into role as director and write notes for yourself, describing how you will present Act 1 Scene 2 from Ferdinand's entrance at line 375 to the end of the scene. Include reasons for your decisions about the style of this scene, the atmosphere you intend to create, and how you will stage particular dramatic moments. Pay special attention to the number of secret conversations that take place – between Prospero and Ariel and between Miranda and Ferdinand – as well as the asides that let the audience know more about what is happening on stage.

b Draw a rough sketch of a stage or use a plain piece of paper to mark out the characters' positions. Annotate (注解) your sketch and draw arrows to show how you want the characters to move and speak at every stage direction in the script opposite. For example, in line 492 for Prospero's aside 'It works', you might like to note that the actor should stay at the front of the stage and turn to the audience to allow only them to hear what he says.

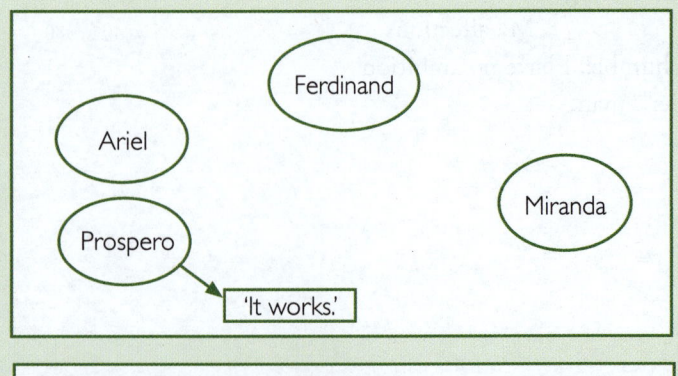

```
        ┌─────────────┐
        │  Ferdinand  │
        └─────────────┘
  ┌──────┐
  │ Ariel│              ┌─────────┐
  └──────┘              │ Miranda │
                        └─────────┘
  ┌──────────┐
  │ Prospero │
  └────┬─────┘
       └──→ 'It works.'

  ┌──────────────────────────────┐
  │          Audience            │
  └──────────────────────────────┘
```

1 nerves 肌肉
2 in their infancy 如婴儿一般柔弱
3 bound up 受到束缚
4 loss 死
5 subdued 被迫屈服
6 but light 只是小事一桩
7 All ... of 让别人拥有世界其他地方
8 unwonted 不寻常

PROSPERO	[*To Ferdinand*] Come on, obey.	
	Thy nerves¹ are in their infancy² again	
	And have no vigour in them.	
FERDINAND	So they are.	
	My spirits, as in a dream, are all bound up³.	485
	My father's loss⁴, the weakness which I feel,	
	The wrack of all my friends, nor this man's threats,	
	To whom I am subdued⁵, are but light⁶ to me,	
	Might I but through my prison once a day	
	Behold this maid. All corners else o'th'earth	490
	Let liberty make use of⁷; space enough	
	Have I in such a prison.	
PROSPERO	[*Aside*] It works. [*To Ferdinand*] Come on!	
	[*To Ariel*] Thou hast done well, fine Ariel. [*To Ferdinand*] Follow me.	
	[*To Ariel*] Hark what thou else shalt do me.	
MIRANDA	[*To Ferdinand*] Be of comfort;	
	My father's of a better nature, sir,	495
	Than he appears by speech. This is unwonted⁸	
	Which now came from him.	
PROSPERO	[*To Ariel*] Thou shalt be as free	
	As mountain winds; but then exactly do	
	All points of my command.	
ARIEL	To th'syllable.	
PROSPERO	[*To Ferdinand*] Come follow. [*To Miranda*] Speak not for him.	500
	Exeunt	

The Tempest
暴风雨

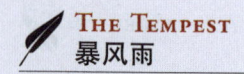

Looking back at Act 1　"第1幕"回顾
Activities for groups or individuals

1 Challenging authority

Act 1 is full of challenges to authority. The Boatswain orders the king and courtiers to leave the deck. Prospero recounts how he was overthrown by his brother Antonio. Ariel and Caliban question Prospero's right to keep them as servants. Prospero accuses Ferdinand of wanting to take the island from him.

- In small groups, discuss each of these examples and decide whether or not the questioning of authority is justified. Then rank each example in order of most unlawful to least unlawful. Find quotations in the script to illustrate each of these challenges, and describe briefly why you have chosen your particular order.

2 Imprisonment

The relationship between imprisonment and powerlessness is a theme that runs through Act 1.

- Write two or three sentences about each of the characters listed below, explaining how they suffer imprisonment or confinement (囚禁). Then develop your ideas into a paragraph, using embedded quotations. Explore who we feel the most sympathy for, and why.
  - Ariel
  - Caliban
  - Ferdinand
  - the crew of the shipwrecked vessel
  - Prospero and Miranda.

3 Prospero's overthrow

Neither television nor newspapers existed in Shakespeare's time. Imagine that they did. Show how *The Milan Times* or *Televisione Milano* reported the news of Prospero's overthrow and banishment (放逐) by his brother Antonio. Remember that Antonio may have seized control of the media to ensure that his story is the only one that is heard. Choose whether you want to write for a broadsheet (大报) or tabloid paper (小报), and give both the official and unofficial version in two reports.

4 Four stories – tell them, show them

In Scene 2, Prospero tells the story of how Antonio stole his dukedom (lines 66–168), and of Ariel's imprisonment by Sycorax (lines 257–93). Ariel describes how he brought about the shipwreck (lines 195–215). Caliban's story explains how he welcomed Prospero, but was condemned to slavery (lines 332–45).

- Prepare a series of three tableaux to depict one of these stories. Present your tableaux to the class and ask others to guess which story you are representing.

5 Caliban on stage

Look at the way in which Caliban has been presented in the photographs opposite. Is he a stereotype (刻板形象) of a savage and deformed slave? Is he even human? How would you choose to portray Caliban on stage?

a Write a description of how you think he should look, move, sound and behave. Draw a sketch if you like, then collect pictures from magazines or draw pictures that represent ideas that you would like associated with him on stage. These could relate to his costume, the props he uses and his appearance.

b Refer back to descriptions of Caliban in the script at Act 1 Scene 2 lines 281–4 and lines 368–71. Note that in the first extract, it is not clear whether 'not honoured with / A human shape' refers to the island or to Caliban; Prospero may mean that except for Caliban, the island had no other human population. However, many directors have portrayed Caliban with some sort of deformity. How else might he be deformed and dehumanised on stage?

43

Gonzalo tries to cheer Alonso up by reminding him of their miraculous survival. Sebastian mocks Gonzalo, deliberately mistaking his words. Alonso begs Gonzalo to be quiet.

剧情简介：为了让额朗佐振作精神，艮扎娄说他们能活下来是一种神迹。塞巴斯田故意曲解艮扎娄的话嘲笑他。额朗佐请求艮扎娄别说话。

Stagecraft 导演技巧

'Beseech you, sir, be merry' (in pairs)

In the previous scene, Prospero praised Gonzalo for his kindness. Now the audience is reintroduced to this character through a carefully constructed opening speech. Gonzalo's lines here are written in **iambic pentameter** (抑扬五音步) (see p. 165), with a deliberate and regular rhythm. Gonzalo is trying to lift the spirits of King Alonso, who is mourning the loss of his son, Ferdinand.

a Look closely at the arguments Gonzalo uses here. Talk together about how you think the actor should deliver lines 1–9.

b Read the rest of the script opposite. Discuss what you think each character wants here and how far they might go to get it.

1 Beseech you 恳求您
2 much beyond 远超过
3 hint 处境
4 woe 不幸
5 The … merchant 某些商船船主和商人
6 preservation 保住性命
7 weigh … comfort 在我们的厄运和活下来的好运之间寻找平衡
8 porridge 豆粥
9 visitor 安抚患者的人
10 give him o'er so 轻易对他罢休
11 winding … wit 给脑瓜子上弦（以座钟为喻）
12 One: tell 一，接着数
13 When … offered 如果把每次遇到的不幸都当回事
14 entertainer 遭遇不幸的人
15 dollar 银币
16 Dolour 难过
17 Fie 呸（表示不满的叹词）
18 spendthrift 铺张浪费的人，话多的人
19 I prithee, spare 拜托您少说两句吧

1 A divided court?

Alonso's courtiers form two distinct groups. Gonzalo, Adrian and Francisco all attempt to comfort their king, trying to find good in what has happened to them. In contrast, Sebastian and Antonio comment cynically about what the others (and in particular Gonzalo) are saying.

a **Exploring character** In groups of six, take parts as Alonso and the five courtiers (remember that Francisco does not speak), and read lines 1–100. Sit or stand in two separate groups as you read, in order to emphasise the differences between the courtiers' characters (see also the photograph on p. 77).

b **Consumed by grief** In the first 100 lines of this scene, the character with the greatest authority – Alonso – speaks only five words. After you have read through this first section of the scene, discuss in groups where you would position this character. Should he overhear what is said by his courtiers, or should he stand apart from the rest of the group, unaware of what is taking place between them? How does he make his grief clear to the audience? In your Director's Journal, write down between five and ten notes for the actor. Then perform the first 100 lines of the scene, focusing on Alonso's role.

c **Mockery** (嘲笑) **and sincerity** (真诚) Divide into pairs and experiment with different ways of delivering the speeches in lines 1–100, ranging from mockery to despair. This will help bring out the sense and humour of the episode.

Act 2 Scene 1
A remote part of the island

Enter ALONSO, SEBASTIAN, ANTONIO, GONZALO, ADRIAN, FRANCISCO *and others*

GONZALO Beseech you[1], sir, be merry. You have cause –
So have we all – of joy; for our escape
Is much beyond[2] our loss. Our hint[3] of woe[4]
Is common; every day some sailor's wife,
The masters of some merchant, and the merchant[5]   5
Have just our theme of woe. But for the miracle –
I mean our preservation[6] – few in millions
Can speak like us. Then wisely, good sir, weigh
Our sorrow with our comfort[7].

ALONSO   Prithee, peace.

SEBASTIAN [*Apart to Antonio*] He receives comfort like cold   10
porridge[8].

ANTONIO [*Apart to Sebastian*] The visitor[9] will not give him o'er so[10].

SEBASTIAN Look, he's winding up the watch of his wit[11],
By and by it will strike.

GONZALO [*To Alonso*] Sir, –   15

SEBASTIAN One: tell[12].

GONZALO   When every grief is entertained
That's offered[13], comes to the entertainer[14] –

SEBASTIAN A dollar[15].

GONZALO Dolour[16] comes to him indeed; you have spoken truer than you
purposed.   20

SEBASTIAN You have taken it wiselier than I meant you should.

GONZALO Therefore, my lord –

ANTONIO Fie[17], what a spendthrift[18] is he of his tongue.

ALONSO I prithee, spare[19].

45

Antonio and Sebastian mockingly bet on which courtier will speak first. They comment cynically on the optimistic remarks of the others. Gonzalo is amazed that everyone's clothes are clean and dry.

剧情简介：安托纽和塞巴斯田嘲讽地打赌哪位侍臣会最先说话，他们讥笑其他人的乐观看法。艮扎娄惊奇地发现他们的衣服竟然干爽整洁。

Themes 主题分析

Utopia (乌托邦，理想国) and dystopia (敌托邦，噩梦国) (in threes)

After the shock of the shipwreck, Adrian and Gonzalo begin to notice how beautiful the island is. In contrast, Antonio and Sebastian only see the imperfections of the island on which they find themselves stranded (搁浅).

- Is the island a utopia or a dystopia – a perfect society or a place where discontent and unhappiness reign? Discuss which view you agree with most.

1 Subjective and objective truth (in pairs)

Gonzalo continues to find the good points of the island, while Antonio and Sebastian see only the bad. Can they both be correct? Subjective truth is something that we believe to be true ('X is brilliant!'). Objective truth is what is clearly true ('The UK is in the Northern Hemisphere').

a Discuss the idea that subjective truth is the only truth that matters, and that objective truth is impossible to prove beyond doubt.

b Choose four objects in your classroom. One person in your pair points out only the positive features of the object, and the other only its negative features. Who is closer to the truth? Join with other pairs to debate the objective and subjective truths of these everyday objects. What conclusions do you reach?

c Now imagine that you have to explain the concept of objective and subjective truth to a class of younger children. Prepare a ten-minute lesson plan that uses lines from *The Tempest* to illustrate the differences between objective and subjective truth. You may want to consider episodes such as the storm, or characters such as Caliban. Use visual aids such as storyboarding (故事梗概图板) to explain your ideas.

Stagecraft 导演技巧

One-word it! (in fours)

The dialogue in the script opposite moves very quickly. Try to make it even quicker, while retaining the sense of Shakespeare's script.

- First, cut back each line to a single word. Then act out the scene several times, choosing different ways of emphasising the words to create different effects.

---

1 wager 打赌
2 crow 开口说话
3 cockerel 小公鸡
4 A match! 一言为定！
5 desert 荒无人烟
6 you're paid 赌注已经赔给你了（因为你笑了）
7 subtle 精致（塞巴斯田却理解为"精明"）
8 temperance 温和的气候 / 女孩名
9 fen 沼泽地
10 save 除了
11 lush 苍翠茂盛
12 lusty 生机勃勃
13 tawny 黄褐色
14 eye 一点儿
15 He misses not much 差不多都让他看到了
16 he … totally 他完全弄错了
17 rarity 稀奇之处
18 beyond credit 难以相信
19 vouched rarities 公认的稀奇之物
20 garments 衣服
21 drenched 湿淋淋
22 notwithstanding 然而，尽管
23 glosses 光亮的外表
24 new-dyed 全新
25 If … lies? 他的衣兜要是会说话，难道不会说他撒谎？

GONZALO   Well, I have done. But yet –   25
SEBASTIAN   He will be talking.
ANTONIO   Which, of he or Adrian, for a good wager[1], first begins to crow[2]?
SEBASTIAN   The old cock.
ANTONIO   The cockerel[3].   30
SEBASTIAN   Done. The wager?
ANTONIO   A laughter.
SEBASTIAN   A match![4]
ADRIAN   Though this island seem to be desert[5] –
ANTONIO   Ha, ha, ha!   35
SEBASTIAN   So: you're paid[6].
ADRIAN   Uninhabitable, and almost inaccessible –
SEBASTIAN   Yet –
ADRIAN   Yet –
ANTONIO   He could not miss't.   40
ADRIAN   It must needs be of subtle[7], tender and delicate temperance[8].
ANTONIO   Temperance was a delicate wench.
SEBASTIAN   Ay, and a subtle, as he most learnedly delivered.
ADRIAN   The air breathes upon us here most sweetly.   45
SEBASTIAN   As if it had lungs, and rotten ones.
ANTONIO   Or as 'twere perfumed by a fen[9].
GONZALO   Here is everything advantageous to life.
ANTONIO   True, save[10] means to live.
SEBASTIAN   Of that there's none, or little.   50
GONZALO   How lush[11] and lusty[12] the grass looks! How green!
ANTONIO   The ground indeed is tawny[13].
SEBASTIAN   With an eye[14] of green in't.
ANTONIO   He misses not much[15].
SEBASTIAN   No, he doth but mistake the truth totally[16].   55
GONZALO   But the rarity[17] of it is, which is indeed almost beyond credit[18] –
SEBASTIAN   As many vouched rarities[19] are.
GONZALO   That our garments[20] being, as they were, drenched[21] in the sea, hold notwithstanding[22] their freshness and glosses[23], being rather new-dyed[24] than stained with salt water.   60
ANTONIO   If but one of his pockets could speak, would it not say he lies?[25]
SEBASTIAN   Ay, or very falsely pocket up his report.

Gonzalo continues to marvel at everyone's dry clothes. Antonio and Sebastian laugh sarcastically about Gonzalo's references to widow Dido and to the location of Carthage. Gonzalo again tries to cheer Alonso.

剧情简介：良扎娄仍然感到惊讶，所有人的衣物都很干燥。安托纽和塞巴斯田讥笑良扎娄提到寡妇荻荁和迦太基的地理位置。良扎娄再次试图宽慰额朗佐。

1 Exploring classical mythology

Gonzalo's lines 65–7 reveal that the court party was returning home from a wedding when the tempest struck. Alonso's daughter Claribel has married the king of Tunis.

- **'widow Dido'** Dido, queen of Carthage, was a famous figure in Roman and Greek mythology. In one version of the myth, she was faithful to her dead husband. In another she had an affair with Aeneas (埃尼斯，特洛伊城沦陷前逃亡意大利的特洛伊王孙，后来与其追随者建立了罗马城), the Trojan prince who founded Rome, and she killed herself when he later abandoned her. Antonio and Sebastian's mockery may, therefore, lie in their amazement at hearing the tragic queen, who killed herself for love, described as 'widow Dido'.

- **'the miraculous harp'** Carthage was close to the city of Tunis (now in ruins). Antonio and Sebastian compare Gonzalo to the legendary Amphian, king of Thebes (底比斯), who raised the city walls by playing his harp. Since Gonzalo mistakes Tunis for Carthage, Sebastian says Gonzalo has built the city out of words (line 83).

To what extent do you think it is important for children to learn about ancient civilisations and their myths? Write a short article for your school magazine or website that argues either that such knowledge is important, or that it should make way for more 'relevant' subjects.

1	Afric = Africa
2	prosper well in our return 归程顺利
3	graced 变得优美
4	paragon 完美的典范
5	Dido 荻荁（迦太基女王）
6	A pox o'that! 胡说！
7	study of that 想一想
8	harp 竖琴
9	kernels 籽，核
10	rarest 最稀罕的
11	Bate 除了
12	doublet 紧身外套
13	in a sort 从某种程度上来说
14	That … for 你这剑鱼捕得不错（这里的sort与sword音近似，sword是swordfish [剑鱼]的简称，安托纽故意曲解良扎娄的意思）

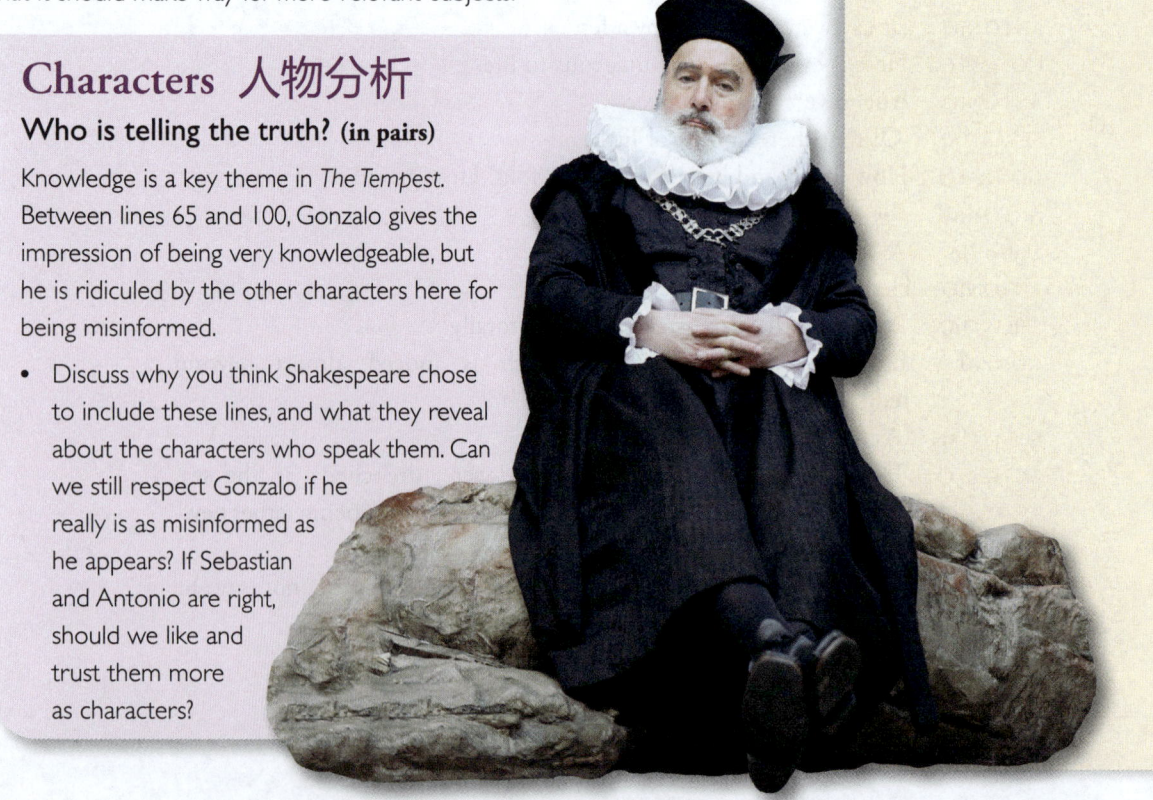

Characters 人物分析

Who is telling the truth? (in pairs)

Knowledge is a key theme in *The Tempest*. Between lines 65 and 100, Gonzalo gives the impression of being very knowledgeable, but he is ridiculed by the other characters here for being misinformed.

- Discuss why you think Shakespeare chose to include these lines, and what they reveal about the characters who speak them. Can we still respect Gonzalo if he really is as misinformed as he appears? If Sebastian and Antonio are right, should we like and trust them more as characters?

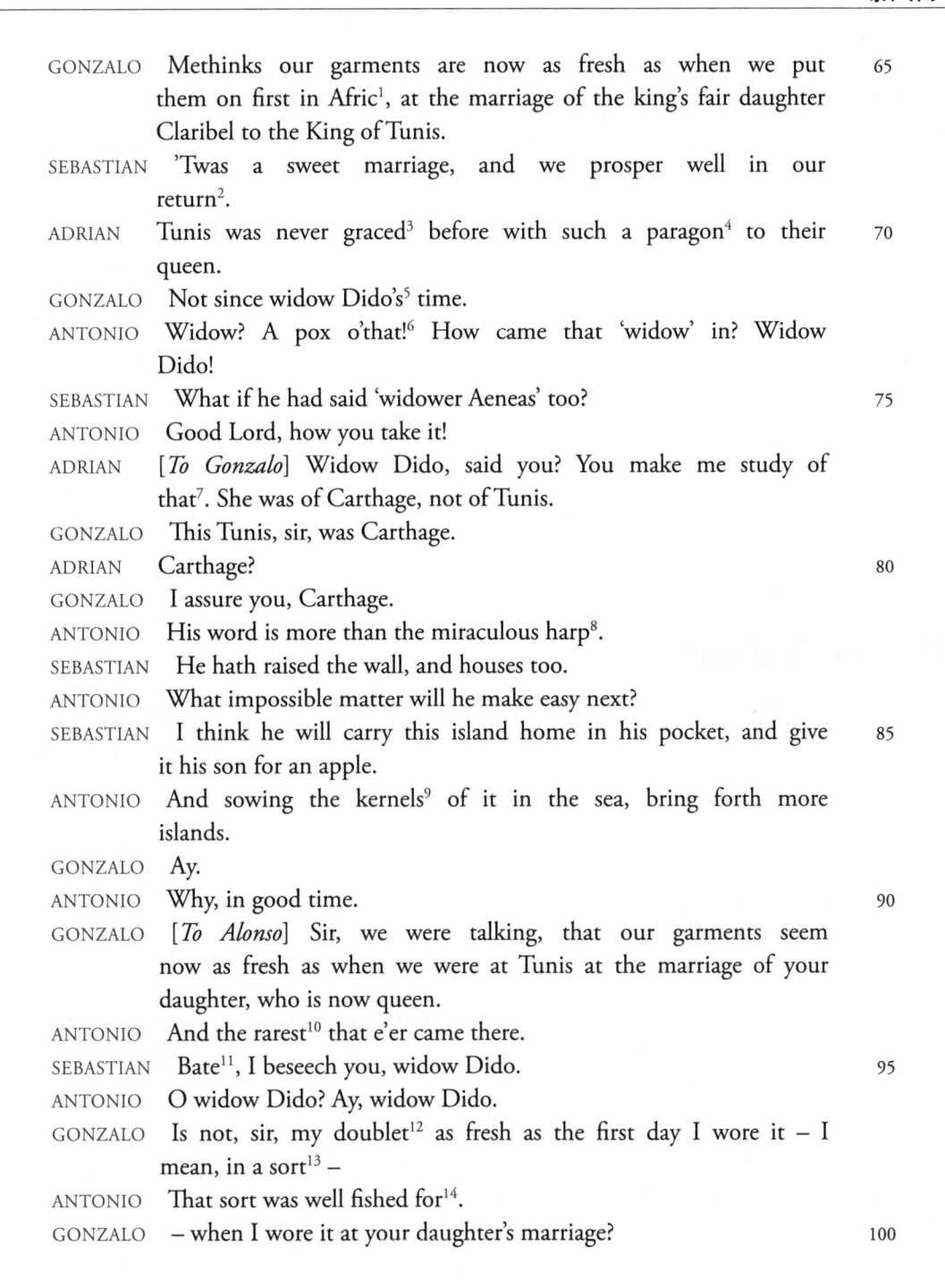

GONZALO	Methinks our garments are now as fresh as when we put them on first in Afric[1], at the marriage of the king's fair daughter Claribel to the King of Tunis.	65
SEBASTIAN	'Twas a sweet marriage, and we prosper well in our return[2].	
ADRIAN	Tunis was never graced[3] before with such a paragon[4] to their queen.	70
GONZALO	Not since widow Dido's[5] time.	
ANTONIO	Widow? A pox o'that![6] How came that 'widow' in? Widow Dido!	
SEBASTIAN	What if he had said 'widower Aeneas' too?	75
ANTONIO	Good Lord, how you take it!	
ADRIAN	[*To Gonzalo*] Widow Dido, said you? You make me study of that[7]. She was of Carthage, not of Tunis.	
GONZALO	This Tunis, sir, was Carthage.	
ADRIAN	Carthage?	80
GONZALO	I assure you, Carthage.	
ANTONIO	His word is more than the miraculous harp[8].	
SEBASTIAN	He hath raised the wall, and houses too.	
ANTONIO	What impossible matter will he make easy next?	
SEBASTIAN	I think he will carry this island home in his pocket, and give it his son for an apple.	85
ANTONIO	And sowing the kernels[9] of it in the sea, bring forth more islands.	
GONZALO	Ay.	
ANTONIO	Why, in good time.	90
GONZALO	[*To Alonso*] Sir, we were talking, that our garments seem now as fresh as when we were at Tunis at the marriage of your daughter, who is now queen.	
ANTONIO	And the rarest[10] that e'er came there.	
SEBASTIAN	Bate[11], I beseech you, widow Dido.	95
ANTONIO	O widow Dido? Ay, widow Dido.	
GONZALO	Is not, sir, my doublet[12] as fresh as the first day I wore it – I mean, in a sort[13] –	
ANTONIO	That sort was well fished for[14].	
GONZALO	– when I wore it at your daughter's marriage?	100

Alonso refuses to be comforted. He fears that his daughter and son are lost for ever. Francisco claims that Ferdinand probably survived. Sebastian blames Alonso for all the disasters, but is reprimanded by Gonzalo.

剧情简介：额朗佐拒绝安慰，他担心自己永远地失去了一双儿女。伏冉希斯寇认为法迪南很有可能还活着。塞巴斯田责怪额朗佐一手造成了所有的不幸，他的做法遭到艮扎娄的谴责。

Stagecraft 导演技巧

Making the most of Francisco's speech

Lines 108–17 (and three words in Act 3 Scene 3, line 40, p.97) are Francisco's only words in the play. His description of Ferdinand swimming strongly is full of active verbs ('beat', 'ride', 'trod', 'flung', 'breasted', 'oared'). He paints an image of the cliff bending over, as if to help Ferdinand (lines 115–16).

- Imagine you are directing a production of *The Tempest*. In your Director's Journal, write a set of notes to the actor playing Francisco, offering advice on how to say these lines. Remember that this is his only chance in the play to make a memorable impression on the audience, so consider carefully how you want him to deliver his speech.

Themes 主题分析

Sebastian challenges the king (by yourself)

In the script opposite, there is another example of a character challenging someone in a position of authority (see also p. 2). In lines 118–30, Sebastian strongly criticises Alonso, claiming that all the courtiers begged him not to permit the marriage of his daughter Claribel to the king of Tunis. Sebastian also asserts that Claribel did not want to marry the African king, but that – as a dutiful (孝顺) child – she obeyed her father's will. Alonso would not listen to either his courtiers or his daughter, with disastrous results.

a Read Sebastian's lines opposite carefully and identify the words or phrases that the actor could emphasise to hurt Alonso's feelings as much as possible.

b Write a paragraph explaining why you think Sebastian speaks harshly to his king here. What motivates him to be so cruel to a man who is obviously mourning the loss of both his son and his daughter?

1 cram 填满
2 against … sense 不看看我有胃口没有（没有心情听那些话）
3 in my rate 在我看来
4 mine heir 我的继承人（法迪南）
5 surges 海浪
6 enmity he flung aside 他抛却仇恨
7 breasted 用胸膛抵挡
8 surge most swol'n 滔天巨浪
9 contentious 凶险
10 oared 划水
11 lusty 强有力
12 his wave-worn basis 海浪拍打的悬崖底部
13 stooping 弯腰驼背
14 Who … on't 谁有理由痛哭
15 kneeled to and impòrtuned 跪下哀求
16 loathness 厌恶，憎恨
17 Which end o'th'beam should bow 秤杆的哪一端会沉下去（beam指秤杆）
18 time to speak it in 说这些话的时机
19 plaster 药膏
20 chirurgeonly 像个外科医生

THE TEMPEST ACT 2 SCENE 1
暴风雨

ALONSO	You cram[1] these words into mine ears, against
	The stomach of my sense[2]: would I had never
	Married my daughter there. For coming thence
	My son is lost, and, in my rate[3], she too,
	Who is so far from Italy removed	105
	I ne'er again shall see her. O thou mine heir[4]
	Of Naples and of Milan, what strange fish
	Hath made his meal on thee?
FRANCISCO	Sir, he may live.
	I saw him beat the surges[5] under him,
	And ride upon their backs; he trod the water	110
	Whose enmity he flung aside[6], and breasted[7]
	The surge most swol'n[8] that met him. His bold head
	'Bove the contentious[9] waves he kept, and oared[10]
	Himself with his good arms in lusty[11] stroke
	To th'shore, that o'er his wave-worn basis[12] bowed,	115
	As stooping[13] to relieve him. I not doubt
	He came alive to land.
ALONSO	No, no, he's gone.
SEBASTIAN	Sir, you may thank yourself for this great loss,
	That would not bless our Europe with your daughter,
	But rather lose her to an African,	120
	Where she, at least, is banished from your eye,
	Who hath cause to wet the grief on't[14].
ALONSO	Prithee, peace.
SEBASTIAN	You were kneeled to and impòrtuned[15] otherwise
	By all of us; and the fair soul herself
	Weighed between loathness[16] and obedience, at	125
	Which end o'th'beam should bow[17]. We have lost your son,
	I fear for ever. Milan and Naples have
	More widows in them of this business' making
	Than we bring men to comfort them. The fault's
	Your own.
ALONSO	So is the dearest of the loss.	130
GONZALO	My lord Sebastian,
	The truth you speak doth lack some gentleness,
	And time to speak it in[18]; you rub the sore,
	When you should bring the plaster[19].
SEBASTIAN	Very well.
ANTONIO	And most chirurgeonly[20].	135

Gonzalo seeks to cheer the king with an account of an ideal world, where everything is opposite to usual social arrangements. Antonio and Sebastian mock Gonzalo. He criticises their empty sense of humour.

剧情简介：艮扎娄设法宽慰额朗佐，向他描绘了一个与世俗社会相反的理想世界。安托纽和塞巴斯田嘲笑艮扎娄，艮扎娄批评他们没有幽默感。

1 'The noble savage' (whole class)

Here, Gonzalo further develops the theme of a utopia, or 'the golden age' (see p. 46). His picture of a society in which ownership of everything is shared ('commonwealth') is heavily influenced by an essay entitled 'On Cannibals', written by the French philosopher Michel de Montaigne (蒙田) (1533–92). Montaigne explored what it meant to be civilised, arguing that the 'savage' societies being discovered in the New World (America) at the time were superior to the sophisticated (先进) civilisations of Europe. The essay (which Shakespeare read) gave rise to the belief in 'the noble savage', for whom harmonious, peaceful and equal relationships were completely natural.

- As a class, discuss what you think it means to be 'civilised' – as a human being, a community and a society. During this discussion, make notes in preparation for the activity below.

1 plantation 殖民地
2 nettle-seed / docks / mallows 荨麻、酸模、锦葵等寻常植物或野草的籽
3 contraries 不按惯例
4 Exècute 处理
5 traffic 商业，贸易
6 magistrate 执法官
7 Letters 文学，教育
8 use of service 雇用奴仆
9 contract, succession 契约、继承
10 Bourn, bound of land, tilth 边界、地界、农业
11 occupation 职业
12 all men idle 人人无所事事
13 sovereignty 君主
14 The latter ... beginning 这番话的结尾与开头相矛盾
15 common 公有
16 felony 重罪
17 pike 长矛
18 engine 武器
19 kind 本性
20 foison 大量
21 whores and knaves 娼妓和流氓
22 T'excel the Golden Age 将超越黄金时代
23 minister occasion 提供机会
24 sensible and nimble 敏感且敏捷（带嘲讽意）

Write about it 写作练习

Describing Utopia

Look at the things that Gonzalo would not permit in his utopian society, such as 'traffic' (trade and commerce) and 'letters' (education). What would be your utopia?

- Write an article for a magazine, outlining your own vision for a perfect society. Include a headline, then describe what would be included and forbidden in your utopia. Think carefully about the implications of each decision.
- Share your ideas with others in your class, then decide which society seems the most utopian. Are there any that you feel are the opposite of a perfect society (dystopian)?

GONZALO	[*To Alonso*] It is foul weather in us all, good sir,	
	When you are cloudy.	
SEBASTIAN	Foul weather?	
ANTONIO	Very foul.	
GONZALO	Had I plantation[1] of this isle, my lord –	140
ANTONIO	He'd sow't with nettle-seed.	
SEBASTIAN	Or docks, or mallows[2].	
GONZALO	– And were the king on't, what would I do?	
SEBASTIAN	'Scape being drunk, for want of wine.	
GONZALO	I'th'commonwealth I would by contraries[3]	
	Exècute[4] all things. For no kind of traffic[5]	145
	Would I admit; no name of magistrate[6];	
	Letters[7] should not be known; riches, poverty,	
	And use of service[8], none; contract, succession[9],	
	Bourn, bound of land, tilth[10], vineyard, none;	
	No use of metal, corn, or wine, or oil;	150
	No occupation[11], all men idle[12], all;	
	And women too, but innocent and pure;	
	No sovereignty[13] –	
SEBASTIAN	Yet he would be king on't.	
ANTONIO	The latter end of his commonwealth forgets the beginning[14].	155
GONZALO	All things in common[15] nature should produce	
	Without sweat or endeavour. Treason, felony[16],	
	Sword, pike[17], knife, gun, or need of any engine[18]	
	Would I not have; but nature should bring forth	
	Of it own kind[19], all foison[20], all abundance	160
	To feed my innocent people.	
SEBASTIAN	No marrying 'mong his subjects?	
ANTONIO	None, man, all idle; whores and knaves[21].	
GONZALO	I would with such perfection govern, sir,	
	T'excel the Golden Age[22].	165
SEBASTIAN	'Save his majesty!	
ANTONIO	Long live Gonzalo!	
GONZALO	And – do you mark me, sir?	
ALONSO	Prithee, no more; thou dost talk nothing to me.	
GONZALO	I do well believe your highness, and did it to minister occasion[23] to these gentlemen, who are of such sensible and nimble[24] lungs, that they always use to laugh at nothing.	170
ANTONIO	'Twas you we laughed at.	

Gonzalo continues to reprimand Antonio and Sebastian. Ariel's music sends some of the courtiers to sleep. Antonio offers to guard Alonso as he sleeps, then hints that Sebastian could become king.

剧情简介：艮扎娄继续谴责安托纽和塞巴斯田。艾瑞尔的音乐让几位侍臣昏昏睡去。安托纽主动提出站岗以保证额朗佐睡觉时的安全，他暗示塞巴斯田有机会成为那不勒斯国王。

1 Gonzalo: sarcastic (挖苦的) or annoyed? (in pairs)

It seems that the mild-mannered Gonzalo finally has enough of Antonio and Sebastian: he turns on them and attacks them for mocking him.

a Do you think Gonzalo shows genuine anger, or does he use a drier, more sarcastic tone? Given what you know of his character, which is the most likely? Discuss this with your partner.

b Experiment with ways of speaking everything Gonzalo says in lines 170–84, and decide on an appropriate style of delivery.

Characters 人物分析

Antonio: opportunist (机会主义的) or evil?

Up to this point, Antonio has come across as a rather mocking, cynical character in the play (remember Prospero's description of him in Act 1 Scene 2). However, at line 200 a more sinister (阴险) side to him seems to emerge as he begins to tempt Sebastian into a murderous plot (谋杀的阴谋).

a Search the script opposite and the rest of Act 2 for evidence of Antonio's character. Do you think he is genuinely evil, or is he an opportunist who is doing what anyone else would do in his situation?

b Imagine that a director of the play wants to portray Antonio as an opportunist, but the actor playing him believes he should be depicted as a manipulative (操纵别人的) murderer. Write a record of their discussion in your Director's Journal, giving the arguments each one makes for their own interpretation of Antonio.

1	blow	侮辱
2	And	如果
3	flat-long	安然无恙（剑的平面，这里指剑落下来时不是刃朝下而是平面朝下）
4	brave mettle	英勇
5	sphere	轨道
6	We … a-batfowling	我们会这么做，然后提着这月亮灯笼去捕鸟
7	warrant	保证
8	adventure my discretion	拿我的谨慎名声去冒险
9	heavy	困乏，打瞌睡
10	I … thoughts	我希望闭上眼睛就可以让我停止思考
11	omit	忽略
12	heavy offer	沉睡的机会
13	drowsiness	睡意，困倦
14	possesses	控制，附体
15	It is the quality o'th'climate	是这里气候的原因
16	disposed to sleep	想睡觉
17	nimble	清醒
18	consent	同意，答应
19	What might	（安托纽看到机会来了，欲提醒塞巴斯田，又不便说出口）
20	Worthy	好……，尊贵的……
21	Th'occasion speaks thee	机会在对您说话（即您的机会来了）

GONZALO   Who, in this kind of merry fooling, am nothing to you; so
you may continue, and laugh at nothing still.   175
ANTONIO   What a blow[1] was there given!
SEBASTIAN   And[2] it had not fall'n flat-long[3].
GONZALO   You are gentlemen of brave mettle[4]; you would lift the moon
out of her sphere[5], if she would continue in it five weeks without
changing.   180

Enter ARIEL [*invisible*] *playing solemn music*

SEBASTIAN   We would so, and then go a-batfowling[6].
ANTONIO   Nay, good my lord, be not angry.
GONZALO   No, I warrant[7] you, I will not adventure my discretion[8] so
weakly. Will you laugh me asleep, for I am very heavy[9]?
ANTONIO   Go sleep, and hear us.   185

[*All sleep except Alonso, Sebastian and Antonio*]

ALONSO   What, all so soon asleep? I wish mine eyes
Would with themselves shut up my thoughts[10]; I find
They are inclined to do so.
SEBASTIAN   Please you, sir,
Do not omit[11] the heavy offer[12] of it.
It seldom visits sorrow; when it doth,   190
It is a comforter.
ANTONIO   We two, my lord,
Will guard your person while you take your rest,
And watch your safety.
ALONSO   Thank you. Wondrous heavy.

[*Alonso sleeps*]   [*Exit Ariel*]

SEBASTIAN   What a strange drowsiness[13] possesses[14] them?
ANTONIO   It is the quality o'th'climate[15].
SEBASTIAN   Why   195
Doth it not then our eyelids sink? I find
Not myself disposed to sleep[16].
ANTONIO   Nor I; my spirits are nimble[17].
They fell together all, as by consent[18]
They dropped, as by a thunder-stroke. What might[19],   200
Worthy[20] Sebastian, O, what might? – No more.
And yet, methinks I see it in thy face,
What thou shouldst be. Th'occasion speaks thee[21], and
My strong imagination sees a crown
Dropping upon thy head.

Sebastian is puzzled by Antonio's words, but begins to see significance in them. He asks Antonio for advice. Antonio says that fear and idleness cause failure, and asserts confidently that Ferdinand has drowned.

剧情简介： 塞巴斯田不理解安托纽的话，但开始明白此事的重要性。他向安托纽讨主意，安托纽说内心胆怯与没有行动导致失败，并断言法迪南已淹死。

Stagecraft 导演技巧

The plot thickens (in pairs)

Antonio has already seized his brother Prospero's throne. Now he begins to encourage Sebastian to do likewise – to usurp Alonso's throne.

a Take it in turns to read lines 194–293. Explore the different ways that these lines could be spoken by considering the following questions.

- Are there long pauses as Sebastian slowly realises that Antonio is prompting him to murder his own brother?
- Do they sit or stand face to face and make eye contact, or does Antonio deliberately avoid meeting Sebastian's gaze except at certain moments?
- How quickly does Sebastian realise what Antonio has in mind (be exact: find the line)?

b Act out the 'ebb and flow' of the conversation between Antonio and Sebastian. Consider the following:

- How might the actors physically show the shifting balance of power between the two characters?
- How does Sebastian's body language change when he realises what Antonio is proposing?

Language in the play 剧中语言

Exploring complex imagery (in pairs)

Lines 215–34 are rich in imagery. For example, Sebastian says he is like 'standing water' (line 217) – when the tide is about to turn and does not withdraw ('ebb') or go forward ('flow'). His own inclination is to ebb, and perhaps to even go backwards. Antonio replies that Sebastian's comparison is more powerful than he thinks, because unsuccessful men ('Ebbing men') are those who are fearful or idle.

a Pick out your favourite images in these lines and represent them visually, using pencil, pen, paint or a computer. You could try to storyboard the lines so that you create a coherent narrative with the words overlaying (覆盖) the images.

b Talk about your choices, considering the different ways that words and pictures convey the meaning of these lines.

---

1 waking 醒着
2 repose 休息，睡眠
3 fast asleep 熟睡
4 Thou … rather 你任由时机睡着——说死去更准确
5 wink'st … waking 醒着的时候偏要（对机会）闭眼睛
6 meaning 深意
7 I … custom 我现在很认真严肃，不像平时
8 if heed me 如果您留心听我说
9 Trebles thee o'er 使你身价涨三倍
10 standing water 静水（非涨潮或退潮）
11 flow 涨潮（这里是双关语，另一意思是"高升"）
12 ebb 退潮
13 Hereditary sloth 天生懒惰（这里是双关语，另一意思是"比兄长晚出生"）
14 the purpose cherish 说中，一语道破
15 stripping 脱衣
16 invest 穿衣
17 Ebbing 没落
18 bottom run 一落千丈
19 setting … cheek 热切的眼神和表情
20 throes thee 使你痛苦
21 Thus 是这样的
22 weak remembrance 记性不好
23 as little memory 没有什么值得记忆的
24 earthed 入土，下葬
25 spirit of persuasion 劝说别人的能手
26 only / Professes to persuade 以劝说为业

SEBASTIAN	What? Art thou waking[1]?	205
ANTONIO	Do you not hear me speak?	
SEBASTIAN	I do, and surely	
	It is a sleepy language, and thou speak'st	
	Out of thy sleep. What is it thou didst say?	
	This is a strange repose[2], to be asleep	
	With eyes wide open; standing, speaking, moving,	210
	And yet so fast asleep[3].	
ANTONIO	Noble Sebastian,	
	Thou let'st thy fortune sleep – die rather[4]; wink'st	
	Whiles thou art waking[5].	
SEBASTIAN	Thou dost snore distinctly;	
	There's meaning[6] in thy snores.	
ANTONIO	I am more serious than my custom[7]. You	215
	Must be so too, if heed me[8]; which to do,	
	Trebles thee o'er[9].	
SEBASTIAN	Well: I am standing water[10].	
ANTONIO	I'll teach you how to flow[11].	
SEBASTIAN	Do so – to ebb[12]	
	Hereditary sloth[13] instructs me.	
ANTONIO	O!	
	If you but knew how you the purpose cherish[14]	220
	Whiles thus you mock it; how in stripping[15] it	
	You more invest[16] it. Ebbing[17] men, indeed,	
	Most often do so near the bottom run[18]	
	By their own fear, or sloth.	
SEBASTIAN	Prithee say on.	
	The setting of thine eye and cheek[19] proclaim	225
	A matter from thee; and a birth, indeed,	
	Which throes thee[20] much to yield.	
ANTONIO	Thus[21], sir:	
	Although this lord of weak remembrance[22], this,	
	Who shall be of as little memory[23]	
	When he is earthed[24], hath here almost persuaded –	230
	For he's a spirit of persuasion[25], only	
	Professes to persuade[26] – the king his son's alive,	
	'Tis as impossible that he's undrowned	
	As he that sleeps here, swims.	
SEBASTIAN	I have no hope	
	That he's undrowned.	

Antonio predicts the fulfilment of Sebastian's greatest ambitions. Alonso's heir, Claribel, is so far distant that destiny itself invites Antonio and Sebastian to act. Sebastian recalls that Antonio overthrew Prospero.

剧情简介：安托纽预言塞巴斯田最远大的抱负会实现。额朗佐的继承人——克莱若贝尔——远在他乡，命运安排安托纽和塞巴斯田采取行动。塞巴斯田想起安托纽曾经推翻了普饶斯普柔。

Characters 人物分析

Antonio – a sinister persuader (in pairs)

Antonio uses a number of different strategies to convince Sebastian to kill his brother:

- **Certainty** (lines 232–4) Despite Gonzalo's cheering words, Ferdinand is believed to be dead.
- **Ambition** (lines 235–9) Ferdinand's death opens up the opportunity for Sebastian's highest hopes to be fulfilled.
- **Hyperbole** (夸张) (lines 242–6) Using extravagant exaggeration, Antonio claims that Claribel has no hope of succeeding to Alonso's throne. He claims she lives too far away ('beyond man's life'); only a messenger moving as fast as the sun could reach her ('unless the sun were post'); the journey would take as long as the time from a baby boy being born until he is ready to shave (notice that in lines 251–4, Sebastian summarises all Antonio has said, but stripped of the hyperbole). It is, he says, 'destiny' that this opportunity should arise.
- **Imagery** (lines 247–50) Antonio ends by using theatrical imagery – 'cast', 'perform', 'act', 'prologue', 'discharge'. Antonio declares the prologue is now history. It is up to them to decide how to perform the plot. As Sebastian begins to respond, Antonio makes his meaning plainer in lines 254–65.

a What does the script opposite tell us about Antonio's character? Discuss how his skilful use of language – especially rhetorical devices – manipulates Sebastian.

b Consider the motivation behind Antonio's speech, then add to the notes you began on page 56 advising the actor playing this character. How should he deliver these lines?

1 Good and bad angels (in threes)

If Antonio is behaving like Sebastian's bad angel, how could you balance this out by being his good angel?

- One of you plays Antonio, another Sebastian and the third takes on the role of an imaginary 'good angel'. Antonio and the good angel put forward their arguments for and against murdering Alonso. What does Sebastian stand to gain? And what does he stand to lose? Who does Sebastian find the most persuasive?
- Did other groups come up with different arguments from yours?

1 that way 一方面（对法迪南来说）
2 pierce … there 多偷看一眼（即抱有更大的希望）
3 grant 同意，赞同
4 Ten leagues 约30英里
5 note 消息
6 post 驿差
7 The man i'th'moon's too slow 让月亮当驿差又太慢（月亮一个月才转完一圈）
8 chins 胡须
9 rough and razorable （胡须）长得多到能刮了
10 cast 吐出来（即又抛上岸）
11 whereof 关于此事
12 what's past is prologue 刚发生的一切是这件事的序曲（即刚才的暴风雨使这件事成为可能）
13 In yours and my discharge 要靠您与我去处理
14 stuff 问题，事件
15 'twixt = between
16 cubit 肘长（古时一种长度计量单位，相当于从肘到中指指端的长度）
17 Measure us back to Naples 让我们一步步回到那不勒斯
18 no … are 不比现在更糟（他们睡觉如同死去了）
19 There … Naples 有人能统治那不勒斯（即您能做那不勒斯国王）
20 prate 唠唠叨叨
21 amply 滔滔不绝
22 chough 寒鸦（喜欢鸣叫）
23 advancement 前进
24 content 默许
25 Tender 喜欢
26 supplant 篡夺，推翻

ANTONIO	O, out of that 'no hope'	235

What great hope have you! No hope that way[1] is
Another way so high a hope that even
Ambition cannot pierce a wink beyond,
But doubt discovery there[2]. Will you grant[3] with me
That Ferdinand is drowned?

SEBASTIAN   He's gone.

ANTONIO   Then tell me,   240
Who's the next heir of Naples?

SEBASTIAN   Claribel.

ANTONIO She that is Queen of Tunis; she that dwells
Ten leagues[4] beyond man's life; she that from Naples
Can have no note[5], unless the sun were post[6] –
The man i'th'moon's too slow[7] – till new-born chins[8]   245
Be rough and razorable[9]; she that from whom
We all were sea-swallowed, though some cast[10] again –
And by that destiny, to perform an act
Whereof[11] what's past is prologue[12]; what to come
In yours and my discharge[13].   250

SEBASTIAN What stuff[14] is this? How say you?
'Tis true my brother's daughter's Queen of Tunis,
So is she heir of Naples, 'twixt[15] which regions
There is some space.

ANTONIO   A space, whose ev'ry cubit[16]
Seems to cry out, 'How shall that Claribel   255
Measure us back to Naples[17]? Keep in Tunis,
And let Sebastian wake.' Say this were death
That now hath seized them, why, they were no worse
Than now they are[18]. There be that can rule Naples[19]
As well as he that sleeps; lords that can prate[20]   260
As amply[21] and unnecessarily
As this Gonzalo; I myself could make
A chough[22] of as deep chat. O, that you bore
The mind that I do! What a sleep were this
For your advancement[23]! Do you understand me?   265

SEBASTIAN Methinks I do.

ANTONIO   And how does your content[24]
Tender[25] your own good fortune?

SEBASTIAN   I remember
You did supplant[26] your brother Prospero.

Antonio points out his gains from overthrowing Prospero. He says that he has no conscience, and proposes the murder of Alonso and Gonzalo. Sebastian agrees, but asks to talk further. Ariel wakens the sleepers.

剧情简介：安托纽点明了推翻普饶斯普柔后他得到的好处。他说自己没有良心，还建议杀死额朗佐和艮扎娄。塞巴斯田同意，但提出从长计议。艾瑞尔唤醒了熟睡的人。

Language in the play 剧中语言
Murderous words (by yourself)

Once again, authority is seen to be challenged on the island, but this time it takes on a much deadlier form. Antonio makes his plan clear: he will kill Alonso so that Sebastian can become king. Sebastian himself must kill Gonzalo to silence any criticism. Antonio implies that he has no conscience, and feels no sense of guilt for illegally seizing Prospero's crown.

a Identify the most striking images used by Antonio in this part of the scene. Write down why you think they are so effective.

b Identify the points in the script opposite where Antonio's mood and tone of voice become increasingly threatening.

c Bring together all the work you have done on Antonio and compose a letter to a well-known actor who you would like to play the part. Explain why you think he would be ideal as Antonio, and provide him with guidance about how to approach this character.

Stagecraft 导演技巧
Raising the tension

Ariel returns as the plotters are finalising their murderous plans. Explore ways of staging this part of the script so that the tension continues to rise. Take into account the points below, and try out some of the movements or gestures you would want the actors to use.

- Sound effects – what music or other sounds would you use here?
- Stage space – how would the actors use this?
- Lighting – would the lighting be changed in any way to reflect the growing seriousness of the situation?
- Pacing – does line 293 ('O, but one word') seem false? How can it be spoken convincingly?
- Movement, expressions and gestures – explore these to best represent Antonio, Sebastian and Ariel at this point.
- Costume and make-up – if you are able, dress up in costumes and make-up that identify the characters on stage. Try to reflect qualities such as each character's status and personality.

1 feater 更高雅
2 fellows 同僚
3 men 下属
4 kibe 冻疮
5 put me to my slipper 逼我穿上拖鞋
6 deity in my bosom 心里的神明
7 candied 外表凝固或结晶
8 melt ere they molest 在它们妨碍我之前早化了
9 obedient steel 听话的短剑
10 lay to bed for ever 使（他）长眠（即杀死对方）
11 doing thus 这样做
12 perpetual wink 长眠，死亡
13 for aye 永远
14 ancient morsel 老东西
15 Sir Prudence 谨慎先生
16 Should not upbraid （如果他死了）就不会批评谴责
17 course （指二人计划的实施）
18 as a cat laps milk 像猫舔牛奶一样
19 tell ... hour 数着钟点，唯命是从（即我们说什么时候该怎么做，他们就会照着去做）
20 case 例子（指安托纽篡夺普饶斯普柔的王位）
21 precedent 先例
22 got'st 得到，夺取
23 tribute 进贡
24 rear 举起
25 project 计划
26 conspiracy 阴谋
27 Shake off slumber 摆脱睡眠（醒来）

ANTONIO	True;	

And look how well my garments sit upon me,
Much feater[1] than before. My brother's servants 270
Were then my fellows[2], now they are my men[3].

SEBASTIAN	But for your conscience?
ANTONIO	Ay, sir: where lies that? If it were a kibe[4]

'Twould put me to my slipper[5]; but I feel not
This deity in my bosom[6]. Twenty consciences 275
That stand 'twixt me and Milan, candied[7] be they,
And melt ere they molest[8]. Here lies your brother,
No better than the earth he lies upon,
If he were that which now he's like – that's dead;
Whom I with this obedient steel[9], three inches of it, 280
Can lay to bed for ever[10]: whiles you doing thus[11],
To the perpetual wink[12] for aye[13] might put
This ancient morsel[14], this Sir Prudence[15], who
Should not upbraid[16] our course[17]. For all the rest,
They'll take suggestion as a cat laps milk[18]; 285
They'll tell the clock to any business that
We say befits the hour[19].

SEBASTIAN	Thy case[20], dear friend,

Shall be my precedent[21]. As thou got'st[22] Milan,
I'll come by Naples. Draw thy sword; one stroke
Shall free thee from the tribute[23] which thou payest, 290
And I the king shall love thee.

ANTONIO	Draw together:

And when I rear[24] my hand, do you the like
To fall it on Gonzalo.

SEBASTIAN	O, but one word.

[*They talk apart*]

Enter ARIEL [*invisible*] *with music*

ARIEL	My master through his art foresees the danger

That you, his friend, are in, and sends me forth – 295
For else his project[25] dies – to keep them living.
      Sings in Gonzalo's ear
  While you here do snoring lie,
  Open-eyed conspiracy[26]
    His time doth take.
  If of life you keep a care, 300
  Shake off slumber[27] and beware.
    Awake, awake.

Sebastian and Antonio explain that their swords are drawn to protect the king from lions. Gonzalo tells that he was woken by a humming noise. The courtiers leave, urged by Alonso to search for Ferdinand.

剧情简介：塞巴斯田和安托纽辩解说他们拔剑是要杀掉狮子保护国王。良扎娄说他被音乐声吵醒。在额朗佐的催促下，侍臣们四下去寻找法迪南。

1 Unconvincing explanations? (in pairs)

Antonio and Sebastian are caught with swords in their hands. They have to provide a plausible (说得通) explanation. Do they sound convincing?

a Explore ways of speaking lines 305–13 to show the two conspirators struggling to sound sincere. Try to bring out the element of humour as well as threat in these lines (for example, in some productions Sebastian makes the audience laugh at line 309 when he changes his story from 'bulls' to 'lions').

b Are there other moments in this scene in which Shakespeare uses humour to relieve the tension on stage?

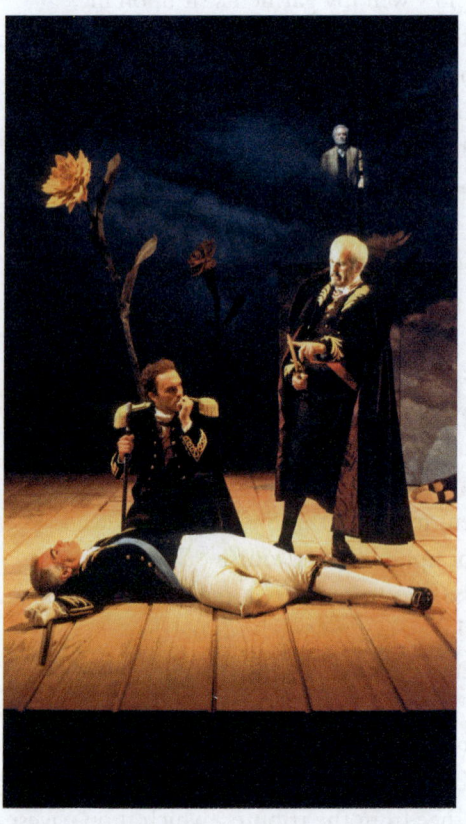

▲ Sebastian (kneeling) and Antonio plot to kill the sleeping Alonso. Choose a quotation from the script opposite that would be a suitable caption (说明文字) for this picture.

1	sudden	迅速
2	preserve	保护
3	drawn	拔出剑
4	Wherefore	为什么
5	ghastly looking	一脸惊恐
6	securing your repose	在您睡觉时守护您
7	bellowing	吼叫
8	din	喧嚣
9	humming	音乐声
10	cried	喊叫
11	verily	真的
12	Lead off this ground	带路离开这里

Characters 人物分析

'Heavens keep him from these beasts'

It is ironic that the dangerous 'beasts' that Gonzalo refers to are, in fact, the 'civilised' Antonio and Sebastian.

- In your opinion, who is the best advertisement for human nature on the island, and who is the least appealing? Choose your two characters and lists their strengths and weaknesses on a sheet of paper.
- Swap your list with a classmate and add to the points they have listed on their chosen characters. Explain your ideas with reference to the script. You will be able to use this work later, in your essay on this act (see p. 76).

ANTONIO	Then let us both be sudden[1].	
	[*Antonio and Sebastian draw their swords*]	
GONZALO	[*Waking*] Now, good angels preserve[2] the king.	
	[*He shakes Alonso*]	
ALONSO	Why, how now? ho! Awake? Why are you drawn[3]?	305
	Wherefore[4] this ghastly looking[5]?	
GONZALO	What's the matter?	
SEBASTIAN	Whiles we stood here securing your repose[6],	
	Even now, we heard a hollow burst of bellowing[7],	
	Like bulls, or rather lions; did't not wake you?	
	It struck mine ear most terribly.	
ALONSO	I heard nothing.	310
ANTONIO	O, 'twas a din[8] to fright a monster's ear,	
	To make an earthquake. Sure it was the roar	
	Of a whole herd of lions.	
ALONSO	Heard you this, Gonzalo?	
GONZALO	Upon mine honour, sir, I heard a humming[9],	315
	And that a strange one too, which did awake me.	
	I shaked you, sir, and cried[10]. As mine eyes opened,	
	I saw their weapons drawn. There was a noise,	
	That's verily[11]. 'Tis best we stand upon our guard,	
	Or that we quit this place. Let's draw our weapons.	320
ALONSO	Lead off this ground[12], and let's make further search	
	For my poor son.	
GONZALO	Heavens keep him from these beasts:	
	For he is sure i'th'island.	
ALONSO	Lead away.	
ARIEL	Prospero my lord shall know what I have done.	
	So, king, go safely on to seek thy son.	325
	Exeunt	

Caliban curses Prospero, saying that Prospero's creatures control and torment him for the slightest offence. Fearing that Trinculo is one of Prospero's spirits, Caliban hides himself under his cloak.

剧情简介：凯力般诅咒普饶斯普柔，说只要自己有一丁点儿冒犯，普饶斯普柔的精灵们就会来控制和折磨他。由于害怕淳丘娄是普饶斯普柔派来的精灵，凯力般吓得躲在斗篷里。

Stagecraft 导演技巧

The first read-through (in threes)

Act 2 Scene 2 can be wonderfully funny both in the theatre and in a reading.

- To gain a first impression, take parts as Caliban, Trinculo and Stephano, and read straight through the whole scene. Don't pause to work out words you don't understand, but just enjoy the energy and humour of the scene. Take it in turns to read different parts if you like.

Themes 主题分析

Justice and injustice (in threes)

Caliban first curses Prospero, then describes the ways in which Prospero torments him for every minor offence ('every trifle').

a One person takes the role of the narrator, and the two others play Caliban and Prospero. The narrator slowly reads lines 1–14, pausing after each torment (there are at least seven). In the pause, Caliban and Prospero argue about the 'crime' and the 'punishment'. To what extent do you think the crimes can be defended? And what do the actions of both characters tell us about them? Afterwards, talk together about whether Prospero or Caliban has the greatest cause for complaint.

b Improvise a trial between Prospero and Caliban, with a third person acting as the judge. Each character puts forward his 'case', defending his actions. At the end, the judge should reach a verdict (裁定) of who is guilty of behaving badly.

1 'I needs must curse' (whole class)

Caliban's language is often powerful, and he uses provocative imagery despite knowing that Prospero's spirits (like secret police) are listening to his words. In fact, Caliban seems compelled (被迫) to 'curse' his master. Why does he feel the need to do so when Prospero's punishments are so cruel?

- Discuss Caliban's determination to keep talking in defiance (违抗) of Prospero. Why might his 'voice' and use of language be important in his struggle against his 'cruel' master? You could extend your discussion to include real-life examples of people who have spoken out against injustice despite attempts to silence them.

1 bogs, fens, flats 泥塘、沼泽、湿地
2 Prosper = Prospero （凯力般对普饶斯普柔的不准确称谓）
3 By inch-meal 一英寸一英寸地
4 urchin-shows 小鬼乱舞
5 pitch me i'th'mire 把我丢进泥潭
6 firebrand 鬼火
7 every trifle 每一个小的冒犯
8 mow 扮鬼脸
9 tumbling 翻滚
10 at my footfall 听到我的脚步声
11 wound with adders 被蝰蛇缠绕
12 cloven 分岔的
13 Lo 瞧
14 Perchance 也许
15 mind 注意到

Act 2 Scene 2
Near Caliban's cave

Enter CALIBAN, *with a burden of wood. A noise of thunder heard*

CALIBAN   All the infections that the sun sucks up
From bogs, fens, flats[1], on Prosper[2] fall, and make him
By inch-meal[3] a disease. His spirits hear me,
And yet I needs must curse. But they'll nor pinch,
Fright me with urchin-shows[4], pitch me i'th'mire[5],   5
Nor lead me like a firebrand[6] in the dark
Out of my way, unless he bid 'em; but
For every trifle[7] are they set upon me,
Sometime like apes, that mow[8] and chatter at me
And after bite me; then like hedgehogs, which   10
Lie tumbling[9] in my barefoot way and mount
Their pricks at my footfall[10]; sometime am I
All wound with adders[11], who with cloven[12] tongues
Do hiss me into madness.

Enter TRINCULO

    Lo[13], now lo!
Here comes a spirit of his, and to torment me   15
For bringing wood in slowly. I'll fall flat,
Perchance[14] he will not mind[15] me.
    [*He lies down, and covers himself with a cloak*]

Trinculo is fearful of the weather. He discovers Caliban, and thinks of using him to make his fortune in England. Hearing thunder, Trinculo creeps under Caliban's cloak. Stephano enters, drunk and singing.

剧情简介：淳丘娄害怕天气变坏。他发现了凯力般，想利用他在英格兰发财。听到雷声，淳丘娄爬到了凯力般的斗篷下面。斯迪法诺醉醺醺地哼着小曲走上来。

Characters 人物分析

Trinculo and Stephano: a comedy double act (in pairs)

The introduction of two new characters who have escaped the shipwreck brings some much-needed comic relief (喜剧场面). Trinculo is Alonso's court jester (俳优).

- Read Trinculo's lines and discuss how you would perform them. Is he rather stupid and scared of everything? Or is he in a state of post-traumatic (受惊吓等心理创伤后) shock, made worse by being in a strange new country? Would you play it purely for laughs (especially with lines such as 'What have we here …?' and 'Misery acquaints a man with strange bedfellows'). Or would you try to portray a darker, more complex character?

Write about it 写作练习

Of monsters and men

The Elizabethan and Jacobean (伊丽莎白一世和詹姆斯一世时期) exploration of the Americas is strongly echoed in *The Tempest*. Explorers sometimes brought inhabitants of the newly discovered countries back to England. These 'Indians' were often cruelly displayed for profit in fairgrounds (露天市场) and other public places. The exhibitors made large profits from this inhuman practice ('There / would this monster make a man' means that Caliban would make him a large fortune).

- Imagine you are one of these captives (俘虏) in Shakespeare's England. Write a letter describing your experiences as a 'monster' on show. What stories can you tell?

1 Playing the drunk (in pairs)

Stephano is Alonso's butler (男管家) or wine steward. He is very drunk, and he sings a rude song – one that contrasts greatly with Ariel's almost heavenly music.

- Even experienced actors find it difficult to play drunks convincingly. Before you attempt Stephano's song, discuss the challenges that such a part might involve. Remember that drunks are not necessarily loud and argumentative (好争吵). Think about other convincing ways of interpreting this state.
- Consider not just the melody and tempo (拍子) of the song, but also what it contributes to the scene overall.

---

1 bear off 遮挡，防护
2 brewing 酝酿
3 bombard 大酒囊
4 pailfuls 成桶地
5 poor-John 腌鳕鱼
6 painted 画在板上招揽顾客
7 holiday-fool 逛假日集市的人
8 make a man 让人发大财
9 doit 铜板，小钱
10 Warm 有体温
11 o'my troth! 我担保!
12 suffered by a thunderbolt 被雷击毙
13 gaberdine 袍子，斗篷
14 acquaints 与……熟悉
15 bedfellows 伙伴
16 shroud 躲在……之下
17 dregs 残余，最后一点
18 scurvy 不中用
19 swabber 甲板清洁工
20 gunner 炮手
21 tang 蛇的信子
22 savour … pitch 焦油或沥青的滋味
23 Yet … itch 但无论身上哪里痒，裁缝都会替她挠（即裁缝与女主顾有性关系）
24 let her go hang! 让她去死吧!

THE TEMPEST ACT 2 SCENE 2
暴风雨

TRINCULO   Here's neither bush nor shrub to bear off[1] any weather at all, and another storm brewing[2] – I hear it sing i'th'wind. Yond same black cloud, yond huge one, looks like a foul bombard[3] that would shed his liquor. If it should thunder as it did before, I know not where to hide my head. Yond same cloud cannot choose but fall by pailfuls[4]. [*Sees Caliban*] What have we here – a man, or a fish? Dead or alive? A fish, he smells like a fish; a very ancient and fishlike smell; a kind of, not-of-the-newest poor-John[5]. A strange fish. Were I in England now – as once I was – and had but this fish painted[6], not a holiday-fool[7] there but would give a piece of silver. There would this monster make a man[8]; any strange beast there makes a man. When they will not give a doit[9] to relieve a lame beggar, they will lay out ten to see a dead Indian. Legged like a man – and his fins like arms. Warm[10], o'my troth![11] I do now let loose my opinion, hold it no longer: this is no fish, but an islander, that hath lately suffered by a thunderbolt[12]. [*Thunder*] Alas, the storm is come again. My best way is to creep under his gaberdine[13]; there is no other shelter hereabout. Misery acquaints[14] a man with strange bedfellows[15]. I will here shroud[16] till the dregs[17] of the storm be past.
   [*He hides under Caliban's cloak*]

   Enter STEPHANO [*carrying a bottle and*] *singing*

STEPHANO   I shall no more to sea, to sea,
   Here shall I die ashore.
This is a very scurvy[18] tune to sing at a man's funeral. Well, here's my comfort. (*Drinks*)
   (*Sings*) The master, the swabber[19], the boatswain and I,
      The gunner[20] and his mate,
   Loved Mall, Meg and Marian, and Margery,
      But none of us cared for Kate.
      For she had a tongue with a tang[21],
      Would cry to a sailor, 'Go hang!'
   She loved not the savour of tar nor of pitch[22],
   Yet a tailor might scratch her where'er she did itch[23].
      Then to sea, boys, and let her go hang![24]
This is a scurvy tune too; but here's my comfort. (*Drinks*)

CALIBAN   Do not torment me! O!

Claiming to be brave, Stephano thinks of making a profit out of the four-legged 'monster'. Caliban cries out in fear. Stephano forces Caliban to drink, but is frightened by the sound of Trinculo's voice.

剧情简介：斯迪法诺自称胆子大，想在这个四条腿的"怪物"身上赚一笔。凯力般害怕地大叫起来，斯迪法诺强迫凯力般喝酒，但被淳丘娄的声音吓了一跳。

Stagecraft 导演技巧
Loud, grotesque (风格奇异) – and funny (in fours)

Lines 59 to 85 are among the funniest in the play: they encourage the actors to emphasise the absurdity (荒谬) of the action, and to turn their characters into grotesques (exaggerated and unpleasant creatures).

- With one member of the group in role as director, experiment with this scene using an old coat or blanket to cover Trinculo and Caliban. Have a quick run-through, in which Stephano's words are slurred (吐字不清), and those of the other two characters – although inaudible and muffled (声音含混，听不清) – convey their mood. Don't forget that Caliban is getting drunk for the first time.
- After your practice session, perform your version of the scene to other groups.

Themes 主题分析
Change and transformation

Caliban and Trinculo are transformed into something non-human here for comic effect. Transformation is one of the play's main themes, ranging from the sea becoming a destructive force, to sober men being transformed into drunks. What other signs of change and transformation can you identify in the play so far?

- On your own, write down as many examples of transformation as you can find.
- Discuss your ideas with a partner.
- Finally, share your jointly agreed points with the rest of the class.

1 men of Ind 西印度群岛的人
2 give ground 让步
3 ague 高烧
4 Where … language? 他从哪儿学会了说我们的语言？
5 for that 为这一点（即会说我们的话）
6 recover 救活
7 present … leather 献给任何一位穿皮鞋的君王的好礼物（neat's leather：母牛皮）
8 fit 发作
9 after the wisest 特别聪明
10 I will … him 我要多高的价也不过分
11 he … soundly 谁想要买他都要付大价钱
12 anon 不久
13 trembling 发抖（像鬼魂附体了那样）
14 shake your shaking 让你不再发抖
15 chops 下巴
16 detract 批评
17 Amen 阿门，够了（即这张嘴已经喝够了）
18 I have no long spoon 我可不想冒险

STEPHANO   What's the matter? Have we devils here? Do you put tricks upon's with savages and men of Ind[1]? Ha? I have not 'scaped drowning to be afeared now of your four legs. For it hath been said, 'As proper a man as ever went on four legs, cannot make him give ground[2]'; and it shall be said so again, while Stephano breathes at' nostrils.

CALIBAN   The spirit torments me! O!

STEPHANO   This is some monster of the isle, with four legs, who hath got, as I take it, an ague[3]. Where the devil should he learn our language?[4] I will give him some relief if it be but for that[5]. If I can recover[6] him, and keep him tame, and get to Naples with him, he's a present for any emperor that ever trod on neat's leather[7].

CALIBAN   Do not torment me, prithee! I'll bring my wood home faster.

STEPHANO   He's in his fit[8] now, and does not talk after the wisest[9]. He shall taste of my bottle. If he have never drunk wine afore, it will go near to remove his fit. If I can recover him, and keep him tame, I will not take too much for him[10]; he shall pay for him that hath him, and that soundly[11].

CALIBAN   Thou dost me yet but little hurt; thou wilt anon[12], I know it by thy trembling[13]. Now Prosper works upon thee.

STEPHANO   Come on your ways. Open your mouth; here is that which will give language to you, cat. Open your mouth; this will shake your shaking[14], I can tell you, and that soundly.

   [*Caliban drinks and spits it out*]

You cannot tell who's your friend: open your chops[15] again.

   [*Caliban drinks again*]

TRINCULO   I should know that voice. It should be – but he is drowned, and these are devils. O defend me!

STEPHANO   Four legs and two voices; a most delicate monster! His forward voice now is to speak well of his friend; his backward voice is to utter foul speeches, and to detract[16]. If all the wine in my bottle will recover him, I will help his ague. Come.

   [*Caliban drinks*]

Amen[17]. I will pour some in thy other mouth.

TRINCULO   Stephano.

STEPHANO   Doth thy other mouth call me? Mercy, mercy! This is a devil, and no monster. I will leave him; I have no long spoon[18].

Stephano pulls Trinculo out from under Caliban's cloak. Trinculo is delighted to find Stephano alive. Caliban thinks that Stephano is a god, and decides to become his servant.

剧情简介：斯迪法诺从凯力般的斗篷下拽出淳丘娄。看到斯迪法诺还活着，淳丘娄高兴不已。凯力般以为斯迪法诺是神，决定当他的奴仆。

Themes 主题分析

Appearance and reality (in pairs)

Shakespeare constantly explores the conflict between appearance and reality in *The Tempest* — perhaps no more so than here, where characters are 'transformed' from men into a strange creature (and back again). What appears to be the truth is often something quite different in this play.

- Identify parts of the script opposite where reality is not quite the same as the appearance. Think about the words, but also about how the characters might be dressed, and how they may behave. Are they completely open with each other?

1 How important is context? (whole class)

As well as the theme of appearance and reality, this part of Act 2 Scene 2 brings together several other key ideas that recur throughout the play. The activity below will help you discover more about these themes.

a Divide the class into three large groups and allocate (分配) each group one of the topics below. In your groups, discuss the theme you have been allocated and answer the question in *italics*.

- **Imperialism** (帝国主义) **and colonialism** (殖民主义) (see pp. 154–5) Caliban's promise to serve Stephano loyally (lines 104–5) seems to echo what happened to Caliban when Prospero first came to the island.

  What is Shakespeare saying about the complex relationship between an indigenous (土著) population and an imperial force?

- **Historical sources** (see pp. 152–3) Stephano's story (lines 101–2) contains an echo of what happened during a real shipwreck that may have inspired Shakespeare to write *The Tempest*. In that shipwreck, too, the sailors heaved barrels overboard.

  How important is context to any interpretation of the play?

- **Religion** Stephano's order to Trinculo and Caliban to 'kiss the book' (line 109) echoes the custom of kissing the Bible when promising to tell the truth, or vowing allegiance (发誓效忠) to a lord. This shows us how deeply embedded religion was in Shakespeare's England.

  How important are faith, spirituality (精神性，精神生活) and religion in this play?

b Each group should appoint a chairperson. After the initial group discussion, each chairperson should present the argument to the class that their group's theme is the most significant.

---

1 pull ... legs 拽这两条细点儿的腿
2 very 正是
3 siege 粪便
4 moon-calf 怪物，傻瓜
5 vent 排泄出来
6 over-blown 吹过去（即平息）
7 turn me about 把我扭来扭去
8 my stomach is not constant 我胃不舒服
9 sprites （普饶斯普柔的）精灵
10 celestial 天上的
11 kneel to 向……下跪
12 butt of sack 白葡萄酒桶
13 heaved 扔
14 subject 仆人
15 earthly 人间的
16 kiss the book 亲这《圣经》一口（这里用《圣经》比喻酒瓶，意为喝一口酒以证实誓言）
17 goose 傻子，笨蛋

TRINCULO   Stephano! If thou beest Stephano, touch me, and speak to me; for I am Trinculo – be not afeared – thy good friend Trinculo.

STEPHANO   If thou beest Trinculo, come forth! I'll pull thee by the lesser legs[1]. If any be Trinculo's legs, these are they.

[*Pulls him out*]

Thou art very[2] Trinculo indeed! How cam'st thou to be the siege[3] of this moon-calf[4]? Can he vent[5] Trinculos?

TRINCULO   I took him to be killed with a thunder-stroke. But art thou not drowned, Stephano? I hope now thou art not drowned. Is the storm over-blown[6]? I hid me under the dead moon-calf's gaberdine for fear of the storm. And art thou living, Stephano? O Stephano, two Neapolitans 'scaped!

[*Embraces Stephano*]

STEPHANO   Prithee do not turn me about[7], my stomach is not constant[8].

CALIBAN   [*Aside*] These be fine things, and if they be not sprites[9]. That's a brave god, and bears celestial[10] liquor. I will kneel to[11] him.

STEPHANO   How didst thou 'scape? How cam'st thou hither? Swear by this bottle how thou cam'st hither. I escaped upon a butt of sack[12] which the sailors heaved[13] o'erboard, by this bottle – which I made of the bark of a tree, with mine own hands, since I was cast ashore.

CALIBAN   I'll swear upon that bottle to be thy true subject[14], for the liquor is not earthly[15].

STEPHANO   Here. Swear then how thou escap'dst.

TRINCULO   Swum ashore, man, like a duck. I can swim like a duck, I'll be sworn.

STEPHANO   [*Gives bottle to Trinculo*] Here, kiss the book[16]. Though thou canst swim like a duck, thou art made like a goose[17].

TRINCULO   O Stephano, hast any more of this?

STEPHANO   The whole butt, man. My cellar is in a rock by the sea-side, where my wine is hid. [*To Caliban*] How now, moon-calf, how does thine ague?

Caliban is totally in awe of Stephano, and swears obedience to him. He promises to serve Stephano by showing him the island's resources. Trinculo mocks Caliban's desire to worship a drunkard.

剧情简介：凯力般彻底被斯迪法诺折服，发誓效忠于他，还答应给斯迪法诺带路去找岛上的资源。淳丘娄嘲笑凯力般把醉鬼当神灵。

Characters 人物分析
Caliban: the human and the inhuman

Stephano and Trinculo do not regard Caliban as a human being like themselves. In one production, Caliban appeared in later scenes with a placard (名牌) around his neck that read 'Monster' (see the picture on p. 86).

a List all the names that Stephano and Trinculo call Caliban in Scene 2. As you read the rest of the play, add to this list and keep a tally (计数) of how many times they refer to him as 'monster'.

b What advice would you give the actor playing Caliban here? How should he both conform to the imagery used by Stephano and Trinculo and retain his humanity? What advice might you give the other actors in this scene – how should they interact with Caliban and with one another?

c Write a psychologist's report on each of the three characters in the script opposite, in which you describe and explain their behaviour. What should they work to change about themselves? Why do they need to change? What do you predict will happen if they don't?

1 Out o'th'moon 从月亮上来的（早期在新世界的定居者对土著说他们是来自月亮的神）
2 when time was 原来，从前
3 My mistress 我的女主人（即蜜兰达）
4 thy dog, and thy bush 你的狗和柴火（传说某人不守安息日，星期天仍去打柴，因而被驱逐到月亮上，带着他的狗和柴火）
5 furnish it anon 很快会装满
6 this good light （指太阳）
7 shallow 浅薄
8 credulous 愚昧
9 drawn 吞咽
10 in good sooth 说实话
11 kiss thy foot 吻您的脚（即完全服从于您）
12 perfidious 不讲信用
13 puppy-headed 狗脑子，猪脑袋
14 scurvy 卑鄙
15 in drink 喝醉酒
16 abominable 讨厌
17 tyrant 暴君
18 bear him no more sticks 再也不给他搬柴

1 A tour of the island (in fours)

- Create a presentation based on lines 137–49, in which you map out the island. In particular, think about where all the characters are situated at this point in the play, while Caliban is pledging his loyalty to Stephano, and note their positions. You can use anything from a computer program to pencils, pens and paint, but make sure it is 'an isle full of noises, sounds and sweet airs', as well as a place of imprisonment and danger.
- Give the rest of the class a guided tour around your version of the island. As one person presents, the other three take parts as Caliban, Stephano and Trinculo. and act out lines 137–49.

CALIBAN	Hast thou not dropped from heaven?	115
STEPHANO	Out o'th'moon[1] I do assure thee. I was the man i'th'moon, when time was[2].	
CALIBAN	I have seen thee in her; and I do adore thee. My mistress[3] showed me thee, and thy dog, and thy bush[4].	
STEPHANO	Come, swear to that! [*Giving him the bottle*] Kiss the book – I will furnish it anon[5] with new contents. Swear.	120

[*Caliban drinks*]

TRINCULO	[*Aside*] By this good light[6], this is a very shallow[7] monster. I afeared of him? A very weak monster. The man i'th'moon? A most poor, credulous[8] monster. Well drawn[9], monster, in good sooth[10].	
CALIBAN	I'll show thee every fertile inch o'th'island. And I will kiss thy foot[11] – I prithee be my god.	125
TRINCULO	[*Aside*] By this light, a most perfidious[12] and drunken monster – when's god's asleep he'll rob his bottle.	
CALIBAN	I'll kiss thy foot; I'll swear myself thy subject.	
STEPHANO	Come on then: down and swear.	130
TRINCULO	[*Aside*] I shall laugh myself to death at this puppy-headed[13] monster. A most scurvy[14] monster. I could find in my heart to beat him –	
STEPHANO	[*To Caliban*] Come, kiss.	
TRINCULO	– but that the poor monster's in drink[15]. An abominable[16] monster.	135
CALIBAN	I'll show thee the best springs; I'll pluck thee berries;	
	I'll fish for thee, and get thee wood enough.	
	A plague upon the tyrant[17] that I serve!	
	I'll bear him no more sticks[18], but follow thee,	140
	Thou wondrous man.	
TRINCULO	[*Aside*] A most ridiculous monster, to make a wonder of a poor drunkard.	

Caliban continues with his promise to serve Stephano and to share with him the secret resources of the island. Stephano decides to become king of the island. Caliban sings about his freedom from Prospero.

剧情简介：凯力般履行诺言，继续效命于斯迪法诺，并且告诉他岛上那些不为人知的资源。斯迪法诺决定在这个岛上称王。凯力般为摆脱普饶斯普柔的奴役而欢唱。

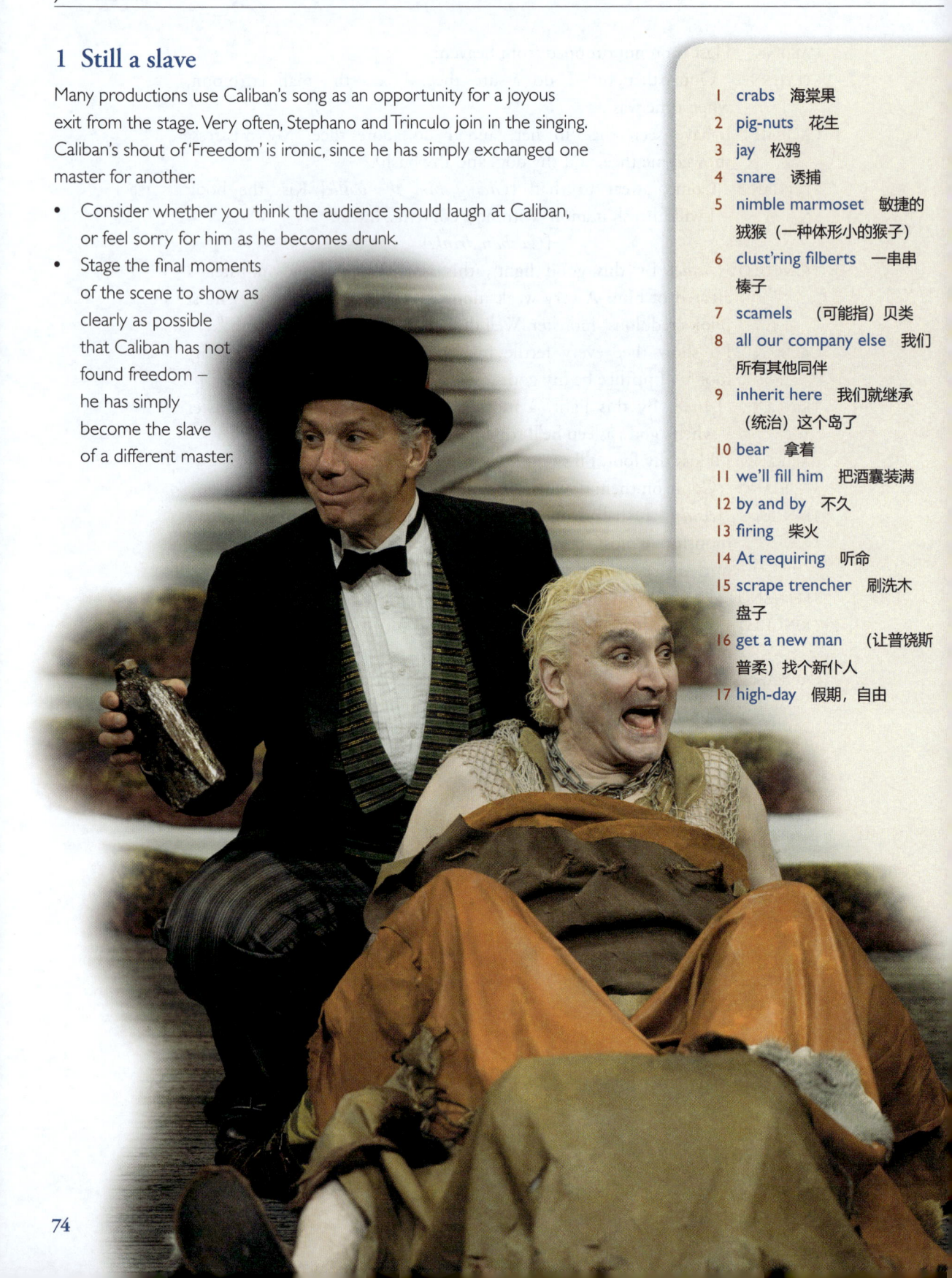

1 Still a slave

Many productions use Caliban's song as an opportunity for a joyous exit from the stage. Very often, Stephano and Trinculo join in the singing. Caliban's shout of 'Freedom' is ironic, since he has simply exchanged one master for another.

- Consider whether you think the audience should laugh at Caliban, or feel sorry for him as he becomes drunk.
- Stage the final moments of the scene to show as clearly as possible that Caliban has not found freedom – he has simply become the slave of a different master.

1	crabs	海棠果
2	pig-nuts	花生
3	jay	松鸦
4	snare	诱捕
5	nimble marmoset	敏捷的狨猴（一种体形小的猴子）
6	clust'ring filberts	一串串榛子
7	scamels	（可能指）贝类
8	all our company else	我们所有其他同伴
9	inherit here	我们就继承（统治）这个岛了
10	bear	拿着
11	we'll fill him	把酒囊装满
12	by and by	不久
13	firing	柴火
14	At requiring	听命
15	scrape trencher	刷洗木盘子
16	get a new man	（让普饶斯普柔）找个新仆人
17	high-day	假期，自由

CALIBAN	I prithee let me bring thee where crabs[1] grow;
	And I with my long nails will dig thee pig-nuts[2], 145
	Show thee a jay's[3] nest, and instruct thee how
	To snare[4] the nimble marmoset[5]. I'll bring thee
	To clust'ring filberts[6], and sometimes I'll get thee
	Young scamels[7] from the rock. Wilt thou go with me?
STEPHANO	I prithee, now lead the way without any more talking. Trin- 150 culo, the king and all our company else[8] being drowned, we will inherit here[9]. [*To Caliban*] Here; bear[10] my bottle. Fellow Trinculo, we'll fill him[11] by and by[12] again.
CALIBAN	(*Sings drunkenly*) Farewell, master; farewell, farewell.
TRINCULO	A howling monster; a drunken monster. 155
CALIBAN	[*Singing*] No more dams I'll make for fish,
	Nor fetch in firing[13]
	At requiring[14],
	Nor scrape trencher[15], nor wash dish,
	Ban, ban, Ca-caliban 160
	Has a new master – get a new man[16].
	Freedom, high-day[17], high-day freedom, freedom high-day, freedom.
STEPHANO	O brave monster, lead the way!

Exeunt

The Tempest
暴风雨

Looking back at Act 2   "第2幕" 回顾
Activities for groups or individuals

1 A mini Act 2

A great deal happens in Act 2, but what are the most important moments? The following activity will help you decide.

- Write out (in continuous prose) the main action and ideas that take place in this act. You must do this in exactly 200 words.
- In pairs, compare your work and agree on which 100 words you would cut and which you would leave. Together, rewrite the remaining action in exactly 100 words.
- Next, cut down this draft to fifty words. Make sure your text remains clear and fluent.
- Cut down these fifty words into a twenty-five word mini summary of Act 2. Read this to the rest of the class.
- Finally, cut down these twenty-five words to a single word that best sums up Act 2. Take it turns to go to a board and write or pin up that word. Then explain your choice and make a note of the ideas behind the other word choices.
- You might try reversing this activity: begin with one word and build it up to 200 words.

2 What is Prospero thinking?

Prospero does not appear in Act 2. However, he uses Ariel to prevent murder in Scene 1, and Caliban's first song in Scene 2 refers to Prospero's 'spirits' following him.

- In groups, imagine that you are these sprites reporting back to Prospero after every scene. Would you portray them as fairies, secret police, children, resentful slaves, or something else? How would you describe what is happening? How do you think Prospero would respond? To what extent is he in charge of them?

3 What does it mean to be civilised?

Act 2 Scene 1 reveals the murderous intentions of the 'civilised' Antonio and Sebastian. Scene 2, which shows Caliban's encounter with Stephano and Trinculo, reflects what happened when Europeans colonised the Americas. The Europeans assumed that they were superior to the native people; they tried to make money out of them, drugged them with alcohol, and made them their servants.

- As a class, discuss whether or not you think Shakespeare is using Act 2 to make ironic and critical comments on colonisation and 'civilisation' (see p. 154 for more information about this).
- Consider the qualities that you think make an individual – and a society – 'civilised'. Debate as a class and agree on a list of ten qualities.
- Afterwards, return to The Tempest – how many of these ten qualities can you find in the script, and who is most closely associated with them?

4 Imprisoned women

We have been 'introduced' to three female characters: Sycorax, Claribel and Miranda (though only the last is seen on stage). Although very different, they seem to share one similarity: they are all restricted or imprisoned, and their fates are decided by men.

- In pairs, discuss why you think Shakespeare has done this and whether it reveals more about the male characters or the female ones.

5 Who has rightful authority?

Act 2 continues to explore the theme of rightful authority.

- Using the notes you have compiled so far, write an essay – using embedded quotations (嵌入式引用) – discussing this theme as it is presented in both Act 1 and Act 2. Remember to plan your essay before you write it.

The Tempest has been adapted for film many times in modern dress. In this 2010 production, we see Alonso, Sebastian, Gonzalo and Antonio exploring the island after surviving the storm.

Ferdinand reflects that his hard labour is pleasurable, because thoughts of Miranda make the work enjoyable. Miranda pleads with him to rest. She says that the logs will weep for Ferdinand as they burn.

剧情简介：法迪南表示他苦中有乐，因为一想到蜜兰莐，苦役也变成乐事。蜜兰莐请求法迪南休息，说他搬运的木头会在燃烧时流下心疼他的眼泪。

1 A 'mean (卑微的) task' (by yourself)

Prospero forces Ferdinand to do exactly the same wood-carrying task as Caliban. Although he is forced to work as a slave, Ferdinand says that this social degradation (落魄，潦倒) is a noble task for the sake of Miranda. How is Ferdinand's response different to Caliban's?

- Imagine Caliban is secretly watching and listening to Ferdinand's speech here. Write out what is going through his head. Refer to specific parts of the script opposite as you try to capture Caliban's tone and perspective.

Language in the play 剧中语言

Weigh the contrasts (in pairs)

Conflict is central to all drama, and Shakespeare uses **antitheses** (对偶) (see 'The language of *The Tempest*', p. 167) throughout this play as a way of expressing contrasts or conflicts. Lines 1–9 contain at least eight contrasts.

a Stand opposite each other and read the lines aloud. Every time Ferdinand makes a contrast, such as 'sports' versus 'painful' or 'labour' versus 'delight', swap places with your partner.

b Read through these lines again. This time, instead of swapping places, devise gestures or movements that embody (体现) this conflict. Pay attention to what your partner's body movement conveys about the conflict in each instance.

c Afterwards, talk together about why conflict is so important to drama in general.

1 sports　游戏，娱乐
2 painful　累人
3 sets off　抵消
4 baseness　苦工
5 heavy　沉重
6 odious　令人厌恶，可憎
7 but　除了
8 quickens　使……有活力
9 crabbed　粗暴，暴躁
10 sore injunction　严格的命令
11 such … executor　这种卑贱的差事从没有让我这样高贵的人干过
12 I forget　我忘记干活了（法迪南只顾说话忘了搬木头）
13 Most … it　干活时只想着蜜兰莐
14 enjoined　被命令
15 burns / 'Twill weep　这些木头燃烧时也会因为你受苦而流泪（木头燃烧时流出树脂）
16 wearied　使……疲倦
17 safe　（父亲不会出来干涉）安全无事

Act 3 Scene 1

Near Prospero's cave

Enter FERDINAND, *bearing a log*

FERDINAND [*Sets down the log*] There be some sports[1] are painful[2], and their labour
Delight in them sets off[3]. Some kinds of baseness[4]
Are nobly undergone; and most poor matters
Point to rich ends. This my mean task would be
As heavy[5] to me as odious[6], but[7]
The mistress which I serve quickens[8] what's dead,
And makes my labours pleasures. O, she is
Ten times more gentle than her father's crabbed[9] —
And he's composed of harshness. I must remove
Some thousands of these logs, and pile them up,
Upon a sore injunction[10]. My sweet mistress
Weeps when she sees me work, and says such baseness
Had never like executor[11]. I forget[12]. [*Picks up the log*]
But these sweet thoughts do even refresh my labours,
Most busy, least when I do it[13].

Enter MIRANDA, *and* PROSPERO [*following at a distance*]

MIRANDA Alas, now pray you
Work not so hard. I would the lightning had
Burnt up those logs that you are enjoined[14] to pile.
Pray set it down, and rest you. When this burns
'Twill weep[15] for having wearied[16] you. My father
Is hard at study; pray now, rest yourself —
He's safe[17] for these three hours.

Miranda wants to carry the logs, but Ferdinand prevents her. Prospero observes that Miranda is in love. Ferdinand declares his love for her. He says that, of all the women he has known, Miranda is without equal.

剧情简介：蜜兰荙想搬木头，但法迪南阻止了她。普饶斯普柔发现蜜兰荙爱上了法迪南。法迪南表达了对蜜兰荙的爱慕之情，说他认识的女性没有一个能比得上蜜兰荙。

1 Catching the plague (瘟疫) of love (by yourself)

Prospero's lines 32–3 compare falling in love with catching a disease ('visitation' means a visit of the plague). A modern equivalent is the phrase 'You've got it bad' (你坠入爱河，不可救药了). Does Miranda share her father's view of love?

- Write out how you think Miranda would respond if she overheard her father say 'Poor worm, thou art infected'. Refer to the script and use your understanding of Miranda's character and experiences.

Characters 人物分析

'Admired Miranda'

Miranda disobeys her father's order and tells Ferdinand her name. In Latin, 'Miranda' means 'to be wondered at'. If you turn back to the young lovers' first meeting, you will find that Ferdinand calls her 'O you wonder' (Act 1 Scene 2, line 425). Ferdinand plays with this meaning in 'Admired' and 'admiration' (lines 38–9). He is punning (使用双关语) on the Latin meaning of her name and using **polyptoton** (同根异形) (the repetition of words from the same root but with different endings).

- Try using language in the same way with the names of other characters. Write a sentence each punning on 'Prospero', 'Caliban', 'Sycorax' and 'Ariel'. Refer to some aspect of their character or circumstances. You might like to imitate the way Ferdinand plays on the meaning of Miranda's name, or you could build your pun (双关语) around a particular quality that a character demonstrates.

2 Playing with absolute sincerity (in pairs)

This is what one actor who played Ferdinand said about lines 38–49:

Ferdinand has been captivated by many women, but found some fault in every one. Only Miranda is perfect. You have to play these lines absolutely sincerely, full of wonder. Although it's not the kind of language you hear nowadays, you can make it ring true (听上去是真的). Your job is to convince the audience you are really in love for the first time. You simply mustn't be embarrassed. The same applies to Miranda's lines too.

- Take the actor's advice as your cue to practise speaking as Ferdinand and Miranda. If you are embarrassed, talk about why this part of the script prompts such a response. Why might Shakespeare have given the characters such language at this point in the play?

---

1 discharge 干完活
2 crack my sinews 拉伤我的肌肉
3 become me 适合我
4 good … against 我是心甘情愿去做，而你是被迫的
5 Poor worm 可怜虫（普饶斯普柔对蜜兰荙的爱称）
6 infected 动情了（被感染了）
7 visitation （瘟疫、疾病的）降临
8 Chiefly 主要是
9 hest 诫令
10 dearest 最珍贵的
11 Th'harmony of their tongues 她们动听的话
12 too diligent 太专注
13 into … ear 迷住了我（专注倾听的耳朵）
14 virtues 美德，优点
15 defect 缺点
16 quarrel with 与……不合
17 put it to the soil 糟蹋了它
18 peerless 独一无二，无与伦比

FERDINAND   O most dear mistress,
            The sun will set before I shall discharge¹
            What I must strive to do.

MIRANDA   If you'll sit down
            I'll bear your logs the while. Pray give me that;
            I'll carry it to the pile.

FERDINAND   No, precious creature,
            I'd rather crack my sinews², break my back,
            Than you should such dishonour undergo,
            While I sit lazy by.

MIRANDA   It would become me³
            As well as it does you; and I should do it
            With much more ease, for my good will is to it,
            And yours it is against⁴.

PROSPERO   [*Aside*]   Poor worm⁵, thou art infected⁶;
            This visitation⁷ shows it.

MIRANDA   You look wearily.

FERDINAND   No, noble mistress, 'tis fresh morning with me
            When you are by at night. I do beseech you
            Chiefly⁸, that I might set it in my prayers,
            What is your name?

MIRANDA   Miranda. – O my father,
            I have broke your hest⁹ to say so.

FERDINAND   Admired Miranda,
            Indeed the top of admiration, worth
            What's dearest¹⁰ to the world. Full many a lady
            I have eyed with best regard, and many a time
            Th'harmony of their tongues¹¹ hath into bondage
            Brought my too diligent¹² ear¹³. For several virtues¹⁴
            Have I liked several women, never any
            With so full soul but some defect¹⁵ in her
            Did quarrel with¹⁶ the noblest grace she owed,
            And put it to the soil¹⁷. But you, O you,
            So perfect and so peerless¹⁸, are created
            Of every creature's best.

Miranda declares her love for Ferdinand, and he describes how he fell in love with her at first sight. He professes his overwhelming love for her. Miranda weeps, and Prospero blesses their love.

剧情简介：蜜兰达表达了对法迪南的爱慕，法迪南倾诉自己如何对蜜兰达一见钟情，并坦言自己无法抑制对蜜兰达的爱。蜜兰达落泪，普饶斯普柔为他们的恋情祝福。

Language in the play 剧中语言
Verse (韵文；诗体) and prose

Ferdinand and Miranda talk together in a way that no one uses in conversation today. Their elaborate verse seems to come from a fairy-tale world. Miranda's speech in lines 49–58 is particularly formal. Where Ferdinand bases his compliments on his experience of women, she praises him from her contrasting ignorance of men.

- Rewrite the verse opposite as prose (for either character) and try to capture the essence of what they say in modern English. As a class, listen to one another's examples and discuss the different effects of verse and prose.

1 Which images can you 'see'? (by yourself)

Which of the following images from the script opposite do you find easy to visualise? Write them in order, ranging from the easiest to the most difficult. Alongside each image, write about the picture it conjures up (使在脑海中显现) in your mind.

- 'The jewel in my dower' (line 55)
- 'This wooden slavery' (line 64)
- 'The flesh-fly blow my mouth' (line 65)
- 'My heart fly to your service' (line 67)
- 'patient log-man' (line 69)
- 'Heavens rain grace / On that which breeds between 'em' (lines 77–8)

Write about it 写作练习
Casting for Miranda

- Look at the pictures of Miranda on pages viii, 18, 34, 38, 123, 134, 160 and 161. Which comes closest to your view of her? In role as director of a new performance, describe the kind of actress you would want to play Miranda. Think about her age, her appearance, her mannerisms (特有的言谈举止) and her previous roles. You may even want a specific actress whom you already admire or who has specific skills or talents.
- Write notes as a casting director, asking one of your assistants to search the agencies on the Internet, or drama schools' websites, to see if they can find someone suitable.

1 glass 镜子
2 good friend 我的爱
3 How features are abroad 外面的男人长什么模样
4 skilless 不知晓
5 modesty 贞洁
6 The jewel in my dower 我嫁妆中的珍宝
7 I prattle / Something too wildly 我信口说来有些过分
8 precepts 嘱咐
9 condition 社会地位
10 wooden slavery 搬木工
11 suffer 忍受
12 flesh-fly 在腐肉上产卵的苍蝇
13 blow my mouth 在我嘴里产卵
14 resides 居住
15 patient 吃苦耐劳
16 bear witness to 为……作证
17 crown 表彰，使圆满完成
18 profess 声称，公开表示
19 kind event 好结果
20 if … mischief 如果我撒谎，就把我的好运变成厄运
21 what else 其他一切
22 encounter 相遇
23 that which breeds between 'em 两人之间产生的爱情

MIRANDA	I do not know

                One of my sex; no woman's face remember,   50
                Save from my glass[1], mine own. Nor have I seen
                More that I may call men than you, good friend[2],
                And my dear father. How features are abroad[3]
                I am skilless[4] of; but by my modesty[5],
                The jewel in my dower[6], I would not wish   55
                Any companion in the world but you;
                Nor can imagination form a shape
                Besides yourself, to like of. But I prattle
                Something too wildly[7], and my father's precepts[8]
                I therein do forget.   60

FERDINAND   I am in my condition[9]
                A prince, Miranda; I do think a king –
                I would not so – and would no more endure
                This wooden slavery[10] than to suffer[11]
                The flesh-fly[12] blow my mouth[13]. Hear my soul speak.   65
                The very instant that I saw you, did
                My heart fly to your service, there resides[14]
                To make me slave to it, and for your sake
                Am I this patient[15] log-man.

MIRANDA   Do you love me?

FERDINAND   O heaven, O earth, bear witness to[16] this sound,   70
                And crown[17] what I profess[18] with kind event[19]
                If I speak true; if hollowly, invert
                What best is boded me to mischief[20]. I,
                Beyond all limit of what else[21] i'th'world,
                Do love, prize, honour you.

MIRANDA   I am a fool   75
                To weep at what I'm glad of.

PROSPERO   [*Aside*]   Fair encounter[22]
                Of two most rare affections. Heavens rain grace
                On that which breeds between 'em[23].

FERDINAND   Wherefore weep you?

Miranda indirectly explains her tears, then openly says she wants to marry Ferdinand. He willingly agrees. Prospero expresses pleasure. In Scene 2, Trinculo comments sceptically on his own and his companions' intelligence.

剧情简介：蜜兰达婉转地说出流泪的原因，接着敞开心扉表示想嫁给法迪南。法迪南欣然同意，普饶斯普柔很欣慰。第二场，淳丘娄质疑自己和两位同伴的智商。

Language in the play 剧中语言
Riddles, plain speech and images of fertility (生育能力)

In lines 79–83, Miranda explains in an enigmatic (高深莫测) way why she is weeping. She dare not offer what she wants to give (herself), but cannot live without what she lacks (Ferdinand). She decides to speak directly ('this is trifling', 'Hence, bashful cunning') and offers herself as wife to Ferdinand.

Some critics have noted that Miranda uses an image of pregnancy to describe how she speaks initially in riddles: 'the more it seeks to hide itself / The bigger bulk it shows.' Ferdinand also uses language that implies growth and abundance in line 93.

a   Write a paragraph describing how the language used here reflects the growing love between Miranda and Ferdinand. Consider the formal verse used earlier and the fruitful language of growth and abundance in the script opposite.

b   Use the Internet to help you compare the formal speeches given by Miranda and Ferdinand with other romantic love poetry written around the same time, such as that by Philip Sidney or John Donne. You could also compare it with less romantic poems, such as 'Come live with me and be my love' by Christopher Marlowe (look also for Sir Walter Raleigh's reply).

Stagecraft 导演技巧
Stage directions in the language (in pairs)

How many implied stage directions can you find in the lovers' pledge (誓言) and farewell (lines 85–93)? At each of these points, write a detailed and explicit stage direction to advise the actors playing the parts of Miranda and Ferdinand.

1 A sneak preview of Scene 2 (in threes)

a   Take parts and read through the whole of Scene 2. Remember – all three men have been drinking heavily, and can probably barely stand.

b   Work out how you would stage the scene, identifying the lines where you would attempt to get the loudest laughs from the audience. For example, Trinculo's sceptical statement in lines 5–6 ('if th'other / two be brained like us, the state totters') usually evokes much laughter.

---

1   unworthiness   不配
2   die to want   少了它我就得死
3   trifling   无用的废话
4   The bigger bulk it shows   越发明显
5   bashful cunning   扭捏羞怯（的样子）
6   prompt   鼓励，提醒（某人说话）
7   die your maid   为你守身而死
8   fellow   伴侣
9   mistress   心上人
10   thus humble   如此顺服（这时法迪南向蜜兰达下跪或深鞠躬）
11   As bondage e'er of freedom   就像囚犯拥抱自由
12   A thousand thousand   千千万万个（再见）
13   surprised   没有预料到，惊喜
14   appertaining   相关
15   butt is out   酒桶空了
16   bear up, and board 'em   干杯（水手的祝酒词）
17   The folly of this island!   这个岛真荒唐！
18   be brained like us   脑子和我们的一样
19   totters   摇摇欲坠，踉踉跄跄

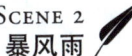

MIRANDA   At mine unworthiness¹, that dare not offer
           What I desire to give, and much less take   80
           What I shall die to want². But this is trifling³,
           And all the more it seeks to hide itself
           The bigger bulk it shows⁴. Hence, bashful cunning⁵,
           And prompt⁶ me, plain and holy innocence.
           I am your wife, if you will marry me;   85
           If not, I'll die your maid⁷. To be your fellow⁸
           You may deny me, but I'll be your servant
           Whether you will or no.

FERDINAND [*Kneeling*]   My mistress⁹, dearest,
           And I thus humble¹⁰ ever.

MIRANDA   My husband then?

FERDINAND   Aye, with a heart as willing   90
           As bondage e'er of freedom¹¹. Here's my hand.

MIRANDA   And mine, with my heart in't; and now farewell
           Till half an hour hence.

FERDINAND   A thousand thousand¹².
                    Exeunt [*Ferdinand and Miranda separately*]

PROSPERO   So glad of this as they I cannot be,
           Who are surprised¹³ with all; but my rejoicing   95
           At nothing can be more. I'll to my book,
           For yet ere supper-time must I perform
           Much business appertaining¹⁴.   *Exit*

Act 3 Scene 2
Near Caliban's cave

Enter CALIBAN, STEPHANO *and* TRINCULO

STEPHANO   Tell not me. When the butt is out¹⁵ we will drink water, not a drop before; therefore bear up, and board 'em¹⁶. Servant monster, drink to me.

TRINCULO   [*Aside*] Servant monster? The folly of this island!¹⁷ They say there's but five upon this isle; we are three of them – if th'other   5
           two be brained like us¹⁸, the state totters¹⁹.

Stephano promises to make Caliban his deputy. Caliban accuses Trinculo of cowardice, and is mocked in return. Stephano threatens to hang Trinculo for mutiny. Ariel begins to create trouble for Trinculo.

剧情简介：斯迪法诺答应凯力般做自己的副手。凯力般指责淳丘娄胆小怕事，却被反唇相讥。斯迪法诺威胁淳丘娄如果反叛就绞死他。艾瑞尔开始给淳丘娄制造麻烦。

Stagecraft 导演技巧
A new master for Caliban (by yourself)

In some performances, Trinculo does not seem to be fully part of the conversation between Stephano and Caliban. His words are mostly directed to the audience until he is drawn into the quarrel at line 23. In contrast, in other performances he argues directly with Stephano.

- In your Director's Journal, make notes advising the actors on how to portray the three characters in the script opposite. How would you depict Trinculo in particular?

1 Trinculo – drunk, but perceptive

Trinculo is drunk, but he sees the foolishness of his companions. He ridicules them each time he speaks in lines 4–28 and uses puns, a language device characteristic of the court jester.

- Find each of Trinculo's puns and explain how it provides cues for comic stage business (see lines 9, 17 and 26).
- Suggest a gesture that Stephano might make to accompany his words when he threatens to hang Trinculo on 'the next tree' (line 31).

1 set （因醉酒两眼）发直
2 brave 不得了（嘲讽口气）
3 set 长在
4 five and thirty leagues （约100英里）
5 off and on 来回
6 standard 掌旗官（即可以直立的人）
7 list = please
8 no standard 站不起来
9 run 逃跑
10 go 走
11 lie 躺下（或说谎）
12 valiant 勇敢
13 I ... constable 我足够勇敢以至于跟治安官打一架都不怕
14 deboshed 喝得烂醉
15 monstrous lie 天大的谎话（怪物说的谎）
16 quoth he 他说
17 natural 蠢材
18 keep ... head 你说话客气点儿
19 mutineer 叛贼
20 the next tree 意思是"走到下一棵树我就绞死你"
21 hearken 听
22 suit 请求
23 Marry 圣母马利亚在上（起誓）
24 cunning 法术，技巧
25 jesting 爱开玩笑，滑稽
26 valiant master 勇敢的主人（即斯迪法诺）

THE TEMPEST ACT 3 SCENE 2
暴风雨

STEPHANO   Drink, servant monster, when I bid thee; thy eyes are almost set[1] in thy head.
TRINCULO   Where should they be set else? He were a brave[2] monster indeed if they were set[3] in his tail.
STEPHANO   My man-monster hath drowned his tongue in sack. For my part, the sea cannot drown me – I swam, ere I could recover the shore, five and thirty leagues[4] off and on[5]. By this light, thou shalt be my lieutenant, monster, or my standard[6].
TRINCULO   Your lieutenant if you list[7]; he's no standard[8].
STEPHANO   We'll not run[9], monsieur monster.
TRINCULO   Nor go[10] neither; but you'll lie[11] like dogs, and yet say nothing neither.
STEPHANO   Moon-calf, speak once in thy life, if thou beest a good moon-calf.
CALIBAN   How does thy honour? Let me lick thy shoe. I'll not serve him, he is not valiant[12].
TRINCULO   Thou liest, most ignorant monster; I am in case to jostle a constable[13]. Why, thou deboshed[14] fish thou, was there ever man a coward that hath drunk so much sack as I today? Wilt thou tell a monstrous lie[15], being but half a fish, and half a monster?
CALIBAN   Lo, how he mocks me. Wilt thou let him, my lord?
TRINCULO   'Lord', quoth he[16]? That a monster should be such a natural[17]!
CALIBAN   Lo, lo again! Bite him to death, I prithee.
STEPHANO   Trinculo, keep a good tongue in your head[18]. If you prove a mutineer[19], the next tree[20]. The poor monster's my subject, and he shall not suffer indignity.
CALIBAN   I thank my noble lord. Wilt thou be pleased to hearken[21] once again to the suit[22] I made to thee?
STEPHANO   Marry[23] will I. Kneel, and repeat it. I will stand, and so shall Trinculo.

Enter ARIEL *invisible*

CALIBAN   As I told thee before, I am subject to a tyrant, a sorcerer, that by his cunning[24] hath cheated me of the island.
ARIEL   Thou liest.
CALIBAN   [*To Trinculo*] Thou liest, thou jesting[25] monkey thou. I would my valiant master[26] would destroy thee. I do not lie.

Stephano threatens Trinculo. Caliban begs Stephano to kill Prospero. Ariel gets Trinculo into further trouble by again imitating his voice. Stephano beats Trinculo, who blames the wine for Stephano's behaviour.

剧情简介：斯迪法诺威胁淳丘娄，凯力般乞求斯迪法诺杀死普饶斯普柔。艾瑞尔再次模仿淳丘娄的声音为其制造麻烦。斯迪法诺动手打了淳丘娄，淳丘娄把斯迪法诺的行为归咎为醉酒。

Themes 主题分析

Comic echoes of usurpation (by yourself)

The three drunkards provide a comic parody (滑稽的模仿) of one of the main themes of the play: usurpation (the overthrow of a rightful ruler). Stephano tries to behave like a king, and demands that his subjects obey him. He has already threatened Trinculo with hanging ('the next tree'). Caliban's plot to overthrow Prospero is a comic reflection of the way in which Antonio seized the throne of Milan from Prospero, and of the courtiers' conspiracy to kill Alonso. Even Stephano's threat to Trinculo, 'I will supplant some of your teeth' (line 43), echoes the theme ('supplant' literally means 'uproot').

- Write a paragraph on how this theme has developed in the play so far, and how it links these two strands of the plot. Remember to use embedded quotations to support your ideas.

Stagecraft 导演技巧

Comedy and slapstick (闹剧)

a Trinculo gets a beating for something he hasn't done. Stephano thinks Trinculo is mocking him, but Ariel is really to blame, getting Trinculo into trouble by echoing his earlier accusation at line 23 and imitating his voice at lines 39, 56 and 67.

- Work out how Ariel moves, how close he stands to Trinculo and how he behaves after he has spoken. In some performances Trinculo reacts with astonishment to Ariel's words; in others he is bemused (茫然) by the accusations from the others, which suggests that he does not hear Ariel.

b Already imagining that he is king of the island, Stephano strikes Trinculo at line 68. Trinculo blames his beating on drink ('This can sack and drinking do' means 'This is what wine makes you do'). In some productions Trinculo speaks angrily, in others sulkily (闷闷不乐), in others fearfully, afraid of another beating.

- Practise speaking Trinculo's lines in the script opposite in different tones and to draw different reactions from an audience. Devise suitable slapstick for this part of the scene, and experiment with pulling off boots, or playing with hats or chairs.

1 supplant 拔掉
2 Mum then 闭嘴
3 this thing 这个东西（指淳丘娄）
4 compassed 实现
5 party 你说的那个人
6 pied ninny 穿花格衣服的傻瓜（即小丑）
7 patch 小丑的戏服
8 quick freshes 水流湍急的清泉
9 stockfish 咸鱼干（制作时要拍打使鱼身变软）
10 give me the lie 说我撒谎
11 pox （一种疾病，常用于诅咒）
12 murrain 瘟疫
13 devil take your fingers 但愿魔鬼咬下你的手指头（淳丘娄诅咒那只打了他的手）

STEPHANO Trinculo, if you trouble him any more in's tale, by this hand, I will supplant[1] some of your teeth.
TRINCULO Why, I said nothing.
STEPHANO Mum then[2], and no more. [*To Caliban*] Proceed.
CALIBAN I say by sorcery he got this isle;
From me he got it. If thy greatness will
Revenge it on him – for I know thou dar'st,
But this thing[3] dare not –
STEPHANO That's most certain.
CALIBAN Thou shalt be lord of it, and I'll serve thee.
STEPHANO How now shall this be compassed[4]? Canst thou bring me to the party[5]?
CALIBAN Yea, yea, my lord, I'll yield him thee asleep,
Where thou mayst knock a nail into his head.
ARIEL Thou liest, thou canst not.
CALIBAN What a pied ninny's[6] this? [*To Trinculo*] Thou scurvy patch[7]!
[*To Stephano*] I do beseech thy greatness give him blows,
And take his bottle from him. When that's gone,
He shall drink nought but brine, for I'll not show him
Where the quick freshes[8] are.
STEPHANO Trinculo, run into no further danger. Interrupt the monster one word further, and by this hand, I'll turn my mercy out o'doors, and make a stockfish[9] of thee.
TRINCULO Why, what did I? I did nothing. I'll go farther off.
STEPHANO Didst thou not say he lied?
ARIEL Thou liest.
STEPHANO Do I so?
[*Strikes Trinculo*]
Take thou that! As you like this, give me the lie[10] another time.
TRINCULO I did not give the lie. Out o'your wits, and hearing too? A pox[11] o'your bottle! This can sack and drinking do. A murrain[12] on your monster, and the devil take your fingers[13]!
CALIBAN Ha, ha, ha!
STEPHANO Now forward with your tale. [*To Trinculo*] Prithee stand further off.
CALIBAN Beat him enough; after a little time
I'll beat him too.

Caliban proposes a plan to kill Prospero. Stephano agrees to do the deed. He says that he will take Miranda as his queen, and will make Trinculo and Caliban his deputies. Stephano apologises for beating Trinculo.

剧情简介：凯力般提出一个杀死普饶斯普柔的计划。斯迪法诺同意动手，还说要蜜兰莶做他的王后，让淳丘娄和凯力般做他的副手。斯迪法诺为打淳丘娄道歉。

Characters 人物分析

Caliban's plot (in pairs)

Caliban urges Stephano to burn the books that give Prospero his magical powers. (The same books probably led to Prospero's overthrow as duke of Milan, because he was so busy studying them that he neglected state affairs.) Caliban also claims that Prospero's spirits loathe (厌恶) their master: 'they all do hate him / As rootedly as I.'

- Experiment with different ways of speaking Caliban's lines 79–95 to reveal his character at this point in the play. Try packing them with anger and resentment – and persuasive power.

1 paunch him with a stake 将木桩戳进他肚子里
2 wezand 气管，喉咙
3 sot 白痴，醉鬼
4 hate him / As rootedly 对他恨之入骨
5 brave ùtensils 精美的器皿
6 deck 装饰
7 nonpareil 绝代佳人
8 become thy bed 正好可以给您侍寝
9 brave brood 很多子女
10 'save our graces! 老天保佑！
11 viceroys 总督
12 jocund 高兴，快乐
13 troll the catch 轮着唱那首曲子，每位歌手都唱一样的曲调
14 but whilere 就在刚才

1 'Ex-cell-ent' – is it sarcasm?

In the 1993 Royal Shakespeare Company (RSC) production of *The Tempest*, Trinculo stretched out his one word in line 102 very slowly and sarcastically: 'Ex-cell-ent'. In other productions, he adopts a sulky (生闷气的) tone that prompts Stephano to try to make amends.

- How would you advise Trinculo to speak this one word? Why?

2 Contrasting episodes

Lines 96–101 make a stark contrast with the tender love scene between Ferdinand and Miranda. Some of the comedy is shown in the photograph below, as the very drunk Trinculo and Stephano offer Caliban alcohol, while Ariel looks on.

- Write a paragraph to explain the effect you would try to create with these lines if you were directing the play.
  What reaction would you want from your audience?

THE TEMPEST ACT 3 SCENE 2
暴风雨

STEPHANO   Stand farther. [*To Caliban*] Come, proceed.
CALIBAN   Why, as I told thee, 'tis a custom with him
           I'th'afternoon to sleep. There thou mayst brain him, 80
           Having first seized his books; or with a log
           Batter his skull, or paunch him with a stake[1],
           Or cut his wezand[2] with thy knife. Remember
           First to possess his books; for without them
           He's but a sot[3], as I am, nor hath not 85
           One spirit to command – they all do hate him
           As rootedly[4] as I. Burn but his books;
           He has brave ùtensils[5] – for so he calls them –
           Which when he has a house, he'll deck[6] withal.
           And that most deeply to consider, is 90
           The beauty of his daughter. He himself
           Calls her a nonpareil[7]. I never saw a woman
           But only Sycorax my dam, and she;
           But she as far surpasseth Sycorax
           As great'st does least. 95
STEPHANO   Is it so brave a lass?
CALIBAN   Ay, lord, she will become thy bed[8], I warrant,
           And bring thee forth brave brood[9].
STEPHANO   Monster, I will kill this man. His daughter and I will be
           king and queen – 'save our graces![10] – and Trinculo and thyself shall 100
           be viceroys[11]. Dost thou like the plot, Trinculo?
TRINCULO   Excellent.
STEPHANO   Give me thy hand. I am sorry I beat thee. But while thou
           liv'st, keep a good tongue in thy head.
CALIBAN   Within this half hour will he be asleep, 105
           Wilt thou destroy him then?
STEPHANO   Ay, on mine honour.
ARIEL   This will I tell my master.
CALIBAN   Thou mak'st me merry. I am full of pleasure,
           Let us be jocund[12]. Will you troll the catch[13] 110
           You taught me but whilere[14]?

The three drunkards sing raucously, but Ariel's music strikes fear into Stephano and Trinculo. Caliban urges them not to be afraid, and describes delightful sounds and wonderful dreams. They follow Ariel's music.

✒ 剧情简介：三个醉汉粗声哑嗓地唱起来，但是艾瑞尔的音乐让斯迪法诺和淳丘娄心生恐惧。凯力般劝他们不必害怕，讲述了那些美妙的音乐和奇妙的梦。他们循着艾瑞尔的乐声去了。

1 Caliban's dream (in small groups)

Stephano and Trinculo are terror-stricken by Ariel's music. But Caliban tells them about the delightful noises of the island and his wonderful dreams. His lines 127–35 are among the best known and most haunting (让人难忘) of Shakespeare's verse. Try the following activities to experience the quality of the poetry.

a **Choral** (合唱，合在一起) **speaking** Devise a way of speaking the lines so that everyone in the group shares them. Use echoes and repetitions.

b **Different emotional tones** Explore ways of speaking the lines in different tones of voice, such as full of wonder and awe, sadly, and/or with musical accompaniment.

c **Accompanying gestures** Work out an action or gesture for one key word or image in each line.

Write about it 写作练习
Poetry and prose

As a general rule in Shakespeare's plays, high-status characters speak in verse (poetry), and comic or low-status characters speak in prose. In lines 127–35, the low-status Caliban speaks some of Shakespeare's greatest poetry. These poignant (令人感到痛苦和辛酸) and memorable lines are delivered by a character whom the others call 'monster'. Does this show another side to Caliban? What effects on the audience do these lines have?

- Write one or two paragraphs to answer these questions, referring closely to this part of the script by using embedded quotations. In particular, you should explore the ideas of nature and nurture (先天与后天) that are among the play's thematic concerns. Consider also the language features Shakespeare uses to create his effects (look for metaphors, alliteration, onomatopoeia and repetition of words or ideas).

1 do reason, any reason 做任何合理的事
2 Flout 'em, and scout 'em 嘲弄他们，讥笑他们
3 tabor 泰伯鼓（一种小鼓）
4 same （指相同的曲子）
5 Nobody 隐身人
6 thou beest 你是
7 show ... likeness 显出你的原形
8 airs 曲子
9 twangling instruments 鲁特琴、竖琴之类的弦乐器
10 hum 发出持续的噪声
11 by and by 很快
12 taborer 敲鼓的人
13 lays it on （鼓）敲得很好

STEPHANO   At thy request, monster, I will do reason, any reason[1]. Come
             on, Trinculo, let us sing.
                [*They sing*] Flout 'em, and scout 'em[2]
                    And scout 'em, and flout 'em.   115
                        Thought is free.
CALIBAN   That's not the tune.
                Ariel plays the tune on a tabor[3] and pipe
STEPHANO   What is this same[4]?
TRINCULO   This is the tune of our catch, played by the picture of
             Nobody[5].   120
STEPHANO   If thou beest[6] a man, show thyself in thy likeness[7]: if thou
             beest a devil, take't as thou list.
TRINCULO   O, forgive me my sins!
STEPHANO   He that dies pays all debts! I defy thee! Mercy upon us!
CALIBAN   Art thou afeared?   125
STEPHANO   No, monster, not I.
CALIBAN   Be not afeared; the isle is full of noises,
             Sounds, and sweet airs[8], that give delight and hurt not.
             Sometimes a thousand twangling instruments[9]
             Will hum[10] about mine ears; and sometime voices,   130
             That if I then had waked after long sleep,
             Will make me sleep again; and then in dreaming,
             The clouds methought would open, and show riches
             Ready to drop upon me, that when I waked
             I cried to dream again.   135
STEPHANO   This will prove a brave kingdom to me, where I shall have
             my music for nothing.
CALIBAN   When Prospero is destroyed.
STEPHANO   That shall be by and by[11]: I remember the story.
                                        [*Exit Ariel, playing music*]
TRINCULO   The sound is going away; let's follow it, and after do our   140
             work.
STEPHANO   Lead, monster, we'll follow. I would I could see this taborer[12],
             he lays it on[13].
TRINCULO   [*To Caliban*] Wilt come? I'll follow Stephano.
                                                                Exeunt

Gonzalo and Alonso are wearied by their wanderings. Alonso gives up hope of finding Ferdinand alive. Sebastian and Antonio again plot to murder Alonso. A banquet magically appears, brought in by Prospero's spirits.

剧情简介：艮扎娄和额朗佐四处游荡，疲惫不堪，额朗佐放弃了法迪南还活在人世的信念。塞巴斯田和安托纽再次密谋要杀掉额朗佐。普饶斯普柔的精灵们安排了一场神奇的宴会。

Themes 主题分析

A moral maze and spiritual journey

Some critics argue that lines 2–3 symbolise the spiritual journey of King Alonso. He is wandering in a labyrinth ('maze'), unable to find his way out. As you read on, keep in mind the idea of Alonso travelling on a symbolic journey where he learns, through suffering, to repent of his wrong-doings. During this time, Antonio and Sebastian remain unchanged – and once again they plan to murder Alonso.

a Suggest how lines 11–17 could be played to emphasise the contrast between the villainy (邪恶) of Antonio and Sebastian, and the vulnerability (脆弱性) of Alonso and Gonzalo.

b Describe how the idea of a moral journey – where a person develops morally and spiritually through experience and suffering – helps you understand each of the characters in this scene. What do you predict will happen next?

1 By'r lakin = by our lady （圣母马利亚在上）
2 forth-rights and meanders 笔直和蜿蜒的路
3 By your patience 求您恩准
4 attached 陷入
5 To th'dulling of my spirits 让我感觉没有希望
6 put off 放弃
7 frustrate 徒劳无功
8 for one repulse 因为我们第一次错失良机
9 forgo 放弃
10 purpose 目标（即掉他俩）
11 advantage 良机
12 throughly 好好地，完美地
13 oppressed with travail 饱受旅途劳顿之苦
14 vigilance 警醒，警觉
15 harmony 乐曲

1 Responding to stage directions (in small groups)

a Every production tries to present the stage directions following lines 17 and 19 as dramatically and imaginatively as possible. The stage directions are an exciting opportunity for you to exercise your imagination. Discuss your response to each of the following:

- *'Solemn and strange music'* Compose your own music or find some music that might fit this stage direction.
- *'PROSPERO on the top'* How could this be shown?
- *'invisible'* How would you suggest Prospero's invisibility?
- *'Enter several strange shapes'* Costumes? Appearance?
- *'bringing in a banquet'* How?
- *'dance about it'* How might they dance to the music you created above?
- *'with gentle actions of salutations'* How do they salute the king?
- *'inviting the king, etc. to eat'* With what gestures and movements?
- *'they depart'* Devise a dramatic departure.

b How would you want a set designer, costume designer, composer and sound-effects team to portray the spirits in the most effective way? Try to capture the wonder, mystery and fear that these shapes would inspire, as well as describing how the stage would be set.

Act 3 Scene 3
A remote part of the island

Enter ALONSO, SEBASTIAN, ANTONIO, GONZALO, ADRIAN, FRANCISCO *and others*

GONZALO By'r lakin[1], I can go no further, sir,
My old bones ache. Here's a maze trod indeed
Through forth-rights and meanders[2]. By your patience[3],
I needs must rest me.

ALONSO   Old lord, I cannot blame thee,
Who am myself attached[4] with weariness   5
To th'dulling of my spirits[5]. Sit down, and rest.
Even here I will put off[6] my hope, and keep it
No longer for my flatterer. He is drowned
Whom thus we stray to find, and the sea mocks
Our frustrate[7] search on land. Well, let him go.   10

ANTONIO [*Drawing Sebastian aside*] I am right glad that he's so out of hope.
Do not for one repulse[8] forgo[9] the purpose[10]
That you resolved t'effect.

SEBASTIAN [*To Antonio*]   The next advantage[11]
Will we take throughly[12].

ANTONIO   Let it be tonight;
For now they are oppressed with travail[13], they   15
Will not, nor cannot use such vigilance[14]
As when they're fresh.

SEBASTIAN   I say tonight: no more.

Solemn and strange music, and [*enter*] PROSPERO *on the top, invisible*

ALONSO What harmony[15] is this? my good friends, hark!
GONZALO Marvellous sweet music.

Enter several strange shapes, bringing in a banquet, and dance about it with gentle actions of salutations, and inviting the king, etc. to eat, they depart

The courtiers wonder at what they have seen, saying it resembled something from mythology or travellers' tales. Prospero comments on the evil of Alonso, Sebastian and Antonio, and hints at further marvels.

剧情简介：侍臣们惊叹于眼前的景象，都说这是神话或游记中描绘的场景。普饶斯普柔评价了额朗佐、塞巴斯田、安托纽的罪恶，并暗示还有更多的奇迹出现。

1 Fantastic animals, birds – and tales (in pairs)

Lines 20–49 are rich in echoes of the fantasies of fable and mythology, and the travellers' tales that the early explorers brought home to Shakespeare's England:

- **'unicorns'** (line 22) Mythical horses with a long, spiked horn.
- **'phoenix'** (lines 23–4) A fabulous bird, only one of which lived at any time. It burned itself upon a funeral pyre (火葬用的柴堆) ('throne'), and arose, new-born, from the ashes.
- **'Travellers ne'er did lie'** (lines 26–7) Explorers brought back incredible stories of what they had seen in distant lands. Their fantastic tales were often ridiculed.

a Imagine the characters in this scene are back safely in Milan and are describing what it was like to be on the island, seeing the food and the spirits, and experiencing the magic, the fear, the sadness and the wonder. Do they stick to the truth of the story or do they embellish (润饰，添油加醋) it with more extravagant accounts of their adventures on the island and the creatures they met there? Discuss this in your pairs.

b In role as one of the characters in the script opposite, tell the story to your partner, or write a diary entry for that character in which they reflect on these events.

Write about it 写作练习

You should have been there …

Almost every line in the script opposite (except Prospero's) contains an expression of wonder or disbelief.

- Write down a word or phrase in each line that the actor could emphasise to express a sense of wonder.
- Use these words to create a few headlines for two newspapers – a tabloid and a broadsheet – that are both featuring the story of the travellers' experiences on the island.

---

1 kind keepers 守护天使
2 living drollery 活人演的木偶戏
3 want credit 缺少可信度
4 certes = certainly
5 human generation 人类
6 muse 惊叹
7 dumb discourse 无声的言谈
8 Praise in departing 还有更多值得赞美的呢 / 等事情完全结束再赞美也不迟（谚语）
9 viands 食物
10 stomachs 胃口
11 moutaineers 山民，住在山上的人
12 Dewlapped like bulls 像牛那样脖子下面垂着皮（dewlap指牛等动物颈下发达的皮肤褶皱）
13 such men 这样的人（旅行者报告说他们看到头缩在胸膛里的人，类似例子见《奥赛罗》第一幕第三场第143–144行中的The Anthropophagi）
14 Each … one 每个拿到5倍奖金的远游人（传说远游人出发前交给经纪人一笔钱，若是能回来并证明确实到过目的地就可以得到5倍的钱，否则原来交的钱归经纪人所有）
15 Good warrant of 确凿的证据

ALONSO	Give us kind keepers[1], heavens! What were these?	20
SEBASTIAN	A living drollery[2]! Now I will believe	

That there are unicorns; that in Arabia
There is one tree, the phoenix' throne, one phoenix
At this hour reigning there.

ANTONIO   I'll believe both;
And what does else want credit[3], come to me   25
And I'll be sworn 'tis true. Travellers ne'er did lie,
Though fools at home condemn 'em.

GONZALO   If in Naples
I should report this now, would they believe me?
If I should say I saw such islanders –
For certes[4], these are people of the island –   30
Who though they are of monstrous shape, yet note
Their manners are more gentle, kind, than of
Our human generation[5] you shall find
Many, nay almost any.

PROSPERO [*Aside*]   Honest lord,
Thou hast said well – for some of you there present   35
Are worse than devils.

ALONSO   I cannot too much muse[6],
Such shapes, such gesture, and such sound, expressing –
Although they want the use of tongue – a kind
Of excellent dumb discourse[7].

PROSPERO [*Aside*]   Praise in departing[8].
FRANCISCO They vanished strangely.
SEBASTIAN   No matter, since they   40
Have left their viands[9] behind; for we have stomachs[10].
Wilt please you taste of what is here?

ALONSO   Not I.
GONZALO Faith, sir, you need not fear. When we were boys,
Who would believe that there were mountaineers[11],
Dewlapped like bulls[12], whose throats had hanging at 'em   45
Wallets of flesh? Or that there were such men[13]
Whose heads stood in their breasts? Which now we find
Each putter-out of five for one[14] will bring us
Good warrant of[15].

剧情简介： 额朗佐、塞巴斯田、安托纽正准备用餐，宴会却消失了。艾瑞尔扮成鹰身怪物警告他们自己不会受到伤害。他指控三人密谋推翻了普饶斯普柔并劝他们忏悔。

1 stand to, and feed 开始，用餐
2 harpy 希腊神话中的妖怪，长着女人的头和身子，鸟的翅膀、尾巴和爪子
3 to instrument 掌管
4 this lower world 下界（即人世间）
5 never-surfeited … you 永远填不满的大海都打饱嗝把你们吐出来
6 you … live （由于你们的罪孽）你们不配活在人世间
7 suchlike valour 这种一时之勇
8 Their proper selves 他们自己
9 elements 材料，材质
10 tempered 铸造
11 with … waters 如同抽刀断水一般
12 dowl 细羽绒
13 plume 羽翎
14 fellow ministers 精灵同伴
15 massy 沉重
16 business 目的
17 requit it 这一罪行已遭到报应
18 powers 上天
19 creatures 生灵
20 bereft 夺走
21 Ling'ring perdition 缓缓的毁灭过程
22 any … once 任何立即执行的死刑
23 nothing but 只有
24 heart's sorrow 内心的忏悔
25 clear life ensuing 今后洗心革面的生活

Themes 主题分析

'You are three men of sin'

After accusing the 'men of sin', Ariel declares them 'unfit to live'. He reminds them of their powerlessness, of their overthrow of Prospero, and of the ruin they now face as a result. Ariel tells them that only sorrowful repentance (悔改，忏悔) and virtuous living can save them now ('heart's sorrow, / And a clear life ensuing').

- Practise ways of speaking Ariel's lines for the greatest dramatic effect. Remember, this speech is in iambic pentameter, so listen out for the underlying rhythmical sound of the verse.

Characters 人物分析

Internal monologues (in small groups)

The notion that God's justice would ultimately prevail was pervasive in Shakespeare's day. It was referred to in legal proceedings and in religious sermons and pamphlets.

- Script an internal monologue for each of the characters as they hear what the harpy (Ariel) says to them. What are they thinking and feeling? Are they sorry, or are they hard-hearted and full of excuses?

THE TEMPEST ACT 3 SCENE 3

暴风雨

ALONSO   I will stand to, and feed[1],
                Although my last, no matter, since I feel   50
                The best is past. Brother, my lord the duke,
                Stand to and do as we.

          Thunder and lightning. Enter ARIEL, *like a harpy*[2], *claps his wings upon
          the table, and with a quaint device the banquet vanishes*

ARIEL   You are three men of sin, whom Destiny –
          That hath to instrument[3] this lower world[4],
          And what is in't – the never-surfeited sea   55
          Hath caused to belch up you[5]. And on this island,
          Where man doth not inhabit – you 'mongst men
          Being most unfit to live[6] – I have made you mad;
          And even with suchlike valour[7] men hang and drown
          Their proper selves[8].
                    [*Alonso, Sebastian, Antonio draw their swords*]
                              You fools! I and my fellows   60
          Are ministers of Fate. The elements[9]
          Of whom your swords are tempered[10] may as well
          Wound the loud winds, or with bemocked-at stabs
          Kill the still-closing waters[11], as diminish
          One dowl[12] that's in my plume[13]. My fellow ministers[14]   65
          Are like invulnerable. If you could hurt,
          Your swords are now too massy[15] for your strengths,
          And will not be uplifted. But remember –
          For that's my business[16] to you – that you three
          From Milan did supplant good Prospero;   70
          Exposed unto the sea – which hath requit it[17] –
          Him, and his innocent child; for which foul deed,
          The powers[18], delaying, not forgetting, have
          Incensed the seas and shores, yea, all the creatures[19]
          Against your peace. Thee of thy son, Alonso,   75
          They have bereft[20]; and do pronounce by me
          Ling'ring perdition[21] – worse than any death
          Can be at once[22] – shall step by step attend
          You, and your ways; whose wraths to guard you from –
          Which here, in this most desolate isle, else falls   80
          Upon your heads – is nothing but[23] heart's sorrow[24],
          And a clear life ensuing[25].

Prospero congratulates Ariel on his performance. Alonso, remorseful, decides to drown himself. Sebastian and Antonio leave to fight the spirits. Gonzalo says all three feel guilty. He sends the younger courtiers after them.

剧情简介：普饶斯普柔祝贺艾瑞尔表现出色。额朗佐满是忏悔，决定投海自尽。塞巴斯田和安托纽离开去跟精灵打斗。艮扎娄说三人都心怀愧疚，他派年轻的侍臣去追他们。

1 A splendid performance (in small groups)

Prospero is delighted with how Ariel has played his part ('Bravely': excellently). His other spirit servants have also put on a splendid spectacle ('with good life / And observation strange': vividly and imaginatively). Just what did the 'shapes' (spirits) do in support of Ariel?

- Form a discussion group for the actors playing Prospero's spirit servants. With the director in charge, discuss what movements and facial expressions might work best in this presentation to Alonso, Sebastian and Antonio. It seems that each spirit does something different, using its particular talents ('several kinds').

Write about it 写作练习

Poison and hidden sin (in pairs)

Prospero's plan is working. Gonzalo sees the frenzy (狂暴) of the three men as a long-awaited consequence of their sin, echoing Ariel's message about delayed justice. He uses the **simile** (明喻) (see p. 166) of slow-working poison to describe the way that their sins are now affecting them.

This part of the play also draws from the belief that sinfulness will always torment those who do not repent. In his guilt, Alonso feels accused by Nature and he experiences a great sense of remorse for wronging Prospero. He believes he has been punished for this by the death of his son Ferdinand, and decides that death by drowning must also be his destiny.

- Discuss how the imagery in the script opposite helps us to understand what Alonso is feeling. Then write one or two paragraphs to describe Alonso's guilt and to explore the effect of the language Gonzalo uses when he sees Alonso's despair.

2 Do Antonio and Sebastian feel guilt? (in pairs)

Sebastian and Antonio are determined to resist. They make no clear expression of guilt, showing only a desire to fight.

a Talk together about whether you think Sebastian and Antonio should show any acknowledgement of guilt. If so, how (for example, by leaving a long pause before speaking 'But one fiend at a time').

b Write a paragraph explaining whether you think Sebastian and Antonio feel any guilt. Use quotations from the script and consider Gonzalo's and Alonso's responses as well as Sebastian's and Antonio's words.

---

1 *mocks and mows* 扮鬼脸、做手势嘲讽
2 figure 角色
3 devouring 吞没一切
4 bated 遗漏
5 So 同样
6 with good life 生动，活灵活现
7 observation strange 认认真真
8 meaner ministers 低等精灵
9 several kinds 各自（扮演）不同的角色
10 distractions 思想上的冲突和烦闷
11 fits 发作
12 billows 波涛
13 deep and dreadful organ-pipe 声音低沉而可怕的风琴
14 bass my trespass （以低沉的声音）吼出我的过失
15 Therefore 为此
16 i'th'ooze is bedded 躺在海底的淤泥里
17 plummet sounded 用铅锤测量线测过
18 fiend 恶魔
19 legion 军团
20 second 支持者，助手
21 desperate 绝望
22 'gins = begins
23 bite 侵蚀
24 of suppler joints 腿脚灵活
25 ecstasy 疯狂

THE TEMPEST ACT 3 SCENE 3

暴风雨

He vanishes in thunder; then, to soft music, enter the shapes again, and dance, with mocks and mows[1], and [then depart] carrying out the table

PROSPERO	Bravely the figure[2] of this harpy hast thou	
	Performed, my Ariel; a grace it had devouring[3].	
	Of my instruction hast thou nothing bated[4]	85
	In what thou hadst to say. So[5], with good life[6]	
	And observation strange[7], my meaner ministers[8]	
	Their several kinds[9] have done. My high charms work,	
	And these, mine enemies, are all knit up	
	In their distractions[10]. They now are in my power;	90
	And in these fits[11] I leave them, while I visit	
	Young Ferdinand, whom they suppose is drowned,	
	And his and mine loved darling. *[Exit]*	
GONZALO	I'th'name of something holy, sir, why stand you	
	In this strange stare?	
ALONSO	O, it is monstrous: monstrous!	95
	Methought the billows[12] spoke and told me of it,	
	The winds did sing it to me, and the thunder,	
	That deep and dreadful organ-pipe[13], pronounced	
	The name of Prosper. It did bass my trespass[14];	
	Therefore[15] my son i'th'ooze is bedded[16]; and	100
	I'll seek him deeper than e'er plummet sounded[17],	
	And with him there lie mudded. *Exit*	
SEBASTIAN	But one fiend[18] at a time, I'll fight their legions[19] o'er.	
ANTONIO	I'll be thy second[20].	
	Exeunt [Sebastian and Antonio]	
GONZALO	All three of them are desperate[21]. Their great guilt,	105
	Like poison given to work a great time after,	
	Now 'gins[22] to bite[23] the spirits. I do beseech you,	
	That are of suppler joints[24], follow them swiftly,	
	And hinder them from what this ecstasy[25]	
	May now provoke them to.	
ADRIAN	Follow, I pray you.	110
	Exeunt	

The Tempest
暴风雨

Looking back at Act 3   "第3幕" 回顾
Activities for groups or individuals

1 Spectacle and drama

Act 3 ends very dramatically. There is the spectacle of Ariel's fellow spirits, who appear as 'strange shapes' and dance, make 'gentle actions of salutations', pull faces ('mocks and mows') and set out a banquet for the courtiers. There is also the description of imagined creatures and spectacular discoveries during voyages of exploration. In addition, there is the drama of Ariel's appearance as a harpy, the frenzied reaction of the 'three men of sin' and their hurried exit off the stage.

- In role as a director, imagine you are having a conversation with a theatre critic. Describe how you would stage the ending of this act. Consider how you would link spectacle and drama with the main themes of the play.
- Script the conversation between these two people. Make sure the theatre critic asks the director some interesting questions about costume, stage design, special effects and the impact on the audience.

2 Three scenes, three minutes

Devise a mini version of Act 3, expressing the essence of each scene in one minute. To prepare, read through the summaries at the top of each left-hand page in Act 3.

3 Different views of the island

a Write a sentence that begins: 'I see this island as …' for each of the following characters at this point in the play: Prospero, Miranda, Caliban, Ariel, Alonso, Antonio, Ferdinand, Stephano, Trinculo, Gonzalo.

b Choose two characters and create a past for them, which fills in the gaps of our knowledge of them so far. Write a first-person account of what their life may have been like. Your aim is to imaginatively re-create their past in order to understand their present behaviour and motivations.

4 Thematic focus

a Look back at the 'Themes' boxes in this act. In small groups, talk about these themes. Draw a chart to show how they interrelate, and support your chart with quotations and examples. Remember that the following themes are linked: the relationship between appearance and reality, illusion and magic, imprisonment and freedom, and how selfishness and ambition relate to authority and power.

b Present a case to the rest of the class. What is the most important single theme? What are the most important combinations of themes? Why did you reach these conclusions? If you were staging a production of the play, which themes would you highlight, and what elements of stagecraft would you employ to emphasise them?

5 Control and surveillance (监视)

Prospero's control and Ariel's surveillance link all three plot strands ([计划、故事等的]部分) in the play (Miranda and Ferdinand; Caliban and the drunken servants; Alonso and the courtiers).

- List all the examples of Prospero's control and Ariel's surveillance in Act 3. Considering what you know about their plots, write out a detailed prediction for what might happen in the next act. Do you think that Prospero will have his enemies killed? Will he enchant them further? Or will he forgive them?
- As you write, consider what you know about the characters so far. Also, think about the genre of the play and conduct further research into the characteristics of a romance play. Justify your predictions about Act 4 by explaining your reasons with reference to quotations and examples from the first three acts of the play.

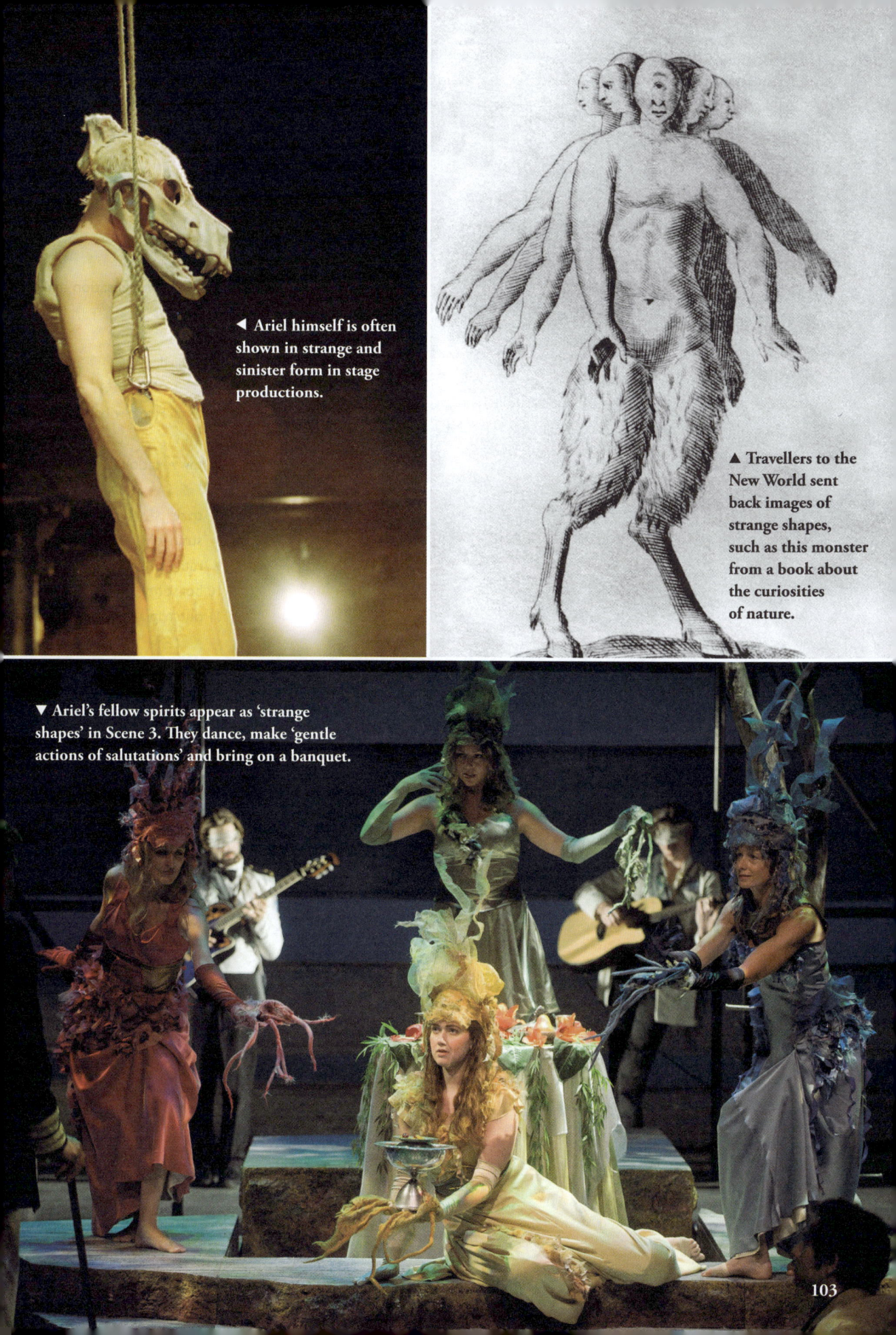

◀ Ariel himself is often shown in strange and sinister form in stage productions.

▲ Travellers to the New World sent back images of strange shapes, such as this monster from a book about the curiosities of nature.

▼ Ariel's fellow spirits appear as 'strange shapes' in Scene 3. They dance, make 'gentle actions of salutations' and bring on a banquet.

Prospero tells Ferdinand that he has successfully endured the testing of his love, and can therefore marry Miranda. Prospero warns against sex before marriage: it will bring misery.

剧情简介：普饶斯普柔告诉法迪南他经受住了爱情的考验，可以娶蜜兰达为妻，同时警告二人不可在婚前有性行为，否则会有苦难。

Characters 人物分析

Prospero: simple pride or greedy ownership? (in pairs)

Act 4 begins with two complex speeches by Prospero. In lines 1–11, he tells Ferdinand that he has proven his love for Miranda, and he gives the couple his blessing as a reward.

a   Read Prospero's words carefully. Do you think he is being over-protective ('that for which I live'), or are his words completely understandable given the circumstances? Why does he refer to her as 'a third of [his] own life'? Discuss this with your partner. Remember that in Shakespeare's day, a girl was considered to be her father's property until she was married.

b   Talk together about how Prospero's speeches opposite add to our understanding of this character. Write down your conclusions to help you with the next activity.

Write about it 写作练习

Act convincingly

In lines 14–22 (from 'But'), Prospero warns Ferdinand not to have sexual intercourse with Miranda before they marry. If he does, says Prospero, discord and hatred will follow. He repeats the warning later, in lines 51–4.

Many people think that Prospero's words show that *The Tempest* was specially performed at the wedding celebrations in 1612–13 of Princess Elizabeth, daughter of King James. At the time, there was a strong belief that premarital sex was undesirable (although many women – including Shakespeare's wife – were pregnant on their wedding day).

- Imagine that you are directing *The Tempest*. The actor playing Prospero writes you a private note: 'I'm having real problems with how to deliver this speech. It doesn't feel right just to play Prospero as such a strict father here, but his words are pretty harsh. I wonder what is motivating him to talk like this. Will you write a paragraph or two to help me, please?' Write your reply.

1   austerely   严厉
2   punished you   使你遭罪
3   Your compensation makes amends   你得到的补偿足以弥补
4   a third … life   我生命的三分之一（即蜜兰达）
5   tender to thy hand   托付给你
6   thy vexations   你所受的皮肉折磨
7   trials   考验
8   strangely   令人诧异
9   ratify   认可
10   boast her of   夸耀她
11   outstrip all praise   超越所有赞美之词
12   halt   蹒跚
13   against an oracle   即便违背神谕
14   purchased   赢得
15   virgin-knot   贞操
16   sanctimonious ceremonies   圣洁的婚礼仪式
17   aspersion   甘露
18   make this contract grow   让你们的婚姻开花结果
19   loathly   令人厌恶
20   Hymen   亥门（希腊神话中的婚姻之神，手里擎着火炬）

Act 4 Scene 1
Near Prospero's cave

Enter PROSPERO, FERDINAND *and* MIRANDA

PROSPERO [*To Ferdinand*] If I have too austerely[1] punished you[2]
Your compensation makes amends[3], for I
Have given you here a third of mine own life[4],
Or that for which I live; who once again
I tender to thy hand[5]. All thy vexations[6]
Were but my trials[7] of thy love, and thou
Hast strangely[8] stood the test. Here, afore heaven,
I ratify[9] this my rich gift. O Ferdinand,
Do not smile at me, that I boast her of[10],
For thou shalt find she will outstrip all praise[11]
And make it halt[12] behind her.

FERDINAND I do believe it against an oracle[13].

PROSPERO Then, as my gift, and thine own acquisition
Worthily purchased[14], take my daughter. But
If thou dost break her virgin-knot[15] before
All sanctimonious ceremonies[16] may
With full and holy rite be ministered,
No sweet aspersion[17] shall the heavens let fall
To make this contract grow[18]; but barren hate,
Sour-eyed disdain and discord shall bestrew
The union of your bed with weeds so loathly[19]
That you shall hate it both. Therefore take heed,
As Hymen's[20] lamps shall light you.

Ferdinand says that he will never do anything to dishonour his marriage with Miranda. Prospero sends Ariel to arrange another dramatic spectacle, then again warns Ferdinand against passion.

剧情简介：法迪南说他决不会让自己与蜜兰达的婚姻有任何污点。普饶斯普柔派艾瑞尔安排另一个盛大场景，再次警告法迪南要控制情欲。

Stagecraft 导演技巧

Ariel: a surrogate (替代的) child? (in small groups)

The relationship between Prospero and Ariel is a fascinating one. Are they simply master and servant, or something more complex? Has Ariel observed Miranda's growing independence and moved in to take her place as Prospero's surrogate child? Think about how Prospero and Ariel might feel towards each other by this stage of the play.

- Discuss how line 48 ('Do you love me master? No?') should be spoken: sadly, fearfully, playfully, or in some other manner?
- Decide how Prospero should speak his reply in line 49 ('Dearly, my delicate Ariel.')

1 A second warning (in pairs)

In lines 51–2, Prospero speaks again to Ferdinand about his conduct towards Miranda, telling him to keep his desires in check ('Do not give dalliance / Too much the rein').

a Talk together about whether you think something in Prospero's character provokes this second warning, or whether Ferdinand and Miranda are giving 'dalliance the rein' (perhaps behaving too intimately too soon). Which seems more likely?

b Imagine that you are a counsellor advising Miranda and Ferdinand on their relationship. Write a short letter to both of them outlining what you think are the key issues and how they might be resolved.

▼ In the 2010 film adaptation of *The Tempest*, Prospero became Prospera and was played by a woman. The director explored the complex relationship between this character and Ariel (played by a man), asking the audience to think about gender, age and emotional attachments.

1 fair issue 漂亮的后代
2 With … now 如果这份感情还保持现在的热度
3 murkiest den 最昏暗的藏身洞
4 oppòrtune 方便，合适
5 suggestion 诱惑
6 worser genius 坏天使
7 edge 食欲的强烈
8 that day 结婚那天
9 foundered 跛
10 When … below 当太阳神 (Phoebus) 的马停下来（法迪南的意思是婚礼那天时间的流逝将放慢）
11 potent 强大
12 meaner fellows 等级低的同类
13 last service （指那消失的宴会）
14 the rabble 一群精灵
15 incite 催促
16 Some vanity of mine art 魔法产生的幻觉
17 Presently = immediately
18 twink 眨眼
19 mop and mow 扮鬼脸做手势
20 conceive 明白
21 true 可敬
22 dalliance 轻浮的举止
23 abstemious 节制
24 good night your vow 同承诺告别（即失信）

FERDINAND   As I hope
              For quiet days, fair issue¹, and long life,
              With such love as 'tis now², the murkiest den³,   25
              The most oppòrtune⁴ place, the strong'st suggestion⁵
              Our worser genius⁶ can, shall never melt
              Mine honour into lust, to take away
              The edge⁷ of that day's⁸ celebration,
              When I shall think or Phoebus' steeds are foundered⁹,   30
              Or night kept chained below¹⁰.
PROSPERO   Fairly spoke.
              Sit then, and talk with her, she is thine own.
              What, Ariel! My industrious servant Ariel!

                        Enter ARIEL

ARIEL   What would my potent¹¹ master? Here I am.
PROSPERO   Thou and thy meaner fellows¹² your last service¹³   35
              Did worthily perform; and I must use you
              In such another trick. Go bring the rabble¹⁴ –
              O'er whom I give thee power – here, to this place.
              Incite¹⁵ them to quick motion, for I must
              Bestow upon the eyes of this young couple   40
              Some vanity of mine art¹⁶. It is my promise,
              And they expect it from me.
ARIEL   Presently¹⁷?
PROSPERO   Ay: with a twink¹⁸.
ARIEL   Before you can say 'come' and 'go',
              And breathe twice, and cry 'so, so',   45
              Each one tripping on his toe,
              Will be here with mop and mow¹⁹.
              Do you love me master? No?
PROSPERO   Dearly, my delicate Ariel. Do not approach
              Till thou dost hear me call.
ARIEL   Well; I conceive²⁰.   *Exit*   50
PROSPERO   [*To Ferdinand*] Look thou be true²¹! Do not give dalliance²²
              Too much the rein. The strongest oaths are straw
              To th'fire i'th'blood. Be more abstemious²³,
              Or else good night your vow²⁴.

Ferdinand promises that his love will overcome his lust. The masque begins. Iris describes Ceres's fertility, and commands her to join Juno in celebration. Ceres asks why she must obey.

剧情简介：法迪南承诺他的爱将会克服情欲。假面舞会开始，爱蕊丝描述熹蕊丝的富饶并命令她与朱娜一道庆祝，熹蕊丝反问为何她必须服从。

Stagecraft 导演技巧
Making it spectacular (in threes)

Masques were spectacular court entertainments, rich in elaborate scenery and gorgeous costumes – much like big production musicals, or blockbuster (大片) movies of today. They involved music, poetry and dance, as well as visual effects. They also used complex stage machinery to create striking illusions.

The masque that Prospero has arranged to impress Ferdinand and Miranda symbolises two major themes of *The Tempest*:

- **Harmony after the storm** The appearance of Iris, goddess of the rainbow, expresses the peace that follows a tempest. Just as a rainbow appears after a storm, so Iris herself is an emblem (象征) of Prospero's plan to see Ferdinand and Miranda married. This union will reconcile (使和解) Milan and Naples after many years of trouble. Notice the words that link Iris to the rainbow: 'watery arch', 'many-coloured', 'blue bow', 'Rich scarf'.
- **Bounty and fertility** Ceres, goddess of the harvest, symbolises the riches that will result from the wedding. In lines 60–9, Iris describes the fertile natural world over which Ceres reigns.

a Imagine you are the costume designer for a new stage production of the play. Sketch costumes for both Iris and Ceres. What would you want the costumes to convey to the other actors, and to the audience? Label and annotate your ideas in discussion with each other. This plan could make an eye-catching wall display.

b Together, write 100 words for the production's programme, in which you outline the symbolism of your designs to a reader. Keep a copy of this in your Director's Journal.

1	warrant	答应，做出保证
2	Abates	减弱
3	The white … liver	我心中那冰雪般的纯洁（即蜜兰达的圣洁）削减了我身体中的激情
4	Well	说得好
5	a corollary	多了一个
6	want	缺少
7	pertly	立即
8	IRIS	彩虹女神
9	Ceres	大地和谷物女神
10	bounteous	富饶，慷慨
11	leas	牧场
12	turfy	绿草覆盖的
13	meads	草场
14	thatched with stover	堆满干草
15	pionèd	挖出
16	twillèd	编织
17	spongy	潮湿
18	hest	命令
19	betrims	装点
20	broom-groves	金雀花丛
21	dismissèd bachelor	失恋的单身汉
22	lass-lorn	没有（女性）恋人
23	pole-clipped	用木桩围起来
24	sea-marge	海边
25	dost air	呼吸新鲜空气以放松
26	queen o'th'sky	天后朱娜（Juno）
27	amain	快速
28	saffron	（金）黄色
29	wings	翅膀（也指彩虹的边缘）
30	bosky acres	树林

1 How do the characters respond?

The spectacle of the masque suddenly makes an audience of the other characters on stage, and Prospero becomes a director as well as a magician.

- If you were directing the play, where would you place the onstage audience at this point in the play? To what extent would you ask them to break down the 'fourth wall' and interact with the spirits? Write brief stage directions to each of the actors. Is Prospero proud of his work? Are the others impressed or afraid?

THE TEMPEST ACT 4 SCENE 1
暴风雨

FERDINAND   I warrant[1] you, sir,
The white cold virgin snow upon my heart   55
Abates[2] the ardour of my liver[3].

PROSPERO   Well[4].
Now come, my Ariel – bring a corollary[5],
Rather than want[6] a spirit; appear, and pertly[7].
Soft music
No tongue! All eyes! Be silent!

Enter IRIS[8]

IRIS   Ceres[9], most bounteous[10] lady, thy rich leas[11]   60
Of wheat, rye, barley, vetches, oats and peas;
Thy turfy[12] mountains, where live nibbling sheep,
And flat meads[13] thatched with stover[14], them to keep;
Thy banks with pionèd[15] and twillèd[16] brims,
Which spongy[17] April at thy hest[18] betrims[19]   65
To make cold nymphs chaste crowns; and thy broom-groves[20],
Whose shadow the dismissèd bachelor[21] loves,
Being lass-lorn[22]; thy pole-clipped[23] vineyard,
And thy sea-marge[24], sterile and rocky-hard,
Where thou thyself dost air[25]: the queen o'th'sky[26],   70
Whose watery arch and messenger am I,
Bids thee leave these, and with her sovereign grace,
Here on this grass-plot, in this very place
To come and sport. Her peacocks fly amain[27].
Approach, rich Ceres, her to entertain.   75

Enter CERES

CERES   Hail, many-coloured messenger, that ne'er
Dost disobey the wife of Jupiter;
Who, with thy saffron[28] wings[29], upon my flowers
Diffusest honey drops, refreshing showers,
And with each end of thy blue bow dost crown   80
My bosky acres[30], and my unshrubbed down,
Rich scarf to my proud earth. Why hath thy queen
Summoned me hither, to this short-grazed green?

Iris tells Ceres that they are meeting to celebrate a wedding. She assures Ceres that Venus and Cupid will not be present, and that they have failed to bewitch Ferdinand and Miranda. Juno and Ceres sing a blessing.

剧情简介：爱蕊丝告诉熹蕊丝她们会面是为了庆祝婚礼，她保证维纳斯和丘比特不会出席，他们没能使法迪南和蜜兰莐中他们的魔法。朱娜和熹蕊丝唱诵了祝福歌。

1 Classical mythology – a presentation (in sevens)

Like most Jacobean (具有詹姆斯一世时期风格) entertainment, Prospero's masque draws heavily upon classical mythology.

a Using the Internet, or any other resources available to you, carry out some research into Jacobean masques. Find out what they consisted of and why they were so popular in Shakespeare's day. Using this research and the information on page 108, put together a presentation to deliver to the class.

b Allocate each member of your group a character from the masque in the script opposite (Ceres, Iris, Juno, Venus, Cupid, Hymen). Find out more about these figures from mythology, and suggest how each one has a particular symbolic significance in *The Tempest*.

c Stage your own performance of the masque.

1 **estate** 赠予，馈赠
2 **Venus** 爱神维纳斯
3 **her son** 她儿子（即丘比特 [Cupid]）
4 **dusky Dis** 冥王蒂斯（又称普路托 [Pluto]）
5 **blind boy** 瞎眼的男孩（丘比特常被刻画为蒙着眼或瞎眼的孩子）
6 **scandalled** 丑闻缠身
7 **forsworn** 发誓断绝
8 **society** 社交圈
9 **her deity** (指维纳斯)
10 **Cutting the clouds** 分开云层
11 **Paphos** 帕福斯（位于塞浦路斯，是维纳斯崇拜者之城）
12 **wanton charm** 邪恶的咒语
13 **no bed-right shall be paid** 不得同房
14 **Mars's hot minion** 战神马斯那个放荡的情妇（指维纳斯）
15 **returned** 返回
16 **waspish-headed son** 头上长毒刺/恶毒的儿子（指丘比特）
17 **be a boy right out** 只做男孩而不是神

18 **gait** 步态（朱娜以风度高雅闻名）
19 **Go with me** 跟我一起
20 **issue** 儿女
21 **Long continuance** 长寿
22 **increasing** 增加（儿女，感情）
23 **foison** 大丰收
24 **garners** 粮仓

IRIS	A contract of true love to celebrate,	
	And some donation freely to estate[1]	85
	On the blest lovers.	
CERES	Tell me, heavenly bow,	
	If Venus[2] or her son[3], as thou dost know,	
	Do now attend the queen? Since they did plot	
	The means that dusky Dis[4] my daughter got,	
	Her and her blind boy's[5] scandalled[6] company	90
	I have forsworn[7].	
IRIS	Of her society[8]	
	Be not afraid. I met her deity[9]	
	Cutting the clouds[10] towards Paphos[11], and her son	
	Dove-drawn with her. Here thought they to have done	
	Some wanton charm[12] upon this man and maid,	95
	Whose vows are, that no bed-right shall be paid[13]	
	Till Hymen's torch be lighted – but in vain.	
	Mars's hot minion[14] is returned[15] again;	
	Her waspish-headed son[16] has broke his arrows,	
	Swears he will shoot no more, but play with sparrows,	100
	And be a boy right out[17].	
	[JUNO *descends*]	
	Highest queen of state,	
	Great Juno comes, I know her by her gait[18].	
JUNO	How does my bounteous sister? Go with me[19]	
	To bless this twain, that they may prosperous be,	
	And honoured in their issue[20].	105
	[*Singing*] Honour, riches, marriage-blessing,	
	Long continuance[21], and increasing[22],	
	Hourly joys be still upon you,	
	Juno sings her blessings on you.	
[CERES]	[*Singing*] Earth's increase, and foison[23] plenty,	110
	Barns and garners[24] never empty,	
	Vines, with clust'ring bunches growing,	
	Plants, with goodly burden bowing;	
	Spring come to you at the farthest,	
	In the very end of harvest.	115
	Scarcity and want shall shun you,	
	Ceres' blessing so is on you.	

Prospero says that the spirits are enacting his fantasies. Ferdinand is full of happy wonder. Harvesters and nymphs dance at Iris's command, but are ordered off by Prospero when he remembers Caliban's plot.

剧情简介：普饶斯普柔说精灵正实现他的幻想，法迪南又惊又喜。收割庄稼的人和仙子在爱蕊丝的命令下跳舞，但被普饶斯普柔大声喝止，因为他想起了凯力般的阴谋。

Characters 人物分析

Ferdinand: shallow, deep or deluded (被骗)?
(in small groups)

In lines 122–4, Ferdinand refers to the island as a 'paradise'. What does this say about him?

- Is he genuinely impressed by his surroundings and the events that have taken place since his arrival? Is he saying that having such a father, and a dutiful wife, are the most important things in a man's life? Or do you think he has fallen under Prospero's spell? Talk about your views of Ferdinand at this point in the play.

1 Choreographing (舞蹈设计) a large cast

The arrival of 'certain reapers' and 'nymphs' means that the stage is suddenly very busy. This presents challenges for the whole cast.

- Imagine that you are in charge of choreography. Draw up a plan of the stage in which you give clear guidelines about where all the actors should be positioned, and when and how they should move. Make sure your design is clearly annotated.

Stagecraft 导演技巧

Making a mini-masque (in large groups)

a Bringing together all the work you have done on the masque, write out a version of Prospero's entertainment in modern prose. Make sure you stick closely to Shakespeare's meaning while still bringing the language up to date.

b Using your modern script, stage your own mini-masque for the rest of the class. Members of your group should take on the roles of Ceres, Iris and Juno, as well as director. You could adapt your script using one or more of the following techniques:

- Explore the story being told through movement, tableaux and sound only.
- Perform the story with a narrator reading out the modern script and a small cast acting out the words.
- Introduce a range of props, and incorporate them into the performance.
- Experiment with other sounds, including singing, clapping or musical instruments.
- Add more characters to reflect the growing scale of the masque.

---

1 Harmonious charmingly 神奇地和谐
2 confines 牢房，禁闭之地
3 fancies 幻景
4 wondered 能创造奇幻
5 marred 破坏，毁掉
6 naiads of the windring brooks 蜿蜒溪流中的仙水
7 sedged crowns 芦苇编的王冠
8 ever-harmless 永远天真无邪
9 crisp 涟漪
10 temperate 圣洁温和
11 sicklemen 收割庄稼的人
12 furrow 庄稼地
13 fresh 纯洁
14 footing 跳舞
15 *properly habited* 穿戴整齐
16 minute （定好的）时刻
17 Avoid! 退下！/ 赶紧离开
18 *heavily* 难过地

THE TEMPEST ACT 4 SCENE 1
暴风雨

FERDINAND   This is a most majestic vision, and
             Harmonious charmingly[1]. May I be bold
             To think these spirits?
PROSPERO   Spirits, which by mine art   120
             I have from their confines[2] called to enact
             My present fancies[3].
FERDINAND   Let me live here ever;
             So rare a wondered[4] father, and a wife,
             Makes this place paradise.
                Juno and Ceres whisper, and send Iris on employment
PROSPERO   Sweet now, silence.
             Juno and Ceres whisper seriously,   125
             There's something else to do. Hush, and be mute,
             Or else our spell is marred[5].
IRIS   You nymphs called naiads of the windring brooks[6],
             With your sedged crowns[7], and ever-harmless[8] looks,
             Leave your crisp[9] channels, and on this green land   130
             Answer your summons, Juno does command.
             Come, temperate[10] nymphs, and help to celebrate
             A contract of true love. Be not too late.

                         Enter certain nymphs

             You sun-burned sicklemen[11] of August weary,
             Come hither from the furrow[12], and be merry,   135
             Make holiday; your rye-straw hats put on,
             And these fresh[13] nymphs encounter every one
             In country footing[14].

   *Enter certain reapers, properly habited[15]. They join with the nymphs, in a
   graceful dance, towards the end whereof Prospero starts suddenly and
                              speaks*

PROSPERO   [*Aside*] I had forgot that foul conspiracy
             Of the beast Caliban and his confederates   140
             Against my life. The minute[16] of their plot
             Is almost come. [*To the spirits*] Well done! Avoid![17] No more.
             To a strange, hollow and confused noise [the spirits] heavily[18] vanish

113

The lovers comment on Prospero's anger. Prospero tells Ferdinand not to be troubled, because everything in the masque is ephemeral, and will fade. Prospero questions Ariel about Caliban and his accomplices.

剧情简介：这对恋人谈论普饶斯普柔的愤怒，普饶斯普柔告诉法迪南不必烦恼，假面舞会上的一切都是昙花一现，终将幻灭。普饶斯普柔向艾瑞尔询问凯力般和他的同伙。

Characters 人物分析

Prospero's anger: real or pretended? (in threes)

Prospero is a magician with great powers: he is able to control the elements and command the spirit world. Yet the thought of Caliban's plot seems to trouble him deeply. Why?

- Draw up a list of possible reasons for his concerns. While doing so, think about whether he might just be pretending to be angry.
- Write notes for an actor playing Prospero, explaining your interpretation and suggesting how he should appear in the transition from the end of the masque up to line 158.

Language in the play 剧中语言

Prospero's famous speech

Lines 148–58 ('Our revels … sleep') are full of words with strong theatrical associations: 'revels', 'actors', 'baseless fabric' (the temporary scenery for a pageant play), 'globe', 'pageant', 'rack' (clouds painted on scenery). Just as the actors have vanished into thin air, so too will everyone and everything else. The lines have become famous as a metaphor (隐喻) for the impermanence (短暂，无常) of human life.

a Talk together about the mood of Prospero's speech. Why does it appear to be so elegiac (悲哀) (an elegy is a sad or reflective poem or song)?

b Work out how an actor could present the lines on stage. Suggest the tone of voice, which words to emphasise, where the actor should pause, and so on.

c You will find lots of versions of this speech online (it was even used in the opening ceremony of the 2012 London Olympics and the closing of the Paralympics). Which version do you feel is the most effective and why? Write down your thoughts in your Director's Journal.

d Why do you think this speech has proven to be so popular? Create a presentation in which you explain the power and significance of these ten lines.

e This is a beautiful speech, filled with rich images. Pick out three of your favourite phrases and explain why they are so striking.

1 passion 激情
2 works 使激动
3 distempered 暴躁
4 movèd sort 担忧的样子
5 revels 欢庆
6 foretold you 之前告诉你了
7 baseless fabric 无地基的建筑
8 all which it inherit 大地继承的一切
9 pageant 戏中的场景
10 rack 一丝烟云
11 on = of
12 vexed 懊恼
13 infirmity 缺点，疾病
14 beating 纷扰
15 Come with a thought! 刚一想就来了！
16 cleave to 遵从
17 prepare to meet 准备与……正面遭遇
18 presented 扮演
19 varlets 恶棍，混蛋

FERDINAND　　This is strange. Your father's in some passion[1]
　　　　　　That works[2] him strongly.
MIRANDA　　　　　　　　　　　Never till this day
　　　　　　Saw I him touched with anger so distempered[3].　　　　　　145
PROSPERO　　You do look, my son, in a movèd sort[4],
　　　　　　As if you were dismayed. Be cheerful, sir,
　　　　　　Our revels[5] now are ended; these our actors,
　　　　　　As I foretold you[6], were all spirits, and
　　　　　　Are melted into air, into thin air;　　　　　　　　　　　　150
　　　　　　And like the baseless fabric[7] of this vision,
　　　　　　The cloud-capped towers, the gorgeous palaces,
　　　　　　The solemn temples, the great globe itself,
　　　　　　Yea, all which it inherit[8], shall dissolve,
　　　　　　And like this insubstantial pageant[9] faded　　　　　　　155
　　　　　　Leave not a rack[10] behind. We are such stuff
　　　　　　As dreams are made on[11]; and our little life
　　　　　　Is rounded with a sleep. Sir, I am vexed[12].
　　　　　　Bear with my weakness, my old brain is troubled.
　　　　　　Be not disturbed with my infirmity[13].　　　　　　　　　　160
　　　　　　If you be pleased, retire into my cell,
　　　　　　And there repose. A turn or two I'll walk
　　　　　　To still my beating[14] mind.
FERDINAND *and* MIRANDA　　　　　We wish your peace
　　　　　　　　　　　　　　　　　Exeunt [*Ferdinand and Miranda*]
PROSPERO　　[*Summoning Ariel*] Come with a thought![15] – [*To Ferdinand
　　　　　　and Miranda*] I thank thee. – Ariel, come!

　　　　　　　　　　　　Enter ARIEL

ARIEL　　　　Thy thoughts I cleave to[16]. What's thy pleasure?
PROSPERO　　　　　　　　　　　　　　　　Spirit,　　　　　　　　165
　　　　　　We must prepare to meet[17] with Caliban.
ARIEL　　　　Ay, my commander. When I presented[18] Ceres
　　　　　　I thought t'have told thee of it, but I feared
　　　　　　Lest I might anger thee.
PROSPERO　　Say again, where didst thou leave these varlets[19]?　　　170

Ariel describes how he led Caliban, Stephano and Trinculo into a stinking pool. Prospero plans to punish them further, and reflects that Caliban is unteachable. Ariel hangs up gaudy clothes as a trap.

剧情简介：艾瑞尔讲述他如何把凯力般、斯迪法诺、淳丘娄引入一个臭泥塘。普饶斯普柔计划继续严惩他们并表示凯力般不可教化。艾瑞尔挂起花哨的衣服来布置陷阱。

1 Ariel's torments: funny or cruel? (in small groups)

Lines 171–84 (to 'O'er-stunk their feet') are full of action and, like other episodes in the play, can be interpreted as both cruel and funny. Work on the following activities to explore how Ariel tormented the would-be assassins.

a One person reads Ariel's lines slowly. The other three members of the group act out the actions of Caliban, Stephano and Trinculo. Depending on the size of your groups, another person could play Prospero – how would he respond to what Ariel is telling him?

b Take it in turns to speak aloud just two or three words from each line in Ariel's speech. Choose the words that you feel convey most powerfully what happened to the conspirators.

Themes 主题分析

Nature versus nurture (whole class)

Prospero's lines 188–90 explore an important theme of the play: can nurture (education, civilisation) change nature? Prospero regrets that, in spite of all his training and art, he has been unable to improve Caliban's nature ('a born devil'). He has succeeded in educating Miranda, but has failed with Caliban. So Prospero decides that he must further punish Caliban and the others ('plague them all, / Even to roaring').

- Hold a class debate on this statement: 'Nature, not nurture, is the major influence on our lives'. One group should argue that the natures we are born with determine what happens to us. The opposing group should argue that education can have a transformative effect on our lives. You might begin the debate by stating whether you think that human nature is essentially good or bad – or neither.
- Before the debate, take a vote on who agrees or disagrees with the statement. Take another vote after the debate has ended. Ask those who changed their minds to explain which arguments persuaded them.

1 red-hot 脸红脖子粗
2 valour 一时之勇
3 smote 打击，挥拳打
4 bending 一心想
5 unbacked colts 未驯服（未被人骑过）的马
6 Advanced their eyelids 睁大了双眼
7 lowing 哞哞声
8 Toothed … thorns 带锯齿的野蔷薇、扎人的金雀花和刺人的荆棘（furze和gorse都指荆豆或金雀花）
9 frail shins 脆弱的胫骨
10 filthy mantled 被污泥烂草覆盖
11 O'er-stunk their feet 比他们的脚还臭
12 trumpery 艳俗的衣物（与193行的glistering apparel 同义）
13 stale 诱捕，做诱饵
14 cankers 感染，溃烂
15 Even to roaring 直到他们鬼哭狼嚎
16 played the jack with us 耍弄了我们
17 in great indignation 很气愤

ARIEL	I told you, sir, they were red-hot[1] with drinking,
	So full of valour[2] that they smote[3] the air
	For breathing in their faces, beat the ground
	For kissing of their feet; yet always bending[4]
	Towards their project. Then I beat my tabor, 175
	At which like unbacked colts[5] they pricked their ears,
	Advanced their eyelids[6], lifted up their noses
	As they smelt music. So I charmed their ears
	That calf-like they my lowing[7] followed, through
	Toothed briars, sharp furzes, pricking gorse and thorns[8], 180
	Which entered their frail shins[9]. At last I left them
	I'th'filthy mantled[10] pool beyond your cell,
	There dancing up to th'chins, that the foul lake
	O'er-stunk their feet[11].
PROSPERO	This was well done, my bird!
	Thy shape invisible retain thou still. 185
	The trumpery[12] in my house, go bring it hither
	For stale[13] to catch these thieves.
ARIEL	I go, I go. *Exit*
PROSPERO	A devil, a born devil, on whose nature
	Nurture can never stick; on whom my pains
	Humanely taken, all, all lost, quite lost; 190
	And, as with age his body uglier grows,
	So his mind cankers[14]. I will plague them all,
	Even to roaring[15].

Enter ARIEL, *laden with glistering apparel, etc.*

Come, hang them on this line.
[*Prospero and Ariel stand apart*]

Enter CALIBAN, STEPHANO *and* TRINCULO, *all wet*

CALIBAN	Pray you tread softly, that the blind mole may not hear a foot fall. We now are near his cell. 195
STEPHANO	Monster, your fairy, which you say is a harmless fairy, has done little better than played the jack with us[16].
TRINCULO	Monster, I do smell all horse-piss, at which my nose is in great indignation[17].
STEPHANO	So is mine. Do you hear, monster? If I should take a displeasure against you, look you – 200

Trinculo and Stephano complain about losing their wine, but Caliban urges them to commit the murder. The gaudy clothes attract the drunkards' interest, much to Caliban's dismay.

剧情简介：淳丘娄和斯迪法诺抱怨丢了酒，但是凯力般催促他们动手杀人。那些艳俗的衣物引起了醉汉的注意，这令凯力般灰心丧气。

1 'Look what a wardrobe here is' (in threes)

Trinculo and Stephano are equally impressed with clothes, and take great pleasure in dressing up in the elaborate costumes they find on the line. The two men are fooled by appearances and, interestingly, it is only Caliban who recognises the garments as 'trash'.

a Research a number of occupations (a judge, a politician, a banker, a manual worker, a doctor, a soldier) and then discuss how much clothes tell us about the people who wear them.

b Find images of celebrities and talk about what their clothing choices reveal about the image they want to project.

c Create a display for your classroom that picks out key figures from different professions and historical periods. Analyse each element of their appearance, including crests (象征家族、机构等的纹章) or logos. You could begin with a school uniform. Make the display as visually attractive as you can and annotate it with appropriate quotations from Act 4.

d Consider how the exchange about clothes in the script opposite links to the theme of appearance and reality that runs through the play.

---

1 lost　不可救药
2 hoodwink this mischance　补偿这一小差错
3 fetch off　捞回来
4 be o'er ears　淹死
5 good mischief　谋杀
6 aye = ever
7 peer　贵族
8 frippery　旧衣店
9 Put off　脱下
10 dropsy　水肿，积水
11 dote thus on　如此痴迷于
12 luggage　废品，累赘
13 Let't alone　把它放回原处
14 jerkin　短外套

TRINCULO	Thou wert but a lost[1] monster.	
CALIBAN	Good my lord, give me thy favour still.	
	Be patient, for the prize I'll bring thee to	
	Shall hoodwink this mischance[2]. Therefore speak softly –	205
	All's hushed as midnight yet.	
TRINCULO	Ay, but to lose our bottles in the pool!	
STEPHANO	There is not only disgrace and dishonour in that, monster, but an infinite loss.	
TRINCULO	That's more to me than my wetting. Yet this is your harmless fairy, monster.	210
STEPHANO	I will fetch off[3] my bottle, though I be o'er ears[4] for my labour.	
CALIBAN	Prithee, my king, be quiet. Seest thou here,	
	This is the mouth o'th'cell. No noise, and enter.	215
	Do that good mischief[5] which may make this island	
	Thine own for ever, and I, thy Caliban,	
	For aye[6] thy foot-licker.	
STEPHANO	Give me thy hand. I do begin to have bloody thoughts.	
TRINCULO	O King Stephano, O peer[7], O worthy Stephano! Look what a wardrobe here is for thee.	220
CALIBAN	Let it alone, thou fool, it is but trash.	
TRINCULO	O ho, monster! We know what belongs to a frippery[8]. [*Puts on a garment*] O King Stephano!	
STEPHANO	Put off[9] that gown, Trinculo! By this hand I'll have that gown.	225
TRINCULO	Thy grace shall have it.	
CALIBAN	The dropsy[10] drown this fool! What do you mean	
	To dote thus on[11] such luggage[12]? Let't alone[13],	
	And do the murder first. If he awake,	230
	From toe to crown he'll fill our skins with pinches,	
	Make us strange stuff.	
STEPHANO	Be you quiet, monster! Mistress line, is not this my jerkin[14]? [*He takes down the garment*] Now is the jerkin under the line. Now, jerkin, you are like to lose your hair, and prove a bald jerkin.	235

Despite Caliban's warning, Stephano and Trinculo are distracted by the gaudy clothes. Spirits disguised as dogs drive the conspirators away. Prospero says his enemies are in his power. He promises freedom to Ariel.

剧情简介：尽管凯力般警告过斯迪法诺和淳丘娄，但他俩被那些花里胡哨的衣服吸引住了。精灵化身为狗，将阴谋者赶跑了。普饶斯普柔说他的仇敌已在自己掌控之中。他答应给艾瑞尔自由。

Stagecraft 导演技巧

The hunting of the conspirators (whole class)

The hunting of Caliban, Trinculo and Stephano can be a very humorous scene in the play. Have a go at performing it for the greatest comic effect.

- First, pick three students to direct three different versions of lines 250–60.
- Select the actors to play the main characters in each version, as well as a number to play the hunting dogs. Groups should rehearse independently of one another, but everyone should know what each director's ideas are before they begin rehearsing, to ensure variety.
- Perform your scenes with the rest of the class as the audience. Which was the funniest, and why? Write up your notes on these performances in your Director's Journal.

Characters 人物分析

Has power gone to Prospero's head?

What do Prospero's lines 252–5 reveal about him by this point in the play?

- Read the lines in as many different ways as you can (joyfully, cruelly, 'tongue-in-cheek' [半开玩笑地]). Then write some notes for the actor playing the part, advising him how best to perform this scene. How do you want the audience to respond to Prospero's words? Is there a way of making them anything other than purely vengeful (图谋报复的)?

1 An alternative view

Trinculo, Stephano and Caliban are clearly foolish (and drunk), but what are they *really* guilty of doing? Is it possible to defend them? Ariel tells us that they are roaring in pain, and so they have already been punished for a crime they are yet to commit.

- Imagine that you are representing these three characters in a court of law. Write a short statement for the defence, in which you argue that they should be set free.
- Extend this activity by considering a case for prosecuting Prospero.

---

1 steal by line and level 偷东西也要守规矩 (line and level 指测量线和水准仪)
2 and't like your grace 如果陛下愿意
3 pass of pate 俏皮话
4 lime 黏液
5 lose our time 错过机会
6 barnacles = barnacle geese （藤壶鹅，即白颊黑雁，传说鹅是从藤壶变来的）
7 foreheads villainous low 额头矮（显得笨）
8 lay to 伸出
9 hogshead 猪头桶，大桶
10 *diverse* 各种各样的
11 Mountain ... Tyrant 各条狗的名字
12 charge 命令
13 goblins 小妖精
14 grind ... cramps 叫他们抽风，痛得像骨节被磨；叫他们浑身痉挛，像老年人抽筋一样
15 pinch-spotted 掐得青一块紫一块
16 pard 豹子
17 cat-o'-mountain 山猫
18 be hunted soundly 被追赶得走投无路

TRINCULO	Do, do; we steal by line and level[1], and't like your grace[2].
STEPHANO	I thank thee for that jest; here's a garment for't. Wit shall not go unrewarded while I am king of this country. 'Steal by line and level' is an excellent pass of pate[3]: there's another garment for't.
TRINCULO	Monster, come put some lime[4] upon your fingers, and away with the rest.
CALIBAN	I will have none on't. We shall lose our time[5], And all be turned to barnacles[6], or to apes With foreheads villainous low[7].
STEPHANO	Monster, lay to[8] your fingers. Help to bear this away where my hogshead[9] of wine is, or I'll turn you out of my kingdom. [*Loading Caliban with garments*] Go to, carry this.
TRINCULO	And this.
STEPHANO	Ay, and this.

A noise of hunters heard. Enter diverse[10] spirits in shape of dogs and hounds, hunting them about, Prospero and Ariel setting them on

PROSPERO	Hey, Mountain, hey!
ARIEL	Silver! There it goes, Silver.
PROSPERO	Fury, Fury! There, Tyrant[11], there! Hark, hark! [*Exeunt Caliban, Stephano and Trinculo, pursued by spirits*] [*To Ariel*] Go, charge[12] my goblins[13] that they grind their joints With dry convulsions, shorten up their sinews With agèd cramps[14], and more pinch-spotted[15] make them, Than pard[16], or cat-o'-mountain[17].
ARIEL	Hark, they roar.
PROSPERO	Let them be hunted soundly[18]. At this hour Lies at my mercy all mine enemies. Shortly shall all my labours end, and thou Shalt have the air at freedom. For a little Follow, and do me service.

Exeunt

THE TEMPEST
暴风雨

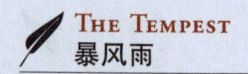

Looking back at Act 4 "第4幕"回顾
Activities for groups or individuals

1 Speedy themes

Act 4 contains many of the key themes in the play, but how well do you understand them?

- Form groups of ten. Look back through the act and write down five key themes on pieces of card. Now feed back to the rest of the class and, together, rank them in order of importance.
- Place five chairs in an outward-facing circle with a 'theme card' on the floor in front of each chair. Place another circle of five chairs around the first circle, so that you have two chairs facing each other with a 'theme card' between them.
- Sit facing each other and, for two minutes, discuss the theme on the card between you. When your time is up, those sitting in the inner circle move to the right and discuss the new theme they find there.
- When you have come full circle, discuss with your original partner any new ideas you might have come up with relating to the first theme.

2 Fathers and daughters

Prospero is the last in a long line of fathers in Shakespeare's plays who seek to control their daughters' choice of husband. Among others are Capulet in *Romeo and Juliet*, Baptista in *The Taming of the Shrew*, the Duke of Milan in *The Two Gentlemen of Verona*, Egeus in *A Midsummer Night's Dream*, Leonato in *Much Ado About Nothing*, Polonius in *Hamlet*, Lear in *King Lear*, Brabantio in *Othello* and Cymbeline in *Cymbeline*.

Shakespeare had two daughters, and it seems likely that he strongly disapproved of Thomas Quiney, the man who married his youngest daughter, Judith (although this was after *The Tempest* was written).

- One person steps into role as Shakespeare. The others question him about why he returns to the father-daughter theme so frequently in his plays. Begin by asking: 'Do you wish your relationship with Judith was like the one between Prospero and Miranda? Why?'

3 Prospero: thesis (正题), antithesis (反题), synthesis (合题)

Write an essay in response to this statement: 'Act 4 shows that Prospero is a megalomaniac (妄自尊大) tyrant, not a kindly old magician.' State one side of the argument (thesis), then put forward an opposing interpretation (antithesis), before bringing both positions together in a balanced and clear conclusion (synthesis). Remember to use quotations to support each of your points.

4 What are the other characters up to?

Several of the main characters in the play – Alonso, Sebastian, Antonio and Gonzalo – do not feature in Act 4 at all. What do you think they have been doing?

- Write a short script in which you imagine what these characters have been doing since the end of Act 3. Write your script in either modern prose or in Shakespearean verse using iambic pentameter.

5 Storyboarding the main action

Act 4 is short but pivotal (关键). Make a storyboard of six to eight images that capture the main points of action in the correct order. Use lines from Act 4 as captions. Which scenes will you choose? What will you decide to leave out, and why?

6 To cut or not to cut?

Some directors cut lines and scenes from Shakespeare's play, but many consider this to be an act of cultural vandalism (故意破坏行为).

- Look at Act 4 and think about which lines you could delete without affecting the audience's enjoyment of

the scene (could the whole of the masque be cut, for example?)
- Hold a class debate in which you discuss your choices and decide whether it is right to cut out lines from a play.

7 What will happen next?

It is widely believed that Shakespeare knew that *The Tempest* would be his final play. It would end a career in theatre unlike anything seen before or since. You are now about to read the final act of his final play.

- What do you think will happen? Jot down (草草记下) the main characters' names and then write two or three lines predicting their fates.
- As you write, think about which themes Shakespeare might have wanted to develop from the first four acts. What feeling might the playwright have wanted to leave us with as the curtain comes down for the last time?

Prospero foresees the success of his scheme. Ariel reports the troubled state of the king and courtiers, and expresses compassion for them. Moved by Ariel's feelings, Prospero says that he, too, will pity them.

剧情简介：普饶斯普柔预见他的计划得以实现。艾瑞尔报告国王和侍臣们的窘境并表示同情。普饶斯普柔被艾瑞尔的怜悯之心打动，说他也会可怜他们。

Write about it 写作练习

Prospero: magician or scientist? (in pairs)

In the first few lines of this scene, Prospero uses the language of a magician and refers to charms, spirits and control of the natural world. His imagery is taken from alchemy, an early 'science' that attempted to change base metal into gold. Here, Prospero seems to see himself as an alchemist who carries out a 'project' (experiment), which will 'gather to a head' (come to the boil) if it does not 'crack' (fail). This language of alchemy, along with Ariel's description of its effect on the 'three men of sin', relates to the idea of a 'sea-change', where a person is transformed or purified through trials and suffering.

a Compile a list of Prospero's magic powers (his 'potent art') and contrast it with a list of the limitations of his power ('this rough magic').

b Write a paragraph or two in which you explore the kind of transformation that is prompted by Prospero's art. To what extent you see him as a benign (和善) magician?

1 Prospero's 'project' (in small groups)

Prospero's project seems to have a number of aims:

- Political ends – (i) uniting Naples and Milan through the marriage of Ferdinand and Miranda; (ii) the regaining of his own dukedom.
- Revenge – the punishment of Alonso, Sebastian and Antonio.
- Repentance – bringing the 'three men of sin' to repent their wrong-doings.
- Reform – overcoming, with nurture, the wicked nature of others.
- Self-knowledge – deepening his own humanity by overcoming his nature and putting mercy before vengeance.
- Reward – releasing Ariel from his service.
- Escape – leaving the island to return to Milan.
- Harmony – achieving unity and peace in personal, social and natural life.

Present Prospero's aims as a diagram, showing the relationships between them. Make it clear which aims you think are the most important. Add quotations and other aims if you can think of them.

---

1 project 计划
2 gather to a head 达到了高峰，到了关键时刻
3 crack 失效，失败
4 Time … carriage 时间过得稳稳当当（指一切按计划进行）
5 as you gave in charge 照您吩咐的
6 line-grove 酸橙树林
7 weather-fends 为……挡风
8 till your release 直到您放了他们
9 abide all three distracted 三个人都疯了
10 eaves of reeds 茅草屋檐
11 works 起了效果
12 affections 感情
13 One of their kind 他们同类中的一个
14 kindlier moved 受感动而变得更人性

Act 5 Scene 1

Near Prospero's cave

Enter PROSPERO *in his magic robes, and* ARIEL

PROSPERO Now does my project[1] gather to a head[2].
My charms crack[3] not, my spirits obey, and Time
Goes upright with his carriage[4]. How's the day?

ARIEL On the sixth hour; at which time, my lord,
You said our work should cease.

PROSPERO I did say so, 5
When first I raised the tempest. Say, my spirit,
How fares the king and's followers?

ARIEL Confined together
In the same fashion as you gave in charge[5],
Just as you left them; all prisoners, sir,
In the line-grove[6] which weather-fends[7] your cell; 10
They cannot budge till your release[8]. The king,
His brother, and yours, abide all three distracted[9],
And the remainder mourning over them,
Brim full of sorrow and dismay; but chiefly
Him that you termed, sir, the good old lord Gonzalo. 15
His tears runs down his beard like winter's drops
From eaves of reeds[10]. Your charm so strongly works[11] 'em
That if you now beheld them, your affections[12]
Would become tender.

PROSPERO Dost thou think so, spirit?

ARIEL Mine would, sir, were I human.

PROSPERO And mine shall. 20
Hast thou, which art but air, a touch, a feeling
Of their afflictions, and shall not myself,
One of their kind[13], that relish all as sharply
Passion as they, be kindlier moved[14] than thou art?

Prospero decides on mercy rather than vengeance. He appeals to the spirits who have helped him to perform miracles, and declares that he will give up his magic powers.

剧情简介：普饶斯普柔决定以宽容代替复仇。他向那些帮他实现奇迹的精灵求助，并宣布他将放弃他的法术。

1 Forgiveness, not revenge (in pairs)

Prospero's lines 20–30 have been seen by some critics as the moral centre of the play. Although his enemies have wronged him deeply, he will forgive them: 'The rarer action is / In virtue, than in vengeance.'

Is Prospero's assertion of his intention to forgive his enemies a result of Ariel's speech, or has this been his intention all along? How would you indicate your decision in a performance of this turning-point in the play? Work out a delivery of lines 1–32 as you consider the following options:

- Prospero is pleased to hear Ariel's description of the sorrow and repentance of his enemies, and reveals his plan for ultimate forgiveness.
- Prospero is moved by Ariel's declaration and feels compassion for the suffering wrong-doers, Alonso, Sebastian and Antonio. He visibly struggles with his conscience, then decides that he, too, feels merciful towards his enemies (line 20).
- Prospero is still angry and bitter, and reluctantly declares that he will forgive his enemies.

Characters 人物分析

Prospero renounces his art (in small groups)

Prospero's lines 33–57 are a kind of invocation (祈求，祷告) or spell, building dramatic effect as he calls on his spirits and describes the astonishing things they have enabled him to perform. His list culminates (达到高潮) in a seeming paradox as he renounces his 'so potent art' and declares he will give up his 'rough magic' and become merely human again (line 51).

a Explore different ways of delivering the lines. Bring out the spell-like qualities, and the importance of Prospero's decision to give up his magic. At what point does he decide to 'abjure' (发誓放弃) his art? Is this spur of the moment (一时冲动), or did he know this earlier in this scene, or even earlier in the play?

b Step into role as Prospero and take turns to sit in the hot-seat*. Answer questions from the rest of your group about why you have changed your view about your powers, and why you have decided to 'break my staff' and 'drown my book'.

---

1 high wrongs 重罪
2 quick 内心最柔弱的部分
3 nobler reason, 'gainst my fury 站在理智的一边，强压怒火
4 rarer 难能可贵
5 sole drift 唯一目的
6 standing 静止
7 with printless foot 不留脚印
8 ebbing Neptune 退潮
9 demi-puppets 小精灵，半大木偶
10 green sour ringlets 仙草圈 (传说是仙子在草地上跳舞会留下环形的印记，实际上是环状聚生的菌类)
11 midnight mushrooms 深夜长出的蘑菇
12 solemn curfew 晚上9点钟声敲响表示夜晚降临 (传说夜里9点以后坟墓打开，精灵开始活动)
13 masters 大臣
14 azured vault 蔚蓝的苍穹
15 fire 闪电
16 rifted 劈开
17 bolt 打雷
18 promontory 海角，陆岬
19 spurs 树根
20 rough 粗暴
21 airy charm 使魔咒生效的音乐
22 plummet 水深仪

* hot-seat 热座位，一种课堂游戏，玩法是请一位同学坐到讲台上的一把椅子上，其他同学轮番给他/她出难题，哪个问题他/她回答不出就算输。

	Though with their high wrongs[1] I am struck to th'quick[2],	25
	Yet, with my nobler reason, 'gainst my fury[3]	
	Do I take part. The rarer[4] action is	
	In virtue, than in vengeance. They being penitent,	
	The sole drift[5] of my purpose doth extend	
	Not a frown further. Go, release them, Ariel.	30
	My charms I'll break, their senses I'll restore,	
	And they shall be themselves.	
ARIEL	I'll fetch them, sir. *Exit*	
PROSPERO	Ye elves of hills, brooks, standing[6] lakes, and groves.	
	And ye that on the sands with printless foot[7]	
	Do chase the ebbing Neptune[8], and do fly him	35
	When he comes back; you demi-puppets[9], that	
	By moon-shine do the green sour ringlets[10] make,	
	Whereof the ewe not bites; and you, whose pastime	
	Is to make midnight mushrooms[11], that rejoice	
	To hear the solemn curfew[12]; by whose aid –	40
	Weak masters[13] though ye be – I have bedimmed	
	The noontide sun, called forth the mutinous winds,	
	And 'twixt the green sea and the azured vault[14]	
	Set roaring war. To the dread rattling thunder	
	Have I given fire[15], and rifted[16] Jove's stout oak	45
	With his own bolt[17]; the strong-based promontory[18]	
	Have I made shake, and by the spurs[19] plucked up	
	The pine and cedar; graves at my command	
	Have waked their sleepers, oped, and let 'em forth	
	By my so potent art. But this rough[20] magic	50
	I here abjure. And when I have required	
	Some heavenly music – which even now I do –	
	To work mine end upon their senses that	
	This airy charm[21] is for, I'll break my staff,	
	Bury it certain fathoms in the earth,	55
	And deeper than did ever plummet[22] sound	
	I'll drown my book.	

The court party enters. Prospero praises and weeps with Gonzalo, criticises Alonso and Sebastian, and though recognising Antonio's evil nature, forgives him. Prospero decides to dress as the duke of Milan.

剧情简介：国王一行上场。普饶斯普柔赞扬良扎娄的美德，二人落泪。普饶斯普柔谴责额朗佐和塞巴斯田；尽管他认清了安托纽的邪恶本性，还是宽恕了他。普饶斯普柔决定穿戴成米兰公爵的模样。

1 Work out the staging (in small groups)

Copy and complete the table below to record your notes for performing the long stage direction and speech in the script opposite. Remember, none of the court party verbally responds to Prospero. He sometimes speaks to different groups or individuals, sometimes to himself and sometimes to the audience. As you complete the table, identify to whom Prospero speaks, his tone of voice, where he pauses and the gestures he could make.

Line	What might happen on stage
Solemn music … frantic gesture … stand charmed … (stage direction)	Alonso clutches (紧紧抱住) his head and tries to run away, while Gonzalo tries to calm him down.
'spell-stopped' (line 61)	
'Fall fellowly drops' (line 64)	
'rising senses' (line 66)	
'Th'art pinched' (line 74)	
'You, brother mine' (line 75)	(e.g. in one production, Prospero slapped Antonio's face before addressing him in these lines.)
'inward pinches' (line 77)	
'I do forgive thee' (line 78)	(e.g. in one production, Prospero paused a long time before saying this line.)
'Begins to swell' (line 80)	
'yet looks on me' (line 83)	
'Fetch me' (line 84)	

1 A solemn air 和谐的音乐（据信可以治疗疯症）
2 unsettled fancy 扰乱的思绪
3 Holy 圣贤
4 sociable to 对……感同身受
5 show of thine 你的样子（良扎娄热泪盈眶）
6 Fall fellowly drops 流下同情的泪水
7 rising senses 逐渐复苏的知觉
8 mantle 笼罩，覆盖
9 graces 恩惠（艮扎娄的美德和他在普饶斯普柔被放逐时提供的帮助）
10 Home 到家（引申义：完全，充分）
11 furtherer 帮凶
12 Th'art pinched for't now 为此你正在受折磨
13 entertained 怀有
14 nature 本性，与生俱来的亲情
15 inward pinches 良心的折磨
16 reasonable shore 理性的海岸
17 rapier 佩剑
18 discase me 脱下我的外套
19 sometime Milan 原来的米兰公爵

Solemn music. [Prospero traces out a circle on the stage.] Here enters ARIEL *before; then* ALONSO *with a frantic gesture, attended by* GONZALO; SEBASTIAN *and* ANTONIO *in like manner attended by* ADRIAN *and* FRANCISCO. *They all enter the circle which Prospero had made, and there stand charmed; which Prospero observing, speaks*

A solemn air[1], and the best comforter
To an unsettled fancy[2], cure thy brains,
Now useless, boiled within thy skull. There stand, 60
For you are spell-stopped.
Holy[3] Gonzalo, honourable man,
Mine eyes, ev'n sociable to[4] the show of thine[5],
Fall fellowly drops[6]. The charm dissolves apace,
And as the morning steals upon the night, 65
Melting the darkness, so their rising senses[7]
Begin to chase the ignorant fumes that mantle[8]
Their clearer reason. O good Gonzalo –
My true preserver, and a loyal sir
To him thou follow'st – I will pay thy graces[9] 70
Home[10] both in word and deed. Most cruelly
Didst thou, Alonso, use me, and my daughter.
Thy brother was a furtherer[11] in the act –
Th'art pinched for't now[12], Sebastian. Flesh and blood,
You, brother mine, that entertained[13] ambition, 75
Expelled remorse and nature[14], who, with Sebastian –
Whose inward pinches[15] therefore are most strong –
Would here have killed your king; I do forgive thee,
Unnatural though thou art. Their understanding
Begins to swell, and the approaching tide 80
Will shortly fill the reasonable shore[16]
That now lies foul and muddy. Not one of them
That yet looks on me, or would know me. Ariel,
Fetch me the hat and rapier[17] in my cell.

                                                        [Exit Ariel]

I will discase me[18], and myself present 85
As I was sometime Milan[19]. Quickly, spirit,
Thou shalt ere long be free.

Ariel sings about a future of everlasting summer, and is sent by Prospero to fetch the sailors. Prospero presents himself to the amazed court. Alonso asks for Prospero's forgiveness, and resigns all claim to Milan.

剧情简介：艾瑞尔歌唱那永远都是夏日的未来，然后被普饶斯普柔派去传唤水手。普饶斯普柔见过各位王公大臣，众人皆惊愕。额朗佐请求普饶斯普柔宽恕，并放弃了他在米兰公国的权利。

Language in the play 剧中语言

Ariel's freedom song (in pairs)

Ariel looks forward to a life without winter or servitude (奴役), in which he will enjoy an endless carefree summer.

- Turn back to Caliban's song of freedom in Act 2 Scene 2, lines 156–62, and compare it with Ariel's. What do you notice about the sound echoes, rhyme, repetition and rhythm in both songs?
- What is the difference between the two songs in terms of the context, content, language and tone?

1 Images of speed

Ariel uses two remarkable images to convey the speed at which he will travel to release the sailors from their enchanted sleep: 'I drink the air before me' and 'Or ere your pulse twice beat'. A modern familiar image is 'as quick as a flash'.

- Make up two more images in the same style as Ariel's to convey the impression of amazing speed.

Stagecraft 导演技巧

How do the wrong-doers react?

Prospero first becomes visible to the court party at line 106. At that moment, the three men who had grievously wronged Prospero twelve years earlier see him in all his finery (华丽的服饰) as the duke of Milan.

a Write detailed stage directions for how you think Alonso, Sebastian and Antonio should react. Invent a different reaction for each man when Prospero first appears (in lines 106–7) and then for when he embraces Alonso to show that he is real (in lines 109–10).

b Work through each phrase of Alonso's lines 111–20, and suggest a movement or gesture for each one.

1 *attire him* 帮普饶斯普柔穿衣
2 *cowslip's bell* 金钟花的花苞
3 *couch* 歇息，安眠
4 *owls do cry* 猫头鹰叫（即夜晚）
5 *dainty* 乖巧（指艾瑞尔的美丽或他歌声的美妙）
6 *So, so so* 行了，行了
7 *Under the hatches* 在船舱里
8 *enforce* 强迫
9 *drink the air before me* 迎风前进，高速飞翔
10 *Or ere* 或在……之前
11 *assurance* 确定性
12 *enchanted trifle* 魔法制造的幻觉
13 *abuse* 折磨或欺骗
14 *Th'affliction of my mind amends* 我不再胡思乱想
15 *crave* 使……产生
16 *Thy dukedom I resign* 你的公国我放弃（额朗佐立刻做出回应，说明他真心悔过）
17 *do entreat* 诚恳请求
18 *my wrongs* 我的种种罪过

ARIEL [*returns with hat and rapier,*] *sings, and helps to attire him*[1]

ARIEL
    Where the bee sucks, there suck I;
    In a cowslip's bell[2] I lie;
    There I couch[3] when owls do cry[4];
    On the bat's back I do fly
    After summer merrily.
    Merrily, merrily, shall I live now,
    Under the blossom that hangs on the bough.

PROSPERO
    Why that's my dainty[5] Ariel. I shall miss thee,
    But yet thou shalt have freedom. [*Arranging his attire*] So, so so[6].
    To the king's ship, invisible as thou art;
    There shalt thou find the mariners asleep
    Under the hatches[7]. The master and the boatswain
    Being awake, enforce[8] them to this place;
    And presently, I prithee.

ARIEL
    I drink the air before me[9], and return
    Or ere[10] your pulse twice beat.   *Exit*

GONZALO
    All torment, trouble, wonder and amazement
    Inhabits here. Some heavenly power guide us
    Out of this fearful country!

PROSPERO
                  Behold, sir king,
    The wrongèd Duke of Milan, Prospero.
    For more assurance[11] that a living prince
    Does now speak to thee, I embrace thy body,
    And to thee, and thy company, I bid
    A hearty welcome.
    [*He embraces Alonso*]

ALONSO
                  Whether thou beest he or no,
    Or some enchanted trifle[12] to abuse[13] me,
    As late I have been, I not know. Thy pulse
    Beats as of flesh and blood; and since I saw thee,
    Th'affliction of my mind amends[14], with which
    I fear a madness held me. This must crave[15],
    And if this be at all, a most strange story.
    Thy dukedom I resign[16], and do entreat[17]
    Thou pardon me my wrongs[18]. But how should Prospero
    Be living, and be here?

Prospero embraces Gonzalo. He reminds Antonio and Sebastian that he knows of their treachery to the king, but forgives them. Alonso regrets the loss of his son. Prospero says he has recently lost his daughter.

剧情简介：普饶斯普柔拥抱艮扎娄，他提醒安托纽和塞巴斯田，说他知道他二人对国王的背叛，但宽恕了他们。额朗佐哀悼遇难的儿子，普饶斯普柔说他也刚失去了女儿。

1 Still under the influence

The courtiers have had such extraordinary experiences that they are unwilling to trust their eyes. Prospero says that this is because they still 'taste / Some subtleties (糕点，甜点) o'th'isle' (lines 123–4). He is referring to sugar-covered sweets and pastries that were served after different courses during a banquet. These 'subtleties' were shaped like mythical figures or buildings, and made a kind of edible masque such as that in Act 4 Scene 1.

- If you had to design these 'subtleties' to represent the characters, events and themes of the play, what would they look like? Perhaps you might include a pastry in the shape of a harpy to represent judgement on the 'three men of sin', or a heart-shaped strawberry tart to represent the love between Ferdinand and Miranda.
- Consider the effect they would have on the person eating them: would they induce nausea (恶心), romance, hallucinations (幻觉), or something else?

2 Forgiveness for the worst offender? (in pairs)

- Script a conversation between an actor and director who have different ideas about how to portray Prospero here. The actor thinks that Prospero says lines 130–2 between clenched teeth (咬牙切齿), as if he is forcing himself to forgive Antonio. However, the director thinks that Prospero's forgiveness is sincere and graciously given.
- As you write, talk with your partner about how you can develop these two interpretations of Prospero. Find quotations from the script opposite (and elsewhere in the play) to support each one.

1	thine age	你上了年纪的身体
2	confined	受限制
3	You … subtleties	你们仍受着魔幻的影响
4	brace	双，对
5	minded	有意（做某事）
6	justify	充分地证实
7	tell no tales	不告发
8	devil speaks	魔鬼在说话（塞巴斯田对普饶斯普柔识破他们的阴谋感到吃惊）
9	rankest	最卑鄙
10	require	以理要求
11	perforce	必然
12	particulars	详情
13	point	刀尖
14	woe	难过
15	soft	怜悯，富于同情心
16	like	相似
17	I have her sovereign aid	我有（耐心）女神的帮助
18	as late	刚发生的
19	dear	巨大
20	means much weaker	（比你）更没有办法

Themes 主题分析

'Loss', 'lost', 'lose' (in pairs)

a Take parts as Alonso and Prospero and read lines 134–52, emphasising the words 'lost', 'loss' and 'lose'. How many times are they used? What action or gesture could you use for each repetition to reflect the feelings of the two men in (supposedly) having lost their children?

b How would you instruct Prospero to deliver his lines. Remember that he could also be punning on the word 'lost' – in what other sense might he have 'lost' his daughter?

PROSPERO	[*To Gonzalo*] First, noble friend,	120
	Let me embrace thine age¹, whose honour cannot	
	Be measured or confined².	
	[*Embraces Gonzalo*]	
GONZALO	Whether this be,	
	Or be not, I'll not swear.	
PROSPERO	You do yet taste	
	Some subtleties³ o'th'isle, that will not let you	
	Believe things certain. Welcome, my friends all.	125
	[*Aside to Sebastian and Antonio*] But you, my brace⁴ of lords,	
	were I so minded⁵	
	I here could pluck his highness' frown upon you	
	And justify⁶ you traitors. At this time	
	I will tell no tales⁷.	
SEBASTIAN	The devil speaks⁸ in him!	
PROSPERO	No.	
	For you, most wicked sir, whom to call brother	130
	Would even infect my mouth, I do forgive	
	Thy rankest⁹ fault – all of them – and require¹⁰	
	My dukedom of thee, which perforce¹¹ I know	
	Thou must restore.	
ALONSO	If thou beest Prospero,	
	Give us particulars¹² of thy preservation,	135
	How thou hast met us here, who three hours since	
	Were wracked upon this shore; where I have lost –	
	How sharp the point¹³ of this remembrance is –	
	My dear son Ferdinand.	
PROSPERO	I am woe¹⁴ for't, sir.	
ALONSO	Irreparable is the loss, and Patience	140
	Says it is past her cure.	
PROSPERO	I rather think	
	You have not sought her help, of whose soft¹⁵ grace	
	For the like¹⁶ loss, I have her sovereign aid¹⁷,	
	And rest myself content.	
ALONSO	You the like loss?	
PROSPERO	As great to me, as late¹⁸; and supportable	145
	To make the dear¹⁹ loss have I means much weaker²⁰	
	Than you may call to comfort you; for I	
	Have lost my daughter.	

Alonso wishes that Ferdinand and Miranda were married, and he was dead. Prospero comments on the courtiers' amazement, then reveals Ferdinand and Miranda playing chess. Ferdinand expresses gratitude to the sea.

剧情简介：额朗佐希望法迪南和蜜兰达成婚而自己去死。普饶斯普柔为朝臣们的惊愕做了解释，并向众人展现正在下棋的法迪南和蜜兰达。法迪南感恩大海。

1 'A most high miracle'

Everyone is astonished at the sight of Ferdinand and Miranda. In 2002, the Royal Shakespeare Company heightened dramatic effect by having the lovers drawn on to the stage while sitting in a boat.

a Suggest other ways in which the 'discovery' of the lovers might be staged to surprise both the courtiers and the audience.

b Explain how you would stage the three responses (from Alonso, Sebastian and Ferdinand) in lines 175–9, describing the tone and gesture each might have at this point. For example, the actor playing Sebastian has an opportunity to explore this character's complex response, which could be sincere or cynical – he certainly has much to lose by the recovery of Alonso's heir.

Themes 主题分析

A game of chess (in pairs)

- Chess was an aristocratic game, and in literary tradition it is often associated with love because of its focus on strategic encounters – using moves and counter-moves to gain the upper hand in a way that could mirror the games lovers play or the proverbial battle between the sexes. The game could also be a reference to Prospero as a chess grand master (象棋大师) manipulating all the players, and an ironic comment on the two lovers who think they are in control of the game.
- Talk together about the significance and symbolism of this game for the play and its characters.

1 mudded in that oozy bed 被埋葬在海底淤泥里
2 admire 惊讶
3 devour their reason 达到吞没理智的程度
4 do offices of truth 眼见为实
5 natural breath 大自然的呼吸（即空气）
6 jostled from your senses 被逼得失去理智
7 thrust forth of Milan 被逐出米兰
8 chronicle of day by day 说来话长的故事
9 relation 讲述
10 none abroad 没有外地人（即都是这个岛上的）
11 requite 回报
12 discovers 让……现身
13 play me false 你耍赖
14 wrangle 争辩
15 If … lose 如果这是岛上的另一个幻境，那我将失去爱子两次
16 A most high miracle 做梦都想不到的奇迹
17 compass thee about 围绕在你身边

▲ In Shakespeare's theatre, Prospero probably drew back a curtain at the rear of the stage to reveal the lovers playing chess. At which line was this photograph taken?

ALONSO	A daughter?	
	O heavens, that they were living both in Naples,	
	The king and queen there! That they were, I wish	150
	Myself were mudded in that oozy bed[1]	
	Where my son lies. When did you lose your daughter?	
PROSPERO	In this last tempest. I perceive these lords	
	At this encounter do so much admire[2]	
	That they devour their reason[3], and scarce think	155
	Their eyes do offices of truth[4], their words	
	Are natural breath[5]. But howsoe'er you have	
	Been jostled from your senses[6], know for certain	
	That I am Prospero, and that very duke	
	Which was thrust forth of Milan[7], who most strangely	160
	Upon this shore, where you were wracked, was landed	
	To be the lord on't. No more yet of this,	
	For 'tis a chronicle of day by day[8],	
	Not a relation[9] for a breakfast, nor	
	Befitting this first meeting. Welcome, sir;	165
	This cell's my court. Here have I few attendants,	
	And subjects none abroad[10]. Pray you look in.	
	My dukedom since you have given me again,	
	I will requite[11] you with as good a thing,	
	At least bring forth a wonder, to content ye	170
	As much as me my dukedom.	

Here Prospero discovers[12] FERDINAND and MIRANDA, playing at chess

MIRANDA	Sweet lord, you play me false[13].	
FERDINAND	No, my dearest love, I would not for the world.	
MIRANDA	Yes, for a score of kingdoms you should wrangle[14],	
	And I would call it fair play.	
ALONSO	If this prove	175
	A vision of the island, one dear son	
	Shall I twice lose[15].	
SEBASTIAN	A most high miracle[16].	
FERDINAND	Though the seas threaten, they are merciful;	
	I've cursed them without cause.	
	[*He kneels before Alonso*]	
ALONSO	Now all the blessings	
	Of a glad father compass thee about[17].	180
	Arise, and say how thou cam'st here.	

Miranda marvels at the sight of the king and courtiers. Ferdinand tells his story, and Prospero urges that sorrows be forgotten. Gonzalo rejoices at the happy outcome of the voyage for everyone.

剧情简介：蜜兰莐看到国王和众侍臣后大为吃惊。法迪南讲述他的遭遇，普饶斯普柔劝大家忘掉悲伤。艮扎娄因为这次皆大欢喜的旅行而喜悦。

1 'O brave new world' (in pairs)

Miranda's words in line 182 reveal her essential innocence, but her wonder at the sight of so many strangers is charged with dramatic irony (戏剧反讽). The 'beauteous mankind' she sees includes usurpers and would-be murderers. Aldous Huxley's novel *Brave New World* uses Miranda's words ironically to describe an inhuman future world. Prospero's four-word response to his daughter's delighted exclamation is very ambiguous.

- Take parts as Miranda and Prospero and try different ways of speaking lines 181–4. Is Prospero's tone heavily ironic, gentle and sympathetic, dismissive (语气轻蔑) or something else? Be prepared to explain what tone you think works best and give your reasons.

2 Design the pillars (in pairs)

Gonzalo enthusiastically recommends that the happy outcome should be recorded 'With gold on lasting pillars'.

- Take Gonzalo's words literally and design your own version of his 'lasting pillars'. Include on them your version of the inscription that Gonzalo has in mind (lines 206–13, from 'O rejoice').

Write about it 写作练习
Sea-change

Gonzalo claims that each person has 'found' themselves as a result of the voyage and shipwreck (lines 206–13). Has each character really gained self-knowledge and understanding from their ordeal? Has each one changed?

a Turn to the list of characters on page 1. Write down each name. Alongside the names, note the way in which they have changed (or if they have not changed at all), and find quotations that support your ideas.

b Use this list to write a paragraph about the kinds of internal and external transformations that have occurred on the island.

---

1 goodly 相貌不凡，好看
2 creatures 人
3 Your ... hours 你认识她最多不过仨小时
4 by immortal providence 感谢上天对我的恩赐
5 renown 大名鼎鼎
6 second life 第二次生命（指溺水后被救）
7 second father 第二个父亲（指岳父）
8 I am hers 我也是她的父亲（指公公）
9 heaviness 悲痛
10 inly 内心
11 chalked forth 指明
12 'amen' 阿门（额朗佐附和艮扎娄的祷告）
13 Was Milan thrust from Milan 米兰公爵被逐出米兰
14 issue 子孙后代（指蜜兰莐的儿女）
15 lasting pillars 千古石柱（如罗马的特洛伊柱，上面刻有描述战争和打了胜仗的文字）
16 When ... own 当没有人知道自己是谁时（失魂落魄）

MIRANDA	O wonder!	

MIRANDA   O wonder!
How many goodly[1] creatures[2] are there here!
How beauteous mankind is! O brave new world
That has such people in't!

PROSPERO   'Tis new to thee.

ALONSO [*To Ferdinand*] What is this maid with whom thou wast at play? 185
Your eld'st acquaintance cannot be three hours[3].
Is she the goddess that hath severed us,
And brought us thus together?

FERDINAND   Sir, she is mortal;
But by immortal providence[4], she's mine.
I chose her when I could not ask my father 190
For his advice, nor thought I had one. She
Is daughter to this famous Duke of Milan,
Of whom so often I have heard renown[5],
But never saw before; of whom I have
Received a second life[6]; and second father[7] 195
This lady makes him to me.

ALONSO   I am hers[8].
But O, how oddly will it sound, that I
Must ask my child forgiveness!

PROSPERO   There, sir, stop.
Let us not burden our remembrances with
A heaviness[9] that's gone.

GONZALO   I have inly[10] wept, 200
Or should have spoke ere this. Look down, you gods,
And on this couple drop a blessèd crown;
For it is you that have chalked forth[11] the way
Which brought us hither.

ALONSO   I say 'amen'[12], Gonzalo.

GONZALO Was Milan thrust from Milan[13], that his issue[14] 205
Should become kings of Naples? O rejoice
Beyond a common joy, and set it down
With gold on lasting pillars[15]: in one voyage
Did Claribel her husband find at Tunis,
And Ferdinand her brother found a wife 210
Where he himself was lost; Prospero, his dukedom
In a poor isle, and all of us ourselves,
When no man was his own[16].

Alonso blesses Ferdinand and Miranda. Gonzalo jokingly greets the Boatswain, who, though dazed, announces that the ship is seaworthy and the crew is safe. Alonso is amazed by everything he sees and hears.

剧情简介：额朗佐祝福法迪南和蜜兰莎。艮扎娄打趣地跟水手长打招呼。不明就里的水手长告诉各位他们的船未受损伤，随时可以出海，全体船员安然无恙。额朗佐对所见所闻感到惊奇不已。

1 Whom does Alonso have in mind? (in pairs)

Alonso condemns anyone who does not wish happiness for Ferdinand and Miranda: 'Let grief and sorrow still [always] embrace his heart'.

- Decide whether Alonso should look directly at Sebastian and Antonio as he speaks lines 214–15. Give reasons for your decision.

2 Reminders of the tempest (in pairs)

Gonzalo's friendly mocking of the Boatswain ('Now, blasphemy [亵渎神明]'), echoes what he said about the Boatswain in the first scene of the play (lines 25–9, 40–3, 50–2).

- Use these lines to explain why Gonzalo now jokes about 'on shore' and 'by land'. Also read what the Boatswain said in the first scene and decide whether or not he is really a blasphemer (someone who speaks irreverently about God or religion). Gonzalo's memory may be playing tricks on him.

3 The Boatswain's story (in small groups)

The story the Boatswain tells is full of striking detail (lines 230–40). He contrasts the horror of being rudely awakened by horrible noises with the sight of the master of the boat dancing for joy at the discovery of his undamaged ship.

a Prepare two tableaux to capture the events that the Boatswain describes. You might like to read specific lines aloud or provide sound effects for your tableaux.

b Discuss why Ariel or Prospero awoke the lower-class sailors in this way, compared to the heavenly music that rouses the aristocrats.

Characters 人物分析

Ariel and Prospero

- Look at the snatches (只言片语) of private conversation between Ariel and Prospero in the script opposite, and think about their relationship at this point compared to earlier in the play.
- How would you want to stage their dialogue to show their feelings towards each other and the fact that no one else on stage can hear their conversation? Write stage directions at lines 225–6 and 240.

---

1 still 一直
2 *amazedly* 难以置信地
3 swear'st grace o'erboard 在船上辱骂神明（以至于船失事）
4 glasses （用沙漏计量的）小时（同186行的hours）
5 since = ago
6 gave our split 宣告船解体
7 tight and yare 滴水不漏，准备扬帆起航
8 bravely rigged 帆缆齐备
9 tricksy 机智，随机应变
10 strengthen 愈加
11 clapped under hatches 关在舱口下面
12 even now 就在刚才
13 several 与众不同，奇特
14 trim 安然无恙
15 Cap'ring to eye her 看到船后高兴得手舞足蹈
16 On a trice 立刻
17 divided from them 跟其他船员分开
18 moping 迷迷糊糊地
19 diligence 勤奋的人
20 more … of 超出自然所为
21 oracle / Must rectify 必须靠神谕才可以让我们明白是怎么回事

ALONSO	[*To Ferdinand and Miranda*] Give me your hands:
	Let grief and sorrow still[1] embrace his heart
	That doth not wish you joy.
GONZALO	Be it so, amen.

Enter ARIEL, *with the* MASTER *and* BOATSWAIN *amazedly[2] following*

O look, sir, look, sir, here is more of us!
I prophesied, if a gallows were on land
This fellow could not drown. [*To Boatswain*] Now, blasphemy,
That swear'st grace o'erboard[3] – not an oath on shore?
Hast thou no mouth by land? What is the news?

BOATSWAIN	The best news is, that we have safely found
	Our king and company. The next, our ship,
	Which but three glasses[4] since[5] we gave out split[6],
	Is tight and yare[7] and bravely rigged[8] as when
	We first put out to sea.
ARIEL	[*To Prospero*] Sir, all this service
	Have I done since I went.
PROSPERO	[*To Ariel*] My tricksy[9] spirit.
ALONSO	These are not natural events, they strengthen[10]
	From strange, to stranger. Say, how came you hither?
BOATSWAIN	If I did think, sir, I were well awake,
	I'd strive to tell you. We were dead of sleep,
	And – how we know not – all clapped under hatches[11],
	Where, but even now[12], with strange and several[13] noises
	Of roaring, shrieking, howling, jingling chains
	And more diversity of sounds, all horrible,
	We were awaked, straightway at liberty;
	Where we, in all our trim[14], freshly beheld
	Our royal, good and gallant ship; our master
	Cap'ring to eye her[15]. On a trice[16], so please you,
	Even in a dream, were we divided from them[17],
	And were brought moping[18] hither.
ARIEL	[*To Prospero*] Was't well done?
PROSPERO	[*To Ariel*] Bravely, my diligence[19]. Thou shalt be free.
ALONSO	This is as strange a maze as e'er men trod,
	And there is in this business more than nature
	Was ever conduct of[20]. Some oracle
	Must rectify[21] our knowledge.

Prospero promises to explain. He sends Ariel to fetch Caliban, Stephano and Trinculo. They arrive. Caliban admires the courtiers. Prospero describes the drunkards and admits responsibility for Caliban.

剧情简介：普饶斯普柔许诺他会解释，他派艾瑞尔将凯力般、斯迪法诺、淳丘娄带来。三人上场，凯力般对众朝臣赞叹不已。普饶斯普柔讲述这几个醉鬼的所作所为，并承认他对凯力般负有责任。

1 'this thing of darkness, I / Acknowledge mine'
(in pairs)

What does it mean for Prospero to 'acknowledge' Caliban? Many critics believe that, in lines 274–5, Prospero means more than 'Caliban is my servant'. They argue that Prospero accepts he also has an evil side to his nature, and believe his exile on the island has taught him that he must control his darker thoughts and desires.

a Experiment with reading aloud lines 271–5. In what tone does Prospero speak, and how might Caliban respond?

b Talk together about whether you think Prospero has an evil side to his nature. What kind of personal or spiritual journey might he have taken during the course of the play?

c Compose a soliloquy (独白) for Prospero, in which he reveals how his feelings and intentions towards his enemies – including Caliban, Antonio and Alonso – have changed because of his time on the island.

1	liege	君主
2	infest	困扰
3	beating on	费心琢磨
4	picked leisure	找个空儿
5	shortly single	很快而且就你我在场
6	resolve you	向你说清楚
7	Which … probable	让你听了觉得合情合理
8	accidents	发生的这一切
9	odd	怪异的
10	Every … rest	自己顾大家（成语本为Let each man shift for himself，意思是"自己顾自己"；这里是斯迪法诺醉酒后的口误）
11	Coragio	= courage
12	bully-monster	怪物大侠
13	spies	眼珠
14	fine	好看（指公爵的衣服）
15	chastise	责怪，惩罚
16	badges	徽章（贵族家仆人通常佩戴该家族的徽章）
17	That could	= That she could
18	make flows and ebbs	造成潮涨潮落
19	And … power	以她（月亮）的名义发号施令，却不经过她允许
20	robbed me	偷我的东西
21	demi-devil	半妖半人
22	own	承认
23	darkness	地狱

▲ 'How fine my master is!' Caliban faces Prospero before the king and courtiers. Antonio and Sebastian are cynical to the end, commenting on Caliban's market value (just as Trinculo and Stephano did in Act 2 Scene 2).

PROSPERO   Sir, my liege¹,   245
Do not infest² your mind with beating on³
The strangeness of this business. At picked leisure⁴,
Which shall be shortly single⁵, I'll resolve you⁶,
Which to you shall seem probable⁷, of every
These happened accidents⁸. Till when, be cheerful   250
And think of each thing well. [*To Ariel*] Come hither, spirit,
Set Caliban and his companions free:
Untie the spell.
                                                    [*Exit Ariel*]

[*To Alonso*]   How fares my gracious sir?
There are yet missing of your company
Some few odd⁹ lads that you remember not.   255

Enter ARIEL, *driving in* CALIBAN, STEPHANO *and* TRINCULO
in their stolen apparel

STEPHANO   Every man shift for all the rest¹⁰, and let no man take care
for himself; for all is but fortune. Coragio¹¹, bully-monster¹², coragio.

TRINCULO   If these be true spies¹³ which I wear in my head, here's a
goodly sight.

CALIBAN   O Setebos, these be brave spirits indeed!   260
How fine¹⁴ my master is! I am afraid
He will chastise¹⁵ me.

SEBASTIAN   Ha, ha! What things are these, my lord Antonio?
Will money buy 'em?

ANTONIO   Very like. One of them
Is a plain fish, and no doubt marketable.   265

PROSPERO   Mark but the badges¹⁶ of these men, my lords,
Then say if they be true. This misshapen knave,
His mother was a witch, and one so strong
That could¹⁷ control the moon, make flows and ebbs¹⁸,
And deal in her command, without her power¹⁹.   270
These three have robbed me²⁰, and this demi-devil²¹ –
For he's a bastard one – had plotted with them
To take my life. Two of these fellows you
Must know and own²²; this thing of darkness²³, I
Acknowledge mine.

CALIBAN   I shall be pinched to death.   275

Trinculo staggers about and Stephano has severe cramps. Ordered by Prospero to behave, Caliban hopes for wisdom and forgiveness. He rejects Stephano. Prospero invites Alonso and the others to hear his story.

剧情简介：淳丘娄跌跌撞撞，斯迪法诺浑身抽搐。普饶斯普柔让凯力般言行守规矩。凯力般希望得到智慧和宽恕，背弃了斯迪法诺。普饶斯普柔请额朗佐和众人听他讲事情的原委。

1 'I have been in such a pickle'

Trinculo and Stephano have little to say, other than expressing their aches and pains.

- Advise them on how to speak each line, how to behave and how to stage their exit. What do they do with their stolen clothes? How do they behave towards each other? (In one production, Stephano viciously rejected Trinculo's friendship.) In your Director's Journal, write detailed notes to the actors explaining what you want from them at this point in the play.

Characters

Caliban's last words – are they sincere? (in small groups)

Lines 292–5 are Caliban's final words in the play. Do they express his real feelings? Has he experienced some kind of moral transformation or a decisive change of heart? Does he lie to Prospero when he promises to behave well and 'seek for grace'? Does he threaten or strike Stephano? Has his attitude towards Miranda changed? What other questions do you have?

- Take turns as Caliban in the hot-seat and answer questions from others in your group. Remember to explain whether you have also gone on a journey of self-discovery, and why you said you were a 'thrice-double ass' to follow Stephano and Trinculo.

2 'Every third thought shall be my grave' (in pairs)

The play seems to be ending happily. Prospero looks forward to his departure for Naples, to the marriage of Ferdinand and Miranda, and to his return to Milan. But, like so much else in *The Tempest*, Prospero's line 309 is enigmatic (神秘，费解). It could mean that he has a sense his life is drawing to a close, or that he will embrace his humanity and meditate on his mortality. Or it might have some quite different meaning.

- Talk together about how you interpret Prospero's thoughts and feelings at this moment, and suggest how you think the line should be spoken. Decide together what would work best on stage.

---

1 **reeling ripe** 头重脚轻，摇摇晃晃
2 **gilded 'em** 使他们红光满面
3 **pickle** 腌菜（引申义：悲惨境地）
4 **fly-blowing** 苍蝇光顾
5 **sirrah** 伙计（不屑、轻蔑的称呼）
6 **sore** 痛苦
7 **disproportioned** 畸形（普饶斯普柔这里的意思是凯力般畸形的外表折射出其内心的扭曲）
8 **manners** 举止
9 **shape** 外形
10 **trim it handsomely** 好好修理一下
11 **grace** 宽恕
12 **thrice-double** 3个双倍（即6倍）
13 **this drunkard** 这个酒鬼（指斯迪法诺）
14 **this dull fool** 这个傻瓜（指淳丘娄）
15 **bestow** 放置
16 **luggage** （指偷来的衣物）
17 **train** 随从
18 **I'll … discourse** 我有一番话说给你们听，来度过（waste）这段时间
19 **nuptial** 婚礼
20 **solemnised** 隆重举行

ALONSO	Is not this Stephano, my drunken butler?	
SEBASTIAN	He is drunk now; where had he wine?	
ALONSO	And Trinculo is reeling ripe[1]. Where should they	
	Find this grand liquor that hath gilded 'em[2]?	
	[*To Trinculo*] How cam'st thou in this pickle[3]?	280
TRINCULO	I have been in such a pickle since I saw you last, that I fear me will never out of my bones. I shall not fear fly-blowing[4].	
SEBASTIAN	Why how now, Stephano?	
STEPHANO	O touch me not! I am not Stephano, but a cramp.	
PROSPERO	You'd be king o'the isle, sirrah[5]?	285
STEPHANO	I should have been a sore[6] one then.	
ALONSO	[*Gesturing to Caliban*] This is as strange a thing as e'er I looked on.	
PROSPERO	He is as disproportioned[7] in his manners[8]	
	As in his shape[9]. Go, sirrah, to my cell;	
	Take with you your companions. As you look	290
	To have my pardon, trim it handsomely[10].	
CALIBAN	Ay that I will; and I'll be wise hereafter,	
	And seek for grace[11]. What a thrice-double[12] ass	
	Was I to take this drunkard[13] for a god	
	And worship this dull fool[14]!	
PROSPERO	Go to, away.	295
ALONSO	Hence, and bestow[15] your luggage[16] where you found it.	
SEBASTIAN	Or stole it rather.	
	[*Exeunt Caliban, Stephano and Trinculo*]	
PROSPERO	Sir, I invite your highness and your train[17]	
	To my poor cell, where you shall take your rest	
	For this one night, which, part of it, I'll waste	300
	With such discourse[18] as I not doubt shall make it	
	Go quick away: the story of my life,	
	And the particular accidents gone by	
	Since I came to this isle. And in the morn	
	I'll bring you to your ship, and so to Naples,	305
	Where I have hope to see the nuptial[19]	
	Of these our dear-belovèd solemnised[20],	
	And thence retire me to my Milan, where	
	Every third thought shall be my grave.	

Prospero promises a favourable voyage to Naples, and sets Ariel free. Alone on stage, Prospero admits that all his magical powers have gone. He asks the audience for applause, and for forgiveness to set him free.

剧情简介：普饶斯普柔保证那不勒斯之旅将一帆风顺并还了艾瑞尔自由。普饶斯普柔独自站在台上，坦言自己的法术都已消失。他请观众鼓掌喝彩，也请他们宽恕他，给他自由。

Stagecraft 导演技巧

'*Exeunt all*': everyone leaves the stage

The way in which characters leave the stage may reflect how they think and feel at the end of the play. Write down your suggestions for each character. Use the following to help your thinking:

- **Ferdinand and Miranda** Do they look forward to the future with total pleasure? Do they leave before the others, or at the same time?
- **Antonio and Sebastian** They have not acknowledged their wickedness, and have spoken no words of repentance. How do they behave?
- **Alonso, Gonzalo and the courtiers** As king, does Alonso expect to leave first? How does his new-found repentance affect him?
- **Ariel** Ariel says nothing when Prospero gives him his freedom. Does he run delightedly into the darkness? Or does he react with anger and hatred, as in a 1993 production where he turned and spat in Prospero's face?

1 Prospero's epilogue (收场辞) – a plea for freedom

It was a convention in many Elizabethan and Jacobean plays for an actor to step out of role at the end and ask the audience for applause. This is the most complex epilogue in all of Shakespeare's plays because the figure on stage is both the character Prospero and the actor playing the part.

a Pick out all the puns and double meanings in the epilogue and discuss how you would show with gesture, tone of voice and position on the stage that it is both character and actor talking?

b Stage your own version of this epilogue. Try to capture the dramatic challenge Prospero throws out to the audience, as well as the ambivalent (情感矛盾的), complex ending the epilogue gives to the play itself.

1 Take the ear strangely 让耳朵听得入神
2 deliver all 把一切都说清楚
3 auspicious gales 一帆风顺
4 expeditious 迅速
5 chick 小乖乖（像对孩子那样的昵称）
6 charge 任务
7 elements 天地之间
8 draw near 靠近
9 here 这儿（既指这座岛，也指戏台）
10 deceiver 骗子（指安东尼）
11 spell （因缺少掌声而产生的）魔咒
12 bands 束缚
13 help of your good hands 借助你们尊贵的手掌（指掌声，掌声可以破咒）
14 Gentle breath 高贵的呼吸（指喝彩）
15 enforce 控制
16 art 法术或戏剧艺术
17 enchant （用法术）降服
18 prayer 我的请求（或观众的祈祷）得到回应
19 indulgence 宽宏大量（即掌声）

ALONSO	I long	
	To hear the story of your life; which must	310
	Take the ear strangely¹.	
PROSPERO	I'll deliver all²,	
	And promise you calm seas, auspicious gales³,	
	And sail so expeditious⁴ that shall catch	
	Your royal fleet far off. [*To Ariel*] My Ariel, chick⁵,	
	That is thy charge⁶. Then to the elements⁷	315
	Be free, and fare thou well. [*To the others*] Please you draw near⁸.	

Exeunt all [except Prospero]

    EPILOGUE, *spoken by* PROSPERO

Now my charms are all o'erthrown,
And what strength I have's mine own –
Which is most faint. Now 'tis true
I must be here⁹ confined by you,
Or sent to Naples, let me not,   5
Since I have my dukedom got
And pardoned the deceiver¹⁰, dwell
In this bare island, by your spell¹¹;
But release me from my bands¹²
With the help of your good hands¹³.   10
Gentle breath¹⁴ of yours my sails
Must fill, or else my project fails,
Which was to please. Now I want
Spirits to enforce¹⁵, art¹⁶ to enchant¹⁷,
And my ending is despair,   15
Unless I be relieved by prayer¹⁸
Which pierces so, that it assaults
Mercy itself, and frees all faults.
As you from crimes would pardoned be,
Let your indulgence¹⁹ set me free.   *Exit*   20

THE TEMPEST 暴风雨

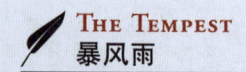

Looking back at the play 本剧回顾
Activities for groups or individuals

1 Harmony – or an uncertain future?

In traditional productions of *The Tempest*, the major themes of the play were presented as being harmoniously concluded. Prospero learns forgiveness and grants mercy to his enemies, reconciliation (和解) is achieved, all characters are set free from their enchantment and the future looks bright for everyone. In contrast, modern productions often end in a mood of uncertainty or even menace (令人恐怖的氛围). In one production, Ariel returned to the stage after Prospero's exit, carrying his staff and clearly intending to take over the island and make slaves of Caliban and the spirits. In another production, Miranda's naïvety was highlighted and the 'brave new world' she thought she saw was questioned by Prospero's brisk remarks, to prevent any heart-warmingly happy ending to the play.

- Think about the final image you would want the audience to see in a modern production. Who is left as master of the island? Write a paragraph or two explaining how you think the play should end, giving reasons for your choice.

2 Press conference

On the return to Naples, a press conference is arranged. All the characters will be closely questioned by press, radio and television reporters. Take parts and stage the press conference. Prospero and Alonso may well have prepared a speech in advance to deliver at the quayside (码头).

3 What happens next?

- **On the island** Step into role as Caliban or Ariel. Write the story of what has happened to you in the year since Prospero and the others sailed back to Naples.
- **Back in Naples** Step into role as Antonio, Prospero, Ferdinand or Miranda. Write about what has happened in the year since you arrived home.

4 Plot the action

A well-known theory of drama (based on the writings of the Greek philosopher Aristotle) states that if a play is to possess aesthetic harmony, it must observe the unities of action, time and place. This means that it should have a single action lasting less than twenty-four hours, taking place in a single location. *The Tempest* is unusual among Shakespeare's plays, as it observes the unities:

Time The action of the play takes place in under four hours (see Act 1 Scene 2, lines 239–41, and Act 5 Scene 1, lines 186 and 223).

Place Apart from Scene 1, everything takes place on the island.

Action All the sub-plots link neatly to the central plot of the usurpation of Prospero and his plan to regain his dukedom.

- Draw a timeline to represent 2 p.m. to 6 p.m., and place the various events in the play on it, from the shipwreck to the final scene. Remember, events in the sub-plot may occur at the same time as events in the main plot.

5 A mini-*Tempest*

- Write a summary of *The Tempest* in exactly 100 words. Now cut it down to exactly fifty words (try to stick to complete sentences); then cut it down to exactly ten words.
- Share these words with the class by posting them on a designated pinboard, by using sticky notes, or by posting them to a class website. Discuss the choices you have made.
- Now choose one word that you think captures the most important element in the play. Draw up a list of everyone's chosen words. Create a series of newspaper headlines (either for a tabloid or broadsheet paper) to capture the main events of the play using these words.

147

THE TEMPEST
暴风雨

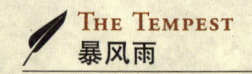

Perspectives and themes 视角与主题

What is the play about?

Imagine that you can travel back in time to around 1611. You meet William Shakespeare a few minutes after he has finished writing *The Tempest*, just before he takes it into rehearsal with his company, The King's Men. You ask him, 'What is the play about?' But like many great artists, Shakespeare does not seem interested in explaining his work, preferring to leave it up to others. He just says: 'Here it is. Read it, perform it, make of it what you will.'

There has been no shortage of responses to that invitation! *The Tempest* has been popular ever since it was first performed. The thousands of productions and millions of words written about it show that there is no single 'right way' of thinking about or performing the play. You will probably have noticed this as you looked at the photographs of different productions in this book. The play is like a kaleidoscope (万花筒). Every time it is performed it reveals different shapes, patterns, meanings, interpretations. For example, you could think about *The Tempest* as:

- the dramatic story of a group of people who are shipwrecked in a great storm
- a moral tale representing the mental and emotional turmoil (动乱，混乱) suffered by nearly all the characters as a spiritual journey that enables them to undergo a 'sea-change'
- a masque to entertain the court through spectacular theatrical effects, music, dance and mythology
- a play that comments on politics in seventeenth-century Europe, with a criticism of colonialism
- a romance play that contains elements of both tragedy and comedy, loss and recovery, mixing fairy-tale improbabilities and fantasies with love, magic, storms, feasts and miracles
- Shakespeare's last play, written as a farewell to the stage when he, like Prospero, gave up his art.

It is unlikely that Shakespeare had a single purpose in mind. As in all his plays, various interpretative standpoints allow different 'readings' of the play. People have interpreted *The Tempest* according to a number of perspectives. These include:

Postcolonial perspectives – looking at power relationships between colonised cultures and people, based on the belief that no culture is better or worse than other cultures.

Cultural materialist perspectives – looking at the way politics, wealth and power strongly influence every human relationship.

Feminist perspectives – gender issues are politicised and critiqued from women's perspectives; this includes looking at the way women are represented and how gender can be both socially and symbolically constructed.

Psychoanalytical perspectives – looking at the unconscious and the irrational, as well as the impact of repressed sexuality and desire.

Liberal-humanist perspectives – freedom and human progress are the goals of life, and final reconciliation and harmony are possible.

◆ In pairs, talk about which of the perspectives described above would be most helpful in exploring *The Tempest* further. Then, in groups, choose a scene and experiment with staging it several times, focusing on a particular perspective each time. Take turns watching other groups' scenes and guess which perspective is being represented.

◆ Alternatively, by yourself or in pairs, write the script for a dialogue between two people with different perspectives on the play. Try to show how their conversation develops, and encourage them to agree or disagree with each other about the meaning of *The Tempest*.

Themes

Another way of answering the question 'What is *The Tempest* about?' is to identify the themes of the play.

Perspectives and themes

Themes are ideas or concepts of fundamental importance that recur throughout the play, linking together plot, characters and language. Themes echo, reinforce and comment upon each other – and the whole play – in interesting ways. For example, it would be difficult to write about illusion and magic without mentioning the themes of change and transformation or forgiveness and reconciliation.

As you can see, themes are not individual categories but a 'tangle' of ideas and concerns that are interrelated in complex ways. When you write about this play, you should aim to explore the way these themes cross over and illuminate each other, rather than simply listing each one. The key themes of *The Tempest* are outlined below.

Usurpation and treachery
The play portrays rebellions, political treachery, mutinies (暴动，叛变) and conspiracies. All kinds of challenges to authority are made at all levels of society – on the boat, on the island and (in the past) back in Naples.

Nature versus nurture
Two major views of nature are explored in *The Tempest*. The first is that when left alone, nature grows to perfection and is inherently good. The second is that nature is inherently bad and therefore must be controlled and educated in order to become good.

The simple contrast between nature and nurture is questioned by Prospero when he says that Caliban is someone 'on whose nature / Nurture can never stick'. In this case, he suggests that it is not a question of whether nature is inherently good or bad, but whether or not nurture can have an influence on it.

Imprisonment and powerlessness
All the characters in the play suffer some kind of confinement, whether as a result of exile, unjust punishment, tests of character, the effects of magic, or their own conscience. Everyone yearns for freedom.

Forgiveness and reconciliation
For much of the play, it is not clear exactly what Prospero intends to do to his enemies. However, at the end he relents, deciding that forgiveness and mercy are better guides to human conduct than dominance and revenge.

Illusion and magic
The Tempest is full of magic and its effects: the opening tempest is itself an enchantment; music is everywhere; strange shapes, fantastic creatures and wonderful illusions appear; everything undergoes an alteration.

Colonialism and exploration
Tales that explorers brought back to England from what became known as the 'New World' are strongly echoed in this play. The Europeans set about what they believed to be their divinely ordained (受天命) task of taking ownership of this New World. Gonzalo's vision of his 'commonwealth' – a dream of what the perfect, utopian society might be like – is in stark contrast (鲜明的对比) to the realities of colonialism.

Sleep and dreams
Prospero sends Miranda to sleep, Ariel causes Alonso and Gonzalo to sleep, and Caliban's dreams are so wonderful that he longs to sleep again. The island itself also has dream-like qualities.

The Tempest
暴风雨

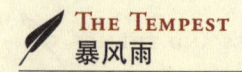

Change and transformation

The turbulence of the storm with which the play begins changes into the apparent peace and harmony of the ending. Many of the characters experience a 'sea-change': Alonso's despair turns to joy; Prospero's wish for vengeance metamorphoses (变形，变质) into forgiveness; and Caliban's evil intentions become a desire for grace.

- ◆ Working in small groups, devise a tableau that shows one of the themes of the play. Present your tableau, frozen for one minute, for other groups to guess which theme is being portrayed.

- ◆ Imagine you are asked to explain what *The Tempest* is about by an eight-year-old child, and also by your teacher/lecturer. Write a reply to each of them, using these pages to help you.

Shakespeare's context and sources

One way of thinking about *The Tempest* is to set it in the context of its time: the world that Shakespeare knew. His imagination was influenced by many features of that world. Layers of dramatic possibilities within the script are built on past performances (such as morality plays, the Italian *commedia dell'arte* [即兴喜剧] and English courtly masques), other literary texts (such as essays by Montaigne on cannibals, or by Erasmus on shipwrecks) and contemporary events or topical concerns (such as the voyages of exploration and settlement in Asia, Africa and America or the impending [即将到来的] marriage of Princess Elizabeth). This layering gives Shakespeare's plays great depth, without limiting them to any single or specific social, religious or political meaning.

▼ The masque scene in the play may have been added later to celebrate a royal wedding.

Writing for a king and his family

In 1611, the first recorded performance of *The Tempest* took place at the court of King James I of England and Ireland (and VI of Scotland). It is likely that the audience included James's wife, Queen Anne (a great patron of the arts), the heir to the throne, Prince Henry, the Princess Elizabeth and Prince Charles, their younger brother.

The play may be Shakespeare's response to the courtly masque, a form of theatre that developed – and was very popular – during King James's reign. Such entertainments contained spectacular theatrical effects, music, dance and bizarre (古怪，怪诞) and mythological characters. The king and his court would have expected a masque to end in the triumph of virtue, peace and beauty, with harmony restored under a rightful monarch. The wedding masque in Act 4 was possibly a later addition to the play to celebrate the princess's marriage to Frederick V in 1613. *The Tempest* was one of the many performances that were held in honour of the occasion.

There are other aspects of this play that would have interested the king and his family. Prince Henry was a great lover of adventure and exploration, although he was never allowed to embark on these voyages himself (it was considered too dangerous for the heir to the throne). He was always fascinated by the tales of discovery brought back by those who did go. He was also very religious, listening carefully to sermons given by those who commanded his attention. Christian ideas of repentance, forgiveness and the movement from sin to redemption through suffering are raised in this play.

These ideas were also found in earlier performances of the mystery and morality plays from the medieval dramatic traditions in England. Such plays portrayed the human struggle to choose between vice (罪行，恶行) and virtue. They personified a range of vices (including the seven deadly sins) and virtues in stories of temptation and conflict between good and evil. The hero, often given a generic name like 'Everyman' or 'Mankind', must choose between them. Although the everyman is led astray (误入歧途) by vice and wallows (沉湎) in sinfulness, he repents and is saved at the end of the play. The point of the plays is that although the hero succumbs (屈从) to sin, God's mercy is always available to one who repents. In this way, the morality plays made the basic elements of Christianity accessible to those who were unable to read the Latin Bible for themselves. The plays taught people to beware the common vices that might tempt them, and to have faith in the mercy of God.

Magic and sorcery in *The Tempest*

In Shakespeare's England, the line between magic and science was not clearly drawn. A magus (术士) could be an alchemist (an early 'scientist' who attempted to change base metals into gold), or an astrologer (占星家) , or a sorcerer (who supposedly communicated with the occult [神秘] or spirit world).

When Shakespeare created Prospero, he may have had in mind Dr John Dee, a famous Elizabethan mathematician and geographer. Some of Dr Dee's work was genuinely scientific, but he was widely regarded as a magus.

Shakespeare may also have had in mind the legend of Dr Faustus, a magician who sold his soul to the devil in exchange for magical powers, and the play *The Tragical History of Doctor Faustus* – written by his contemporary Christopher Marlowe.

Prospero may be seen as a magus. He has devoted his life to secret studies in order to gain magical powers – what he refers to as his 'art'. When he decides to renounce these powers at the end of the play, he recalls all the miracles he can perform: dimming the sun, commanding the winds, making storms at sea, splitting oaks with lightning bolts and causing earthquakes. He can also raise the dead from their graves, raise and calm tempests, command his spirits to produce fantastic banquets and masques, make himself invisible, and control Caliban with cramps and pinches.

The Tempest
暴风雨

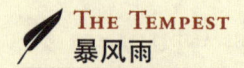

However, Prospero's magic powers are limited: he sometimes depends on luck to help him and although he can control the natural world, he cannot ensure that human nature will change. He cannot make Ferdinand and Miranda fall in love. He cannot cause his enemies to experience remorse and repentance for their deeds. His magic is unable to force Sebastian or Antonio to undergo a change of heart for their misdeeds. Despite its limitations – or perhaps because of them – Prospero's magic art is contrasted with the evil magic of Sycorax, Caliban's mother, and her god, Setebos. Whereas, arguably, Prospero uses his art to achieve virtue and goodness, Sycorax's sorcery is devilish (邪恶) and destructive.

◆ Just what were the books that Prospero brought with him from Milan, and from which he acquired his magic powers? Make up a list of possible titles for the books in Prospero's library. Choose one book and design it, showing the cover illustration, binding, contents page, and how the inside pages would be written and illustrated.

Sea voyages and shipwrecks

In writing *The Tempest*, Shakespeare was probably influenced by a true story that was the talk of London in 1610. In May 1609, a fleet of nine ships set out from England. Five hundred colonists were on board. Their destination was the newly founded colony of Virginia, where the settlers intended to begin a new life. They hoped for fabulous fortunes because of everything they had heard about the natural riches of America. But disaster struck.

The *Sea Venture*, the flagship carrying the expedition's leader, Sir Thomas Gates, became separated from the fleet in a great storm. The ship was driven onto the rocks of Bermuda – a place feared by sailors and known at the time as the Devil's Islands ('the still-vexed Bermudas' of Act 1 Scene 2, line 229). The rest of the fleet sailed on. On reaching Virginia, it sent back news of the loss of the expedition's leader with all of his 150 companions.

▼ This Royal Shakespeare Company performance in 1998 used a model ship on stage during the opening tempest.

For almost a year, England mourned. Then, in late summer of 1610, astonishing news arrived. The lost colonists had miraculously survived and reached Virginia. Apparently, the *Sea Venture* had run aground close to shore. All the passengers and crew had escaped safely, and were able to salvage (抢救) most of the supplies from the ship. They had discovered that Bermuda was far from being the desolate and barren place of legend. It had fresh water and a plentiful supply of food in the form of fish, wild pigs, birds and turtles. The survivors had set about building two boats so that they could sail on to Virginia.

It seemed as if providence smiled, but human nature had soured the good fortune of the survivors, and mutiny had broken out. There were attempts to seize the stores. Malicious rumours had spread, and a bid was made to murder the governor and take over the island. Only after great difficulties had Sir Thomas Gates and his companions set sail for Virginia. Even then, two mutineers had elected to stay behind on Bermuda.

◆ Imagine you are William Shakespeare and that you met one of the survivors of the wrecked *Sea Venture* and heard their stories. What questions did you ask them and what were your own feelings about what they said? Write your diary entry to record what you learnt from this conversation and how it affected you.

Accounts of the tale

Shakespeare probably found the inspiration for *The Tempest* in pamphlets written in 1610–11, which described the misadventures of the would-be colonists. The following extracts suggest how Shakespeare's dramatic imagination might have been stirred by this miraculous tale of loss and rediscovery, of the benevolence of nature, and of mutinies against an island's leader.

> On St James's day, a terrible tempest overtook them, and lasted in extremity forty-eight hours, and wherein some of them spent their masts, and others were much distressed.
>
> From Council of Virginia pamphlet, 1610

> An apparition of a little round light, like a faint star, trembling and streaming along with a sparkling blaze half the height upon the mainmast, and shooting sometime from shroud (横桅索) to shroud … And for three or four hours together, or rather more, half the night it kept with us, running sometimes along the main yard to the very end, and then returning …
>
> The shore and bays round about, when we landed first, afforded great store of fish … Fowl (飞禽 [以下出现了很多水鸟的名字]) there is in great store, small birds, sparrows fat and plump like a bunting, … White and grey heronshews [herons], bitterns, teal, snipes, crows, and hawks … cormorants, baldcoots, moorhens, owls and bats, in great store … A kind of web-footed fowl there is, of the bigness of an English green plover, or sea-mew …
>
> Yet was there a worse practice, faction (内讧) and conjuration afoot, deadly and bloody, in which the life of our governor, with many others, were threatened.
>
> From a pamphlet written by William Strachey, 1610

◆ National newspapers did not exist in Shakespeare's time, so news was often spread by pamphlets. Can you see any elements of the characters and events of *The Tempest* in the descriptions above? Try to find quotations from the play that relate to the passages from the pamphlets. How has Shakespeare developed the ideas and language used here?

▼ An engraving (版画) showing the *Sea Venture* running aground in Bermuda in 1609.

The Tempest
暴风雨

Colonialism

The history of the colonisation of the Americas was a story of horror and savagery. For some, the prospect of unlimited wealth and a life of ease prompted them to embark on an adventure to the New World. In their greed, they viewed the native peoples as little more than beasts, fit only to be slaves. There are sombre (阴暗，忧郁) echoes of this in the portrayal of Caliban. Others felt confident that they were educating the uneducated, bringing spiritual enlightenment to the heathen (野蛮人), and extending the domains of their European monarchs. Along with these aims went the profitable exploitation of what was seen as a wilderness, neglected by its existing inhabitants.

The native people must have viewed this invasion very differently. They saw their freedom vanish as they were forced into virtual slavery. Their lands were seized, their old religions destroyed and their languages eliminated. In *The Tempest*, Caliban is marked out as a savage because he cannot speak a recognised language such as English. He expresses the resentment of the enslaved:

You taught me language, and my profit on't
Is, I know how to curse.

This supplanting of his own language ('gabble' in Miranda's eyes) seems to articulate the deliberate process of linguistic control that English settlers often exercised not just in the new colonies, but also in neighbouring countries such as Ireland, Scotland and Wales.

Although some Europeans tried to uphold the principle of benign civilisation, the overwhelming evidence points to brutal conquest. European greed was a driving force of so-called 'civilisation' and the Europeans sought to profit by exploiting the rich resources of the New World. Such attitudes are reflected in the play when Trinculo (along with Stephano, Sebastian and Antonio) wonders how much money he could get for exhibiting Caliban at an English fair.

Europeans believed in their ethnic superiority over the native races of the Americas. These people were regarded as 'savages' or cannibals ('Caliban' is almost an anagram of 'cannibal'). But did the Europeans have the right to take possession, by gun and sword, of the native inhabitants' land? (Prospero's name is also almost an anagram of 'oppressor'). Resentful of Prospero's take-over, Caliban claims, 'This island's mine', to which Prospero replies, 'Thou most lying slave'.

The notion of social hierarchy was firmly fixed in the European mind, and most people believed it to be God-given. At the top of this social hierarchy was the king, who claimed to rule by divine right. Below him were aristocrats and courtiers, and so on, down to the lowest peasant. The 'masterless man' — a person without a superior — was seen as a terrible threat to social order. The European colonists of the New World brought back reports that

Perspectives and themes

the natives lived without a rigid social hierarchy. Caliban can be seen to represent this potential anarchy (无政府状态) that needs to be controlled by harsh punishment.

In the eyes of Europeans, debauchery (放荡) and vice flourished without control among the natives, and the marriage customs of Europe were unknown in the Americas. To the Europeans, such free love was abhorrent (令人憎恶) and Caliban's attempted rape of Miranda is evidence of his fundamentally evil nature, justifying constraint and harsh punishment. From the same viewpoint, Prospero's strict control of the sexual relations between Miranda and Ferdinand expresses a higher state of civilisation, characterised by restraint, abstinence (节制，禁欲) and self-discipline.

There were other perspectives, however, and the French philosopher Michel de Montaigne wrote an essay entitled 'On Cannibals', arguing that 'savage' societies were in many ways superior to the 'sophisticated' civilisations of Europe. He introduced the idea of 'the noble savage' who was free from 'civilised' greed, ambition and lust for power: 'The very words that import lying, falsehood, treasons, envy, dissimulation; covetousness (贪婪), detraction, and pardon were never heard.'

◆ Give Caliban a chance to tell his side of the story, starting with how the master/slave relationship quickly replaced that of teacher/pupil. Compose an account of what happened from his perspective.

▼ An engraving of Europeans arriving in the New World. Like Caliban, the native inhabitants often revealed the natural resources of their lands to the newcomers. Think about how the picture can help your understanding of *The Tempest*, and find one or two lines from the play to make a suitable caption.

The Tempest
暴风雨

Characters 人物分析

How are characters created?

The process of creating characters is called 'characterisation'. In *The Tempest*, Shakespeare does this in three major ways:

By their actions – Prospero creates a storm; then he brings the courtiers to him and arranges for his daughter, Miranda, to marry Alonso's son Ferdinand.

By what is said about them – amongst other things, Prospero is called 'great master' by Ariel, 'dearest father' by Miranda, 'mine own king' by Caliban and 'the wrongèd Duke of Milan' by himself.

Through their own language – how they speak to each other and, through long speeches and **soliloquy**, what they say to themselves when alone.

Each of these is equally important. Long speeches and soliloquies allow us to gain a deep insight into the innermost thoughts of the speaker, but other characters provide us with different views, and a character's proof of their qualities. Every character has a distinctive voice, and part of Shakespeare's genius is to explore it while allowing it to both change (as events affect the character's mind) and remain unique and recognisable.

Characters evolve over the course of the play – some more than others. However, unlike many of Shakespeare's plays (particularly the tragedies), *The Tempest* does not demonstrate particularly extreme changes in character.

◆ In small groups, discuss which characters change over the course of the play. Which of their actions most influence how you view them?

◆ Which speeches by Prospero and Caliban offer the greatest insight into their personalities? Collect key quotations that show the changes in these two characters over the course of the play. Display your choice of quotations on a large piece of paper, with images that symbolise these significant moments.

Prospero

Historically, Prospero was portrayed as a well-intentioned magician – a serene (安详, 和蔼) old man whose 'project' was to restore harmony and achieve reconciliation. However, over the past fifty years, many productions have shown Prospero as a much more ambiguous figure. He has been depicted as harsh and demanding, impatient and deeply troubled. Opinions about this character vary widely. Below are some interpretations of Prospero.

Enabler – Prospero is Latin for 'I cause to succeed, make happy and fortunate'. Bearing this definition in mind, how appropriate do you think Prospero's name is?

Magus and scholar – Prospero successfully learns to practise magic. His books and his spirits enable him to control the natural world, but to what extent can he control human nature – his own and others'?

Prince – Prospero's self-centred pursuit of study caused him to neglect his civic duties as duke of Milan, and subsequently led to his overthrow. When he is reinstated in this position, will he devote himself single-mindedly to good government ('Every third thought shall be my grave')?

Father – is Prospero a loving, kind and devoted father to Miranda? Or is he bad-tempered, dictatorial (独断专行) and irritable?

Revenger – Prospero pardons his enemies at the end of the play, but was his original plan to seek revenge for his overthrow and banishment?

Man – at the end of the play, Prospero admits to his weakness as a fallible human being:

> Now my charms are all o'erthrown,
> And what strength I have's mine own

What has he learned in the course of the play?

Master – Prospero controls Caliban harshly with cramps and pinches. He does not have a single good word to say about his slave. Is Prospero a colonialist exploiter, or a benevolent ruler of the island?

Actor-manager – Prospero is like a theatre director. He stages the opening tempest. He ensures that Gonzalo and Alonso sleep, thus provoking a murder attempt. He is the unseen observer of his daughter and his enemies. He also produces the banquet and the masque. Is Prospero the puppet-master? Are all the other characters merely his 'actors'?

Shakespeare – Some people believe that Shakespeare wrote the part of Prospero as a self-portrait, particularly in his farewell to his 'art' at Act 5 Scene 1, lines 33–57. Knowing what you know about Shakespeare, how does this affect your reading of this character?

- ◆ Rank these interpretations in order, with the one that best matches your own understanding of Prospero at the top.

- ◆ In small groups, discuss which of these interpretations of Prospero gives you the greatest insight into his character. Share your discussions with the rest of the class.

- ◆ Look at the production photograph of Prospero below. Compare how he is presented here with his portrayal in the pictures elsewhere in this book. Write a description of how you would present this character on stage.

THE TEMPEST
暴风雨

Ariel

Ariel is described in the list of characters as 'an airy spirit', and has been played by both male and female actors. Ariel appears in different guises: a flaming light in the storm, a nymph of the sea, a harpy at the banquet, Ceres in the masque. At Prospero's command, Ariel performs near-impossible feats, such as fetching 'dew / From the still-vexed Bermudas', treading 'the ooze / Of the salt deep' and running 'upon the sharp wind of the north'.

Imprisoned by Sycorax for refusing to obey her orders, and freed by Prospero's magic, Ariel yearns for freedom throughout the play. Prospero's attitude to his spirit-servant is ambiguous. Sometimes he seems affectionate, calling Ariel 'bird', 'chick', 'my fine spirit'. But, at other times, he calls Ariel 'moody' or 'malignant thing'. When Ariel demands 'my liberty', Prospero threatens him with twelve more years of imprisonment.

Ariel's language often expresses rapid movement and breathless excitement. There is a childlike eagerness to please in 'What shall I do? Say what? What shall I do?' But there is greater depth to the character if we look closer: is it Ariel who teaches Prospero forgiveness and pity? Describing the plight (困境) of Prospero's enemies, Ariel says that the sight of them would make Prospero feel compassion (Act 5 Scene 1, lines 18–20):

> ARIEL   That if you now beheld them, your affections
>   Would become tender.
> PROSPERO   Dost thou think so, spirit?
> ARIEL   Mine would, sir, were I human.
> PROSPERO   And mine shall.

Some critics think that Ariel exists only in Prospero's mind. Others see him as Prospero's chief informer and secret policeman. At the end of one production, Ariel picked up Prospero's broken staff, put it together again, and assumed the role of ruler of the island.

◆ **What is your view of Ariel? Think about the following:**
- Male, female – or something 'other'? Some productions emphasise Ariel's asexuality (无性别). Are there benefits to seeing Ariel as either male, female or androgynous (雌雄同体)?
- Does Ariel serve Prospero with eager and spontaneous willingness, or with reluctance and bad temper?
- Does Ariel love Prospero, or fear and detest him, or feel other emotions? Do these feelings change? If so, where exactly are these turning points?
- What are Prospero's feelings for Ariel: genuine love, or a harsh master's demand to have his every wish instantly performed?

◆ **After considering the questions above, design a poster in which you visualise Ariel. You may find it helps to base your representation on one line or an episode from the play. Find quotations to support your interpretations and use them on your poster.**

▲ 'On the bat's back I do fly.' A poster advertising a theatre production of *The Tempest*.

# Characters

Caliban

Caliban is described as a 'savage and deformed slave' in the list of characters, and in all kinds of uncomplimentary ways in the play – 'filth', 'hag-seed', 'misshapen knave' and 'monster'. On stage, he has been played as a lizard, a dog, a monkey, a snake and a fish. In one production, he was a tortoise, and was turned over onto his back by Prospero when he became unruly.

In the eighteenth century, the comic aspects of the role were emphasised. Caliban was a figure of fun, not to be taken seriously. In recent times, performances have emphasised Caliban's human and tragic qualities, not just his wickedness. He has increasingly been seen as a native dispossessed of his language and land by a colonial exploiter.

To help you form your own view of Caliban, think about each of the following:

Victim? A ruthless exploiter takes over Caliban's island, forcing him into slavery. He is seen by the shipwrecked Europeans as an opportunity to make money.

Savage? Caliban is brutish and evil by nature, incapable of being educated or civilised ('on whose nature / Nurture can never stick'). His plot against Prospero reflects his violent and vindictive (复仇，报复) nature.

Servant? Caliban deserves to be a servant. He merely exchanges a harsh master (Prospero) for a drunken one (Stephano), and wants to serve as a 'foot-licker'.

Contrast? Caliban's function in the play is to act as a contrast to other characters. For example, lust versus true love (Ferdinand), or the natural malevolence (恶意，狠毒) he exhibits towards Prospero versus the civilised and calculating evil of Antonio.

Noble savage? Until Prospero arrived, Caliban lived in natural freedom. He loves the island, and his language eloquently expresses some of the most haunting poetry in the play when he responds to Ariel's music: 'the isle is full of noises'.

Symbol of wickedness? Shakespeare's contemporaries believed that deformity was a sign of the wickedness of parents. Prospero claims that Caliban is the son of a witch and the devil. It is also suggested that he tried to rape Miranda. How would you define 'wicked' in the context of the play?

Term of abuse? The word 'Caliban' has entered the English language as a derogatory (贬义的) description. To call someone 'a Caliban' is to imply that they are wicked, violent and sinister.

Sensitive and perceptive? In Act 3 Scene 2, it is Caliban who describes the island so beautifully, and it is he who in Act 4 sees the clothes that Trinculo and Stephano are so taken by as 'trash'. Having suffered so much by being judged on his appearance, Caliban is able to look deeper.

The Tempest
暴风雨

Other characters

Miranda

Miranda appears to be a pure and innocent character, obedient to her father, Prospero. Her first words express compassion for the shipwreck's victims. She falls in love at first sight with Ferdinand (just as Prospero had hoped). She seems like a maiden in a fairy-tale or romance.

However, Shakespeare complicates her character. She assures her father that she is listening to his story, but the rest of the play suggests that she has not paid attention (because she never links Ferdinand or the other shipwrecked characters with the story Prospero has told her). She directs an apparently uncharacteristic torrent of abuse (连珠炮似的漫骂) at Caliban, and she stands up for Ferdinand when Prospero treats him harshly. She also disobeys her father by secretly meeting Ferdinand and telling him her name.

Feminist critics have seen Miranda – the only female character we see on stage – as a feeble representation of women, who seemingly exists to serve first her father and then Ferdinand.

This lack of any distinct female identity is extended to the other women referred to in the text: Caliban's mother, Sycorax, Miranda's mother, and Alonso's daughter Claribel are all marginalised and often subservient (恭顺) to male desires and demands.

Sycorax alone seems to have had some power, but when the play begins she is already dead and demonised by Prospero. Claribel has been given away by Alonso to the king of Tunis (a parallel, perhaps, with the interracial 'union' between Miranda and Caliban that Prospero has thwarted), and Miranda's mother is barely present as a memory for her daughter.

Although for some critics, then, Miranda is barely realised as a character, she does draw together many complex ideas. Many modern directors and actors seek to explore this on stage. It is Miranda who is seen as a possession by Prospero, and one who is given away by him so that he can regain power once removed from the island. It is she who is used by others like the pawn (兵，卒) in the game of chess she plays with Ferdinand.

◆ Think about how complex this character is. How would you describe Miranda's qualities to someone who has not read the play?

Ferdinand

Ferdinand also seems to be a stock figure (常见的人物) of romance: the noble prince who undergoes harsh ordeals, but finally marries a pure maiden. He is first seen enchanted by Ariel's music, but still grieving for the father whom he believes is drowned. He falls instantly in love with Miranda, and patiently endures the hard tasks that Prospero imposes on him. His betrothal to Miranda and his final words help strengthen the reconciliation of Alonso with Prospero.

The Tempest
暴风雨

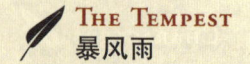

Gonzalo

Gonzalo appears to be precisely as he is described in the list of characters – 'an honest old councillor'. Just as he had helped Prospero, he is loyal to Alonso, seeking to cheer him in his grief. His integrity and sincerity contrast with Sebastian's and Antonio's treachery and cynicism, and he resists their mocking. Always unselfish and optimistic, at the play's end he rejoices that harmony has been restored. He is often played as a rather elderly, ineffectual (无能，软弱) idealist, easily mocked by Antonio and Sebastian.

Antonio and Sebastian

Antonio seems to be a selfish schemer (阴谋家), a character who betrayed his brother Prospero and seized his dukedom. On the island, he and Sebastian mock Gonzalo, then plot together to kill Alonso. When that plot is foiled by Ariel, they again agree to carry out the assassination. Highly disturbed by Ariel's accusation, they resolve to fight, but become spellbound (被咒语控制住) until Prospero releases them from their distraction. Neither man expresses remorse for his evil deeds and intentions. Their last words in the play are as cynical as their first. Is it possible to distinguish between the two characters? Is Antonio the more manipulative, or do we dislike Sebastian more because he is so easily led?

Stephano and Trinculo

These are the comic counterparts (对应角色) of Antonio and Sebastian. Although they add much humour to the play, they both hope to make money out of Caliban, and the drunken Stephano makes him his slave. At Caliban's prompting, Stephano agrees to murder Prospero and become king of the island. Their absurd desire to dress in gaudy clothing leads to their downfall, and – hunted by Prospero's spirits – they end up dishevelled (衣衫不整) and drunk, their foolishness clear to everyone.

What do you think these characters offer the audience beyond the obvious humour? Do you think that we judge them too quickly (and too harshly)?

▼ Stephano and Trinculo (pictured here with Ariel – with his arms raised – and Caliban) provide the comedic element of the play.

◆ Study the pictures on these pages. In groups, talk about what each of these images conveys about the characters.

◆ One person steps into role as one of the characters and takes his or her place in the hot-seat. Group members ask this character questions about why they behave the way they do. Keep the tightly focused so that each character has the same amount of time.

◆ In pairs, write or improvise a dialogue between Prospero and another character, reflecting on their relationship and what they want or need from each other. Other members of your class could watch and give feedback, commenting on how true to the spirit of both characters your interpretations are.

◆ In small groups, write one question each on the relationship between any two characters. Use questions such as 'To what extent would you agree that …?' Choose from Prospero, Caliban, Ariel or Miranda. Select the strongest overall question and draw up a group answer in the form of an essay plan. Deliver your essay plans in a presentation to the rest of the class. Keep the presentation succinct (简洁), using six to eight slides, with each slide representing a different part of the essay.
The slides should contain only key words: it is up to you to talk the class through your answer in more detail.

How real are the characters?

◆ The Shakespeare critic L. C. Knights wrote a famous essay entitled 'How many children had Lady Macbeth?' In it, he mocked the way that some people approach a study of Shakespeare's plays as if the characters were real human beings. How do you feel about what L. C. Knights claims? In groups, discuss your views. Do you see the characters not just as figures in a play, but as real human beings with past lives and familiar emotions?

The Tempest 暴风雨

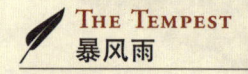

The language of *The Tempest* 《暴风雨》的语言

Imagery

The Tempest abounds in **imagery** (sometimes called 'figures' or 'figurative language'). Imagery is created by vivid words and phrases that conjure up emotionally charged mental pictures or associations. Imagery provides insight into character, and stirs the audience's imagination. It deepens the dramatic impact of particular moments or moods.

In Act 2 Scene 1, as Antonio tempts Sebastian with his murderous plan, he says that he will kill Alonso with 'this obedient steel', instead of 'this sword'. When he assures Sebastian that Naples is so far away from Tunis that it would take a message many years to travel the distance, he uses a striking image: 'till new-born chins / Be rough and razorable' (the time from when a baby boy is born until he begins to shave).

The imagery used to describe change is made more striking in the image that extends over several lines in Ariel's account of the 'sea-change' undergone by people when they die. Ariel also describes how the skeleton of the drowned king has turned to coral and his eye sockets have filled with pearls:

> *Full fathom five thy father lies,*
> *Of his bones are coral made;*
> *Those are pearls that were his eyes;*
> *Nothing of him that doth fade,*
> *But doth suffer a sea-change*
> *Into something rich and strange.*

The sea, dreams and spirits are recurring images in the play and contribute to its strange, dream-like world that causes both terror and wonder.

◆ **In role as a film director, write out your ideas for how the imagery in certain passages might be visualised in a film production. Prepare a storyboard or part of a film script to illustrate your ideas.**

The images that recur throughout the play include:

The sea The play begins in a storm and ends with the promise of calm seas. In between, images of the sea frequently occur: 'sea-sorrow', 'sea-change', 'sea-swallowed', 'never-surfeited sea' (suggesting the infinite appetite of the ocean), 'still-closing waters', and so on. Prospero speaks of the tempest that he and Miranda endured when they were banished from Milan: 'th'sea, that roared to us'. In Act 2 Scene 1, lines 217–24, the sea's ebb and flow is reflected in the exchange in which Antonio tempts Sebastian: 'I am standing water', 'I'll teach you how to

The language of The Tempest

flow', 'Ebbing men, indeed'. In Act 5 Scene 1, lines 79–81, Prospero – about to release his enemies from their enchantment back to sanity (神志正常) – declares:

> Their understanding
> Begins to swell, and the approaching tide
> Will shortly fill the reasonable shore

The theatre Shakespeare's interest in the theatre is evident throughout *The Tempest*. There are the spectacular dramatic events of the shipwreck, the banquet and the masque. The language is full of echoes of acting and plays. Ariel is like a stage-manager as he 'performs' the tempest and arranges the banquet and the masque. When he seizes control in Milan, Antonio is like an actor who would 'have no screen between this part he played, / And him he played it for' (Act 1 Scene 2, lines 107–8). Later, as he plots Alonso's murder, Antonio uses the language of the theatre: 'cast … perform … act … prologue … discharge' (Act 2 Scene 1, lines 247–50). Prospero reflects on the way in which life itself is like a stage pageant, whose actors and theatre, 'the great globe itself', vanish into thin air (Act 4 Scene 1, lines 147–58).

Nature The play's language evokes the rich variety of the natural world: sea, air, earth and wildlife, thunder and lightning, wind and roaring water. Every scene contains aspects of nature, both benign and threatening. Caliban's language expresses his intimate knowledge and love of the island as he describes the 'fresh springs, brine-pits, barren place and fertile', 'pig-nuts' and 'jay's nest', while Ariel delights that he has led the drunken conspirators through 'Toothed briars, sharp furzes, pricking gorse, and thorns' to the 'filthy mantled pool'.

Verse and prose

The verse of *The Tempest* is mainly **blank verse** (无韵诗，素体诗): unrhymed verse with a five-beat rhythm called iambic pentameter. This is a rhythm or metre in which each line has five **feet** (groups of syllables) called **iambs** (抑扬，即前音节轻，后音节重), which have one unstressed (×) and one stressed (/) syllable:

> ×   / × / × / × / × /
> So, king, go safely on to seek thy son.

By the time he came to write *The Tempest* (around 1610), Shakespeare used great variation in his verse. He sometimes wrote lines of more or fewer than ten syllables, sometimes changed the pattern of stresses in a line, and sometimes used rhyming couplets for effect. He ensured that the rhythm of the verse was appropriate to the meaning and mood of the speech: reflective, fearful, apprehensive, anguished or confused.

These rhythmic patterns are what distinguish verse from prose, not whether the lines rhyme. Prose is different from blank verse: it is everyday language with no specific rhythm, metric scheme or rhyme. Shakespeare uses prose to break up the verse in his plays, to signify characters' madness or low status, or to draw attention to changes in plot or character. It is easy to tell the difference: verse lines all begin with a capital letter and the lines do not reach the other side of the page, whereas prose passages have lines that stretch across the page and only use capital letters at the beginning of sentences.

Shakespeare also used **caesura** ([诗行中的] 切分处，停顿处) and **enjambement** (跨行) to add to the rhythm of his blank verse. A caesura is where a phrase ends in the middle of a line to create a pause or a break in the dialogue or action. With enjambement, the phrase carries over into the next line of poetry. In so doing, phrases spill over and build up from one line to the next, increasing the emotional or dramatic impact of the script.

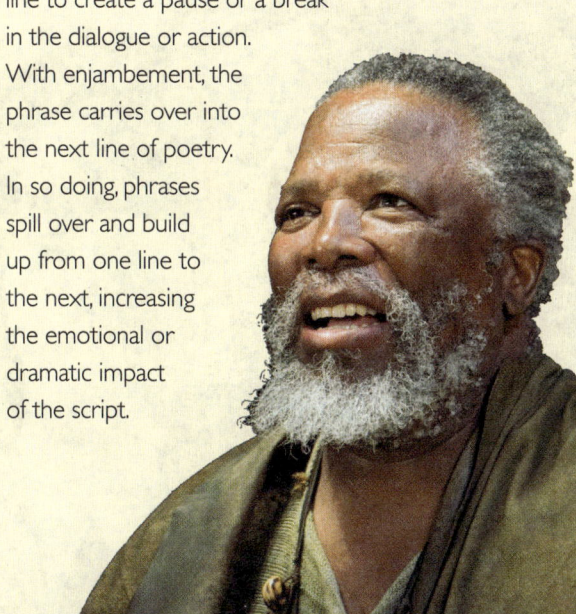

The Tempest
暴风雨

Prose was traditionally used by comic and low-status characters. High-status characters generally use verse. There are exceptions, however. Sebastian and Antonio, despite their high status, use prose as they taunt (奚落) Gonzalo. Similarly, Caliban, despite his very low status, speaks verse – some of it of extraordinary beauty. He uses prose in his first encounter with Stephano and Trinculo (low-status and comic characters), but ends the scene with haunting poetry as he resolves to leave Prospero and serve Stephano:

> *Be not afeared; the isle is full of noises,*
> *Sounds, and sweet airs, that give delight and hurt not.*

- ◆ The human heartbeat has an iambic rhythm. Put your hand on your heart to hear the basic rhythm of weak and strong stresses.
- ◆ Choose a verse speech. Iambic pentameter, with five stresses, will be easy to find, while tetrameter, with four beats, is found only in the songs. Explore ways of speaking it to emphasise the metre. You could clap your hands, tap the desk or walk five paces to accompany each line, for example. Afterwards, write eight or more lines of your own in the same style.

Metaphor, simile and personification

Shakespeare's imagery uses **metaphor**, **simile** or **personification**. All are comparisons.

A simile compares one thing to another using 'like' or 'as'. For example, Trinculo exclaims that Caliban 'smells like a fish'. Ariel compares Gonzalo's weeping to rain falling from a thatched roof: 'His tears runs down his beard like winter's drops / From eaves of reeds'.

A metaphor is also a comparison, suggesting that two dissimilar things are the same. Prospero describes the leaky boat in which he and Miranda were set adrift as 'A rotten carcass of a butt'. His image for the tears he wept on the voyage becomes 'I have decked the sea with drops full salt'.

The language of The Tempest

Personification turns all kinds of things into persons, giving them human feelings or attributes, such as when Prospero declares 'bountiful Fortune, / Now my dear lady, hath mine enemies / Brought to this shore'. Here, he sees Fortune as his goddess or his friend.

Antithesis (对偶) and repetition

Antithesis is the opposition of words or phrases to each other, and it expresses the conflict that is at the heart of the play and that is the essence of all drama. Ferdinand, discovering his father is alive, not drowned, gratefully exclaims, 'Though the seas threaten, they are merciful'. A similar antithesis is set up between Caliban and Ariel, who represent earth versus air, and Prospero and Sycorax, where the former's magic 'art' is superior to the witch's evil sorcery. Antithesis is especially powerful in *The Tempest*, where good is set against evil and where illusion and magic are major themes.

Shakespeare used **repetition** to give his language great dramatic force. Perhaps the most obvious example of repetition is found in Ariel's songs, which please the ear by being rich in the repeated sounds of rhyme and the hypnotic effects of rhythm. At other points in the play, repeated words, phrases, rhythms and sounds add to the emotional intensity of a scene. This repetition can occur on many levels.

Repetition of words

Sometimes the same word is repeated in a short space of time in order to increase pace and tension. This is shown in the following extract from the play's dramatic opening scene:

> 'We split, we split!' – 'Farewell, my wife and children!' – 'Farewell, brother!' – 'We split, we split, we split!'

At other times, a word (such as 'loss' or 'lost') is repeated throughout a passage so that the idea can be developed or extended:

> ALONSO   You the like loss?
> PROSPERO   As great to me, as late; and supportable
>   To make the dear loss have I means much weaker
>   Than you may call to comfort you; for I
>   Have lost my daughter.

Repetition of sounds

Alliteration is the repetition of consonant sounds at the beginning of words:

> *Foot it featly here and there,*
> *And sweet sprites the burden bear.*

Assonance (半谐音，半韵) is the repetition of vowel sounds in the middle of words:

> *Come unto these yellow sands,*
> *And then take hands*

Rhyming couplets, which often end long speeches in blank verse or signal the end of a scene, also show this repetition of sound:

> *Sea-nymphs hourly ring his knell,*
> *Hark, now I hear them, ding dong bell.*

These repetitions are opportunities for actors to intensify emotional impact.

Repetition of patterns

Anaphora is the repetition of the same word at the beginning of successive sentences:

>   *Hast thou forgot*
> *The foul witch Sycorax, who with age and envy*
> *Was grown into a hoop? Hast thou forgot her?*

Epistrophe (尾词重复) is the repetition of a word or phrase at the end of a series of sentences or clauses:

> *Hourly joys be still upon you,*
> *Juno sings her blessings on you ...*
> *Scarcity and want shall shun you,*
> *Ceres' blessing so is on you.*

Polyptoton is repetition of words derived from the same root word, but with different endings or forms: 'Admired Miranda, / Indeed the top of admiration'.

- ◆ Turn to any two or three pages of *The Tempest* and identify all the ways in which Shakespeare uses repetition in those lines. Look especially at sections of Act 1 Scene 2 and Act 4 Scene 1.

- ◆ Try out different ways of speaking the lines to discover how emphasising or playing down the repetition can contribute to dramatic effect.

The Tempest
暴风雨

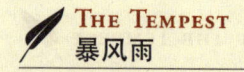

Soliloquies and asides

A **soliloquy** is a monologue – a kind of internal debate spoken by a character who is alone (or assumes he or she is alone) on stage. It gives the audience direct access to the character's mind, revealing their inner thoughts and motives. Ferdinand's soliloquy at the beginning of Act 3, as he stops carrying the logs to think about Miranda, is one example.

An **aside**, on the other hand, is a brief comment or address to the audience that gives voice to a character's inner thoughts, unheard by other characters on stage. The audience is taken into this character's confidence or can see deeper into their motivations and experiences. Asides can also be used for characters to comment on the action as it unfolds. Prospero has many asides, but his language rarely gives direct access to his thoughts. He tells stories, gives orders, comments on the action, and renounces his magic in long, spell-like speeches. Yet, unlike many of Shakespeare's other major characters – such as Hamlet or Iago – he does not have a soliloquy in which he reveals what is really on his mind.

- Identify some of the play's soliloquies and asides. Choose one and write notes on how you would speak it on stage to maximise its dramatic effect.
- Think about possible reasons why Shakespeare did not give Prospero such a soliloquy. Identify a suitable place for a soliloquy for Prospero in the play, then try your hand at writing it to reveal this character's most private thoughts.

Language and power

Throughout history, conquerors and governments have tried to suppress or eliminate the language of certain groups, defining it as 'inferior'. The ancient Greeks called anyone who did not speak Greek a 'barbarian' (speaking 'baa-baa' language). The word itself is onomatopoeic, like 'double-Dutch' or 'mumbo-jumbo', and suggests what the Greeks saw as 'nonsense' language.

In Shakespeare's time, most Europeans believed that only their own languages were civilised. Foreign languages were 'gabble', without real meaning. (Interestingly, however, it was not until the late 1300s that English was considered to be a civilised language.) The mark of savagery was not knowing English or Spanish or some other European language.

Lost words and new words

The Tempest is full of unfamiliar words that have disappeared from use today or that Shakespeare made up as he wrote the play. The meanings of unfamiliar words can sometimes be understood from their context. For example, just what are the 'Young scamels' that Caliban promises to bring to Stephano (Act 2 Scene 2, line 149)? 'Scamels' may be seagulls or clams, or may have meant something quite different in Shakespeare's time. Today, no one really knows. The word reflects the nature of *The Tempest* itself: enigmatic and not able to be tied down to a single meaning.

Furthermore, in this play of improbable happenings, Shakespeare frequently uses the hyphen to create compound words that conjure up vivid images. He puts words together to present new challenges to the imagination.

- Discuss what some of the following compound words might mean:

    'blue-eyed' • 'brine-pits' • 'fresh-brook'
    • 'hag-born' • 'hag-seed' • 'o'er-prized'
    • 'over-topping' • 'sea-change' • 'sea-nymphs'
    • 'sea-sorrow' • 'sea-storm' • 'side-stitches'
    • 'sea-swallowed' • 'pinch-spotted'
    • 'sight-outrunning'

You may notice that these words are vividly powerful, but cannot be pinned down to a single, exact meaning. Shakespeare may have used these hyphenated words because their instability expresses the sense of wonder and ever-changing reality that runs through the play.

- Prospero calls Caliban 'hag-seed', which means seed (child) of a witch. Make up a few hyphenated words of your own to describe Prospero or other characters of your choice.

The language of The Tempest

THE TEMPEST
暴风雨

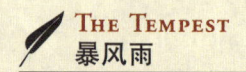

The Tempest in performance 《暴风雨》的演出

Performance on Shakespeare's stage

Shakespeare probably wrote *The Tempest* around 1610. Only two performances of the play are known for certain to have taken place during his lifetime – both at the court of King James. The first recorded performance was on 1 November 1611.

In Shakespeare's lifetime, *The Tempest* was almost certainly performed in two theatres: the Globe Theatre and the better-resourced Blackfriars Theatre. It seems likely that Shakespeare took full advantage of the facilities that the Blackfriars Theatre offered when he was writing the play. This indoor arena came with a group of musicians (which might explain why there is so much music in the play). It also allowed him the opportunity of using greater 'special effects' (for example, the dramatic opening storm, as well as the masque). Both theatres were owned by Shakespeare's acting company, The King's Men.

During Shakespeare's lifetime, plays in outdoor amphitheatres (圆形露天剧场) like the Globe were performed in broad daylight during the summer months. So, at 2 p.m. audiences would assemble with food and drink to watch a play with no lighting and no rule of silence for the audience. There were high levels of background noise and interaction during performances, and audience members were free to walk in and out of the theatre.

Shakespeare seems to want to grab his audience's attention from the very first line of the play: the storm is spectacular, and to some extent threatens to make the subsequent action something of an anti-climax. However, Shakespeare's most 'magical' of plays uses spectacle throughout: Ariel's appearance as a harpy in Act 3, the masque in Act 4, and the chasing pack of dogs in the final scene of the same act, mark this out as a play intended to 'wow' the audience.

The Tempest has music at the heart of its action: not only are there songs, but characters make reference to hearing music (In Act 1, Ferdinand talks of music creeping 'by me upon the waters', and Caliban's famous speech in Act 3 describes an island that is 'full of noises / Sounds and sweet airs, that give delight and hurt not'); and of course Stephano and Trinculo resort to drunken singing. Although all these elements certainly add to the sense that *The Tempest* was intended to be a spectacle, they also pose practical challenges for the actors on stage: for example, how do the actors deliver these lines, and how is the momentum of the plot maintained when elaborate performances are taking place?

- Look at some of the most dramatic moments in the play – the opening scene, the masque, the vanishing banquet. Imagine you are the director of a school production: how would you perform these successfully? Experiment with different ways of staging these episodes, keeping in mind the themes being explored by Shakespeare in each scene.

Shakespeare included many clues for his actors in his scripts. These clues are known as 'embedded stage directions' because of the coded instructions they give to the actors about who to talk to, when to move or gesture and when to exit. Clues about setting, weather, clothing, other characters' appearances and onstage action were also placed in the scripts. For example, in Act 1 Scene 2, we are introduced to Miranda as she is responding to the tempest that has just taken place. The dialogue that follows contains a number of embedded stage directions that help the actors establish the relationship between the two characters. What clues does Shakespeare provide the actors with in order to ensure these lines are successful? Later, in Act 2 Scene 1, the plotting pair of Sebastian and Antonio are brought to the point of killing the other courtiers, and their language is filled with coded signals, conveying meaning that only willing conspirators would receive favourably.

Embedded stage directions were incredibly valuable for early actors, because they had little time to rehearse and almost no opportunity to study the whole play before a performance. When a play was written, a scribe would make a copy. This was cut up and each actor was given a

The Tempest
暴风雨

scroll with his speeches stitched together, along with basic cues and stage directions. The actors would memorise their lines, taking particular care that they knew their cues so they would be sure of when to enter and speak. A summary of the play, known as a 'backstage plot', was hung up backstage so actors would know the main story and the context for their entrances and exits. Players who knew only their parts and a plot summary relied heavily on their cues and embedded stage directions to piece together information about what was going on, who they were addressing and who was going to respond.

- There are many activities in the book that ask you to think about how the script should be staged. Look closely to see if there are embedded stage directions that might have been more fully developed (some examples might include Act 1 Scene 2, lines 22–87; Act 2 Scene 1, lines 1–180; Act 3 Scene 1, lines 22–98; Act 4 Scene 1, lines 194–260; and Act 5 Scene 1, line 215).

- Discuss with a partner what a modern director might say to actors at these points. Are all of them necessary on a modern stage? Would you consider cutting some lines if they are not necessary? How should the actors perform the lines?

This pressured system of rehearsal and performance was confusing for new actors, especially young ones, who were sometimes apprenticed to older actors while they were new to the workings of the stage. The apprentices, aged between about six and fourteen, learned the art of acting from more established actors.

In Shakespeare's day, Miranda, the spirits and Iris, Juno and Ceres were played by boys because women were not allowed to act on stage. There were no elaborate sets on the bare stage of the Globe Theatre, and even with the additional facilities of the Blackfriars Theatre, sets were limited in terms of scenery and lighting. As a result, Shakespeare included detailed and often poetic descriptions of the time and place in various scenes. Audiences needed to use their imagination to compensate for the bare stage!

However, actors wore lavish costumes, usually the fashionable dress of the times, and a range of visual and sound effects were used to add spectacle to a performance: for example, animal organs may have been used on stage, including pig's bladders filled with animal blood during murder scenes; cannon balls were rolled along tracks behind stage to simulate thunder. Storm scenes such as the opening of *The Tempest*, or the scenes on the heath in *King Lear* and *Macbeth* were probably accompanied by such sound effects. Bells, trumpets, and drums were also used, as were a range of songs, background instrumental music and dance music. The space above the stage, the upper structure known as the 'heavens', was decorated on the underside with stars and zodiac signs and used for characters to descend and ascend during a performance.

▲ In a reversal of how the play would have been performed in Shakespeare's day, this performance had women playing Prospero and Ariel.

The Tempest in performance

Performance after Shakespeare

In 1667, *The Tempest* was rewritten as *The Enchanted Island*. Only one-third of Shakespeare's play was included, and a great deal was added. Caliban and Miranda were given sisters. A male character – Hippolito, Duke of Mantua – appeared. He had never seen a woman, and would be under a curse if he *did* see one. The masque and the role of Sebastian were left out entirely, although much more comedy, dance and music were inserted. Expensive stage machinery created spectacular effects, particularly in the storm scene and in the flying of Ariel and the other spirits.

This version of *The Tempest* was revived in many adaptations during the eighteenth and nineteenth centuries, with every production aiming at enthralling (吸引) the audience with theatrical spectacle. One version shifted the shipwreck to the start of Act 2, so that latecomers to the theatre would not miss the elaborate stage effects contained in this scene. Another version contained thirty-two songs.

▼ A scene from the play, published in 1857.

These operatic and balletic versions of *The Tempest* attracted large audiences, but were often criticised for being more like pantomimes (哑剧). In 1815, one famous critic, William Hazlitt, was outraged by what he saw, calling it 'travesty (拙劣的模仿作品), caricature (夸张而怪诞的描述) … vulgar and ridiculous … clap-trap sentiments (哗众取宠的情感表达) … heavy tinsel (华而不实)'. He was tempted never to see another Shakespeare play.

▶ This illustration shows how Caliban was portrayed in an 1850 production of *The Tempest*.

The Tempest
暴风雨

In spite of all the criticism, the spectacular version of *The Tempest* was always popular with audiences. Each new production was hugely successful, and very profitable. It was not until the mid-nineteenth century that serious attempts were made to present the play as Shakespeare had written it.

William Charles Macready's Covent Garden production of 1838 proved a turning point in the performance history of the play. Here, the director used a script that was closer to Shakespeare's original text, cutting down dramatically on the excesses introduced in the previous century during the reign of Charles II (1660–85).

In 1897, William Poel directed an Elizabethan Stage Society production that attempted to present a version of the play that was as close as possible to the original. Twentieth-century productions – at the Old Vic and by the Royal Shakespeare Company – continued this tradition.

William Bridge-Adams's production for the RSC in 1919 staged a simple production that had at its centre the Jacobean court masque. Coming just after the end of World War I, this production – which looked back to perhaps a simpler, less destructive age – was very popular.

Later productions for the RSC, including those by Peter Brook (1957) and Clifford Williams (1978), explored the complexity of Prospero's character. John Gielgud, directed by Brook, portrayed Prospero as a rather sinister figure obsessed with his own personal demons. Williams's direction of Michael Hordern's Prospero emphasised a kinder character, but the staging – bleak and empty – showed the limitations of both his world and his power.

Derek Jacobi played Prospero in 1982. In this production, Prospero is initially motivated by a strong sense of outrage; Jacobi believed that Prospero wants 'to teach these people a lesson now they're in his power'; ultimately, though, he relents, but does not fully forgive those he has made suffer. Jacobi thought deeply about the motivation behind Prospero's actions. He said:

> I think there is a strong feeling for revenge, for the wrong that was done him, the hideous wrong that was done him. Because he was meant to die, so was the girl meant to die, and the girl was a baby. She is fifteen in the play. He wants to provide for her, he wants her certainly to have the future that those wicked men were going to deny her.

The actor believed that Prospero is an 'improviser' (即兴创作者): he adapts to changing conditions throughout his life, including Miranda's falling in love with Ferdinand. Such an interpretation places limitations on his power because we see that he cannot control everything.

◆ To what extent would you agree with this view of Prospero? Does he have total control of his domain, or is he more limited – reacting to events, rather than creating them? How does such an interpretation change your view of the character and of Shakespeare's thoughts on nature?

▼ Derek Jacobi as Prospero in the 1982 production.

The Tempest in performance

The Tempest today

Today, most stage productions of *The Tempest* make only minor changes to Shakespeare's script, and try to avoid the sentimental escapism of earlier versions. They take the opportunities that Shakespeare provides to explore the many ambiguities and conflicts that exist in the script. Even in modern versions, however, special attention is paid to the opportunities for dramatic spectacle.

The Tempest has always been a source of inspiration for other artists, too. Mozart planned an opera based on it, but died before he could turn his plan into music. Many novelists have written 'island stories'; examples are Daniel Defoe's *Robinson Crusoe*, William Golding's *Lord of the Flies* and Marina Warner's *Indigo*. Poets have been especially attracted by the play. Shelley, T. S. Eliot and W. H. Auden all drew on *The Tempest*, and in the poem 'Caliban upon Setebos' Robert Browning made Caliban extremely eloquent and intelligent. Aldous Huxley's novel *Brave New World* imagines a horrific future society in which people are little more than robots.

The Tempest has lent itself to the shifting developments in intellectual and political thought over time. Modern productions have emphasised the postcolonial nature of the play, with Caliban increasingly presented as not only fully human, but also dignified, articulate and with a legitimate grievance against Prospero. Ariel is often portrayed as a resentful and sometimes alienated figure, preoccupied with gaining his freedom from a repressive master.

Race has featured strongly in some productions, such as Jonathan Miller's 1988 production, in which the courtiers were played by white actors and the spirits by black actors. Other productions have stressed different elements of the play: Braham Murray's 1992 production at the Royal Exchange in Manchester saw Prospero's book-lined study on set throughout the performance, and other productions have explored the charged relationship between Prospero and the sexually ambiguous Ariel. From the early eighteenth century until the 1930s, Ariel was played by a female actor.

▼ Trinculo, Caliban and Stephano in Jonathan Miller's 1988 production.

The Tempest
暴风雨

The Tempest has also proven popular with film makers, but most have taken it as a source of inspiration rather than as something to be faithfully interpreted. There were short filmed scenes made in the early twentieth century and the play was made into a BBC television series starring Michael Hordern in 1979. *The Tempest* has received radical interpretations by directors as diverse as Derek Jarman (*Tempest*, 1979) and Peter Greenaway (*Prospero's Books*, 1991).

Other screen and stage adaptations include the Hollywood science-fiction movie *Forbidden Planet* (made in 1956), and *Return to the Forbidden Planet*, a 1980s rock musical. More recently, in 2010 Julie Taymor directed Helen Mirren as a female Prospero (called Prospera) in a well-received film version of the play.

One of the main reasons for *The Tempest*'s popularity with directors and actors is because the main characters can be interpreted so differently: Caliban, Ariel and Prospero are emotionally rich characters, but the themes they allow us to explore bring an additional level of complexity. Caliban in particular allows for radically different approaches from the actor and director. For much of the play's history this character was portrayed as something sub-human, and it was not until the early

▼ The 1956 film adaptation set the story on a distant planet rather than a remote island.

The Tempest in performance

twentieth century that he was depicted as not only human-like but relatively civilised. The changes, of course, had occurred in society, rather than in the play itself.

Beerbohm Tree's 1904 production saw Caliban as an 'elemental man' – a figure seemingly at one with the world around him, who was becoming increasingly educated. Although his original identity was changing, it was not seen as entirely negative. This positive view of colonialism was to some extent echoed in Wilson Knight's performance of Caliban in 1938. Later productions have framed Caliban within a more overtly political context: he is seen as very much the victim of a conquering power.

Some postcolonial productions originating in former colonies of the British Empire have stressed that Caliban is exploited by the conquering European forces represented by Prospero and the shipwrecked courtiers. Not only is his land taken from him, but so too is his indigenous identity. Directors point to the exchange between Miranda and Caliban in which she tells him how she taught him to speak. Caliban's response is grudging (see Act 1 Scene 2).

Increasingly throughout the twentieth and twenty-first centuries, interpretations and productions of *The Tempest* have stressed the contrasts and conflicts between Prospero and Caliban, between colonist and native inhabitant. A 1970 production of *The Tempest* presented the play as a story of colonial exploitation. The director, Jonathan Miller, described it as 'the tragic and inevitable disintegration of more primitive culture as the result of European invasion and colonisation'. He compared Stephano and Trinculo to foreign soldiers, who patronise or bully the native population: 'they shout loudly at the people to make them understand, make them drunk and get drunk themselves'. Caliban was 'the demoralised, detribalised, dispossessed, suffering field-hand'. Miller's interpretation was in sharp contrast to the traditional image of Prospero as a benevolent ruler.

◆ Do you think that Shakespeare's *The Tempest* is a justification of colonialism or a criticism of it – or does it not express any point of view about colonisation?

THE TEMPEST
暴风雨

Like many of Shakespeare's plays, *The Tempest* acts as a mirror reflecting the shifting values of society. Just as Caliban has evolved from a creature that is barely human to a figure that symbolises repressed indigenous peoples, directors and actors have drawn out different themes within the play in order to explore ideas current at the time.

The complex relationship between Prospero and his daughter has proven fertile ground for directors and actors who wish to explore the psychoanalytical aspects of the script. In some productions, the staff that Prospero wields is represented as a phallic symbol (阳具象征) symbolising masculine dominance.

Sex, and attitudes towards it, are powerfully charged themes to explore on stage. Perhaps influenced by the work of Sigmund Freud, directors have suggested that at the heart of the father-daughter relationships (Ariel is often played by a female actor) in this play is an unconscious Elektra complex (伊莱克特拉情结，恋父情结): Prospero's often angry statements are seen as a result of his inner conflict with his desire for Ariel and Miranda and an acceptance that he has to release both from his control.

Other interpretations that have drawn from psychoanalysis see Ariel as symbolic of the super-ego, with Prospero as the controlling ego and Caliban the untamed, primitive id (本我) . (You may want to spend some time researching Freudian terms and their relevance to this play, as well as to other plays by Shakespeare.)

- Race and gender are often divisive issues in society and this is usually why directors are so keen to explore them on stage: they can ask searching questions of both the script and the audience's own views. In small groups, discuss how important you think the race of the actors is in this play. Think about how racial identity might change the audience's interpretation of the play's key themes.

- Consider how important the actor's gender is: what difference does it make if Prospero is female? Which male characters could easily be played by female actors, and which could not without radically changing how they are perceived? Discuss your thoughts in groups.

The Tempest remains one of Shakespeare's most popular plays: it is regularly performed in schools (by younger and older students), and new productions by professional theatre companies appear every year. It has not only been the source of inspiration for films and musicals, but for all forms of art, including literature, manga (日本漫画) texts, dance, songs, cartoons, blogs and fan fiction (同人小说).

The play's popularity can be explained in a number of ways: it has a relatively straightforward story, complex characters, powerful themes with universal – and modern – appeal, and a sense of scale and spectacle that can entrance an audience.

The Tempest in performance

The Tempest
暴风雨

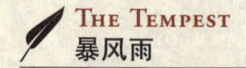

Whose *The Tempest* is it?

As you have seen in the various activities in this edition, if we wish to interpret an episode in a particular way then we do so by focusing on key passages in the script. It is rare to see productions (other than those in translation) that change Shakespeare's language, but this has not always been the case.

◆ Hold a class discussion on how much freedom directors and actors should have in adapting *The Tempest*. Should every word remain untouched? Or is it permissible to cut scenes if they are not felt to be necessary (or by Shakespeare), such as the masque? Is it right to make the play overtly political? Is it possible to separate it from the society in which it is performed? Who judges such changes a success – the director, the cast, the critics, or the audience?

The Tempest on stage and on film

The Tempest is best experienced live, but if you are unable to see a production, or take part in one, then there are many different versions available to watch at home. Take time to find different versions, but remember to view each actively, rather than passively. If you are analysing a film adaptation, take notes on:

- Camerawork (angles, movement, shot type)
- Sound (dialogue, sound effects, music)
- Lighting (back light, key light)
- Editing (simple cuts, montage, fade-out shots, dissolve cuts)

For each of these points, consider what their effect is on the viewer, and how they add to (and sometimes detract from) the original script.

◆ Try reviewing different versions of *The Tempest*. You could compare and contrast two film versions, or two theatre productions. It might help to read film and theatre critics' reviews of past productions so that you can get a sense of what they focus on and of their depth of analysis. There are many radically different interpretations of this play, so remain open-minded about each.

◆ As you watch the productions, ask yourself what each is saying about its own time and culture. As you assess the various qualities of the performances you watch, think about how each differs from your own society, but also how it reflects ideas and attitudes that are still familiar today.

Posters

Promotional posters provide a 'snapshot' of a production. Their layout, typography (版面设计) and use of images convey the qualities of the film or play, as well as the period and culture in which they were created.

◆ Look at the posters and discuss in small groups what you think the differences between the productions might be.

◆ Stay in your groups and design your own poster to promote a production of *The Tempest* that conveys the main values of a particular community. This community could be a school, an area of a town, a financial district, or a whole society. Think carefully about the images and text you would include, and why they are relevant to *The Tempest*.

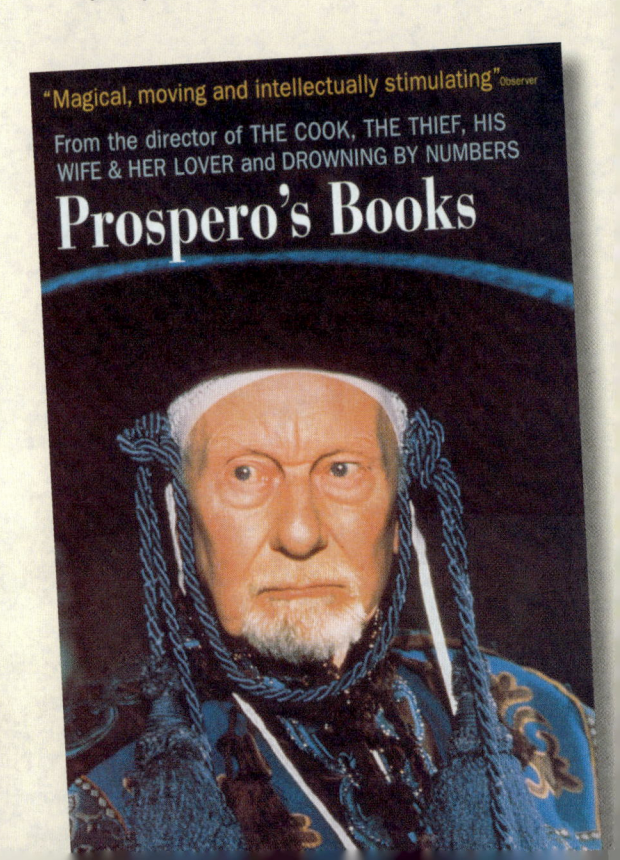

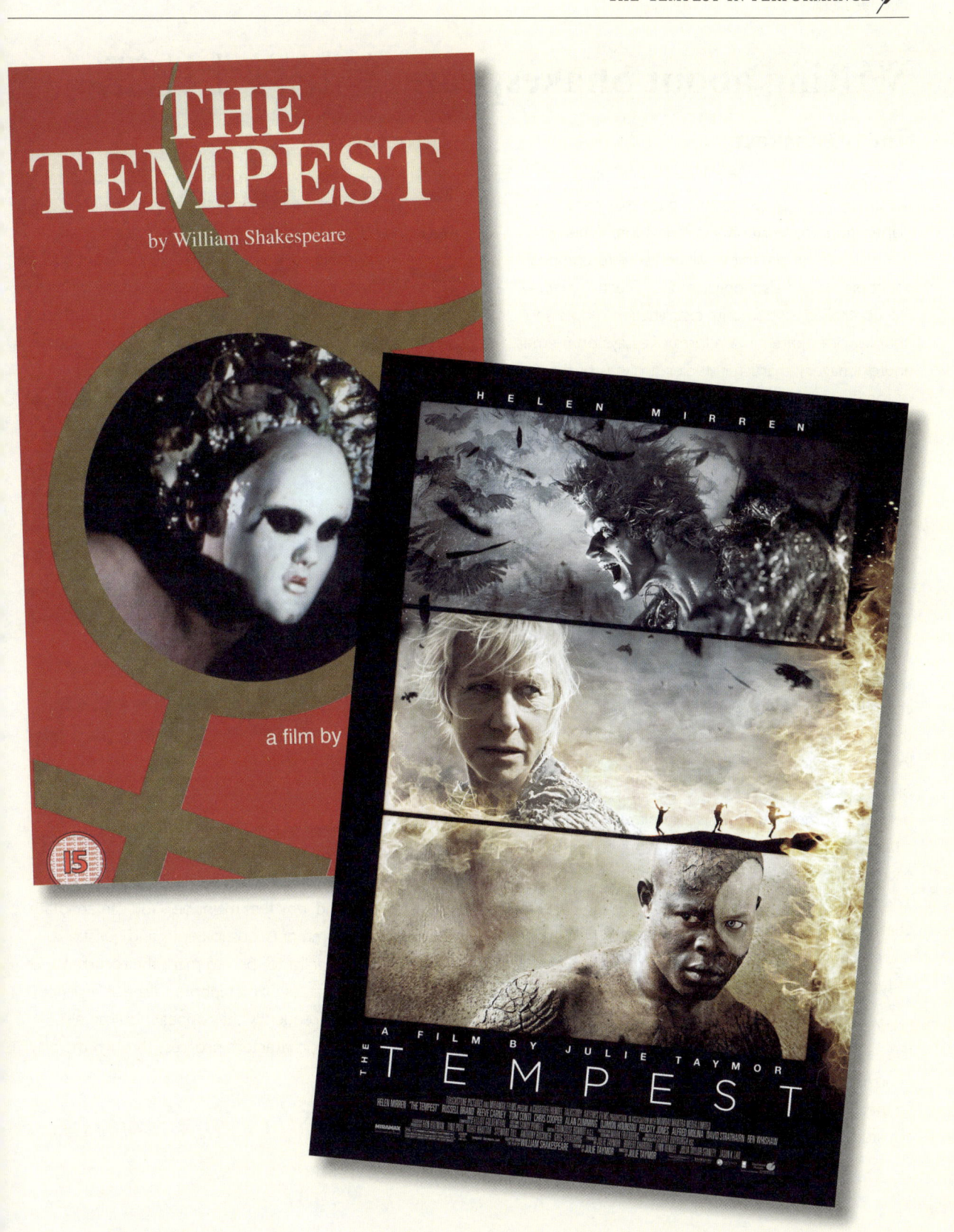

The Tempest in performance

The Tempest
暴风雨

Writing about Shakespeare 笔论莎士比亚

The play as text

Shakespeare's plays have always been studied as literary works — as words on a page that need clarification, appreciation and discussion. When you write about the plays, you will be asked to compose short pieces and also longer, more reflective pieces like controlled assessments, examination scripts and coursework — often in the form of essays on themes and/or imagery, character studies, analyses of the structure of the play and on stagecraft. Imagery, stagecraft and character are dealt with elsewhere in this edition. Here, we concentrate on themes and structure. You might find it helpful to look at the 'Write about it' boxes on the left-hand pages throughout the play.

Themes

It is often tempting to say that the theme of a play is a single idea, like 'death' in *Hamlet*, or 'the supernatural' in *Macbeth*, or 'love' in *Romeo and Juliet*. The problem with such a simple approach is that you will miss the complexity of the plays. In *Romeo and Juliet*, for example, the play is about the relationship between love, family loyalty and constraint; it is also about the relationship of youth to age and experience; and the relationship between Romeo and Juliet is also played out against a background of enmity between two families. Between each of these ideas or concepts there are tensions. The tensions are the main focus of attention for Shakespeare and the audience; this is also how the best drama operates — by the presentation of and resolution of tension.

Look back at the 'Themes' boxes throughout the play to see if any of the activities there have given rise to information that you could use as a starting point for further writing about the themes of the specific play you are studying.

Structure

Most Shakespeare plays are in five acts, divided into scenes. These acts were not in the original scripts, but have been included in later editions to make the action more manageable, clearer and more like 'classical' structures. One way to get a sense of the structure of the whole play is to take a printed version (not this one!) and cut it up into scenes and acts, then display each scene and act, in sequence, on a wall, like this:

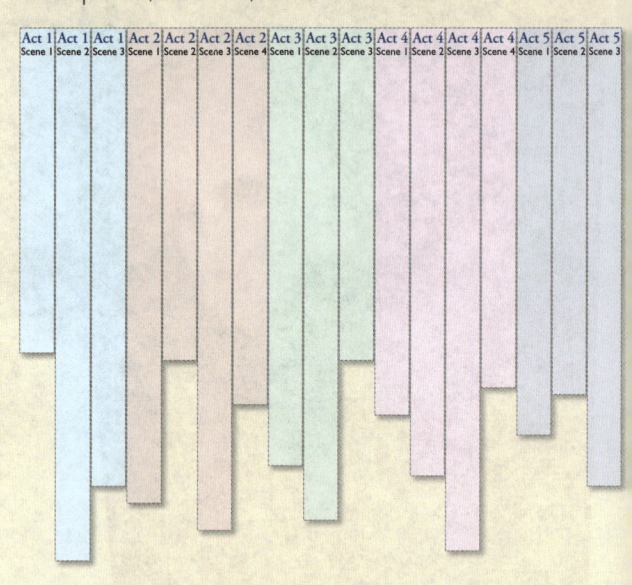

| Act 1 Scene 1 | Act 1 Scene 2 | Act 1 Scene 3 | Act 2 Scene 1 | Act 2 Scene 2 | Act 2 Scene 3 | Act 2 Scene 4 | Act 3 Scene 1 | Act 3 Scene 2 | Act 3 Scene 3 | Act 4 Scene 1 | Act 4 Scene 2 | Act 4 Scene 3 | Act 5 Scene 1 | Act 5 Scene 2 | Act 5 Scene 3 |

As you set out the whole play, you will be able to see the 'shape' of each act, the relative length of the scenes, and how the acts relate to each other (such as whether one act is shorter, and why that might be). You can annotate the text with comments, observations and questions. You can use a highlighter pen to mark the recurrence of certain words, images or metaphors to see at a glance where and how frequently they appear. You can also follow a particular character's progress through the play.

Such an overview of the play gives you critical perspective: you will be able to see how the parts fit together, to stand back from the play and assess its shape, and to focus on particular parts within the context of the whole. Your writing will reflect a greater awareness of the overall context as a result.

The play as script

There are different, but related, categories when we think of the play as a script for performance. These include *stagecraft* (discussed elsewhere in this edition and throughout the left-hand pages), *lighting*, *focus* (who are we looking at? Where is the attention of the audience?), *music and sound*, *props and costumes*, *casting*, *make-up*, *pace and rhythm*, and other *spatial relationships* (e.g. how actors move around the stage in relation to each other). If you are writing about stagecraft or performance, use the notes you have made as a result of the 'Stagecraft' activities throughout this edition of the play, as well as any information you can find about the plays in performance.

What are the key points of dispute?

Shakespeare is brilliant at capturing a number of key points of dispute in each of his plays. These are the dramatic moments where he concentrates the focus of the audience on difficult (sometimes universal) problems that the characters are facing or embodying.

First, identify these key points in the play you are studying. You can do this as a class by debating what you consider to be the key points in small groups, then discussing the long-list as a whole class, and then coming up with a short-list of what the class thinks are the most significant. (This is a good opportunity for speaking and listening work.) They are likely to be places in the play where the action or reflection is at its most intense, and which capture the complexity of themes, character, structure and performance.

Second, drill down at one of the points of contention and tension. In other words, investigate the complexity of the problem that Shakespeare has presented. What is at stake? Why is it important? Is it a problem that can be resolved, or is it an insoluble one?

Key skills in writing about Shakespeare

Here are some suggestions to help you organise your notes and develop advanced writing skills when working on Shakespeare:

- Compose the title of your writing carefully to maximise your opportunities to be creative and critical about the play. Explore the key words in your title carefully. Decide which aspect of the play — or which combination of aspects — you are focusing on.
- Create a mind map of your ideas, making connections between them.
- If appropriate, arrange your ideas into a hierarchy that shows how some themes or features of the play are 'higher' than others and can incorporate other ideas.
- Sequence your ideas so that you have a plan for writing an essay, review, story — whichever genre you are using. You might like to think about whether to put your strongest points first, in the middle, or later.
- Collect key quotations (it might help to compile this list with a partner), which you can use as evidence to support your argument.
- Compose your first draft, embedding quotations in your text as you go along.
- Revise your draft in the light of your own critical reflections and/or those of others.

The following pages focus on writing about *The Tempest* in particular.

The Tempest 暴风雨

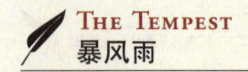

Writing about *The Tempest* 笔论《暴风雨》

Any kind of writing about *The Tempest* will be informed by your responses to the play. Your understanding of how characters, plot, themes, language and stagecraft are all interrelated will contribute to your unique perspective. This section will help you locate key points of entry into the play so that your writing will be engaging and original. The best way to capture your reader's attention is to take them with you on a journey of discovering a new pathway into *The Tempest*.

But first, how do you find your unique perspective? You may want to start with a character – say, Prospero. From here, allow yourself to make free connections with the rest of the play. If you think about the development of his character and the way he controls what happens on the island, this might lead you to consider his motivation and goals. Prospero's plan to isolate his enemies and confront them with their treachery points towards a plan of revenge. However, at the end of play Prospero chooses forgiveness instead of vengeance. This kind of spiritual journey is reflected in the moral development of the king and his courtiers. It is also symbolised in the tempest that follows.

You may also find yourself thinking about the way in which the play links imprisonment and freedom with forgiveness and reconciliation. The idea of forgiveness versus revenge is evident in an antithesis that Prospero uses when he decides to be merciful towards his enemies: 'The rarer action is / In virtue, than in vengeance'. This may lead you to consider the language he uses: how does it create a charmed and dream-like atmosphere? Or does he use language, along with his magic art, to control and manipulate? You might want to compare Prospero's language with the broken, strained speeches of his slave Caliban. As you do, you will notice that Caliban, too, uses some striking poetry, especially when he describes the island that means so much to him.

As you can see, your own perspective on the play will begin to develop as you think about what you are interested in and as you allow yourself to make connections between the dramatic, contextual, linguistic and thematic features of the play.

As you develop and extend your ideas into a coherent piece of writing, by using mind maps and essay plans, remember to refer back to the characters and events in the play, and to quote from the play to develop and extend your ideas further.

- Generate five of your own titles for writing about *The Tempest*. Try to compose your 'dream' questions that will give you plenty of scope to pull together all your ideas about the play and will take you into new and interesting areas. These could be a mixture of creative and analytical questions: be as open-minded as possible. For example, you could start with 'Ambition, power, revenge: what motivates Prospero?'

- Once you have five titles, work with your partner or in a small group to build up ten titles that are varied and clear, and that inspire you to write an essay in response.

Creative writing

At different times during your study of *The Tempest*, and during assessments and examinations, you will be writing about the play and about your personal responses to it. Creative responses, such as those encouraged in the activities on the left-hand pages in this book, can allow you to be as imaginative as you want. This is your chance to develop your own voice and to be adventurous as well as being sensitive to the words and images in the play.

The Tempest is a rich, multi-layered text that benefits from many different approaches, both in performance, and in writing. Don't be afraid of larger questions or implications that cannot be reduced to simple resolutions. The complex issues that have no easy answers are often the most interesting to write about.

Writing about The Tempest

The Tempest (the director's cut)

◆ Imagine that you are directing a movie version of *The Tempest* and the producers want it to have additional scenes. In pairs, look at each act and think about where an extra scene could be used to develop key themes. Would you add a scene that explains what life was like for Caliban and Ariel before Prospero and Miranda arrived on the island? Or would you include a scene that showed what life was like for the characters once they were back in Naples? Now choose one and write it yourself in Shakespeare's language (using iambic pentameter if you can).

◆ As part of the promotional material, the characters themselves are going to be interviewed so that they can explain their actions and give their views on the others. In pairs, write ten questions that you would like to ask the characters. Then, in small groups, conduct the interviews. If you can, film them so that the rest of the class can view them.

Essay

Some responses, such as essays, have a set structure and specific requirements. Writing an essay gives you a chance to explore your own interpretations, to use evidence that appeals to you, and to write with creativity and flair. It allows you to explore *The Tempest* from different points of view. You can approach the play from a number of critical perspectives or in relation to different themes. You can also explore the play in its social, literary, political and cultural contexts. This includes considering the range of possible effects on audiences from the play's original production (Shakespeare's day) and its ongoing reception (today or at any point since Shakespeare's day).

An essay can be seen as an exploration of the play in which you chart a path to illuminate ideas that are significant to you. It is also an argument that uses evidence and structural requirements to persuade your readers that you have an important perspective on the play. You must integrate evidence from the script into your own writing by using embedded quotations — and by explaining the significance of each quotation and reference to the play. Some people like to remember the acronym PEA to help them here. P is the POINT you are making. E is the EVIDENCE you are taking from the script, whether it is a direct quotation, a summary of what is happening, or a reference to character, plot and themes. A is the ANALYSIS you give for using this evidence, which will reflect back on the point you are making and will contain your own personal response and original ideas.

◆ Put the following essay questions in order of difficulty (with number one being the most challenging) and discuss with others why you put them in that order. Choose one and construct a detailed essay plan that reflects the advice given in these two pages.

1. Magic in *The Tempest*: good or evil?
2. Why is Act 3 Scene 3 so dramatically effective?
3. How do the themes of transformation and self-discovery relate to Ariel's idea of a 'sea-change'?
4. Who do you think should be in control of the island? Does one character have more right to it than the others?
5. Miranda is the only female character in *The Tempest*. Why is this significant and what does her presence contribute to your understanding of other characters, events and thematic concerns?
6. Discuss the significance of the play's original context for understanding some of its themes and characters.

The Tempest
暴风雨

William Shakespeare 莎翁年表
1564–1616

1564	Born Stratford-upon-Avon, eldest son of John and Mary Shakespeare.
1582	Marries Anne Hathaway of Shottery, near Stratford.
1583	Daughter Susanna born.
1585	Twins, son and daughter Hamnet and Judith, born.
1592	First mention of Shakespeare in London. Robert Greene, another playwright, described Shakespeare as 'an upstart crow beautified with our feathers'. Greene seems to have been jealous of Shakespeare. He mocked Shakespeare's name, calling him 'the only Shake-scene in a country' (presumably because Shakespeare was writing successful plays).
1595	Becomes a shareholder in The Lord Chamberlain's Men, an acting company that became extremely popular.
1596	Son, Hamnet, dies aged eleven. Father, John, granted arms (acknowledged as a gentleman).
1597	Buys New Place, the grandest house in Stratford.
1598	Acts in Ben Jonson's *Every Man in His Humour*.
1599	Globe Theatre opens on Bankside. Performances in the open air.
1601	Father, John, dies.
1603	James I grants Shakespeare's company a royal patent: The Lord Chamberlain's Men become The King's Men and play about twelve performances each year at court.
1607	Daughter Susanna marries Dr John Hall.
1608	Mother, Mary, dies.
1609	The King's Men begin performing indoors at Blackfriars Theatre.
1610	Probably returns from London to live in Stratford.
1616	Daughter Judith marries Thomas Quiney. Dies. Buried in Holy Trinity Church, Stratford-upon-Avon.

The plays and poems

(no one knows exactly when he wrote each play)

1589–95	*The Two Gentlemen of Verona, The Taming of the Shrew, First, Second* and *Third Parts* of *King Henry VI, Titus Andronicus, King Richard III, The Comedy of Errors, Love's Labour's Lost, A Midsummer Night's Dream, Romeo and Juliet, King Richard II* (and the long poems *Venus and Adonis* and *The Rape of Lucrece*).
1596–99	*King John, The Merchant of Venice, First* and *Second Parts* of *King Henry IV, The Merry Wives of Windsor, Much Ado About Nothing, King Henry V, Julius Caesar* (and probably the Sonnets).
1600–05	*As You Like It, Hamlet, Twelfth Night, Troilus and Cressida, Measure for Measure, Othello, All's Well That Ends Well, Timon of Athens, King Lear.*
1606–11	*Macbeth, Antony and Cleopatra, Pericles, Coriolanus, The Winter's Tale, Cymbeline,* **The Tempest**.
1613	*King Henry VIII, The Two Noble Kinsmen* (both probably with John Fletcher).
1623	Shakespeare's plays published as a collection (now called the First Folio).

Acknowledgements 鸣谢

Cambridge University Press would like to acknowledge the contributions made to this work by Rex Gibson.

Picture Credits

p. iii: Ninagawa Company/Barbican Theatre 1992, © Donald Cooper/Photostage; p. v: Shakespeare's Globe 2000, © Donald Cooper/Photostage; p. vi top: Shakespeare's Globe 2000, © Donald Cooper/Photostage; p. vi bottom: Dhaka Theatre, Bangladesh, Shakespeare's Globe 2012, © Donald Cooper/Photostage; p. vii top: Ninagawa Company/Barbican Theatre 1992, © Donald Cooper/Photostage; p. vii bottom: Old Vic Theatre 1988, © Donald Cooper/Photostage; p. viii top: Shakespeare's Globe 2000, © Donald Cooper/Photostage; p. viii bottom: Almeida Theatre 2000, © Donald Cooper/Photostage; p. ix left: RSC/Courtyard Theatre 2009, © Donald Cooper/Photostage; p. ix right: RSC/Royal Shakespeare Theatre 1998, © Clive Barda/ArenaPAL; p. x: RSC/Royal Shakespeare Theatre 1988, © Donald Cooper/Photostage; p. xi top: Baxter Theatre Centre (Cape Town) in association with RSC/Courtyard Theatre 2009, © Donald Cooper/Photostage; p. xi bottom: RSC/Royal Shakespeare Theatre 1993, © Donald Cooper/Photostage; p. xii top: RSC/Royal Shakespeare Theatre 1998, © Donald Cooper/Photostage; p. xii bottom: Shakespeare's Globe 2000, © Donald Cooper/Photostage; p. 6: Ninagawa Company/Barbican Theatre 1992, © Donald Cooper/Photostage; RSC/Royal Shakespeare Theatre 1993, © Donald Cooper/Photostage; p. 22: Theatre Royal Haymarket 2011, © Geraint Lewis; p 26: RSC/Royal Shakespeare Theatre 1998, © Donald Cooper/Photostage; p. 34: Ninagawa Company/Barbican Theatre 1992, © Donald Cooper/Photostage; p. 38: Nottingham Playhouse 2004, © Donald Cooper/Photostage; p. 43 top: RSC/Royal Shakespeare Theatre 1993, © Donald Cooper/Photostage; p. 43 bottom left: West Yorkshire Playhouse 1999, © Donald Cooper/Photostage; p. 43 bottom right: Old Vic Theatre 2010, © Geraint Lewis; p. 48: Shakespeare's Globe 2013, © Geraint Lewis; p. 52: Plan of Utopia, from Thomas More's *Utopia* 1518, © Topfoto; p. 54: Still from the film *The Tempest* 2010 © Touchstone Pictures/The Kobal Collection; p. 62: RSC/Royal Shakespeare Theatre 1993, © Donald Cooper/Photostage; p. 68: RSC/Royal Shakespeare Theatre 1998, © Donald Cooper/Photostage; p. 74: Jonathan Epstein (Stephano), Rocco Sisto (Caliban) in a Shakespeare & Company production 2012. Photo by Kevin Sprague. p. 77: Still from the film *The Tempest* 2010 © Touchstone Pictures/The Kobal Collection; p. 78: RSC/Royal Shakespeare Theatre 1998, © Donald Cooper/Photostage; p. 86: RSC/Royal Shakespeare Theatre 1993, © Donald Cooper/Photostage; p. 90: RSC/Royal Shakespeare Theatre 1998, © Donald Cooper/Photostage; p. 98: Old Vic Theatre 2010, © Geraint Lewis; p. 103 top left: Almeida Theatre 2000, © Donald Cooper/Photostage; p. 103 top right: Illustration from Caspar Schott's *Physica Curiosa* 1697, © Fortean/Topfoto; p. 103 bottom: Stephanie Hedges, Casey McShain, Jennifer Young, Monica Giordano (Spirits) in a Shakespeare & Company production 2012. Photo by Kevin Sprague; p. 106: Still from the film *The Tempest* 2010 © Touchstone Pictures/The Kobal Collection; p. 110: RSC/Royal Shakespeare Theatre 1993, © Donald Cooper/Photostage; p. 118: Rocco Sisto (Caliban), Jonathan Epstein (Stephano), Timothy Douglas (Trinculo) in a Shakespeare & Company production 2012. Photo by Kevin Sprague; p. 123 top: RSC/Royal Shakespeare Theatre 1988, © Donald Cooper/Photostage; p. 123 bottom: RSC/Courtyard Theatre 2009, © Geraint Lewis; p. 134: Barbican Theatre 2011, © Donald Cooper/Photostage; p. 140: RSC/Royal Shakespeare Theatre 1993, © Donald Cooper/Photostage; p. 147 top: RSC/Barbican Theatre 1983, © Donald Cooper/Photostage; p. 147 bottom left: RSC/Royal Shakespeare Theatre 1993, © Donald Cooper/Photostage; p. 147 middle right: Ninagawa Company/Barbican Theatre 1992, © Donald Cooper/Photostage; p. 147 bottom left: Rocco Sisto (Caliban), Olympia Dukakis (Prospera), Kristin Wold (Ariel) in a Shakespeare & Company production 2012. Photo by Kevin Sprague. p. 149: Theatre Royal Haymarket 2011, © Geraint Lewis; p. 150: Jericho Hands/St Giles Cripplegate 2011, © Jane Hobson/LNP/Rex Features; p. 151: Theatre Royal Bath 2012, © Geraint Lewis; p. 152: RSC/Royal Shakespeare Theatre 1998, © Donald Cooper/Photostage;

The Tempest
暴风雨

p. 153: 'Admiral Somers runs his ship ashore, Bermuda 1609' 1880, © Print Collector/HIP/Topfoto; p. 154: Sahkespeare's Globe 2013, © Geraint Lewis; p. 155; 'Roanake Landing, 1585', © The Granger Collection/Topfoto; p. 156: RSC/Courtyard Theatre 2009, © Geraint Lewis; p. 157: Open Air Theatre, Regent's Park 1996, © Donald Cooper/Photostage; p. 158: Poster for The Tempest at His Majesty's Theatre c. 1920, © Michael Diamond, ArenaPAL; p. 159: RSC/Royal Shakespeare Theatre 1998, © Donald Cooper/Photostage; 160: RSC/Royal Shakespeare Theatre 1998, © Donald Cooper/Photostage; p. 161: Merritt Janson (Miranda), Ryan Winkles (Ferdinand) in a Shakespeare & Company Production 2012. Photo by Kevin Sprague; p. 162: RSC/Royal Shakespeare Theatre 1993, © Donald Cooper/Photostage; p. 163: Theatre Royal Bath 2012, © Geraint Lewis; p. 164: RSC/Royal Shakespeare Theatre 1998, © Donald Cooper/Photostage; p. 165: Baxter Theatre Centre (Cape Town) in association with RSC/Courtyard Theatre 2009, © Geraint Lewis; p. 166: Baxter Theatre Centre (Cape Town) in association with RSC/Courtyard Theatre 2009, © Geraint Lewis; p. 169: Old Vic Theatre 2010, © Geraint Lewis; p. 170: Shakespeare's Globe 2000, © Donald Cooper/Photostage; p. 171: Dhaka Theatre, Bangladesh, Shakespeare's Globe 2012, © Donald Cooper/Photostage; p. 172: Shakespeare's Globe 2000, © Donald Cooper/Photostage; p. 173 top: 'Caliban in The Tempest' 1850, © Topfoto; p. 173 bottom: Lithograph of a scene from The Tempest 1857, © 2006 Charles Walker Topfoto; p. 174: RSC/Royal Shakespeare Theatre 1982, © Donald Cooper/Photostage; p. 175: Old Vic Theatre 1998, © Donald Cooper/Photostage; p. 176: Poster for the film Forbidden Planet 1956, © MGM/The Kobal Collection; p. 177: Old Vic Theatre 2010, © Geraint Lewis; p. 178: Shakespeare's Globe 2013, © Geraint Lewis; p. 179: RSC/Royal Shakespeare Theatre 1998, © Donald Cooper/Photostage; p. 180: Poster for the film Prospero's Books 1991, © Moviestore Collection Ltd/Alamy; p. 181 left: Poster for the film The Tempest 1979, © Moviestore Collection Ltd/Alamy; p. 181 right: Poster for the film The Tempest 2010, © Tempest Production/Topfoto.

Produced for Cambridge University Press by White-Thomson Publishing
+44 (0)843 208 7460
www.wtpub.co.uk

Managing editor: Sonya Newland
Designer: Kim Williams (320 Design)
Concept design: Jackie Hill